BONE MUSIC

BONE MUSIC

ALAN RODGERS

LONGMEADOW PRESS

Stamford, Connecticut

Published by Longmeadow Press, 201 High Ridge Road,
Stamford, Connecticut 06904. All rights reserved. No part
of this book may be reproduced or utilized in any form or by any means,
electronic or mechanical, including photocopying, recording or by
any information storage or retrieval system, without permission
in writing from the Publisher.

Longmeadow Press and the colophon are trademarks.

Cover illustration copyright © 1995 by Tom Canty.

Library of Congress Cataloging-in-Publication Data

Rodgers, Alan, 1959-
    Bone music / Alan Rodgers.
        p.   ca.
    ISBN: 0-681-10086-9
    1. Johnson, Robert, d. 1938–Fiction. 2. Blues musicians–United
States–Fiction. 3. Hoodoo (Cult)–United States–Fiction.
I. Title.
PS3568.03467B66   1994
813'.54–dc20   95-15526
                                                                    CIP

Printed and bound in the United States of America.
First Edition.
0 9 8 7 6 5 4 3 2 1

For Kay McCauley
who walks on water

BONE MUSIC

Long before anybody else figured it out, Lisa knew how big it was, the thing that was wrong with her. She was only eight, and she was only a girl, and she was dying, but even so, she knew: even back before she died she knew about the Hoodoo Doctors and the Seven Kings and even the Eye of the World.

Partly she knew from the dream she had the night she died. Santa Barbara weighed her that night in the place between dead and alive — she whispered to Lisa, and *touched* her.

But even more she knew hoodoo because the magic and the music lived inside her heart, and she breathed and drank them both even when she was alive.

That was the thing about Lisa: the music was inside her, and when she died she lived and died and lived again. Because she knew both sides of death so well, she knew the song they call *Judgment Day* as though she were a Hoodoo Doctor. She loved that song, and sometimes she sang snatches of it in her head. But she knew better than to sing it aloud. Of course she did! Anybody who's got the sense to hear that song knows what it will do, come *Judgment Day*: They know that it will open up the Eye of the World, and Hell will cry upon the Mississippi Delta when she sings.

Lisa loved that song. But she never ever sang the tune.

●

Now Robert Johnson, *he* sang the tune. But Robert Johnson was a young man when he sang it — brash and vainglorious, and when he sang *Judgment Day* he sang because he knew that he was dying and he thought that was the end of the world. Such a fool, that Robert Johnson! Everybody with the talent knows no bluesman ever lived to be a Hoodoo Doctor without dying first. But that was Robert Johnson for you: He lived and he died and when he was dead Hell spat him out, because not even Hell can abide vanity vast enough to swallow the world.

•

Before the world broke open there were seven kings — seven hoodoo wizards who ruled the Mississippi lowlands from the Delta all the way north to Chicago. Oh, they didn't rule so you could see — there were mayors and governors and presidents for that. But those men weren't true powers in the Delta. The real powers were the Wizard Kings of Hoodoo, and the lesser hoodoo men — Hoodoo Doctors — sworn to them.

You and I know these hoodoo wizards as great blues singers, dead and buried. But they are not dead — only hidden, pulled away from the world.

•

After he was dead awhile, Robert Johnson repented. But Hell never did forgive him.

•

The first time Lisa Henderson saw *the goddess who repented* was in the hospital when she was still alive. She was in her sunny room in the children's ward, and it was dusk with the sun streaming in across the river to make the room brighter than it was all day, and the *goddess* whispered to her.

Lisa, she said.

Lisa's hair stood on end the moment she heard the *goddess* say her name. Not just because the room was empty and alone — Lisa got an awful chill the moment that she heard it because she recognized that voice, even though she'd never heard it.

Because all her life she'd heard the old ladies talking on the tenement stoops. And she knew about Santa Barbara, who they sometimes call Shungó or *the goddess who repented.* And the moment Lisa heard that voice she knew that no matter what the doctors did, no matter how her mother prayed, no matter how the nurses nursed and Mama Estrella came to give a blessing — no matter how it happened Lisa was about to die.

She turned to face Shungó and she looked the *goddess* in the eye. She was so beautiful, Lisa thought. More beautiful than any goddess ought to be; more beautiful than a demon loa like Shungó could ever be — when Lisa saw her she knew she was a *santa,* good and true, a *santa* so beautiful that she could only be Santa Barbara, the virgin with the sword. None of the other stories mattered to Lisa — none of the horrible tales that surrounded *the goddess who repented* made any difference at all.

Because Lisa loved Santa Barbara. She didn't hesitate: she took the *santa's* outstretched hand and followed her into a dream.

But the dream was no dream at all — only the blackness of an hour's sleep while the nurses came to take away her untouched dinner.

When she woke she felt calm and rested. She already knew what would happen that night, and in her heart she was prepared.

At nine her mama came back to be with her, and Lisa was glad. She wanted Mama with her tonight, because even if she was prepared to face the darkness she wasn't ready to face it alone.

"I love you, Mama," Lisa said.

Mama kissed Lisa's forehead and sat in the recliner beside the hospital bed.

"How was your dinner, child?" Mama asked.

Lisa smiled and lied. "It was wonderful, Mama."

Mama knew that was a lie. She looked at Lisa disapprovingly, and Lisa knew she was about to get another lecture, and oh but she hated lectures.

"Child —" Mama said, and then she just stopped. Lisa waited for her to go on, but she never did.

"I'm sorry, Mama," Lisa said. "I tried to eat it. I really did. I was hungry! But the food here is so gross. . . ." She patted her stomach as she spoke, to emphasize her hunger.

That was a bad idea. Because the cancer was a mound beside her stomach, and when her fingers brushed across the roundness where it bulged against her skin, the tumor throbbed painfully, and kept throbbing. Then suddenly the pain became unbearable, and Lisa screamed. She writhed against the mattress, twisting the sheets as she tried to push the agony away from her — grabbed her hips with her hands, pulled herself tight, tried to press out the fiery mass that was her cancer . . . closed her eyes and *pushed* the way she saw Lily Fernandez push the day she had her baby on the tenement stair.

When she opened her eyes again there was blood everywhere just like when Lily had her baby. For a moment Lisa thought she'd done it — pushed the throbbing burning out of her, but no, no, it was only the tube from her arm pulled loose and blood was jetting everywhere from the broken tube and the torn vein, pulsing blood went everywhere with every excruciating throb in her abdomen.

Then something deep inside her stomach surged and *broke,* and the pain metamorphosed into a sensation so terrible and consuming that Lisa lost sight of everything but the cancer as she *screamed* —

And screamed, and screamed.

She was alone with the cancer for a long time after that. The world receded; her mother disappeared; if the doctors came to tend to her she never saw them. The part of her that could think was certain she was dying. Any moment now the world would turn to night and the *santa* would take her hand to lead her through the darkness between this world and the next.

But the night and the *santa* never came. Instead the world swam back into focus as the doctors poured their medicines into her, and Lisa saw them everywhere crowding around her, nurses, doctors, people in uniforms she didn't recognize.

"We need to operate," someone said. "She's hemorrhaging."

The medicine was cold comfort dripping down into the veins of her right arm. It turned the pain into an abstraction, and pushed the world so far away . . . so far away that Lisa hardly screamed when she saw the doctors cut her tummy with their knives. She felt the pressure where they cut her, and she felt the flesh peel open as it parted from the scalpel's edge. She heard the Velcro sound as the surgeon pulled the skin of her abdomen away from the cancer that bulged out of her like a leathery grey egg, and she saw blood roiling away from the tumor, and she wanted to reach out to touch the mottled surface of the cancer. But the medicine was too much for her; when she tried to lift her hand she found she did not have the strength to move it.

One of the doctors reached into her open stomach with a clamp; after a moment the blood stopped welling from her abdomen.

"I've stopped the hemorrhage," her surgeon said. "But — something's wrong. This is impossible." He reached into her again, and Lisa felt him lift the cancer, saw him peer at its underside. "The tumor has grown into her femoral artery. It's got to be impeding blood flow from her heart."

The doctor beside him swore. "What're you talking about? Tumors don't grow into arteries. It just doesn't happen."

"Look for yourself."

The second doctor swore again. "I see it," he said.

"The growth has weakened the arterial wall — look at it, it's going to tear soon." The first doctor paused, gestured at the perspiration beading on his forehead. An orderly tamped the moisture with white gauze. "There's no way to remove it. When it tears, the girl is dead."

Lisa wanted to give that doctor a piece of her mind. *I'm not dead,* she wanted to say. *I'm not! I'm alive!* But her voice betrayed her just as her hand had betrayed her, and she was silent.

"She's still breathing, Jim. Hell, her eyes are open. For all you know she may be awake enough to hear you."

"It doesn't matter. There's nothing we can do."

The second surgeon sighed. He sounded angry. "You're wrong," he said. "Stand aside and let me work."

Someone twisted the sphincter on Lisa's IV, and more cold leaked down into her forearm through the plastic tube.

When the coldness reached her wrist, the world went away for the last time. First there was darkness, and cold, and then the *santa* kissed her.

Took her hand and led Lisa away into the darkness where there are no stars.

•

Anyone with half an ear for magic can hear the eerie melody deep inside the blues. Lisa's mother, Emma Henderson, heard it every time she listened. She only listened when she was afraid.

•

After Lisa's life was over and before her death had come to her, Santa Barbara walked with her in the place between this life and the next.

When most people die they pass those steps so quickly that

the trauma of the passage leaves no memory on them. But Lisa stumbled in that place, and as she fell the *santa* held her by the hand and kept her from tumbling into the emptiness.

Lisa looked up at the *santa* through the light that was no light but darkness visible, and she almost started to cry. "I'm scared, *santa*," she said.

Santa Barbara didn't answer, but the power of her silence reassured Lisa. After a moment she drew her flaming sword from the sheath that hung at her belt, and as the blade came free its fire illuminated the corridor that carries children through the Kingdom of Death toward the gates of Heaven and Hell.

Lisa saw where she was, and she had to ask her fate before it found her. "Where am I going?" she asked.

The *santa* frowned.

"It isn't time for you to go, child," the *santa* said.

"I don't understand," Lisa said. "What do you mean?"

The *santa* let go Lisa's hand, wrapped her arm around the girl's tiny shoulder, and drew her to her breast.

"Don't tremble, child," she said. "There's nothing to fear."

The *santa*'s reassurance frightened Lisa.

"I don't understand," Lisa said. "Tell me what you mean."

Santa Barbara frowned. "The world still needs you, child."

"I'm just a girl," Lisa said. "I don't want the world to need me."

The *santa* kissed her on the forehead.

"That's why it needs you most of all," the *santa* said. "God loves the humble most of all."

When the *santa* said God's name her sword shone brightly as the sun, and Lisa felt God's Love enfold her in a way that living children hardly can imagine.

"I don't want to go back," Lisa said.

The *santa* nodded. "I know you don't, child."

"I won't go," Lisa said. "I won't, I won't."

The *santa* frowned again. "Listen to it, girl." She gestured at the darkling haze at the near end of the hall. "That's the music of the world, calling you back into the elements of life. Could your heart deny that song?"

Lisa tried to answer. She wanted to say *Yes, yes, it could, it will,*

I won't go, do you hear? but it wasn't any use: she was already gone.

•

Our Lady of Sorrows: Santa Barbara, the virgin who carries the sword.

You can find her shrines in lawns and niches all through Florida, the northeast; everywhere folks have immigrated from the Caribbean. Uninitiated folks might mistake them for shrines to the Virgin Mary — but that's a serious mistake. For Santa Barbara is nothing but nothing at all like the Mother of the Lord.

Some say she is no saint at all, but rather a voodoo demon loa whose secret name is Shungó. Others say she is a saint, bloodthirsty and vindictive but touched with the righteousness of Heaven.

No ordinary man could ever say for certain which she is — though there are those who think they know. Those who truly know would never say: questions like that aren't meant to answer.

Wise men know and fear her; honor and respect her, no matter what they call her.

Only fools dare to cross her.

•

There is a song all bluesmen know: they call it the song for Judgment Day.

Some of them know it in bits and pieces; others know it nearly whole. The oldest, greatest, deepest talents among them know the song as it truly will be sung — but none of them would ever sing it just that way.

None of them would dare.

As bluesmen and lady blues singers learn their craft they come to know this song a little at a time; as they master the blues the song comes to them more and more clearly. If and when they grow to be Hoodoo Doctors (and few of them ever do) they know it by heart, and in their hearts — no matter how they've never heard it sung.

No Hoodoo Doctor who knew the song would ever play it.

Not *exactly*. He wouldn't dare: anyone who hears the song enough to know it knows what it will do.

If you listen to much blues you've probably heard bits and pieces of it, worked and reworked into blues standards (some of which have gone on to be rock 'n' roll standards) — but even if you've heard them all you've only seen the shadows that this song casts. There's no way plain uninitiated folks can imagine the original from its parts.

The bluesmen of the Delta call the song *Judgment Day* — because that's when they'll sing it. Gabriel will blow his horn, and all the Hoodoo Doctors everywhere will hear, and they'll sing *Judgment Day*. And the sound and the resonance that rise up from their truest song will shatter the Eye of the World.

When it shatters the Apocalypse will be upon us.

Terrible things that weigh on a song — things that would hang like doom impending if *Judgment Day* were just another simple four-four melody. But *Judgment Day* it isn't just a song; it's an unmasterable riff that lives only in the deepest secret hearts of Hoodoo Doctors. Only one man alive has ever deduced the song and sung it *just exactly* so — and that man was Robert Johnson, and what he sang and when he sang it are the deep root beneath this tale.

Greenville, Mississippi
August 1938

Robert Johnson played the bar in Greenville, Mississippi, for two weeks before he got in trouble. Some say he should've wound up dead even sooner than he did — and God knows those folks may be right. Certainly Johnson spent those weeks begging for trouble. He played up to the owner's lady, snarled at the customers — and worst of all he let his music fill the air with possibility and magic. Every moment Johnson played, men found themselves enraptured by women not their wives, and women found the mystery inside their hearts that leaves love an unrequited question, and families broke on the altar of love and possibility that was Robert Johnson's bone guitar.

The owner didn't take it well. He wasn't any hoodoo man, but he knew enough about the blues to see what Johnson was about. By the time Johnson played his club three days that man had to wish he'd never heard of any Robert Johnson.

But no matter how he felt, he never said a word. Maybe the

man was too used-up inside to care, or maybe he had a long fuse.

Or maybe the man who owned the Greenville bar spent those weeks giving Johnson rope enough to hang himself.

On what was to be Johnson's last night in Greenville — Saturday, August 13, 1938 — Sonny Boy Williamson joined him on the club's lineup. Williamson got to Greenville two hours after sundown, took a room in the local boardinghouse, stowed his gear, and headed to the bar. He got there near the end of the first set, just a moment after Johnson began to sing his "Terraplane Blues."

Williamson had been hearing about Johnson for years, but till that moment he'd neither seen nor heard the man.

What he saw and heard when he entered the bar astounded him. First he saw the owner — a small, dark, nasty-looking man who'd come to Memphis in July to book them both — saw the owner glowering at Johnson from behind the bar.

And then he saw Johnson, standing on a stage at the far end of the room, playing his guitar.

The room from here to there was thick with hoodoo, and the hoodoo man was Robert Johnson. His music was in the smoky half-lit air, and the air held the crowd the way the river holds the land; everyone who heard him knew him, and they owned him as he owned them. Drifts of smoke writhed and twisted through the air, following the hoodoo currents swirling through every heart and ear; Johnson howled and the mirrors brayed back to him, echoing his song.

Sonny Boy Williamson was only a journeyman bluesman in 1938, but even then he had the sight and the talent to see Johnson was a hoodoo man. He worked his way to the front of the room, where he stood watching from the shadows left of stage.

Johnson saw him watching.

He knew who Williamson was, and he reveled in the awe he saw in Williamson's eyes; he played to it just as he'd played all week to the desire in the heart of the owner's lady.

Halfway through "Terraplane" he began to improvise, bending the long mournful howls that punctuate the lyrics until they dominated the song, metamorphosing the blues into an animal cry in the half-lit darkness of the bar.

Three wolves howled to answer him from the hills above Greenville. Someone gasped; when Williamson turned toward the gasp he saw the owner's lady staring at Johnson with eyes full of desire, fear, and awe.

She shivered as Johnson's song rose to harmonize with the howling of the wolves.

Williamson took it all in uneasily. Johnson was getting himself in deep — deeper than anybody but a Hoodoo Doctor ever ought to go. And no matter what kind of talent Johnson had, he wasn't any Hoodoo Doctor.

Of course he wasn't any Hoodoo Doctor! Robert Johnson was *alive.*

When the set was over Johnson went to the owner-lady's table and ordered a bottle of whiskey. Williamson looked up just in time to see the owner gaping at the sight of Robert Johnson sitting down beside his wife. The owner's face was a mask of rage, and Williamson knew what was in that man's heart. He didn't need no hoodoo to see it, either: the owner man was mad enough to kill, and maybe he meant to do it.

"Williamson!" Johnson shouted, knocking back the last dregs of an old glass of whiskey. "Sonny Boy Williamson!"

He waved Williamson to the table, pushed a chair toward him.

Williamson hesitated for a moment. Johnson was a gloater; he had the kind of vanity that makes some men lord it over everyone they find. Williamson had already seen enough to know Johnson was about to run a line of shit on him. He didn't want to sit for it — but when he thought a moment he knew there was no way to avoid it short of walking out of the room, away from the bar, getting back in his beat-up car, and driving away from Greenville.

Williamson wasn't ready for that. He needed the money he'd make in Greenville — needed it *bad.* So he left the shadows beside the stage to join Johnson and the owner-lady. He smiled at Johnson, and he tried to make it friendly, but that wasn't any use: Williamson dreaded Robert Johnson, and both men knew it.

"I been hearing about you, Sonny Boy," Johnson said, all

coy and patronizing, like a nice white planter coddling his *boys*. "I hear you know your licks."

Then he laughed just a little and so quietly, like they both knew it didn't matter worth a damn whether Williamson could play or not, because there was a *talent* in the room, very near a Hoodoo Doctor made whole alive, and that was Robert Johnson in the flesh.

Williamson laughed long enough to be polite, but he thought Johnson was out of his mind. Johnson had the *gift*, all right — but he was *alive*. No one ever lived to be a Hoodoo Doctor, and everybody who ever tried ended up in hell — or someplace worse.

When Johnson was done laughing at him, Williamson leaned forward across the table to look him in the eye. "I know that tune," Williamson said, whispering. "But I wouldn't ever sing it."

The song he meant was *Judgment Day*, and they both knew it. It was a lying boast: Williamson didn't really know *Judgment Day*. Three times in the summer of 1937 he'd heard whispers of the melody inside his head, but he'd never imagined the whole, and would not yet conceive it for a lifetime.

"I bet you do," Johnson said, derisively. "You know it all, don't you, Sonny Boy?" He laughed again, this time mocking Williamson openly.

Williamson scowled and swore. "You know I do," he said. "Day going to come you wished you had a little respect."

Robert Johnson pushed his chair away from the table. "My ass," he said. He grabbed his guitar and started toward the stage.

Before he got out of reach Williamson grabbed his arm and pulled him back toward the table. It wasn't hard; Johnson (for all his bluster) was a scrawny man where Williamson was muscle-bound and stocky.

"This is my set," Williamson said. "Don't you need to rest your chops?" He stood, put his free arm on Johnson's back, and eased him into a chair. Lifted his guitar by the handle on the case, and stepped up to the stage.

There wasn't a day in his life where Sonny Boy Williamson could hold a candle to Robert Johnson, but God knows he tried to lift the light that evening. He played "Honest Woman

Blues" and "Jackweed" like he'd never played them in his life. As he sang three verses of *Judgment Day* came to him, and he sang around them, moving the melody of "Jackweed" sideways and away until the tune metamorphosed toward the chords whispered in his ear, and though the words he sang were words from "Jackweed," everyone who heard Sonny Boy Williamson sing that night saw the Eye of the World weeping in his dreams.

When "Jackweed" was over the applause was thunderous, and even Robert Johnson — still watching angrily from the owner's table — regarded him with a measure of respect.

But Williamson faltered in his third number, when he heckled Robert Johnson with three mocking verses of Johnson's own "Hellhound on My Trail." Williamson should have known better, even in 1938: using the music for ridicule makes a mockery of the *gift*. Someone snickered halfway through the second verse of "Hellhound"; before he could sing another line the spell that bound the room to "Jackweed" was broken. Johnson sneered at him, and gestured; Williamson knew he was defeated. He played the third verse to a close, climbed down from the stage, and rejoined Johnson at the owner's table.

When he got there Johnson was whispering in the owner-lady's ear. She was smiling, glowing satisfied triumphant like she was his and he was hers, like she owned him and she liked it.

That man is going to get himself in some awful kind of trouble, Williamson thought as Johnson kissed the owner-lady too long too deep too intimate right there in the open where her fuming husband had to watch. He thought about Johnson sneering at him, thought about a gesture he'd made toward Williamson on the stage. And he wanted to think *It'll serve that bastard right,* but he didn't have the heart. Williamson was a bluesman, even if he was only a journeyman in 1938, and he loved the *gift* with all his heart. It wasn't in him to wish evil on a man who had the *gift* in him so strong as Johnson did.

And maybe Johnson heard him thinking what he thought. Because the dark thin man got to his feet as Williamson approached the table, and he greeted Williamson warmly. "You ain't all bad," he said. He didn't say it nasty or derogatory, the way Williamson would've thought. Just the opposite, in fact: Robert Johnson reached out to take Williamson's hand. He slapped the big man on the back and smiled. "You ain't bad at all, Sonny Boy," he said, and he said it like he meant it. "Barmaid!" he shouted. "What happened to my whiskey?"

Almost like she'd known he was about to call her, the bar girl came around the corner with the whiskey on a tray. She set the bottle and three glasses on the table and left without meeting their eyes.

The seal on the bottle was cracked and oh-so-carefully nestled back in place. It looked plain enough, and any everyday man would have took it for a ordinary whiskey bottle. But both bluesmen had the *sight,* and they could see the poison sifting through the liquor where the owner-man had poured it in.

Robert Johnson laughed. "That fool thinks he's going to kill me," he said. He laughed again, laughed like he'd just told the sweetest joke he'd ever heard.

And maybe it was — but if it was, Williamson didn't see the humor. "You ought to have a care," he said. "It doesn't do a man no good to gather hate like that."

Johnson took the bottle from the table and twisted off the cap. "You know who I am," he said. "You think I'm afraid?"

Williamson scowled. "I think you ought to be."

Hoodoo Doctors eat poison all the time. It doesn't touch them, and wouldn't hurt a one of them, even if he were alive — because the truth in the music inside a Hoodoo Doctor is enough to purify any poison. But Robert Johnson wasn't any Hoodoo Doctor, no matter how he held himself in high regard.

"I'm not afraid," Johnson said. "The *gift* is in me. The *gift* will purify me, no matter what the poison is." And he hefted back the bottle, and opened his mouth to drink —

But before the liquor touched his lips Williamson was on his feet, knocking the bottle from Johnson's hand. It tumbled to the floor and shattered; in three places the whiskey caught fire as it spread across the floorboards.

Johnson stared at Williamson, stunned and angry. For a moment Williamson thought he was about to attack him. "You got to watch yourself, Robert Johnson," Williamson said, tamping out the fire on the floorboards with the leather sole of his boot. "Just because you got a *gift* don't mean the ones who hate you don't got theirs."

The owner-lady pushed her chair away from the table and hurried away.

Johnson didn't even notice. He scowled and swore, reached across the table and grabbed the big man by the collar. He shook Williamson three times — hard and masterfully, as though their sizes were reversed. Then he pulled him across the table and whispered angrily. "I swear to God, *boy,*" he said. "I swear to God, you ever do a thing like that to me again, I'll peel your hide right off your bones. I swear to God I will." He eased Williamson back into his seat. "Barmaid," he shouted, "we got a mess over here. And we need more whiskey."

The second bottle was poisoned, just as the first had been. Johnson didn't care; he opened the bottle, threw away the cork, and drank deeply of the poison. Williamson tried to stop him — not because he didn't fear the threat, because he knew damn well Johnson could make it good — Williamson tried to stop him because he could see Johnson and the poison, and he knew that no matter what kind of bluesman Robert Johnson was, he wasn't any Hoodoo Doctor. And there's no way a decent man can stand by and watch while a fool poisons himself.

But it didn't matter how he tried. Because Johnson had a hoodoo on him, and no matter how he struggled he could not leave his chair. He watched Robert Johnson lift the bottle to his lips, watched the flames that only he could see swirling ripple in the whiskey where the owner's *giftie* poison corrupted good brown mash. And he wanted to shout, but couldn't do that, either. All he could do was watch Robert Johnson drink the fiery poison down.

Johnson caught fire before the bottle was half empty. Williamson kept expecting him to open his eyes and see the hoodoo flames around him, but he never did. Later when he thought back he realized that Johnson never saw them — that he was too young and vain and reckless to realize that the barkeeper had a gift of his own, even if it was a petty gift for poison. He never saw the ripping sheets of flame that Sonny Williamson saw consume him; he never imagined he was going to die until the last drop of whiskey was inside him and the flames consumed his heart. But his eyes went wide when he felt his center burning, and the bottle fell from his hand to shatter and disintegrate as the hoodoo poison broke the shards again and again, and now there were no shards of glass across the filthy barroom floor, no shards of glass but only glassy grains of sand as Robert Johnson died.

Slowly, slowly, the poison and the hoodoo burning and reburning, consuming the man and his heart and his gift. He fought the poison as best he could, but it wasn't any use. He stumbled, caught himself on a table, backed away and stumbled into a wall.

On the wall there was a kerosene lantern. Johnson brushed against it as he fell to the ground — upsetting the reservoir, sending the wick and the glass tumbling in opposite directions.

That was bad.

Bad bad.

Because the wick, still burning, found its way to a bale of straw someone had brought in the night before to use as wallflower seating. In a moment the hay caught fire, and now the fire found the spilled kerosene soaking in the floorboards.

Now the whole bar was on fire.

Sonny Boy Williamson lifted Robert Johnson from the fiery floor where he lay dying, and carried him to safety.

And watched over the man, as best he could, as he lay sweaty and convulsing all night in the dewy Mississippi grass.

Not long before morning the owner-lady found them. She was bruised and bloody, and the moment Sonny Boy Williamson saw her he knew that that small and angry husband of hers had beat her half to death. She looked hateful and vengeful, like she meant to do her husband something even worse than he'd done her.

"You follow me," she said, and Williamson lifted half-dead Robert Johnson up onto his shoulder and carried him into the hills. "I got a shack up here," the owner-lady said. "It come to me through my mamma. That man don't even know it."

She led them to a tiny weather-beaten place that looked down on Greenville from the ridge above the town. Inside, the shack was spare but tidy — there wasn't any furniture, wasn't anything at all but a sooty lantern and a worn straw mattress. But there was a *gift* in that place, and Williamson could feel it — the kind of gift that a mother passes to her daughter, and to her daughter, and to her daughter unto her, and he knew just what that place was. He couldn't see it the way he could see the fire still flickering to consume Robert Johnson, but he could feel it, and he knew that it was there.

"He's going to be okay," the owner-lady said as Williamson set Robert Johnson to rest on the mattress. She stopped to whisper in the sick man's ear. "You're going to be fine, Robert Johnson, I know you are," she said. That sounded like a lie, but it wasn't a lie Williamson was going to argue with. "I'm going to call a gospel man. He'll make you right with God," she said. "He's a man who knows how to stop a hoodoo."

Williamson shook his head. "This man needs a Doctor," he said. They both knew he wasn't talking about any physician from the white doctor school.

"The gospel man knows Doctoring," she said. "He knows it best of all."

"He ain't going to do no good," Williamson said. "There's a graveyard by the crossroads. Go there tonight. Clap the bones three times and tell them Robert Johnson needs him a Doctor."

"I already called the gospel man from Beaumont," she said. "That's all I'm going to say."

"I don't care who you got coming," Williamson said. "He needs the man you call from the boneyard. If you can't call for him I'll have to call myself."

The owner-lady left, just as she promised, without saying another word. But that night she traveled to the crossroads, and rolled the bones beneath the moon, where only dead eyes see.

●

Toward midmorning Robert Johnson began to recover. Bit by bit he sweated out the poison, and the flames Sonny Boy Williamson saw burning his heart began to flicker and go still. A little while after noon the carrion flies lost interest in him.

He woke around three in the afternoon, asking for water. His voice was weak and uncertain, but it was stronger than it'd been last night as he'd murmured in his dreams. He drank the water Williamson held to his lips, and came away gasping for air.

"I told you that poison couldn't hurt me," Johnson said, still trying to find his breath. It was a brave front, but it didn't fool either one of them. No matter what Robert Johnson said, they both knew he was scared out of his mind.

He was right to be scared, too. Because it didn't matter if his gift could damp the hoodoo poison; he was still just a man. The poison had laid him low seventeen hours, and in those hours an infection had found him.

If there'd been a city doctor around, he would have told Robert Johnson he'd caught bacterial pneumonia, but he wouldn't have been able to do anything about it. In those days before penicillin, bacteria were the masters of men, and once a body fell to them there wasn't much to do but die.

Deep in his heart Robert Johnson probably knew what was happening to him. He had his *gift*, after all, and he had the *sight*, and now he had the first measure of humility he needed to use them. But knowing didn't do him a damn bit of good. Because there was nothing he could do by then — nothing but hang tough and die proud.

But even if Robert Johnson had learned the humility that comes to men who swallow poison, he didn't have the grace to die without a tantrum. (He learned it later, when the door to Hell had slammed shut in his face — but that was years and years away.)

●

Three hours after dark the owner-lady came back with hot stew and blankets and Robert Johnson's guitar. She didn't say much and she didn't stay long. Sonny Boy Williamson could feel in his gut how she had a plan she was pursuing, and he tried to figure what it was, but he couldn't figure. It was a long time before he did — ten years, maybe more. And when he did it was a realization from hindsight, and in hindsight he had to wonder how he ever missed it.

When she was gone Williamson could hear the faintest sound like singing, and he heard a chord he knew but never dared to sing. He looked back and forth, trying to find the source of the music — and what he saw was Robert Johnson breathing hard and wheezy, and that was the music, wasn't it? The music was the sound of wet pneumonia singing down in Robert Johnson's lungs.

Williamson tried not to react as he realized what he heard. Because he knew what it meant — seven times in his life he heard that wheezy music as a chest began to fill with fluid. And of all those times there was only once where he'd seen the lady get well and walk away from the disease that ailed her. Six other times what started as a mild illness — a cold, really, just a cold gone down to the chest — six other times what started as a mild illness turned into a death watch.

"What is it?" Robert Johnson asked, demanding. "She told you something, didn't she? — I know she did. I can see it in your eye."

Williamson shook his head. "She didn't tell me anything," he said. "You're the one she whispered to."

Johnson scowled. "Mind your business," he said. "Ain't no concern of yours."

Williamson shrugged. Took his stew plate to the window that looked down on Greenville, and watched the landscape as he ate.

Johnson was still brave the next morning, but by then even he could hear the wheezing. He woke smiling uncertainly. He didn't look Williamson in the eye. "See, Sonny Boy," he said, "that poison couldn't hurt me." He sounded scared out of his mind. They both could hear it.

"I just got a cold, that's all," Johnson said. He coughed raggedly, reached into the pocket of his jacket, found a cigarette, lit it. "I've got a cold but it'll clear out soon enough. I'm going to be fine."

Williamson nodded, patted Johnson on the back. "You going to be fine," he said — but the lie was so plain there was no mistaking it.

"Yeah."

"Need to get you a Doctor," Williamson said. "Got to get you right with the world."

Johnson laughed. " 'Get right with God,' " he said.

" 'He will show you how,' " Williamson responded. He

didn't laugh because it wasn't any joke.

"Get on with you," Robert Johnson said. He coughed, and the cough became a hacking snarling fit that wouldn't end. When he finally cleared his throat he looked Williamson in the eye uneasily. "It ain't like that at all. I'm going to be fine," he said, like he hadn't just coughed himself half to death.

Williamson didn't reply right away, and when he did he didn't really respond. "Yeah," he said. "I got to take a walk, okay? I got some business."

The business he meant to see to was to repeat the exhortation the owner-lady had made in the graveyard at the crossroads outside Greenville.

But he never did attend to it.

Because there was a blind man waiting at the door when Sonny Boy Williamson opened it. A blind man who cleared his throat and brushed past him just like he was sighted, and maybe he was sighted, this way or another. For the man at the door was the gospel man lately from Beaumont.

Robert Johnson's bluster crumbled the moment he set eyes on the blind man.

"Blind Willie," he said, sobbing.

The blind man crossed the room toward him — steadily, purposely, with a sureness that said he knew every step he meant to take.

There are those who say Blind Willie Johnson was a bluesman, and those who say he was too righteous to sing music as feral and ungodly as the blues. He would've told you that his own self, if you'd cared to ask him. He called himself a gospel songster, and maybe that's the best way to describe him. Bluesmen sing the songs that please them, and sometimes they sing wicked songs — but Blind Willie never sang a song that could please the Devil. He sang fire and brimstone, and sometimes stories from the Bible — but he sang with the driving power of a master bluesman. Does it really matter, in the end? Whether he called it hoodoo or the blessing of the Lord, Blind Willie had the *gift*. He had the *gift* like no other man alive, including Robert Johnson.

The *gift* was so strong in him, in fact, that like Robert Johnson he had the presence of a Hoodoo Doctor even when he was still alive. But he wasn't Robert Johnson, and he didn't pretend to *gifts* or gets he didn't have. He didn't act like a Hoodoo Doctor, and he didn't ask to be treated like one; he used his *gift* for the ends of the Lord, shedding light into the hearts of the faithful and onto the sins of the profane. Anyone who talked to him about hoodoo was likely to be beaten with his cane.

"You've got to help me, Blind Willie," Robert Johnson said. "I got the cough, and it's trying to consume me."

Blind Willie didn't answer right away. Instead he knelt at Robert Johnson's bedside, and laid his hands upon him. He held Robert Johnson for the longest time.

•

Blind Willie Johnson — no relation to Robert Johnson, or if there was a relation it's lost in the fog of Texas abolition — was a legend among songsters, and among all of those who listened in the markets and in the churches of the Mississippi lowlands. He sang fire-and-brimstone gospel with a driving thunder like it was the blues, and he sang with a voice that sounded like the end of the world whispering on the wind. He was a blind man, but Blind Willie had the sight — partly the sight that comes from the *gift,* the sight that lets those who have it see things no eyes could ever tell them. But he also had the sight because he was born sighted, and for the seven years that he could see he'd watched the world carefully, almost as though he was born knowing what would happen in his seventh year.

If he did know, he must've damned the knowledge. Because what happened to him his seventh year should never happen to anyone, least of all a child: that year his mother died, and his father took a second wife. One day while his father was in the field his stepmother was with another man. Blind Willie's father came in from the field early that day, and found his woman with the other man. In his rage he beat them both, and stormed away from the house.

The lover skulked away when Willie's father was gone. And then Willie was alone with his stepmother wailing indignity and pain and rage. He tried to hide from her, but it wasn't any use: she found him hiding in the woodshed, and vented her rage on the boy — beating him with a switch, and then with her bare hands. When she was done she was still trembling, wailing with rage. She grabbed the boy by the wrists, dragged him to her kitchen, and poured scalding lye into his eyes.

His father came back in time to save his life, but too late to save his sight.

•

"I'm scared to die, Blind Willie," Robert Johnson said. "You're going to save me, aren't you?"

Blind Willie frowned. Shook his head. Stooped and *stared* at Johnson through his blind eyes cloudy-clear with scar.

He scowled and swore.

"You got to save me. I'm not ready yet, I know that now. I'm not ready and I'm afraid."

"You ought to be," Blind Willie said.

"I am, Blind Willie. I am! Save me!"

Blind Willie shook his head. "It ain't no curse that ails you, Robert Johnson. You got the cough, and you got to get rid of it for yourself — there's nothing I can do for you."

He stood, rubbed his hands against one another. Turned and started toward the door, like he was about to leave.

Robert Johnson called after him, terrified and enraged, but Blind Willie didn't listen. He would have walked out of the shack and got himself home to Beaumont if there hadn't come a knock on the door before he could reach it.

When he heard the knock Blind Willie swore again — profanely this time. Somewhere down in Hell the Devil had a laugh at his expense.

"Lemon!" he said, a moment before Sonny Boy could open the door. He was right, of course — it was Blind Lemon Jefferson standing in the doorway, no matter how he was supposed to be nine years dead in his casket in the Texas soil. "Go back to your grave, Blind Lemon. You don't belong among the living."

The Hoodoo Doctor ignored him. "You called me," he said to Williamson.

Sonny Boy nodded toward Robert Johnson in his sickbed, and saw Johnson trembling. Did the mojo scare him that badly? Did he see his own illness reflected in the Doctor's eyes?

Williamson wasn't sure.

"Someone put a bad hoodoo on him," Williamson said. "Poison. Like to kill him."

The Doctor nodded. He seemed to watch Robert Johnson through his dark blind-man glasses; when he crossed the room toward Johnson's bedside he moved even more purposely than Blind Willie had. When he reached the bedside, he knelt beside it, just as Blind Willie had.

"It's my chest, Doctor," Robert Johnson said. "I feel like the river tried to flood inside me."

Blind Lemon chuckled. "I bet it do," he said. "Listen to it — your lungs are singing to you."

They both had a laugh at that, but it was a bad laugh — because it started Robert Johnson's cough all over again. The man coughed and coughed and coughed, till now he folded over himself heaving and gasping like a drunk who'd lost his stomach, only it was his lungs clutching not his stomach, and the man was breathless like to die, sucking for air, choking and gasping and all he could draw was his own watery phlegm.

The hoodoo man slapped him on the back, whispering words of comfort. But that comfort was a lie — for as he whispered he looked up at Blind Willie and shook his head.

They both knew what he wasn't saying. They both knew Blind Lemon had seen into Robert Johnson's fate, just as Blind Willie had, and there was no hope for him: the man was touched by destiny, and his destiny was death. He was going to die tomorrow. There wasn't any hope for him, just comfort.

"You need to find your faith, Robert Johnson," Blind Willie the Gospel Man said. "Your faith will make you strong."

Robert Johnson looked up terrified from his gasping. He tried to plead for his life, but he couldn't find the wind to say a word.

"You need to put you right with God."

Blind Lemon scowled. "There's always hope," he said. "You got to keep your hope alive."

Robert Johnson reached up to take Blind Lemon's hand. "You got to help me, Doctor," he said. "Doctor, I don't want to die."

Blind Lemon was nine years dead, and he could have told

Robert Johnson that Hell ain't no place to scare a bluesman, but he didn't do anything like that. Maybe he took pity on Robert Johnson, or maybe he thought the man was as damned as he was doomed. Whatever the reason, he did a thing that made Blind Willie's cloudy eyes go wide with shock and indignation: he reached into the pocket of his suit coat and brought forth a packet of rare earth.

It was terrible, terrible dirt — soil from the Bright Spring boneyard in Arkansas, which is no boneyard at all but the ruin of a death-pit where the skeletons of children poke through the thin Ozark soil into the light of day like necrotic daisies reaching for the sun. Some say that a pervert killer spent a lifetime killing children, and always threw their bodies in that pit. Others say some demon monster of a white man went killing every Negro child he could find in the days before Juneteenth — they say he killed ten thousand children and their mothers, killed their grandmothers and grandfathers, too, and when he'd murdered them he heaved their bones into an open pit high up in the mountains. Worms and buzzards ate them all summer long, till winter covered them with snow, and the spring wash covered them with dirt.

No one knows for certain. But to this day those three mountains, southmost of the Ozarks, are a frightful place. The angry ghosts of children crowd those hills, and haunt them in the summer.

The soil that covers their bones is magical stuff, potent and ungodly.

But no matter how magical that soil was, it wasn't enough to save Robert Johnson. It never could be, not after the bacteria had found him. Bacteria don't care about hoodoo or music or magic or the rhythm of the blues: they only live to thrive, and no charm ever could dissuade them.

"Take this dirt," Blind Lemon said, "and make you a tea. Drink it when the sun goes down, and then again when the moon is rising. If the cicada sings past midnight drink it then again."

Blind Willie tried to protest — so far as he was concerned the hoodoo man was talking mumbo jumbo, plain and simple, and the gospel man couldn't abide a lie that deliberate. But

Blind Lemon had slipped a hoodoo on him while he wasn't looking, and that year was before Blind Willie gained the strength to break a hoodoo set on him by a dead man. (Later it was different — but *everything* was different then.)

Robert Johnson took Blind Lemon's cold dry hand and kissed his ring. "I owe you, Doctor," he said. "I love you like my life."

Blind Lemon nodded. "You take better care of yourself, Robert Johnson," he said. "You're a man too young to die."

"I will, Doctor," Robert Johnson said. "I swear I always will."

Blind Lemon smiled. "See that you do," he said. And with that he took Blind Willie by the arm and led him down through the cotton fields to Greenville.

Blind Willie tried to protest, but it didn't do him any good — not till they were halfway back to Greenville.

"What in the name of the Lord do you think you're doing, Blind Lemon Jefferson? That man's going to die tomorrow, sure as I can say my name. He needs to get religion! He needs to save his soul! — and here you got him thinking he can save himself by drinking dirty tea."

Blind Lemon scowled again. "It never hurt a man to give him hope," he said.

"It never did no one no good to let 'em live a lie," Blind Willie told him. " 'The truth will set you free.' "

The hoodoo man scowled, hooted derisively. "Shit," he said.

And for the longest moment he tried to go on — but that was all the answer he could find.

•

Blind Willie was right, of course. There are lies and there are damned lies — and there are lies about damnation, and the lies about damnation are the most terrible lies of all. It was damnation Blind Lemon lied about, no matter how he thought it was just the light of hope he cast on Robert Johnson's bedside.

Robert Johnson drank his graveyard sludge three times that night, just like the Hoodoo Doctor told him. He drank it at dusk, then again two hours later when the moon came up — and when the cicadas opened up in the small hours of the morning, Robert Johnson roused himself from his uneasy sleep and made that foul black tea again.

It didn't do nothing for him but give him a vapor.

Come the cock-crow he still didn't feel no better, so Robert Johnson emptied the last of the packet into his water pot and drank until he like to choke the stuff up.

It still didn't do no good. Just the opposite, in fact — bit by bit Robert Johnson could feel himself getting worse. Now by and by it was hard to breathe, partly because he had a belly full of dirt weighing down his innards, partly because the disease that had ahold of him continued to consume him.

And by and by Robert Johnson come to realize the Doctor man had played a trick on him.

A trick.

A nasty, ugly trick like you'd play on a drunk too stupid to see after himself, and the more Robert Johnson thought on that the angrier he got.

I'm going to die, Robert Johnson thought, and he knew that it was true, and he knew that there wasn't anything in the world he could ever do to stop it, and as he knew those things he grew so furious he like to burst from rage no body could contain.

●

An hour after sunrise the first straight rays of day touched the muddy dregs in the bottom of Robert Johnson's water pot, and as the daylight struck them the foul things caught fire. They burned brilliantly for a long hard moment, and when the flames were gone the muddy dregs were gone, too — vanished into smoke that left no ash, no scent, no sign that there'd ever been anything inside that pot at all.

That made Robert Johnson wonder what would happen to him when he was gone, and as soon as he wondered he knew that he'd leave no trace of himself upon the surface of the earth, because he knew that when the Giftie judged him He would surely find him wanting.

And the more he thought the more he mourned and moaned himself, mourned and mourned till now he could hear three chords from *Judgment Day* ringing in his skull.

More and more he thought about *Judgment Day,* and a vision of the final tumult roiled over him. As he contemplated that terrible apparition Robert Johnson made a mistake more terrible still:

He mistook his own end for the end of the world.

Such a hubris had that Robert Johnson!

Oh, he wasn't the first to think such a thing, and God knows he won't be the last. But few before Robert Johnson ever had the *gift* he had, and no other living soul could ever sing the song he sang; and when he mistook his own doom for the Battle at the End he did a thing no other man has ever done:

He sang a song to make it true.

•

Williamson spent that night in his room in the Greenville boarding house. When he climbed back up to the shack in the morning he found Robert Johnson picking at his guitar, humming bits of a song we all know but none of us want to admit. Johnson looked scared — scared for his life. When Williamson saw that, he knew that Blind Lemon's hoodoo hadn't been enough, and that there wasn't any hoodoo in the world that could save Robert Johnson from his fate.

When Johnson saw him enter the shack, he broke down crying — piteously, wheezing and coughing, as he wailed, gasping for air.

"It ain't working, Sonny Boy," he said. The wheezing got worse when he tried to speak — it got so bad, in fact, that his voice seemed to harmonize with itself. "The cough is going to kill me."

He fished another cigarette from the pack in his shirt pocket, lit it, took a long deep drag. Two puffs in he broke into a spasmodic coughing fit. For a moment Williamson thought he was going to strangle on his phlegm and die right there on the mattress, still clutching his cigarette, heaving over his guitar as he convulsed in the sun that streamed through the window of the shack.

And then he found his wind, and the fit subsided. Or receded, anyway. Not that it mattered; Johnson was dying, and when his cough finally went still they both knew that nothing could save him.

Johnson took another drag on his cigarette and swore quietly because he didn't have the voice to swear out loud.

"They aren't going to kill me so easy, Sonny Boy," Johnson

said. "I'm going to make them sorry that they ever tried."

"What?"

"So damn sorry."

And he started to sing.

And what he sang was *Judgment Day.*

•

If either of the blind hoodoo men had thought Robert Johnson could sing *Judgment Day,* there's no way either one of them would have left his side before he died. If anybody thought he could, they would have watched him like a hawk, like he was a disaster waiting to happen. Which he was, and had been for at least two years.

Maybe Lemon would have killed him on the spot. All things considered, it would have been the prudent thing to do.

•

Sonny Boy Williamson was still young enough that he scarcely conceived of the song that they call *Judgment Day.* But even so he knew the music when he heard it. And deep in his heart he had a vision of Gabriel blowing on his trumpet, and he knew just what it meant. His vision told him that the song Robert Johnson sang would end the world — if nobody could stop him. Here and now, this shack on this hill that looked down at Greenville, Mississippi, and the river beyond it: this was the end of the world, and there was no one on earth in that room to stop that terrible song — no one but Sonny Boy Williamson his own self.

And he tried! He tried to stop it for all he was worth. Tried to dash across the room, seize the guitar from Robert Johnson's arms, and heave it out the window.

But it was a wasted effort.

For *Judgment Day* transfixes all but the greatest of those who hear it, and hard as Sonny Boy Williamson tried there was no way he could so much as move a muscle. And even if he could have crossed that room it would have made no difference, for not even the guns that blast the field of Armageddon will steal the song from *Judgment Day.*

•

The Lady who the Witches of Isla Beata call *the goddess who repented* heard Robert Johnson sing. She was an ocean away when she heard him, and there was no way that she could stop his song. By the time she reached him the Eye of the World was already open, crying its Hell-blue tears into the Mississippi River. She did the only thing she could do, then: she grasped the shattering lens that was Eye of the World and held it whole.

Or nearly whole.

All six of the Wizard Kings of Hoodoo — Leadbelly wasn't yet a king among them in 1938, and wouldn't be until the late 1940s — all six of the Kings of the Delta heard Robert Johnson sing, but they were scattered up and down the length of the Mississippi Valley, too far away to do anything but hear and swear. Each one of them laid a curse, trying to stop Johnson — but it did no good. They were all too far away — all of them but Blind Lemon Jefferson.

Blind Lemon tried to stop the song. He ran like an athlete through the planted fields below the shack, shouting curses as he went. No one who saw him would have took him for a blind man, unless they looked into his scarry eyes.

But it didn't matter how fast he ran. Because even close as he was down in Greenville, he was still too far away.

•

Blind Willie — who'd spent the night in the same boarding-house where Sonny Boy Williamson had stayed, and was in his room waiting for the twelve-noon bus that would take him back to Beaumont — Blind Willie heard Robert Johnson singing, too.

He heard and he wailed and he knew that there was nothing he could do, so he got down on his knees, and he prayed.

And who can say? He may have done more good than Sonny Boy Williamson, Blind Lemon, and the *santa* put together.

•

Hoodoo coalesced around Robert Johnson as he sang *Judgment Day*. Later when he went to Hell he told three people how it felt to sing that song, and they carried the tale far and wide, among the living and the dead: Robert Johnson felt the world spin around him as he sang. He felt hoodoo roiling around him, like it was puffy little clouds of mist, and he could feel and hear and see all of the people running toward him, trying to stop his song.

He heard Blind Lemon curse him, and the cursing made him sad. He saw Blind Willie praying, and the prayer he heard made him even sadder. He saw the *santa* high above the river, trying to hold the Eye secure; he saw a little girl look back at him from half a century away and ask *Why, Robert Johnson, why would you do such a thing?* and it made him sad to know he had no answer for her.

But no matter how sad they made him, it didn't change a thing. In his own heart Robert Johnson was a dead man, and he meant to mourn himself. That was Robert Johnson for you: no matter what kind of talent he had, he was young and self-absorbed, and when he saw his fate awaiting him he took it for the end of the world.

And he sang *Judgment Day.*

When he saw that there were good, decent, sensible people who wanted him to stop, he sang that much harder — and more righteously, too.

Clouds boiled out of nowhere, crowding the sky that had shone clear and bright only moments before; thunder pealed as lightning flickered around the shack.

And Robert Johnson *sang.*

Lightning struck, setting the shack afire, throwing Sonny Boy Williamson (still petrified) into the planted cotton below. But it didn't stop Johnson. There is no force in the world that can stop a man a-singing *Judgment Day,* not the rain, not the wind nor fire nor explosive force of any tumult. Not even the Eye of the World could stop him, appearing as it did in the clouded sky above them; not even as it opened bloodshot with lens-bursting fractures to reveal Our Lady of Sorrows standing on the lens trying to hold it whole.

And Robert Johnson sang.

So glorious, so beautiful, that song! Two dozen people standing near and far could hear him, and they all savored the beauty in the verses, no matter how they swore at him.

●

Sonny Boy Williamson lay transfixed, still paralyzed in the cotton, staring at the open Eye, looking through the lens at Hell thick and blue and thriving like a jungle, hordes and hordes of demons struggling against the lens, all of them yearning to be free, and three of those demons saw him watching, and pleaded, begging him to kill *the goddess who repented.* That was a crazy thing for them to do, of course. Williamson was paralyzed, and they could have seen that if they'd looked. And even if he'd been whole and hale there's nothing a man like him could do to stop the *santa* holding whole the Eye — they should have known that, too. But they didn't know, or they didn't think, and they raged at Williamson. All three of them marked him, and they bedeviled him for the rest of his natural life.

Some people say their curses were a blessing, for their attention made Williamson's natural *gift* grow thick and hard — like calluses on his soul. But Williamson never thought so. He swore whenever he saw them, from the day they first cursed him until the day he died. When he could, he fought them; when he couldn't fight he cursed them back, and his curses plagued the devils as hard as they plagued him.

●

Blind Lemon reached the shack just before it began to crumble. He stopped before the door and shouted for silence, but Robert Johnson ignored him.

"I warn you, Robert Johnson," the Doctor said. "I warn you now for certain."

The door of the shack fell from its hinges as he spoke — maybe because it was afraid to stand between Blind Lemon and the fourth chorus of *Judgment Day.* Maybe because the fire had charred away the frame that held it home.

Blind Lemon Jefferson raised his cane above his head and started singing counterpoint, trying to break the Apocalyptic melody. He raised his free hand to command the fire which so far had avoided Johnson — it hadn't so much as scorched his bedclothes. Jefferson pushed the fire toward the singing man, but no matter how he pushed it never touched Johnson.

And that's the way it ought to be, isn't it? When the Doctors sing *Judgment Day* at the end of time, nothing should harm them, and nothing should impede them. It only stands to reason that the song itself should shield the singers as though it held them in the hand of God — and maybe it does, or maybe it will, but the theologers are uncertain.

So Blind Lemon abandoned magic the way he should've done the day before, and stepped into the burning room, walked into the fire through the embers and the flames to wrap his mortal hands around Robert Johnson's throat and strangle that man to death.

It might've worked if there'd been time.

Certainly Blind Lemon's strangling hands had more effect on *Judgment Day* than anything else the hoodoo man had done. Three verses from the end Robert Johnson choked and hesitated, coughed and cleared his throat — and started singing again, singing just a whisper, just the faintest hint, a ghost of Armageddon, but the song was *Judgment Day* and nothing that ever lived could stop it three verses from the end.

As Robert Johnson sang.

Flames roared up around them, but the flames didn't matter. How could they matter? Blind Lemon was dead long since, and fire could never touch him again. Robert Johnson was dying of pneumonia and strangulation, and the fire couldn't kill him any faster than he was about to die.

But the flames did steal something real: they consumed Robert Johnson's guitar, the only mortal instrument that ever played *Judgment Day,* and that's a loss so dear the world can scarce afford it.

Now came the thunder that was no thunder but the Crack of Doom that sounded as the Eye of the World shattered high above them, above the river, above America and the world at the end of time — cracked so wide it like to shatter and it would have burst asunder if the *santa* had not wrapped her arms around it to hold the fragments secure to one another.

But she did hold them, and the lens stayed whole no matter what breach might divide it, as the *santa* held on dear till now with might courage and righteousness she sealed the sundered lens and closed the Eye around it.

When she was done Blind Lemon Jefferson stood alone in the smoldering wreck that once had been the owner-lady's shack. His hands still wrung Robert Johnson's neck, but that made no difference now: Robert Johnson was a dead man, and his body was as light and empty as cotton when it's blowing on the wind.

•

Later Lemon went down to Hell to find that man and make him answer for the destruction he'd wrought against the Eye, the world, and even the *santa*. But hard as Lemon searched the corridors of Hell, he could not find Robert Johnson in that awful place.

•

Our Lady of Sorrows fused the shattered lens of the Eye of the World, but she could not fuse it well enough. On the far side of the lens of the Eye there lies Lucifer's great chamber-room, the room that holds his throne and lets him rule everything from Purgatory to Damnation.

As Santa Barbara fused the Eye, ten thousand demons — ten thousand among the horde that always crowd the great chamber, supplicating themselves before the Devil — ten thousand minor devils watched the *santa* as she sealed the eye. As she worked, they tried to stop her; and when she was done they set out to destroy her work.

The *santa* saw them, of course. She saw them and she cursed them and warned them all to flee — but she could not stop them.

The devils pounded on the broken Eye for years. After a time they wore away the *santa*'s handiwork. The *santa* tried to shore it up, of course — but when she did she found that something deep and fundamental had changed in the substance of the Eye of the World, and nothing she did to the shattering fragments had any effect on them at all.

Spanish Harlem
The Present

Emma went drinking the night after the cancer finally got done with her daughter Lisa. Lisa was eight, and she'd died long and hard and painful, and when she was finally gone what Emma needed more than anything else was to forget, at least for a night.

The bar Emma went to was a dirty place called the San Juan Tavern. It was only four blocks from home — two blocks in another direction from the hospital where Lisa died. A lot of people who lived where Emma did drank at the San Juan.

She liked to tell herself she went to the San Juan for the music, and it was true the music at that place was special, music like from down home in the Delta. But the truth about the San Juan wasn't music at all: the truth was Emma Henderson went to the San Juan Tavern when she needed to drink. And that night she needed something terrible to drink.

Not that she did it with a clear conscience. Just the opposite: It made her feel dirty to be drinking with her daughter not three hours dead. Twice she thought about stopping, paying up her bill, going home and going to sleep like someone who had a little decency. But the need for succor stopped her. Instead of going home she drank more and more till now the hunger for tobacco overtook her, and she knew she'd gone too far.

Just after one in the morning she went to the machine beside the lavatory and bought Marlboros. By then her hands were trembling so bad she ripped three cigarettes opening the pack, and she couldn't wait, couldn't wait a moment because she had to smoke *now*, and she lit her first cigarette from the candle on her table even though that made the smoke taste waxy.

Emma didn't usually smoke at all — when times were good she didn't even like the smell of tobacco. But she got a taste for the stuff when things went bad, and lately she needed it all the time.

As the night wore on she smoked cigarettes end on end, lighting one from the other from the other, smoking them so hard they almost burned her lips. But they didn't help. Neither did the wine. When she was halfway through her third tumbler of the cheap red stuff the barmaid served when you didn't think to ask for something special, Mama Estrella Perez sat down across from her and clomped her can of Budweiser onto the Formica tabletop. The can tottered back and forth a couple of times like it was going to fall over and spill, and for half a moment Emma was sure the can was going to tumble to the floor — but it didn't.

Things like that happened around Mama Estrella all the time. It was like there was something in the air around her that made all the ordinary probabilities run awry.

And maybe they did. Emma had seen the *botanica* down in

Mama Estrella's store — she'd been there lots of times, even though she'd never bought anything from that part of the store. Emma didn't need that kind of stuff! She was a Baptist, not some Santeria Catholic! She'd been into Mama Estrella's store because it was right downstairs from her apartment and most of the rest of it was just a bodega. It wasn't like she could avoid the place, anyway; Mama Estrella she owned the building, which made her Emma's landlord. And besides, her bodega wasn't like most of them. It was big and clean and well lit, and it didn't *really* matter that there was a big *botanica* in the back, because nobody sensible took that stuff serious. So what if there were love potions and strange waters and things she couldn't figure out because she couldn't read Spanish very well? Emma always thought it was cute.

Then somebody told her Santeria was Cuban voodoo, and she didn't like it so much.

"Your daughter died today," Mama Estrella said. "Why're you out drinking? Why aren't you home, mourning?" Her tone made Emma feel as cheap and dirty as a streetwalker.

Emma shrugged. She knocked back the last of the awful wine in her glass, then refilled it from the bottle the bartender had left for her.

Mama Estrella shook her head and finished off her beer; someone brought her another can before she even asked. She stared at Emma. Emma kept her seat, held her ground. But after a few minutes the taste of the wine began to sour in her throat, and she wanted to cry. She knew the feeling wasn't Mama Estrella's doing, even if Mama Estrella was some sort of a voodoo woman. It was nothing but Emma's own guilt, coming to get her.

"Mama Estrella, my baby *died* today. She died a little bit at a time for six months, with a tumor that finally got to be the size of a grapefruit growing in her belly, almost looking like a child that was going to kill her before it got born." She caught her breath. "I want to drink enough that I don't see her dying like that, at least not tonight."

Mama Estrella was a lot less belligerent-looking after that. Ten minutes later she took a long drink from her beer and said, "You okay, Emma." Emma poured herself some more wine, and someone brought Mama Estrella a pitcher of beer, and they sat drinking together, not talking, for a couple of hours.

About three A.M. Mama Estrella got a light in her eye, and for just an instant, just long enough to take a breath and let it out, Emma got an awful feeling, a feeling like she ought to excuse herself and run away as far and as fast as her drunken legs could carry her.

No one lives long in Harlem without learning when to run, and Emma knew as well as anybody. But she was drunk, too drunk to know she ought to be afraid. Instead of running away she leaned forward and whispered: "What's that, Mama Estrella? What're you thinking?"

Mama Estrella sprayed her words a little as she answered. "I just thought: hey, you want your baby back? You miss her? I could make her alive again." She was even drunker than Emma was. "No, that's wrong. Not alive. More like . . . you know what a zombie is? A zombie isn't a little girl, but it's like one. It moves. It walks. It breathes if you tell it to." She took another long drink from her beer can. "I can't make your baby alive," she said. "But I can make what's left of her go away more slowly."

It was a terrible, terrible idea, and even in her grief Emma knew that from the moment Mama Estrella suggested it. But she was drunk, and she was brooding, and the parts of her with prudence and good sense were drowned in grief and wine.

"A zombie. . . ?"

She missed her little girl so bad — she didn't think. How could she think? Every time she tried to think her head was full of images, like the image of the awful dead-faced men who'd come to wheel Lisa's body from the room, all cold and businesslike. Emma had wanted to shout at them until they acted like she felt, but she couldn't find the heart.

She closed her eyes again, and another image came to her — the image of her darling baby Lisa whimpering in pain, and now she saw the awful hemorrhaging rain of blood that burst from Lisa just before she died.

It would've been better if she'd died herself, Emma thought. Dead is better than alive if you have to live without your little girl you love beyond all measure.

Mama Estrella offered Emma a handkerchief, and Emma realized she was crying. She didn't feel like she was crying. She didn't feel anything but numb, but the tears were there, and when she wiped them away they welled up all over again. She tried to stop, but it was no use. "I love my baby, Mama Estrella," she said. She tried to say more, but the words wouldn't come to her.

Mama Estrella looked grim. She nodded, picked up her beer, and poured most of it down her throat. "We go to the hospital," she said. "Get your Lisa and bring her home." She stood up. Emma took one last swallow of her wine and got up to follow.

It was hot outside — high in the eighties long after midnight, hot as summer even though it was still early in the spring.

When they got to the hospital service door Mama Estrella told Emma to wait and she'd go in and get Lisa. Emma wanted to say no, no, I'm going home I'm going to mourn my girl in peace, but she lost the words before she could speak them, and where she should have turned and run she stood at the service door shivering despite the heat, wishing she were someplace else, anyplace else at all. . . .

But she wasn't anywhere else. She was outside that awful hospital, waiting and waiting in the too-quiet night. She raised her head to look up at the sky and saw the full moon, and it looked so wrong. And it *was* wrong — it shone bright as bone china on star-shot black cloth where most nights the city moon is pale and wan, where the city's lights diminish the stars in the sky until they vanish in the greyness of the night.

Even the steamy air was silent, as though it knew a secret too terrible to hide.

Twice as Emma waited men came out the door carrying red plastic bags of garbage from the hospital. Once Emma heard a siren, and she thought for a moment that somehow she and Mama Estrella had been found out and that the police were coming for them. But that was silly; there were always sirens sounding in the Harlem night.

After twenty minutes the service door opened again, and it was Mama Estrella carrying poor dead little Lisa with her skin so pale, her eyes so hazy white with death. . . . It was too much.

"You okay, Emma?" Mama Estrella asked. She looked worried.

"I'm fine, Mama Estrella. I'm just fine." That was a lie, but Emma tried to make it true.

"We need to get to my car," Mama Estrella said. "We need to go to the graveyard."

Mama Estrella kept her car in a parking garage around the corner from the San Juan Tavern.

"I thought we were going to take her home," Emma said.

Mama Estrella shook her head. She didn't say a word.

> *Among the Saint Francois Mountains*
> *Of Southeastern Missouri*
> *August 1938*

When the sky was quiet the Lady who some people call *the goddess who repented* closed the Eye and sealed it shut. Then she set it back into its place above the great wide river, and looked on it, examining her handiwork.

When she looked on it she had a vision that chilled her to the bone.

She saw a vision of the world, the Eye, and Hell; she saw hateful ardors growing in the breasts of innocents, and breeding everywhere inside the hearts of men and women.

Our Lady of Sorrows cried when she saw that vision. She cried because the people are dear to her, and precious — but she did not turn away from it. She knew she didn't dare.

When the vision was done she shuddered and sobbed and ran to the arms of the great King, partly for comfort, partly for succor, and partly too because he and his fate were terrible keys to the vision.

She found him in his Mansion high upon the Mountain, sitting in his study where a roaring fire burned inside the great black stove. She found the Right and Left hands of the Lord, Dismas and Gestas, in his study with him, offering their counsel.

The Lady ignored them. She went to the King and shed her tears upon his shoulder until her heart could cry no more. Then she said, "I had a vision, King — a terrible terrible vision."

The King held her close, and rubbed her softly near the spine. "I saw a glimmer of it too," he said. "Your sorrow reflected on the jewel."

The jewel he meant was a tiny simulacrum of the Eye of the World that hung from a leather cord around his neck. The Lady gave that to him not long before he died; he never removed it under any circumstance.

"I saw my handiwork undone," she said. "I saw the Eye would break three times. Once now when I have sealed it; once again when that seal wears away. I saw a way to remake it then — but the only way will cost the world its soul. And even then the binding will not hold! I saw you and yours, everything that we hold dear, cast into the deep pit of oblivion. And no matter how that price was paid, the Eye still broke again. The world will fall into corruption, and then when no one can stand tall enough to stop it, damnation falls onto the world, unstoppably."

The King, the Lady, and the good Hands of the Lord stood quiet after that for the longest time, mourning against the destiny that lay before them.

"If I'm going in the pit, I'll go there unafraid. But I won't go without a fight. Is there any hope? Is there nothing we can do to fight the dark?" the King asked at last.

The Lady shook her head. "Nothing. No hope at all! No matter how we rail against the darkness, it will consume us."

And then it got quiet again. Until at last the Left Hand of the Lord spoke to them unbidden:

"You're wrong," he said. "There's always hope, no matter how it may grow faint."

The Lady arched an eyebrow; the King turned to face the Left Hand of the Lord, put a hand upon his shoulder, and spoke to him demandingly. "Tell me," the great King said. "Tell me what you see."

"Hope is a thing," the Left Hand said, "that grows in the hearts of the faithful as they struggle to survive. No matter how they suffer it never abandons them."

The great King laughed. "That's an easy moral," he said. "But I never seen a man come to good depending on rules without arrangements. Be forthright for me — tell me what to do."

The Right Hand of the Lord shook his head. "The Lord helps those who help themselves," he said. "Salvation is a thing that comes from the heart. No machination we could give you could ever salve the Eye."

"Then what do you mean?" the Lady asked. "Riddles aren't salvation, either."

The Left Hand of the Lord sighed impatiently. "Look at the world," he said. "Look into your hearts. Know the history and the mystery that's gone before you, and make salvation where you find it. There isn't any other way."

And then the Hands were gone, disappeared as thoroughly as though they'd never sat beside the King.

When the air was still again the Lady said, "They always talk in riddles. I can make no sense of them."

The great King nodded. "I can't either," he said. "But I'm going to try."

With that he opened the door to the black iron stove, and fed three good hickory logs into the fire. Took his Hammer from its place beside the book case, and tuned it, adjusting the pegs that were made from bits of his own bones.

And then he played, long and loud and hard to charm a prophecy from the roaring fire. The prophecy it gave him wasn't hope, exactly, and in most respects it made him grievously sad. But no matter how grim the news it gave him, it also gave a possibility, a shadow of a hope that grew out of the ashes like a free-bird come to season.

And no matter what it cost him, the great King took that vision to his heart. And faced the doom it made for him.

Spanish Harlem
The Present

Emma took Lisa's body from Mama Estrella and carried it to the garage. She cradled it in her arms so carefully, so lovingly — in her imagination the corpse was Lisa, alive and sleeping soundly, her beautiful delicate head resting on Emma's shoulder. When they reached Mama Estrella's car Emma stretched dead Lisa across the back seat and lingered above her for the longest while, savoring the sight of her. After a moment she stooped, kissed the dead girl's forehead, squeezed her cold limp hand.

Closed the back door, got in the front passenger seat, and watched Mama Estrella ease the car out of its parking space, out of the garage, onto the city street. She kept thinking of all the beer, and how drunk Mama Estrella had to be, but there was no sign of drunkenness in her driving. Just the opposite, in fact: she handled the car with a sureness most sober people can't manage when they're navigating Harlem.

She drove quickly, too — twenty minutes after they'd left the garage they were out in Brooklyn, driving through the cemetery's broken gate, past great grandiose monuments that crowded one another in columns without order, like unearthly soldiers run riot. They cast long shadows underneath the full-bright moon.

Emma knew those shadows hid the worst sins in the world.

She didn't like that place, not one damn bit. She didn't like bringing her precious little girl into it, either. There are things, Emma thought, that even a dead child ought never have to see — and maybe she was right. But by the time Mama Estrella's five-year-old Escort rolled into that cemetery, Lisa had seen worse things already.

And worse things still lay ahead of her.

Mama Estrella drove half a mile through the cemetery's twisting access roads, and then pulled over in front of a stand of trees. "Are there others coming, Mama Estrella? Don't you need a lot of people to have a ceremony?"

Mama Estrella scowled. She shook her head and lifted a beer from a bag on the floor of the car, opened the can and took a long pull out of it.

"You wait here until I call you, Emma," she said. She got out of the car, lifted Lisa from the back, and carried her away.

After a while Emma noticed that Mama Estrella had started a fire on top of someone's grave. She made noise, too — music, almost. Chanting, banging, shuffling her feet like a bluesman keeping time. There were other sounds, too, sounds that weren't music or even counterpoint. Emma recognized those noises, but she couldn't remember what they were, no matter how she tried. Then she heard the sound of an infant scream-ing, and she couldn't help herself anymore — she got out of the car and ran toward the fire.

By the time Emma got to the grave, it looked like Mama Estrella was already finished.

When she saw Emma she got annoyed. "You shouldn't be here," she said, scowling.

"I thought I heard a baby screaming," Emma told her.

She stepped away from Lisa for a moment, looking for something on the ground by the fire, and Emma got a look at her daughter. Lisa wasn't breathing, but her eyes were open, and as Emma looked at her she blinked.

Emma's heart lurched.

Lisa. Alive.

She could see Lisa was all empty inside, like a shell pretending to be a little girl, but even so Emma wanted to cry or pray or sing or something, anything. She ran to Lisa, grabbed hold of her and sang into her dead cold ear. *"Lisa, Lisa, my darling baby Lisa."* When her lips touched Lisa's ear it felt like butchered meat, but all the same she cried wet tears of joy.

As she cried her tears fell onto Lisa's face, into her eyes. And after a moment Lisa reached up to wrap her arms around Emma, and she said "Mama," in a voice that sounded like dry paper brushing against itself.

Emma heard Mama Estrella gasp behind her, and looked up to see her standing over the fire, trembling. "Something's inside her," Mama Estrella said.

Emma shook her head. "Nothing's inside Lisa but Lisa." Emma was sure. A mother *knew* these things. "She's just as alive as she always was."

Mama Estrella scowled. "She shouldn't be alive at all," she said. "It isn't good, a soul alive in a dead body." She frowned. "Her soul could die forever, Emma."

"What do you mean?"

"It isn't right," Mama Estrella said. "We need to put her back to rest."

Emma felt herself flush. "You're not going to touch my baby, Mama Estrella. I don't know what you're thinking, but you're not going to touch my baby."

"Emma —"

Emma pulled her daughter away. "Damn you, woman!" she

said. "Damn you straight to hell!"

Mama Estrella gaped at her. Emma thought she was going to say something, or do something, or — something. But she didn't. She didn't say a word, in fact. Didn't so much as move a muscle.

After a moment Emma took Lisa's hand. "Come on, child," she said, and she led Lisa out of the graveyard, out through Brooklyn, back toward Harlem and their home. It was a long, long way — longer than Emma would've imagined back in the cemetery when she'd walked away from Mama Estrella and her car. Lisa never complained about the distance, but a mile after they'd left the cemetery Emma began to worry about her walking that far in nothing but her bare feet, and she took the girl in her arms. After that she carried Lisa most of the way to Fulton Street, where Emma hailed a livery to drive them home.

When they got home, Emma put Lisa to bed, even though she didn't seem tired. It was long past her bedtime, and God knew it was necessary to at least keep up the pretense that life was normal.

Twenty minutes after that, she went to bed herself.

Marlin, Texas
November 1948

Blind Willie Johnson died ten years after Robert Johnson broke the Eye of the World. He died of pneumonia quietly and humble in the same Marlin Texas hovel where his mother had borne him. When he was gone his wife called on the men from the burying ground to take him and put him in the soil.

For three days he rested still as stone in the Texas dirt, dead as any deadman waiting for the Second Coming.

And then Peetie Wheatstraw came for him.

He paid the gravemen good money to dig with shovels — hard, slow, careful work that lasted hours where the backhoe could have dragged the coffin up in the time it would have took to soften up a wad of chaw.

Peetie Wheatstraw had good reason to be careful.

When the gravediggers' shovels scraped Blind Willie's coffin, Peetie Wheatstraw made them stop, change tools, and clear the remainder with garden spades.

Then the coffin was clear, and they lifted it gently to set it on the grass beside the open grave.

Wheatstraw himself hammered out the nails that held the lid secure. When they were gone he pried it free to expose Blind Willie's carcass to the light of day.

Peetie Wheatstraw stooped over the open coffin, peering at the corpse. After a moment he murmured derisively. "Get up," Peetie Wheatstraw commanded the corpse. "Ain't no sense you lying there, Blind Willie. It ain't the time for you to go to no reward."

The gravediggers sidled away from Wheatstraw; one of them mumbled something about a burial he needed to attend to.

The corpse lay silent, still as stone.

"Get on with you, Blind Willie! Ain't no use you try to lie there. The angel Death already come for you, took you home, and brought you back. She left you here on earth where you belong."

Blind Willie didn't answer.

One of the gravediggers cleared his throat. "He's dead, Mister. Can't you see?"

Peetie Wheatstraw looked up. "You think I don't know? *I* know a dead man when I see one." He shook his head. "Jesus Christ Almighty, what do you think I am?"

The grave digger gave no more answer than the carcass had.

"You got to understand," Peetie Wheatstraw said. "This isn't any ordinary body. Blind Willie — he's a *Hoodoo Doctor.* Being dead ain't no problem for a hoodoo man."

And suddenly the corpse sat bolt upright in its casket.

"Damn you!" Blind Willie shouted. "Damn your hide to Hell, Peetie Wheatstraw!"

Peetie Wheatstraw laughed so hard he like to fall into the open grave. Two of the gravediggers turned and ran for their lives; the third would've run with them if he hadn't been too scared to move.

Blind Willie scowled; he mumbled curses so quiet that only the Devil heard them — but those curses were so foul that the Devil took delight to hear Blind Willie speak them.

"Your time has come and gone, Blind Willie. But the world still needs you, and you're here. You better get used to the idea."

Blind Willie wouldn't hear it. "Go away," he said. "You want to talk to me, I'll see you at the *rapture.*"

That got Peetie Wheatstraw started laughing all over again.

"It ain't a going to work, Blind Willie. The blues have got you, and they've made you to a Doctor."

"I never sang no blues," Blind Willie said. "I sang to serve the Lord."

Peetie Wheatstraw rolled his eyes. "We all serve the Lord," he said. "God makes us who we are."

"You're wrong," Blind Willie said. "I seen the light, and I seen the darkness. I seen the halls of hell and I seen what folks who dwell there. God never made a place like that for anyone He loves."

Now suddenly Wheatstraw grew serious and sober, and when he spoke he spoke so quietly that even Blind Willie — dead and alive with the hoodoo that consumed him despite every good intention — so quietly that Blind Willie hardly heard him. "God loves us all so dear He makes us free to grow as great as we can dare."

"Free to be wrong, you mean. Free to sin!"

"Damn right."

"You better get yourself religion, boy," Blind Willie said. "You better learn to serve the Lord."

Wheatstraw didn't answer right away, and when he did answer he answered at right angles to the point. "Get up, Blind Willie. That grave no longer can contain you."

Blind Willie didn't answer that at all. He sat perched still as stone in his coffin, staring at the horizon for the longest time.

And then he began to pray.

On toward late afternoon a cold wind came down off the plains, and now the boneyard took a chill as deep as death. After a while Peetie Wheatstraw put his arm around the gravedigger who was still too terrified to move, and led him back to town.

Spanish Harlem
The Present

Everything should've been great after Lisa came back. It should have been fine and wonderful and true; it should have been a renewal that gave them life where life had slipped away. But it didn't work that way, because life never works that way: Lisa woke to her new life as angry as a jaybird frightening a pigeon.

It was hard to see at first, because she was still in her heart a good little girl who spoke politely and minded what her mother told her — but underneath the goodness and the deference the girl had a *temper.*

A bad, bad temper.

Emma first saw it the morning after Lisa's resurrection. She'd put her coffee on to brew and gone to Lisa's room to tell her breakfast was ready, and found Lisa awake in bed, playing with a mouse. God only knew how the girl had caught the thing, and damn the exterminator who'd promised to rid the building of mice two months ago, but there it was, acting like some child's darling pet, crawling back and forth across Lisa's papery hands. Such a darling little dear, Emma thought, maybe they ought to buy a cage and keep this one mouse as a pet — and then the creature stumbled, hissed, and bit deep into Lisa's left thumb.

Emma swore and rushed to her daughter's side to nurse the wound.

As Lisa screeched.

Grabbed the mouse with her free hand.

Closed her hand around it and crushed it to a pulp.

"Lisa!"

Lisa glanced over her shoulder, still angry; she looked surprised to see her mother.

"It bit me, Mama," Lisa said. And then she glanced back at the red wet goo that sopped down from her hand into the bedclothes. She sobbed. "It never should have bit me."

She sounded like she wanted to cry, but she sounded angry, too.

Emma bit her lip, tried to make her stomach be still. "The mouse is dead, Lisa," she said. Emma wasn't sure why she chose those words, but they were the only ones she could find. "You need to wash yourself, child."

Lisa looked from her mother to the dead mass in her hand and back again.

"Yes, Mama," Lisa said. She sounded like she wanted to say something else, too, but whatever it was she kept it to herself.

Emma led her to the bathroom, where she flushed the bloody mass down the toilet and washed Lisa's hands in the sink.

"I don't know what's got into you, child," Emma said. "I never seen you hurt a fly before."

Lisa frowned.

"I'm sorry, Mama," she said, rinsing and rinsing her hands in the water. And then her face seemed to crumble, and suddenly she was sobbing, sobbing and crying like a baby lost alone. "I miss my friend," she said. "I want him back."

"The mouse is dead, Lisa."

"He never should have bit me," Lisa said. And then she cried some more.

•

The mouse bite oozed pus for three long days, and when it stopped oozing Lisa's whole thumb hardened stiff as wood.

It was like — like she was still dead. She didn't eat except when Emma told her to, and every time she did the food came back up a few hours later, smelling like death. Lisa smelled like that, too, sometimes — like meat left to sit in the sun for days. And her breath! So sulfury and strange, like brimstone burning closer than you want to think.

One night Emma dreamed that the stinking rotten thing in her daughter's bedroom wasn't Lisa at all — it was some *dead* thing, a zombie, just like Mama Estrella said. It was a monster inhabited by demons, and the only peace she'd ever know was if she burned it in a bonfire.

But there was courage in her heart, and she knew the difference between her convictions and her fears.

And she knew Lisa was her daughter, her precious little girl who'd suffered a terrible miracle, and she knew that if she kept the courage of her faith the Lord would see her through.

There are some — like Mama Estrella — who would say Emma was a foolish woman, and that she should have put her daughter down to rest before she died forever. And there's reason in those words, no question. But there are times when courage and faith are better guides than reason, and this was one of those.

Emma's heart told her this was just that time. But Mama Estrella told her different. She called on the telephone over and over, trying to frighten Emma, trying to persuade her.

"Your baby's going to die, Emma," Mama Estrella would say as Emma lifted the receiver. "She's going to die forever, girl."

But Emma didn't frighten easy.

"You're wrong," she said. And she hung up the phone.

•

What *did* worry Emma was Lisa's temper. There were times it seemed unnaturally inspired, and other times it seemed natural but out of all proportion.

The night she had that awful dream Emma wandered into the kitchen for a glass of water and found Lisa by the sink, killing roaches and painting pictures with their innards around the edges of the drain.

"Lisa!" Emma had shouted, all bleary and confused, "What are you *doing*, child?"

When Lisa saw her mother she looked ashamed.

"Just killing bugs, Mama, that's all," she said, and her voice sounded guilty and repentant even if her words tried to make out like it wasn't something heinous and disgusting she'd been doing.

"Why would you *do* such a thing, child?"

And Lisa had looked up at her mother like she was about to cry. "I just get so mad, is all," she'd said. "Sometimes I get so angry I don't know what to do."

And all that night after Emma went back to bed she lay awake wondering which was real, the demoniac thing that drew her daughter to *hurt* those bugs, or the little girl who did such things even though they shamed her.

She never knew for certain.

•

The next day Mama Estrella and her sisters came looking for Lisa while Emma was away at work. She knocked three times, demanding to be let into the apartment, and when there was no answer she used her master key to open the door.

Lisa heard her, and she hid in the back corner of the closet, terrified of the chanting women and their incense. They looked and looked all through the apartment, but Lisa lay still as stone down in the dirty laundry, and they never found her.

When Emma came home she found Lisa still hiding terrified in her closet. Emma asked the girl what she was doing hiding there, and when Lisa told her Emma hit the roof.

She got on the phone and gave that Santeria Lady a piece of her mind.

But Mama Estrella didn't hear a word of it.

"Emma," Mama Estrella said, "your baby could die forever."

Emma took the phone into the living room and closed the door as much as she could without damaging the cord. When she responded her voice was even angrier than she meant it to be. "You stay away from Lisa, Mama Estrella Perez. My Lisa's just fine, she's going to be okay, and I don't want you going near her. Do you understand me?"

Mama sighed. "When you make a zombie," she said, "when you make a real one from someone dead, I mean, you can make it move. You can even make it understand enough to do what you say. But still the body rots away. It doesn't matter usually. When a zombie is gone it's gone. What's the harm? But your Lisa is inside that zombie. When the flesh rots away she'll be trapped in the bones. And we won't ever get her out."

Emma felt all cold inside. She'd seen the rot; she knew what was happening to her little girl. But there was a truth in her heart, a knowledge and certainty that rose above all argument and justification. She reached into her heart and trusted what she found, and when she answered the Santeria Lady her voice was a crucible of rage. "Don't you say things like that about my Lisa, Mama Estrella," she said. "My Lisa's *alive*, and I won't have you speaking evil of her." She opened the door and slammed the phone into its cradle before Mama Estrella could say another word.

Marlin, Texas
November 1948

Blind Willie finally left his open grave an hour after midnight. For a few moments he considered heading to the northern outskirts of town, to find his mourning wife and comfort her, but when he thought on that long enough he knew that she could never take him in her arms again, because the death that separated them was a final thing no matter how he came back to the earth.

Later he reconsidered this, and went home to look for her, but he never should have done it. It happened just the way he'd known it would as he'd stumbled from his grave: she wouldn't hear of him now that he was gone. And when he stood before her she took him for a ghost, no matter how he tried to reassure her.

When he thought about that for a while he decided she was right, and went back to the ridge over Memphis where he'd built the home that was his new existence.

But that was later — much later. That night when he left his grave he wandered into Beaumont, into the worst parts of town. He found a saloon there he never frequented, and it was doing a brisk business in bad liquor and painted women. He didn't like that place at all, but he knew he had to go there. Because he knew what he would find there, and he knew he had to face it.

And he did face it. He only hesitated a moment outside the barroom door, and then he pushed in, past the drunkards and the devil-music and the party women with their wide smiles and their hearts and eyes so full of self-contempt; through the pool-hall on the far side of the bar, into the back room where the real money was.

He found Peetie Wheatstraw there, sitting at a table with five other gentlemen, playing cards for stakes even deadmen can't afford.

The gamblers glared at Blind Willie as he burst into their room. One of them made to draw his pistol, but Blind Willie waved that threat away with a gesture of his hand.

"You woke me, William Bunch. Tell me what you want so I can return to my rest."

Peetie Wheatstraw threw his cards down on the table and pushed his stake into the pot. "It took you long enough, Blind Willie," he said. "You're a stubborn kind of man."

"You're ignoring my request, William Bunch. I mean to get this done."

Peetie Wheatstraw took Blind Willie by the arm and led him through the back-room door, into the bar. "There's something you don't understand," he whispered.

Blind Willie didn't answer that; instead he glared at Peetie Wheatstraw, waiting for him to go on.

"I can't tell you here," he said. "We need to go where we can talk."

He led Blind Willie out of the bar, into the night; through the empty streets of Beaumont to the boneyard Blind Willie had walked away from not an hour earlier.

As they went the deadman who sometimes called himself the Devil's Son-in-Law hummed a little tune, and though it was no melody Blind Willie could name, he recognized the tune.

Because it was the shadow of the music of the world, and Blind Willie was a part of it, same as you and me. But his part was a large one, very clear; it sang him like a refrain, some ways, because Blind Willie was a crucial bit of everything to happen.

Before they reached his grave Blind Willie knew what lay ahead of him, and he knew why he had woken. He knew Peetie Wheatstraw hadn't been the one to wake him at all, but only a deadman come to greet him; he knew that he was damned to life on Hell and earth, no matter how piously he'd tried to live his life.

And he accepted all of that, because he had the Grace and Faith to accept the fate he never meant to find.

"Tell the King he knows where he can find me," Blind Willie said. And then he walked away to find the wreck of his subsistence on the surface of the world.

Spanish Harlem
The Present

As the summer wore on it grew hotter and hotter in the tenement — hotter than any Harlem summer Emma ever lived.

The heat went bad on Lisa.

Her skin drew chalky, greasy; her hair fell away in clots. Her eyes shriveled in their bony sockets until they hung free, trembling as she moved. The ichorous mound that once had been the cancer in her belly swelled and bloated till Lisa's tiny desiccated form became a caricature of a pregnant corpse.

When the rot had all but consumed her, Lisa had a dream. In the morning, she told her mother about it.

"The Lady came to me last night, Mama," Lisa said.

Emma Henderson frowned. "What lady is that, Lisa?"

"The Lady from my *dream,* Mama."

Emma didn't like it, not one bit. "What did she say, Lisa?"

"She told me not to be afraid, Mama." She looked out the window. "I'm going to die again, aren't I, Mama?"

Emma pursed her lips, set her teeth. When she spoke she spoke carefully, trying not to show how scared she was. "I'm not going to let you die, child," she said. "Don't you worry about that."

Lisa took that in, but she didn't look like she believed it.

"The Lady took me through a city," Lisa said. "She held my hand and showed me all the stuff along the River. Factories and dockyards, old houses with the rot. One place there was a well covered up with stones, and she said it went so deep they drink from it in Hell."

Emma rubbed her temples. She didn't want to think about dreams like that. She didn't want to *know* about them.

Not that she had a choice.

"By the well there was a man with a guitar," Lisa said. "He played music so beautiful it made me want to cry."

"Tell me," Emma said. "Tell me what he sang." She didn't want to know the song, no more than she wanted to think about the dream. But she knew she had to hear.

"He sang about Damnation," Lisa said, "and all about the Eye of the World. But before he told it all he stopped, and the Lady said his song was *Judgment Day.*"

She said that like her mother ought to know just what that meant, and Emma did know, of course, because everybody down home in the Delta knew there was a song called *Judgment Day.* But Lisa hadn't ever gone down home, and Emma couldn't figure where she could have heard of such a thing.

"Don't you ever sing that song, child," Emma told her daughter. "I don't care why you think you need to. I don't want you dreaming about it, neither."

As if there was any way the girl could stop a dream.

"Yes, Mama," Lisa said, obedient as ever, no matter how her mother asked a thing no child could deliver.

"It isn't right, you growing up like this," Emma said. "We've got to set this house in order." And that wasn't right, because the house was tidy as could be, no matter how the stink of Lisa rotting overwhelmed the air. "You need a normal life, child. School and play, Girl Scouts in the afternoon. You need to go to church on Sundays, and get right with the Lord."

Lisa laughed when her mother said those words, *get right with the Lord.*

"I'm serious!" Emma said. "If we were home I'd take you to a revival tent!"

Lisa laughed and laughed, and after a while Emma started trying to think about the churches here in Harlem, and wondering if there was any of them that weren't full of politics and welfare, and maybe it really was time to find religion.

But then Emma realized how wonderful it was to hear her daughter laughing, to see the girl's dead-eyed face alive with sunshine and delight, and the thought of church got lost in the beauty of the afternoon.

By the time Emma found it again it was too late for any preacher in the world to help them.

●

Because everything went to hell early the next morning, and by the time the dust had settled nothing was the same. It started when Emma gave her girl a kiss on the cheek, early in the morning. It never really ended.

"I love you, darling," Emma said, and she stooped and braced herself to give her putrefying girl a kiss. And she did it, too — but when she did it went all wrong. Big oozy flakes of the girl's cheek came away on Emma's lips, and before she could make herself be still Emma screamed and screamed again. It was too much, too damn much, and the faith that'd given her the courage to tell Mama Estrella to go away the day before evaporated in a binding moment made from terror —

And Lisa looked so hurt.

So hurt.

Then Emma got a grip on her heart, and she made herself be silent as she wiped the liquefying flesh away from her lips.

"We need to do something, baby girl," Emma said.

"I know, Mama."

Emma bit her lip and tried to think, but all she could think was how they had to clean her daughter up. The moment she had that thought she knew it was trouble, that it was the worst thing she could do. It ran against common sense, cleaning up a girl who'd begun to fall apart!

Emma shook her head and went back to the kitchen for more coffee.

Lisa followed her.

"I'm scared, Mama," Lisa said.

Emma bit her lip. She wanted to wail, or shout, or — *something*. She wanted to find God and ring his ears for letting her daughter fall into such a state.

She really did.

And as she thought that blasphemy, the last bits of her faith slipped away from her so quietly she didn't even notice.

She bit her lower lip.

"I'm frightened too, child," she said. She kept trying to think. Rot was about germs, wasn't it? And germs hate heat, and they hate disinfectants.

That was no help at all. What was she going to do, boil her daughter? Pickle her in rum?

And that was when it came to her, the terrible idea that she never should have thought.

Alcohol.

There was rubbing alcohol in the cabinet, wasn't there? Emma stepped into the bathroom, opened the cabinet, and found a half-empty bottle of rubbing alcohol.

Not enough. Half a bottle of alcohol wasn't enough to wash a girl falling apart with the rot. They needed more — a whole tub full of the stuff. "You wait here in the closet, baby," Emma said. "I've got to go to the grocery." She stooped, kissed Lisa's forehead — and felt more tiny fragments of Lisa's skin flake away on her lips.

They tasted like cured meat.

Emma tried not to think about the flavor, because the more she thought about it the more she wanted to get sick, but whether she thought about it or not the taste of preserved meat followed her all the way to the store.

And home again to Lisa, huddled and crumbling in her closet. Lisa was asleep there when Emma got back.

"Lisa?" Emma said. She pulled the clothes aside and looked into the closet. Lisa was curled up in the corner of the closet with her head tucked into her chest and her hands folded over her stomach. "Lisa, are you awake, honey?"

Lisa looked up and nodded. The whites of her too-small eyes were dull yellow. "Mama," she said, "I'm scared." She *looked* afraid, too. She looked terrified.

Emma bit into her lower lip. "I'm scared too, baby. Come on." She put up her hand to help Lisa up, but Lisa didn't take it. She stood up on her own, and when Emma moved aside she walked out of the closet.

"What're you going to do, Mama?"

"I'm going to give you a bath, baby. With something that'll stop what's happening to your body." Emma said. "You get yourself undressed and get in the bathtub, and I'll get every-thing ready."

Lisa looked like she didn't really believe what Emma was saying, but she did as her mother asked all the same. When Emma got to the bathroom with the shopping bag Lisa had her nightgown up over her head. She finished taking it off and stepped into the tub without even turning around.

"Put the stopper in the tub for me, baby," Emma said. She took a bottle of alcohol from the bag, carried it to Lisa.

And something down in her heart started shouting at her, telling her she was about to make a terrible mistake.

A terrible, terrible mistake.

But that was silly, wasn't it? Silly. Lisa was sick and she was falling apart and Emma had to do something, didn't she? Something, anything to save her?

The voice in her heart said it was better to do nothing, but that had to be wrong, didn't it?

Had to be.

And so despite the best counsel of her heart Emma doused her daughter in spirit liquor.

Spirit liquor.

The old word, the *real* word, for the alcohol in liquor is *spirit*.

The reason we use that word is lost so far back in time and drunkenness that very few recall it, but it's no mistake — there's magic deep in alcohol, and not just intoxication.

Lisa was a dead girl made live by necromantic sacrilege, as magical as anyone who's ever walked the earth. When Emma washed her in that *spirit liquor* she made a mistake she never stopped regretting.

"This may sting a little," Emma said. "Hold out your hand and let me make sure it doesn't hurt too much."

Lisa extended her hand, and Emma poured the spirit on her.

"What does that feel like?"

"It doesn't feel like anything at all, Mama. I don't feel anything anymore."

"Not anywhere?"

"No, Mama."

Emma shook her head, gently, almost as though she hoped Lisa wouldn't see it. Not feeling anything? That was dangerous. The whole idea frightened Emma.

"Close your eyes, baby. This won't be good for them even if it doesn't hurt." She held the bottle over Lisa's head and tilted it. Clear fluid streamed out of the bottle and into the girl's hair. After a moment it began to run down her shoulders in little rivulets. One of them snaked its way into the big open wound of Lisa's belly and pooled in an indentation on the top of the cancer. For a moment Emma thought something horrible would happen, but nothing did.

Emma poured all ten bottles of *spirit liquor* onto Lisa. When she was done the girl sat in an inch-deep pool of the stuff, soaked with it. Emma — who still didn't realize the awful thing she'd done — thought the girl needed to soak awhile, so she left Lisa in the tub and went to the kitchen to make another pot of coffee.

Poured a cup, sat in a chair at the kitchen table, and opened a magazine she'd bought three months ago and never got the chance to read.

Took a cigarette from the pack she kept on the shelf above the kitchen table, lit it, smoked. It'd been two months since she'd had a cigarette, and the pack was very stale, but Emma didn't care. She needed a cigarette, and stale cigarettes were better than none.

After twenty minutes Lisa screamed. In the middle of her scream she abruptly went silent. Emma bolted out of her seat, rushed to the bathroom —

"Mama," Lisa said. Her voice was so still and quiet . . . it gave Emma a chill. "I'm *melting.*"

She held out her right hand, and Emma saw Lisa's too-thin fingers — they looked like wet clay soaked in water. Milky fluid dripped from them.

Lisa stood up in the tub, and slime drizzled down her butt and thighs. She glared up at Emma, and her shrunken little eyes turned hard and mean and angry, and she screamed again.

Where before she'd screamed in terror, now her scream was murderous rage, and Emma was certain the girl was going to kill her.

"Mama," she shouted, and she launched herself at Emma. "Stupid, stupid, *stupid* Mama!" She raised her fist up over her head and hit Emma square on the breast, and *hard.* Harder than Lisa's father'd ever hit her, back when he was still around. Lisa brought her other fist down, just as hard, then pulled them back and hit her again, and again, and again.

Emma couldn't even move herself out of Lisa's way. She didn't have the spirit for it.

For a moment it didn't even look like Lisa beating on her. It looked like some sort of a monster, a dead zombie-thing that any moment would reach into her chest, right through her flesh, and rip out her heart. And it would eat her bloody-dripping heart while it was still alive and beating, and Emma's eyes would close, and she'd die.

"All your *stupid* fault, Mama! All your *stupid, stupid* fault!" She grabbed Emma by the belt of her uniform skirt and shook her and shook her. Then she screamed and pushed Emma away, threw her against the wall. Emma's head and back hit too hard against the rock-thick plaster wall, and she fell to the floor. She lay on her side all slack and beaten, staring at her daughter, watching to see what she'd do next.

Lisa stared right back at her, her shriveled eyes and cracking lips contorted in a mask of rage. For a moment Emma thought the girl would kill her —

And then something happened on Lisa's face.

Her expression shifted — crumbled, almost. Suddenly she looked all slack and beaten, and her legs dropped out from under her, and she fell to the floor.

She started to cry. Sob, sob, sob, big gasping tortured bleats, broken and pathetic and so sad it like to break Emma's battered heart. The sound of it melted Emma's terror, and after a moment turned it to tenderness.

And what could she do?

What could she do?

She crawled to Lisa's side and put her arms around her.

And held her for the longest time.

"It's okay, baby," Emma said. "Mama loves you." One of her hands brushed across the open cancer in Lisa's belly, and Emma felt an ominous electric throb. She wanted to screech, to flinch away, but she knew that if she did that it'd be like pushing Lisa away, so she clenched her teeth and made herself be still. Lisa's little body heaved with her sobs; her back pressed painfully against Emma's bruised breasts. "Mama loves you."

Emma looked at Lisa's hands, and saw that the flesh had all crumbled away from them. They were nothing but bones, like the skeleton one of the doctors at the hospital kept in his office.

"I want to die, Mama," Lisa said. Her voice was all quiet again.

Emma squeezed her, and held her a little tighter. *I want to die, Mama.*

And Emma thought, *She's right, she's right, my baby needs to die,* and because her faith had left her she couldn't see how false that was. *Mama Estrella is right. It's wrong for a little girl to be alive after she was dead.*

"Baby, baby, baby, baby, I love my baby," Emma cooed. Lisa was crying even harder now, and she'd begun to tremble in a way that wasn't natural at all.

"You wait here, baby. I got to call Mama Estrella." Emma lifted herself up off the floor, which made everything hurt all at once.

Emma went to the kitchen, lifted the telephone receiver, and dialed Mama Estrella's number. As the phone began to ring Emma wandered back toward the bathroom, watching Lisa, trying to save her memory forever.

The girl lay on the bathroom floor, shaking. The tremor had gotten worse, much worse, in just the time it'd taken Emma to dial the phone. As Emma watched it grew more and more intense, till finally Emma thought the girl would shake herself to pieces.

As Mama Estrella finally answered the phone.

"Hello?"

"Mama Estrella?" Emma said, "I think maybe you better come up here."

Mama Estrella didn't say anything at all; the line was completely silent. The silence felt bitter and mean.

"I think maybe you were right, Mama. Right about Lisa, I mean." Emma looked down at the floor and squeezed her eyes shut. She leaned back against the wall and tried to clear her head. "I think . . . maybe you better hurry. Something's wrong. I don't understand."

Lisa made a little sound halfway between a gasp and a scream, and something went *thunk* on the floor. Emma didn't have the heart to look up to see what had happened, but she started back toward the kitchen to hang up the phone.

"Mama Estrella, I got to go. Come here *now,* please?"

"Emma . . ." Mama Estrella started to say, but Emma didn't hear her; she'd already hung up, and she was running back to the bathroom, where Lisa was.

Lisa was shivering and writhing on the bathroom floor. Her left arm, from the elbow down, lay on the floor not far from her.

Emma took Lisa in her arms and lifted her up off the floor.

"You've got to be still, honey," she said. "You're going to tremble yourself to death."

Lisa nodded and gritted her teeth and for a moment she was pretty still. But it wasn't anything she could control, not for long. Emma carried Lisa to her bedroom, and by the time she got there the girl was shaking just as bad as she had been.

There was a knock on the front door, but Emma didn't pay any attention. If it was Mama Estrella she had her own key, and she'd use it. Emma sat down on the bed beside Lisa and stroked her hair.

After a moment Mama Estrella showed up in the bedroom doorway, carrying some kind of a woody-looking thing that burned with a low flame and smoked something awful.

Mama Estrella went to the window and closed it, then drew down the shade.

"Water," she said. "Bring me a kettle of hot water."

"You want me to boil water?" There was smoke everywhere already; it was harsh and acrid and when a wisp of it caught in Emma's eye it burned like poison. Lisa wheezed and coughed as the smoke drifted toward her, coughed and coughed and coughed no matter how she hadn't drawn a breath she didn't need to speak since she'd died.

"No, there isn't time. Just bring a kettle of hot water from the tap."

Then Mama Estrella bent down to look at Lisa, and suddenly it was too late for hot water and magic and putting little girls to rest.

The thick smoke from the burning thing settled onto Lisa's face, Lisa began to gag. She took in a long wheezing-hacking breath, and for three long moments she choked on it, or maybe on the corruption of her own lungs. Then she began to cough, deep, throbbing, hacking coughs that shook her hard against the bed.

Mama Estrella pulled away from the bed. She looked shocked and frightened and unsure.

"Lisa, be *still!*" Emma shouted, and Lisa sat up, trying to control herself. But it only made things worse — the next cough sent her flying face-first onto the floor. She made an awful smacking sound when she hit; when she rolled over Emma saw that she'd broken her nose.

Lisa wheezed, sucking in air.

She's breathing, Emma thought. *Please, God, she's breathing now and she's going to be fine. Please.*

But even as Emma thought it she knew that it wasn't going to be so. The girl managed four wheezing breaths, and then she was coughing again, and much worse — Emma saw bits of the meat of her daughter's lungs spatter on the hardwood floor.

She bent down and hugged Lisa, hugged her tight to make her still. "Be still, baby. Hold your breath for a moment and be still. Mama Estrella loves you, Lisa." But Lisa didn't stop, she couldn't stop, and the force of her wracking was so mean that her shoulders dug new bruises in Emma's breast. When Lisa finally managed to still herself for a moment she looked up at Emma, her eyes full of desperation, and she said, *"Mama . . ."*

And then she coughed again, so hard that her tiny body pounded into Emma's breast, and her small, hard-boned chin slammed down onto Emma's shoulder.

Slammed down so hard that the force of it tore free the flesh of Lisa's neck.

And Lisa's head tumbled down Emma's back, and rolled across the floor.

Her head rolled over and over until it came to a stop against the leg of a chair. Lisa's eyes blinked three times and then they closed forever.

Her body shook and clutched against Emma's chest for a few more seconds, the way a chicken does when you axe it. When the spasming got to be too much to bear Emma let go, and watched her daughter's corpse shake itself to shreds on the bedroom floor. After a while the tumor-thing fell out of it, and everything was still.

Everything but the cancer. It quivered like grey, moldy-rotten pudding that you touched on a back shelf in the refrigerator because you'd forgotten it was there.

"Oh my God," Mama Estrella said.

Emma felt scared and confused, and empty, too, like something important had torn out of her and there was nothing left inside but dead air.

But even if Emma was hollow inside, she couldn't force her eye away from the cancer. Maybe it was morbid fascination, and maybe it was something else completely, but she knelt down and looked at it, watched it from so close she could almost taste it. There was something about it, something wrong. Even more wrong than it had been before.

"She's dead, Emma. She's dead forever."

Emma shuddered, but still she couldn't force herself away. The tumor began to still, but one of its ropy grey veins still pulsed. She reached down and touched it, and the whole grey mass began to throb again.

"What is it, Mama Estrella? Is it alive?"

"I don't know, Emma. I don't know what it is, but it's dead."

Then the spongy grey tissue at the tumor's crest began to swell and bulge, to bulge so far that it stretched thin and finally split.

"Like an egg, Mama Estrella," Emma said. "It almost looks like an egg when a chick is hatching. I've seen that on the television, and it looks just like this."

Emma reached over toward the split, carefully, carefully, imagining some horrible monster would reach up out of the thing and tear her hand from her wrist. But there was no monster, only hard, leathery hide. She set the fingers of her other hand against the far lip of the opening and pried the split wide so that she could peek into it. But her head blocked what little light she could let in.

Small gurgling sounds came out of the darkness.

Emma crossed herself and mumbled a prayer too quiet for anyone else to hear.

And reached down, into her daughter's cancer.

Before her hand was halfway in, she felt the touch of a tiny hand. It startled her so badly that she almost screamed. To hold it back she bit into her lip so hard that she tasted her own blood.

A baby's hand.

Then a baby girl was crawling up out of the leathery grey shell, and Mama Estrella was praying out loud, and Emma felt herself crying with joy.

"I love you, Mama," the baby said. Its voice was Lisa's voice, just as it'd been before her sickness.

Emma wanted to cry and cry and cry, but instead she lifted her baby Lisa out of the cancer that'd borne her, and she held her to her breast and loved her so hard that the moment felt like forever and ever.

Among the Saint Francois Mountains
Of Southeastern Missouri
August 1938

The great King played his Hammer as the fire roared inside

the iron stove there in his study, and as he played a vision
flowered in the fire. It was like the vision that the Lady saw
when she looked into the Eye of the World, but it was different,
too, because the great King's song touched it, and changed it.

That was the nature of the great King's song: it twisted in
upon the music that is the world, and subtly bent the beat into
the melody until it grew in ways no other songster could
imagine: he made his song into the music of the world until
he made that song his own.

His song found the meekest people at the periphery of the
world, and whispered to them in their dreams until they woke
to stand tall, casting ominous shadows on the destiny of the
world. It found poor doomed damned Robert Johnson, cast
from Hell to spite his hubris, and helped him find the light;
it found a boy in Los Angeles with half a gift too small for the
ambition he could never grow to fill, and it whispered greatness
to him; it found a woman who'd loved the King more dearly
than her own life, and guided her through Hell.

It found the hapless boy who would inherit from the great
King, and tried to make him strong enough to bear the load
that fell to him — but it hardly could attempt to make the boy
that strong.

It found the great King's rivals, the Blind Lords of the
Piedmont, and whispered to them pleadingly, begging for
succor; but they could hardly give it.

It found a tiny girl across two generations, and twisted her
heart into a bitter, angry thing, filled with rage and spite. It
turned her into an awful thing that was three parts child and
one part demon, but it made her strong, too, and made her
tough and brave enough to face the awful lot that fell to her.

It spoke to the Hands and the Lady, and it persuaded them
that there was hope inside damnation, no matter what it cost.

When the song was done, the Lady knew that there was hope,
but still she grieved. Because the only hope would cost her and
the world everything she loved, and even then it was only half
a possibility, fainter than the shadow of salvation where it falls
upon the Damned in Hell.

But no matter how she grieved, no matter what she lost, the
Lady stood true, and made her world as best she could. And

in the end that's all there is, isn't it? Is there anything more that any one of us can do?

Outside Memphis, Tennessee
July 1948

When Robert Johnson died he went to Hell — everyone who dies unrepentant goes to Hell, and there was no aspect of Robert Johnson's hubris that could except him from damnation.

Robert Johnson went to Hell, and the Devil looked into his heart to see the hubris that had near destroyed the world, and he cast Robert Johnson out from the pit.

Robert Johnson tried to get back in — more than once. Of course he did! Hell ain't Heaven, but it's a better place for sinners than wandering the world. But no matter how Robert Johnson tried, no matter how he sang nor what the song, no matter the greatness of his craft nor the truth inside his blues, he could not charm the Hell-door open.

Later — years later — he grew great enough to walk back and forth across the threshold of damnation as you and I step through ordinary doors. But that was years away.

Because he could not go to Hell, Robert Johnson wandered the world with no purpose plan or destination.

Like a ghost, but more real.

Sometimes he played his guitar, and other times he didn't; music is like that for deadmen. They like the sound, the music and the magic, but only when it pleases them — they have no passion for performance. That's just as well, the way it happens: things *happen* when deadmen sing. Hoodoo things. Robert Johnson wasn't any Hoodoo Doctor, but he was deader than the best of them, and his music had a magic all its own.

As the years wore on his purposeless meandering reduced him to a derelict — but that reduction taught him, too, in the way that indignity can show a man the error of his ways, and bit by bit Robert Johnson came to see the falseness of his pride.

One night he found himself in a trainyard long after midnight, sitting around a bonfire with two vagabond thieves who'd followed him halfway across a continent.

He looked at the bums, the fire, the half-open can of beans

warming in the embers, and he shut his eyes. Pulled his guitar over his shoulder onto his lap, and just sat there for the longest time, listening to the music of the world.

After a while he plucked two and seven on his guitar, and he heard the blues metamorphosing into a waltz.

As he heard that metamorphic sound he heard the echo of his wasted life.

Hearing, he looked back on his life and his wandering past death in a way his vanity had never let him see before that moment.

And he said, *I'm a fool.*

And then he thought, *I was wrong.*

And the moment the words whispered on the inside of his head he knew how true they were, and he felt ashamed and small and broken and afraid.

I could have torn the world in two, he thought, but that was only the half of it. *Lordie Lordie please forgive me,* he thought, and then he sang those words.

Now, when the damned repent they can move on to their reward, and because they can the Devil takes the act quite personal. He pays repentant sinners special mind.

Every demon down in Hell pays mind, in fact.

The Devil had scarcely thought of Robert Johnson since he'd cast him out of Hell, but he thought of him that day. Worse, he went to earth to watch him (as the Devil always can, because in the truest way there is the Devil is always at our backs). And the Devil saw Robert Johnson sing *"Lordie Lordie please forgive me."*

The Devil hates that song most of all.

As Robert Johnson sang the vagabond thieves who'd been his companions for so many months transformed miraculously into their true selves, and Robert Johnson saw they were repented sinners too, and their names were Dismas and Gestas, and they were the thieves who died on crosses at the Right and Left Hands of the Lord.

On the far side of the fire the Pearly Gates of Heaven opened out before him, and Robert Johnson saw he was redeemed.

He lurched to his feet and stumbled toward the Gates of Heaven, not even noticing when he stepped into the bonfire.

He was too intent on the Majesty of Heaven, the splendor he could almost see through the pearly haze so thick around the gate, and anyway the fire didn't burn him because he'd found a state of Grace few of us will ever know.

As he approached the open gate Saint Peter stepped out to welcome Robert Johnson with open arms.

Robert Johnson cried for joy.

When his tears dried Saint Peter took his hand and told him seven Mysteries. Robert Johnson listened because he'd learned the humility to listen when the blessed voices speak, but he hardly understood.

And is that any wonder? Few can think of Mysteries when the sight of Heaven lies waiting just a hazy fog beyond their vision.

When the Mysteries were spoken Saint Peter looked Robert Johnson in the eye, and he told him what he couldn't bear to hear.

"You can go to your reward," Saint Peter said, "if that's what you really want."

There was something in the saint's voice that told him that he shouldn't. Robert Johnson asked him what he meant.

"The world isn't done with you," Saint Peter said. "It needs you now in ways it never could before."

Robert Johnson couldn't figure what he meant. "I don't understand," he said. "What am I supposed to do?"

The saint frowned and shook his head. "I can't tell you that," he said, "because it isn't certain yet. But the world will need your gifts."

Robert Johnson heard Saint Peter, and the words hurt him worse than he could say, but he took them to heart all the same. He nodded and he turned around and walked back into our world, through the fire and into a clear cold day in 1948.

When the last of the fire was behind him Robert Johnson stood five hundred miles from the trainyard, on a fateful ridge above Memphis, Tennessee.

When he looked into the sky over Memphis he could see the ghost of the Eye of the World, just as he'd seen it the day he cracked its lens and died.

When he saw the Eye he heard a scream behind him — a

terrible, terrible scream, the most terrible sound he'd ever heard, alive or dead or in between, no matter that he'd walked to corridors of Hell before the Devil cast him out.

And he turned around to look behind him, and saw the Devil who'd watched him all this time.

As the Devil screamed in terror to see the bright face of the Eye of the World — he can only bear to look upon the nether Eye, which hung that year above the mantel of his great room in the Mansion called Defiance down in Hell. When he saw the good face of the Eye, the Devil lunged into the sky to steal it, but before he could it vanished like a dream.

And then the Devil vanished, too.

•

When the Devil and the Eye were gone, Robert Johnson wandered down along the ridge toward Memphis. When he was halfway down, he met Blind Willie.

Blind Willie was a deadman, a Hoodoo Doctor, and Robert Johnson knew that the moment he set eyes on him. And Robert Johnson thought that was so funny, to see the gospel man transubstantiated by the Devil's music and made into a hoodoo man. He laughed as he saw Blind Willie. Blind Willie frowned at him in turn.

"You wouldn't help me, Blind Willie," Robert Johnson said. "I needed you."

Blind Willie shook his head; he tried to smile, but it didn't really come off — partly because he wasn't pleased, partly because a smile isn't a pleasant expression when it's forced onto the face of a deadman. "No," Blind Willie said, "you're wrong. I wouldn't *lie* to you, Robert Johnson. You wouldn't help yourself."

Robert Johnson scowled. He said, *"Shit."* But he knew the gospel man was right.

Blind Willie ignored the swear word. "Follow me, Robert Johnson," he said, and he led him off the Memphis trail, into the pine forest that grew on the ridge slope. After a while they were deep in a woods so dense and dark that it was hard to see the river or the sky. Now here before them was a hobo shack, and Blind Willie opened the door and showed Robert Johnson in.

Robert Johnson could've mistook Blind Willie for a sighted man if it weren't for the empty sockets of his eyes half-visible through his dark blind man's glasses.

"Have a seat," Blind Willie said, "and I'll put on the coffee."

Robert Johnson wasn't sure why the gospel man had led him to this place, and by and by now he began to grow uneasy.

"Why have you taken me here?" Robert Johnson asked. "What is this place?"

"Just my home, that's all," Blind Willie said. "You like your coffee black?"

"I like cream," Robert Johnson said. "Why are we here?"

Blind Willie crossed the room as graceful as a dancer, coffepot and cream pitcher in one hand, two empty mugs in the other.

"The Lady came to me last night," he said. "She came to me in a dream, and she told me things."

Robert Johnson snorted. "She tell you where to find me?"

Blind Willie smiled deadly.

"As a matter of fact, she did."

"What else she tell you?"

A dead little laugh, now, hollow and echoy but full of good humor.

"She told me. . . ." Blind Willie said, and then he hesitated. "She told me that you'd know seven Mysteries, but you wouldn't know what to do with them."

Robert Johnson went all stiff and tense, frightened-like, and you'd be surprised how natural and easy that posture looks when a deadman does it.

"She said that, huh?"

"She didn't say those words."

"I hope she didn't."

Blind Willie set the cups and coffee on the kitchen table, sat down in one of the chairs, poured two cups of coffee. "Go ahead," he said, "have some coffee. Set a spell."

Robert Johnson hesitated before he took a chair, but only for a moment. He sat, took the coffee, and waited for Blind Willie to ask him for the Mysteries.

But Blind Willie never did.

After a while Robert Johnson got tired of waiting. He went

ahead and said the first of them without waiting to be asked.

"A bone is a thing that binds a body to the soil," Robert Johnson said.

Of course that made no sense, but Blind Willie understood it anyway. Oh how he understood!

"Of course," Blind Willie said. He smiled ruefully. "I always knew that in my heart."

"You lie," Robert Johnson told him.

But that just wasn't so. Blind Willie never lied; there wasn't a solitary falsehood in his heart. "I wouldn't lie about the truth," he said. "Nobody could do that."

Robert Johnson scowled. "Shit," he said, two syllables, just like a boy responding to a tall tale.

"Go on," Blind Willie said. "What else?"

Robert Johnson eyed him coldly. "Music is a song you hear but never play."

Blind Willie looked at him uncertainly. "Are you sure about that?" he asked. "You got that wrong, I think. It sure ain't right."

Robert Johnson swore; he looked surprised. "The song you hear," he said, "is the music in your heart. The chords it plays are the music of the world."

Blind Willie rolled his eyes. "I *know* that one. Everybody does! I want the mysteries from heaven, Robert Johnson. It's important. Ain't right for you to lead me wrong."

"If I tell you," Robert Johnson said, "you got to tell me what it means."

Blind Willie didn't answer right away. When he finally did answer he didn't look happy at all.

"I tried to do that once," he said. "But nobody ever heard. You know what I mean? It's like, if you understand, you understand it in your heart, soon as you hear. And if you don't you ain't yet meant to hear, and no one could ever tell you."

Robert Johnson stood up suddenly, violently. His chair went flying away from him. "I'm leaving here, old man," he said. "I ain't never coming back."

Blind Willie looked very, very sad.

"Suit yourself," he said. "God speed you on your way."

●

Robert Johnson lied, of course. He came back banging on Blind Willie's door before an hour had elapsed. Blind Willie didn't notice right away, that was how deep he was thinking of the one mystery Robert Johnson had told him, so deep in contemplation that the ridge could have dropped down into the river and he wouldn't even notice.

"Robert Johnson!" Blind Willie said as he finally heard the door. "Come in, come in."

"I need your help, Blind Willie," Robert Johnson said. "I got lost in this damned woods of yours."

Blind Willie was still in his chair at the kitchen table. He had his guitar on his lap, and he was picking a song Robert Johnson knew in his heart but couldn't remember no matter how he tried. He thought, *That's* Judgment Day, *it has to be, it has to be a snatch from* Judgment Day *to do that to my heart.* But it wasn't *Judgment Day* at all, and Robert Johnson knew that better than anyone else.

"What's that, Blind Willie?" Robert Johnson asked. "I never heard that song."

Blind Willie grinned.

"It's a mystery," he said. "Will you give me your secrets if I tell you the tune?" He wasn't serious, and they both knew it.

Robert Johnson scowled. "Get on with you," he said. "Where did you get that song?"

Blind Willie laughed.

"You ought to get yourself a hymnal, Robert Johnson," he said. He was still picking out the melody, strumming quietly on his guitar. "It's called 'The Ode to Joy.'"

Robert Johnson snorted. "Ain't nothing in no hymnal sounds like that," he said, pulling his guitar off the strap where it hung on his back; moving his hands across the strings; picking up the refrain.

He was right, of course. Blind Willie had reworked "The Ode to Joy" considerably — he'd syncopated the beat, rearranged the phrases, rebuilt the structure until it grew bluesy. It was strange, powerful music; it made the world around them irresistibly beautiful. They say God whispered in Beethoven's ear as he wrote "The Ode to Joy"; everyone who ever heard Blind Willie play his version of the ode said he heard the word from God.

And maybe those people *did* hear. Certainly Robert Johnson heard. The sound was nearly dear enough to call him back to Heaven.

It might've called him, too, if Blind Willie hadn't let go his guitar and reached up to take hold of Robert Johnson's arm.

"Don't let it carry you away," he said. "This ain't the time for that."

Robert Johnson laughed derisively, like to say *what makes you think such a foolish thing?*, but he really didn't carry it off. Blind Willie knew all sorts of things — some of them because he had the sight and could see for himself; some because he'd heard the word about a lot of things to come. He patted Robert Johnson on the back and told him not to be afraid.

Johnson hardly even heard him. How could he hear Blind Willie when his mind's eye was showing him the Pearly Gates of Heaven?

No way at all, plain and simple.

"I got lost in your woods, Blind Willie," Robert Johnson said. "How do I get out of here?"

"If you need to know the way," Blind Willie said, "that's what I'll show you."

Robert Johnson snorted. "I bet you will," he said.

"I never gamble," Blind Willie said, standing in the doorway, looking Robert Johnson blindly in the eye. "You want to follow me or not?"

He stood and started toward the door.

Robert Johnson let out a breath; the sound wasn't a sigh, exactly, and it wasn't a gasp, either. Defeated, or tired, or exasperated — it was something like that. He followed Blind Willie out of the shack, into the swept yard beneath the pines.

Three paths led away from the shack. None of them led directly back toward Memphis.

"If you need to come this way again," Blind Willie said, "remember that the best way is the hard way. Some of the other paths work if you know how to follow them, but it's easy to get lost when you go those ways." As he spoke he gestured, first at the rocky path that led up toward the crest of the ridge, then at the other two trails, one of which led down toward the river, the other straight north along the side of the ridge.

"I *went* that way," said Robert Johnson. "It didn't take me anywhere I want to go."

Blind Willie smiled. "Sometimes it seems that way, don't it?"

Robert Johnson swore. "Talk sense," he said.

Blind Willie didn't say another word. He started up the rocky path, and walked it quickly, like a sighted man; he didn't slow until they reached the north edge of the forest and the trail that led down the ridge toward Memphis.

All that time Robert Johnson kept expecting Blind Willie to ask a price for his guidance, the way he'd hinted he would when Robert Johnson first told him he was lost. But if there was a price to pay, Blind Willie never asked it.

That made Robert Johnson especially suspicious, because no man ever puts such a debt on you as the man who helps you without mentioning his price.

"You asked me for the Mysteries," Robert Johnson said. "Is that the price I owe you for your help?"

Blind Willie laughed.

"You pay me what you want," he said. "You don't have to pay me anything at all."

"I bet I don't," Robert Johnson said. "What you mean, old man?"

"I mean exactly what I said, and not another word. You pay me what you like," Blind Willie said. "Or pay me nothing at all, if that's what pleases you. If I wanted to put a geas on you, I would have asked you for it long ago."

Robert Johnson knew he was stepping into a trap, and he wanted to step away from it. But his heart was stingy, and it wanted to get by paying his debt as cheaply as he could.

So he gave Blind Willie just one more mystery, and he tried to let it go at that.

"The blood that goes in the ground," he said, "is the Devil's sacramental wine."

Blind Willie frowned, and he looked away. There was an expression on his face like he'd heard a thing so vile that he could not bear to listen to it.

"Even Satan lives to serve the Lord," Blind Willie answered.

"God bless you, Robert Johnson."

And so, even though Robert Johnson had cheated him — giving him the wisdom he'd seen as the Devil cast him out of Hell instead of the transcendent whisper-word from Heaven — even though Robert Johnson cheated him Blind Willie set him free from the debt.

But that never works the way it should. Because a geas isn't a thing that a body puts on another nor one he could remove: a geas is a thing that grows in your own heart when someone does you a turn that makes you grateful. The geas that Robert Johnson felt was a thing he'd put upon himself, and there was no way he could remove it with a frugal generosity.

Robert Johnson wasn't stupid; it didn't take him long to realize the mistake he'd made. But not too long was plenty long enough: by the time he'd come to understand the burden he'd put on himself he was halfway down the ridge to Memphis, and Blind Willie was unfindably deep inside his haunted forest.

And there was not a solitary thing he could do to change the fate he'd already set in motion.

•

Robert Johnson took a name for himself when he reached Memphis, and the name he took was Hinky Tom. He was a deadman and he didn't dare to play for money, but all the same he picked a little now and then, down to the corner, setting out a cup before him; and when he picked the power of the songs he did not play enraptured every passerby, till none of them who heard him could help but drop ten coins into his cup.

That was how Robert Johnson made his way those months in Memphis as he waited for his fate to come to him: for the first time since his death he made his coin with his guitar, and with the coin the world bestowed on him he cleaned himself and dressed himself, took himself a room in a boardinghouse and made a life as though he'd never died.

And waited for his destiny.

But the destiny he felt awaiting him never came, no matter how he waited. Because that life in Memphis under the name of Hinky Tom *was* his destiny. It made him, molded him, and shaped him in ways he never intended and surely did not understand. He moved through the city and the world, following the song he heard in his heart — and mostly that song was a thing that came from deep within him, a thing that he was born to because of who he was and what he was, but partly too it was the great King's song, whispering in his dreams across the miles and the years.

But Robert Johnson didn't know that. He only thought that he was waiting, day by day all through the fall and into winter for a Destiny to come a calling; and it never did, no matter how he waited. After a while he began to wonder why Saint Peter said the world still needed him, and there were days he picked "The Ode to Joy" softly in his room all by himself, hoping he could learn to play it just the way Blind Willie did to let them see the Pearly Gates of Heaven.

But no matter how he tried, his music would not transubstantiate, and now day by day he found himself growing hungry and eager, felt himself yearn for things he hadn't yearned in all the years since the wet pneumonia took his life.

And the day came when he woke as if from a deep sleep, and he looked himself in the mirror and saw that he needed a shave.

That was when he knew that the lust and the hunger and the yearning were real, and he like to cry when he realized that. Because they meant he was no deadman but alive, and no matter how he wanted otherwise Robert Johnson had to face the world as all men do, to struggle and survive, to thrive or die beneath the sun.

And he cried and cried, but not because of any sadness: Robert Johnson cried to be alive because the joy had overwhelmed him and it like to break his heart.

●

That night Robert Johnson took himself to church and got himself a baptism. When the baptism was over he stood beside the choir, and sang with them, singing *hallelujah* loud among the choir as the preacher screamed and shook so fine, and though his song made magic in the air, it caused no necromancy — it only called the clear pure transcendent Spirit of the Lord.

And that was good.

But the goodness didn't last for long. It never does, does it? Two hours after Robert Johnson got religion he was wandering back to his boardinghouse in the docklands with his heart all full of joy and celebration, and a voice spoke to him from the shadows of an alley.

"Robert Johnson," the voice said, calling him by his born name where everyone in his new life knew him by the name of Hinky Tom.

"Call me Hinky Tom," said Robert Johnson. "That's what they call me now."

The voice ignored him. "I'd like a word with you, Robert Johnson."

Robert Johnson recognized that voice. It was a beautiful voice — a ragged, gnarled, bluesy voice, a voice the *giftie* made unlike all others — and Robert Johnson would have known it in a maelstrom.

"Is that so?" he asked, peering into the shadows, trying to see if it could really be the one whose voice he knew, wondering why that man would come a-looking for him in the dark.

Then he saw that cursed bluesman walking toward him in the uncertain light of the rising moon, and he said, "Leadbelly, why are you here?"

But Leadbelly didn't answer.

Leadbelly was still alive in those days, though the days that remained to him were numbered. He didn't always answer with the truth.

"It's good to see you, man," Robert Johnson said. He lowered his guard — not all the way down, but just about. He'd known Leadbelly almost as long as he'd breathed, and he held him in high regard. Back when Robert Johnson was alive, he and Leadbelly were two of a kind, because both of them had felt the *touch divine* and still went with the Devil.

Robert Johnson didn't think about the things that separated them, now that he'd died and come alive, born again; now that he'd redeemed himself and stood before the Pearly Gates, and returned to the world only because Saint Peter told him that the world still needed him. He didn't see an enemy who lived to serve the Devil, but rather saw a friend, a companion, and man he loved the way great bluesmen love the rivals they respect.

When Robert Johnson looked at Leadbelly, he saw a friend. He would have welcomed him whether he was alive or dead or if he'd been returned from Hell, because there's that kind of brotherhood among those who learn their craft together — but he would have been a fool to do it.

That was Robert Johnson: he was nothing if he wasn't a fool.

And where Robert Johnson was a fool, Leadbelly was a scoundrel.

"I heard you was around," Leadbelly said. "Thought I'd see for myself."

Robert Johnson could hear Leadbelly was lying — the lie was clearer to him than any lie had ever been, partly because the repentance and salvation in his heart made the truth more clear to him. And partly because the Devil was about that man more distinctly than Robert Johnson had ever seen before. The Devil leaves a special mark on those he wraps his arms around, and because the Devil is the Prince of Lies his falsehood colors the words of everyone who serves him.

"Tell me the truth," Robert Johnson said. "Why are you here?"

Leadbelly smiled unaffectedly, like it didn't bother him to get caught in a lie. "What the hell you think?" he asked. "You afraid I come to kiss you for the Devil?" and then he laughed uproariously, as if that were the most outrageous humor.

Robert Johnson wanted to say, *I wouldn't put it past you,* but held his tongue. He was still new to his repentance, and averse to giving deliberate offense — even where more seasoned righteous people call folks as they see them. "I don't know what to think," Robert Johnson said. "Why don't you tell me what I need to know?"

Leadbelly smiled all bright and wide, and Robert Johnson knew he was in trouble.

"I just want to see how you been doing," Leadbelly said. "I heard a story you was dead, and then I heard somebody saw you alive in Memphis. Of course I had to see."

"Just a story," Robert Johnson said. "I don't look dead to you, do I?"

What he meant to say by that was, *Look at me. Do I look like a deadman Hoodoo Doctor walking on the earth?* and of course the answer to that was *no*. Robert Johnson wasn't a Hoodoo Doctor and he wasn't dead, either. But he wasn't entirely innocent of those things, either. Robert Johnson was dissembling — deliberately clouding the truth by answering at right angles to it.

That was his second mistake. Because even if it isn't a lie when a man dissembles, it breeds a lie, and a lie is a lie, any way you get to it.

Ain't no way no man can win, lying to the Devil's henchmen. The Devil is the Prince of Lies, and commands all of those who lie to him; a man who answers him truthfully will almost always face him down, and those who hold their tongues beat him almost as often.

But when a man lies, the Devil laughs, and he knows he'll have his way. He had his way with Robert Johnson that night, that's for sure.

"You look like Robert Johnson, that's a fact," Leadbelly said. Leadbelly's born name was Huddie Ledbetter, but everyone knew him as Leadbelly. There were people who knew why to call him that, and there were those who called him Leadbelly without knowing why. But there were very few who knew the story of his name and called him by it too. "But you ain't the man I know."

Robert Johnson cocked an eyebrow. "Is that so?"

"You know it is."

"Speak for yourself. I'm the man I was born, and the man I'll die. You got me confused with someone else, that's none of my concern."

Leadbelly raised his face to look toward the sky, rolled his eyes toward the heavens. As he did his neck rode up above the scarf he wore around it, and Robert Johnson saw the wide white line of scar that cut across his throat. Johnson knew about that scar; everybody knew about it. He knew about the night in the bar down in Tupelo, and the awful fight that'd left Leadbelly bloody and broken on the floor where the barman slit his throat. And they knew how the barman had left him there when he closed the place, thinking that the rats would eat his rotting corpse. But Leadbelly was Leadbelly, and he wasn't a man you could trust to die just because you'd slit his throat.

When the bar was empty Leadbelly climbed out of his pooling blood, wrapped his shirt around his oozing throat, and stumbled out across the cotton fields toward home.

Even when he was alive, Leadbelly was hard to kill. Lots of men tried lots of ways to kill him, but no one ever hurt him.

"I just mean you changed," Leadbelly said. "That's all."

"I guess I have," Robert Johnson said.

They were walking, now — toward Robert Johnson's boardinghouse, the way it happened, but they could have been walking anywhere, any place there ever was.

"Tell me more," Leadbelly said. "I need to know."

When Leadbelly said that Robert Johnson heard, *I need to hear the good word of the Lord.* And what could he do? No good man who's ever been a sinner can deny a request like that — especially when the person asking is one who needs redemption as dearly as Leadbelly did.

So Robert Johnson said, "I heard the Word," and gave him the news for all mankind. Leadbelly took it all in like he was the dry land and Robert Johnson's testimony was the blessed rain. But he didn't take it the way Robert Johnson meant it — not for a moment. He listened at the corners of every word that Robert Johnson told him, picking out the details of Johnson's history and salvation, just as the Devil instructed him.

Before that night the Devil knew just three things about Robert Johnson: the avaricious life that had killed him and sent him to Hell; the vanity so great that even the Devil himself despised it, and cast him out of Hell; and the moments after his Redemption, when Scratch saw the Eye of the World watching him intently.

The Eye of the World still watched Robert Johnson, albeit more discreetly. The Devil didn't know that, and Leadbelly couldn't learn it for him — because Robert Johnson didn't even know it himself.

But Leadbelly heard every one of Robert Johnson's secrets that he thought to ask for. He heard about the years Robert Johnson spent wandering the country, looking for a thing he didn't know and couldn't name and could not bear to lose; he heard about the music and the magic, and what you hear when

you pick two and seven and *listen* as you sit before a bonfire
between the Left and Right Hands of the Lord. He heard about
the Pearly Gates, Saint Peter, and the Mysteries, but neither
Leadbelly nor the Devil could make a lick of sense from them.
(Is it any wonder? All those things, and the Mysteries especially,
depend upon a State of Grace not available to the unrepentant — a state that's often just beyond the reach of the Lord's
most righteous children.)

When they'd talked for hours Leadbelly took a flask from
the pocket of his coat and offered Robert Johnson *spirit liquor.*

Now Robert Johnson hadn't touched the demon rum since
the night he brought the vengeance of a cuckold husband down
upon himself. Mostly he'd avoided the stuff because he was
dead, and everybody knows the terrible things that happen
when deadmen touch that awful stuff.

But Robert Johnson wasn't dead anymore. He was alive, and
the truth was that even if he'd repented the folly of his sinful
ways, he still had a taste for good brown mash. And is that
such a crime? Lots of righteous gentlemen imbibe a measure
now and then; it doesn't turn them into demons when they
drink in moderation.

Robert Johnson thought, *What could it hurt?*, and then he
made a terrible mistake.

He said, "Sure, sure, I'll take a lick," and he took the cask
of *spirit liquor* from Huddie Ledbetter.

And drank that poison down.

●

Robert Johnson woke on a dock above the Mississippi in
the small hours of the morning. He couldn't remember nothing after the drink he took from Leadbelly's flask of mash, but
he remembered that drink so clearly: it was the savor of every
sip of whiskey he'd ever drank, distilled into a moment richer
than the warmth of morning sunshine on a deadman's cold
dewey-slick skin; it was half the sight of Heaven half-obscured
in the clouds that surround the Pearly Gates; it was greater than
the doomed damned majesty of Lucifer's throne in the Mansion called Defiance along the shore of the Lake of Fire where
it reaches down to Hell.

Spirit liquor was a lover he'd always known but never thought to cherish. When he woke on the dock, bloody and aching like to die, he knew he loved that *liquor* so dearly that he never dare to touch the stuff again.

"Lordie Lordie Lord," he said, and as he spoke he heard his words rasp and burble in and out his throat, and it began to sink through to him how dire were his circumstances, "dear God please forgive me."

And he reached up so carefully to touch the wound he could feel cut across his throat.

And felt with the tips of his fingers the same terror he heard burbling around his words:

He felt his throat cut open wide where Leadbelly had slit him open to the bright light of the moon.

And left him on the dock where his blood gathered in a pool that drizzled slowly into the river, draining toward New Orleans and the sea.

Robert Johnson should have died the moment Leadbelly cut him. If he lived even a moment after he never should have had the strength to wake and see the horror that became of him. But he did wake, aching bloody terrified and alone, and he saw the river; saw the blood and the bright moon high above him; and he saw the Eye of the World.

It hung in the sky brilliant as a red second moon — no, brighter, infinitely brighter than the first — and it watched Robert Johnson through its shattered lens.

Robert Johnson saw the deep bright cracks in the lens of the Eye of the World, and all he could think was *I did that, I broke the Eye of the World, I was so full of myself and now I'm so ashamed.* When he saw the Eye he saw his own hubris, and it shamed him. You can't say a thing about a man that marks the change in him as clearly as that marked Robert Johnson. The man he'd been the day he died would have seen the Eye and wondered what it meant to him, and meant about him. But that night as he lay on the dock clasping his throat, trying to stop his blood spurting and leaking into the river, it didn't even occur to him to wonder why the Eye watched him. He didn't think to wonder why he was alive, or why Leadbelly drugged him, or even why the river whispered his name so softly as it lapped the shore.

"I'm sorry, Lord," Robert Johnson said, still looking at the Eye, still mourning the consequences of the song he'd sung a lifetime ago. "Lordie Lordie please forgive me."

As he wrapped his shirt around his open throat and stumbled away from the river, away from the dockyards, toward the hospital in Memphis where seven doctors gasped in fear and wonder when they saw him.

They rushed him to their operating room and sewed his throat together. When they were done an orderly wheeled him into a hallway and left him there where the doctors could watch him until they were ready to put him in a room.

But Robert Johnson wasn't having any of that. The moment their eyes were off him he pushed himself up off the stretcher, got to his feet, and staggered down the hall. He followed the hall through seven heavy doors until he found the hospital's bright wide entrance. That led him onto the streets of Memphis, where the sun was rising and the birds were calling and the day was wide and full of possibility.

Robert Johnson shambled through the morning streets of Memphis until they led him home. When he reached his room he fell into his bed; in a moment he was sleeping.

It was days before he woke again.

The Ballad of John Henry

When John Henry was a little baby boy
Sitting on his mother's knee
He pointed straight at a piece of steel
Said that steel's gonna be the death of me
Yes, yes
That bridge and tunnel, that bright wide steel
Are gonna be the death of me
Yes, yes
They're gonna be the death of me

Some people say John Henry was born in Texas,
Some say he was born in Maine,
But he really came from the hills of Carolina
That's the last place that he went to 'fore he died
Yes, yes
That's the last place that he went to 'fore he died.

John Henry told his Captain one day
Says, A man ain't nothing but a man
Before I be beat by your steel-driving gang
I'm going to die with this hammer in my hand.
That's what he said,
I'm going to die with this hammer in my hand

Well, the paymaster loved to see John Henry,
Water boy loved to hear him sing,
Most of all what the paymaster loved
Was to hear John Henry's hammer ring.
Made his hammer ring like it was a bell
And it rang so clear, rang yes baby
And it rang

John Henry knew a woman
Her name was Polly Ann
When he got so sick that he lay abed
You know Polly she drove steel just like a man.
Polly she drove steel just like a man.

One day John Henry got a notion
And he had to climb the hills
His Captain said, John Henry, those hills are sinking
  in!
He said shut up, Cap'n, you don't know what you saw
It wasn't nothing but my hammer sucking wind
Lord yes,
That wasn't nothing but my hammer sucking wind.

That day John Henry told his shaker
I declare you a better pray
If I miss this steel with this ten-pound maul
Tomorrow is going to be your burying day
Yes, yes
Tomorrow's going to be your burying day
Lord knows.

John Henry looked at the sun one day
And the sun had done turned red,
And he looked over his shoulder Lord
And he seen his partner falling dead dead
Then John Henry went to the Mansion
Tell the head of his hundred-car fire
Crying, George just pick 'em up and let 'em down
    again!
We're going to work until we die
Yes, yes
We're going to work this line until we die.

John Henry worked until he died.
When he fell they carried Johnny up the Mountain
Up on the Mountain so high
The last words he said to the water boy
Was, Give me a cool drink of water 'fore I die.
Lord yes,
Give me a cool drink of water 'fore I die.

When the woman in the west
Learned of John Henry's death
She came awake in her bed
She was dressed in white
She was dressed in red
She wailed for old John Henry
He was dead dead dead
John Henry

Just give me one cool drink of water before I die.

When the world was whole and the Wizard Kings still ruled the Delta, there was a King who stood foremost among them. He was first because he'd come before them, and also because he was the wisest, truest, and greatest of them all.

His name was John Henry, and he could make his hammer ring like a bell.

In his time he talked to God and he talked to the Devil; he got religion and gave it back; and then learned the error of his ways.

Some people say he was a scoundrel bloodthirstier than Leadbelly. Others say he was a saint as holy as Sister O. M. Terrell. The truth is probably somewhere in between — for though hoodoo men always serve the Lord (just like the blues that breeds them) they serve Him most often at cross-purposes, perversely.

His history is a mystery made of legends that everybody knows and everyone denies. His story is the glory of the nation and the wonder of the world: everyone who knows John Henry celebrates him, and no one does him wrong.

•

Three times in those months he spent in Memphis, among redemption and salvation but before he had the chance to go astray, Robert Johnson went hiking up on the bluff above the city, searching the woods for Blind Willie's shack. But he never found it, maybe because he never took the hardest way.

•

On Fat Tuesday, Peetie Wheatstraw came looking for Robert Johnson.

He found him in a cheap café not far from the riverfront — the kind of two-bit place where dockhands go for breakfast and no one orders anything but eggs, potatoes, coffee, toast, and grits. It wasn't a fancy place, nor even an especially good one, but it was a place where a man can drink his coffee slow enough to read a paper and no one really minds. Robert Johnson went there a lot in the months when he lived in Memphis under the name of Hinky Tom, and the waitresses knew him for a regular.

Robert Johnson knew Peetie Wheatstraw, too — the moment he set eyes on the Doctor he recognized him for a deadman. Robert Johnson had that kind of sight, and he didn't lose it just because he came alive.

"What you want?" Robert Johnson asked, as if he didn't know. "I been waiting for you."

"I bet you have," the Hoodoo Doctor said.

"Waiting for a long time."

"Good, then," Peetie Wheatstraw said. "That makes it simple."

Peetie Wheatstraw was the youngest of the Kings (who weren't yet seven, but five). Because he was youngest he was their arms and legs, and spoke for them just as Blind Lemon had spoken for the kings through the 30s. When he was alive and singing he called himself "Peetie Wheatstraw, the Devil's Son-in-Law," but William Bunch was his born name. He was born in the low country of Alabama, which is a province of the Delta Kingdom, but he spent most of his life up north. He knew the Lords of the Piedmont (who govern the high country in the east as the Seven Kings ruled the Delta, but differently), and paid them the respect they were due.

William Bunch who was Peetie Wheatstraw died in a car wreck in 1941, four years after the accident that killed Bessie Smith.

After he died he was always Peetie Wheatstraw, and William Bunch was dead and gone forever.

"What do you want from me?" Robert Johnson asked.

Peetie Wheatstraw grinned wide and wicked as the Angel Death. "I only want to *help* you, Hinky Tom," he said, and he laughed perfidiously.

"The hell you say," said Robert Johnson. "You want to help me like a buzzard wants to help a sojourner."

Peetie Wheatstraw pushed himself away from the table. He looked offended.

"You got me wrong, Hinky Tom," he said. "I come to seek you for the King."

Robert Johnson eyed him uncertainly. He knew (as all bluesmen know) who the Kings were, and he respected them. But he also knew they serve their own ends, and when his preacher railed against them during the Sunday service, Robert Johnson took his words to heart. "I got religion now, Peetie Wheatstraw. When I play I sing to serve the Lord."

"So?"

"So I got no business with the Devil's Son-in-Law."

Peetie Wheatstraw swore.

"You got me wrong," he said. "And you're doing worse by the King. John Henry is an upright man."

Robert Johnson thought about Leadbelly and the music and the Good Word of the Lord, and he wanted to help because he thought he could. But the Lord don't want nobody acting like a fool, and that's a simple truth. "When he died he got religion, that's what they say," he said. "You can't prove it by me either way."

"I never said I could," Peetie Wheatstraw said.

"What do you want from me?"

Peetie Wheatstraw didn't answer straight away. He just sat there, staring at Robert Johnson so young and healthy and alive sitting across the table from him, and maybe the Devil's Son-in-Law envied him his life and his health, and maybe he only wondered how a man could die such a colossal fool and still find redemption and the miracle of life. Whatever it was that went on in his head, he shrugged it away. And sighed, and leaned close across the table to whisper at Robert Johnson.

Robert Johnson smelled his breath before he heard his words. It was deadman's breath, cool and stale, and somewhere hidden in the staleness there were hints of brimstone and decay.

"John Henry wants to see you," Peetie Wheatstraw said. "He sent me here to bring you back."

I'll go, he thought, even though he was half afraid it was a terrible mistake. Because there was something in his heart that told him that he had to — maybe it was the song that is the music of the world, or maybe it was the song the great King whispered in his ear across the years and miles. But his heart told him to trust it, and it wasn't wrong.

"Where is he?" Robert Johnson asked Peetie Wheatstraw.

"He lives up on the Mountain," Peetie Wheatstraw said. "Everybody knows that — I don't know why you got to ask."

Robert Johnson shrugged. "Just uneasy," he said. "I got to say a reason?"

The Devil's Son-in-Law smiled. "Don't got to say nothing you don't want," he said, getting up from his seat. "We best get started — it'll take us a few days to get there."

"All right," Robert Johnson said.

They went to West Memphis — in Arkansas, on the far side of the river — three hours later, and took the afternoon train bound north toward Chicago.

Spanish Harlem
The Present

The night after Lisa came alive for the third time, her mother told her it was time she got herself back to school.

Lisa never liked school, and she never liked kids, either. She didn't want to go.

"Oh Mama," Lisa said, "I can't go to school! They don't have schools for babies."

Lisa's mother frowned.

"Child," she said, all frustrated and flustered. She didn't like it when Lisa talked back, but she abided it. She liked it even less when Lisa was right.

"I'll go to school when I get big again," Lisa said. She looked up at her mother with her wide and tiny baby eyes and pouted like she had to cry. "I promise I'll go then, Mama."

Her mother crossed her arms and gave Lisa the eye. "You're mistaken, young lady," she said, "and you've got a lot to learn."

"I'm not! I don't!"

"Say that if you like," her mother said. "But you're going to school. I've made arrangements with a day-care center. You start tomorrow."

And Lisa got *so mad.*

So mad!

"Mama! You can't send me to nursery school! I won't go."

"You will," her mother said. She sounded like she didn't want to hear another word about it.

"No," Lisa said, "I won't."

And suddenly her mother's eyes went wide with indignation, and she swore under her breath. "That's enough from you, young lady. To your room! I don't want to hear another word about it."

Lisa did as her mother said, but she didn't like it, not one bit. She stumbled toward her room on her tiny baby legs that still felt so uncertain under her.

When she got there she closed the door behind her, climbed up on the bed that still stunk like Lisa dead and rotting even though her mother had spent all day laundering the bed-clothes. The whole *room* stank, and it probably always would, no matter how her mother scrubbed the floors and washed the walls, no matter what she took down to the laundry and wrung through the machine.

"I hate you, Mama," Lisa whispered. That was how mad she was, hateful mad, like she wanted to hurt everything she could wrap her tiny hands around.

But the moment she heard herself say those words, *I hate you, Mama,* she wanted to cry. Because they were so ugly, so untrue. She loved her mama. She'd always love her mama!

But she still felt hateful mad.

She didn't know why she felt that way, but she felt it so intense, sharp as vinegar when you drink it from a cup, but commanding like she had no choice. She felt a lot of things she didn't understand and didn't even mean — she'd felt a lot of things like that ever since she died.

Sometimes Lisa thought she got those things from the music. All her life she'd heard the music of the world inside her head, but since she'd died the song had been a thing consuming her. Enfolding her, leading her — and saving her, too, because there were times when the music was the only thing that kept her from doing something awful.

Awful.

Really awful.

Sometimes Lisa got a want to do something so terrible she couldn't stand herself.

When her head was clear she didn't want to do those things. But other times the desire was on her like a demon she could not deny.

And sometimes she thought: *Of course I feel those ways! I'm a zombie girl, and zombies are dead things that do the worst things in the world.*

Lisa never meant to be a zombie. She never meant to die, she never meant to live and die and die again; she never meant to become a thing that looked like a baby with a devil in her heart. But she became all those things, or they happened to her, or however you want to think about it.

Lying in her stinking bed still and quiet as a dead baby staring at the ceiling, Lisa swore she'd never be angry or cruel ever again. But it was a false promise, and Lisa knew that even as she swore it to herself: *I'm a monster,* she thought. She couldn't change what she was any more than a tenement could be a mansion.

After a while she began to cry, and swore she wasn't any monster, wasn't wasn't wasn't, she was just a little girl with hopes and fears and dreams, aspirations and afflictions, and the terrors that suffused her weren't anything she meant to become.

But she became them all the same, and Lisa wasn't wrong when she called herself a monster.

Someone screeched outside her window, and then the screech turned into laughter. It was those girls again, those teenage girls who thought it was so funny to scream to see who noticed. Lisa never understood why they did that, but she'd known girls like that all her life — it was a common thing for teenage girls in Harlem, screaming for the joy of it to see who'd look out at them. It never bothered her when she was alive, but when she'd died something had changed inside her ears, and the sound of the girls screaming was a thing that made the bones rattle in her head. Lisa hated that so bad.

She rolled out of bed, stumbled to her window. Climbed up onto her toy box she kept in front of the window and pushed the window open. Leaned out into the child-guard to get a look at the girls.

"You be quiet out there," Lisa shouted, and she saw one of the girls look up at her agog. "It isn't nice to scream without a reason."

The goggy-eyed girl turned to her companion, who was staring up at Lisa now, too. "What is she?" the girl asked. "Babies never talk."

The girl laughed fearfully. "Some kind of freak," she said, and the girls stared at one another for the longest time, wide-eyed and terrified and fascinated until one of them suddenly went running away down the block, leaving her companion alone with Lisa who stared at her angrily and for just that moment the girl stared back —

— and then she screamed.

And took off running after her companion, running like her life depended on it even though her scream metamorphosed to laughter before she was gone halfway down the block.

There was a noise behind Lisa, and she turned in time to see her mother push open the bedroom door.

"What's going on in here?" Mama asked.

Lisa lied.

"Nothing, Mama."

But her mother saw the open window; she could figure out what happened.

"I *bet* nothing happened," she said. "Child, someone's going to have to teach you how to tell a lie. But it won't be me."

Lisa tried to go to sleep when her mother closed the door, but it wasn't any use. She was too angry. Too mad! She wanted to find those girls and wring their necks, she really did.

After a while she sat up and looked out the window. And heard the sound of screaming somewhere in the distance.

I'm going to hurt those girls, I am, I swear I am, Lisa thought. She pushed herself off the bed, stumbled toward the window on her baby legs too small to walk too stumpy to balance too new to understand. When she got to the window she climbed up on the toy box and peered sidelong down the street trying to see as far as she could around the edge of her window. She kept thinking that if she could just see a little farther she'd find the screaming girls.

But they were nowhere in sight.

They're in the park, I bet, Lisa thought. The north edge of Central Park was three blocks south of them; when Lisa looked as hard as she could she could just barely see the high edges of the tallest trees. *I bet I know exactly where they are.*

If Lisa would've given it a little thought there's no way she would have started after them. The whole idea was crazy — little baby Lisa wandering off into Harlem without the protection of an adult!

But she didn't think. She just got up onto the toy box,

pushed her window the rest of the way open.

Climbed out onto the fire escape and into the world.

I'm going to make those girls so sorry, Lisa thought. She really really was.

Down the fire escape, onto the sidewalk. It was late, now, and Lisa's part of Harlem was all but deserted; there was no one on the street as far as Lisa could see in either direction.

They went to the park, Lisa thought. *I know they did.*

She hurried awkwardly toward the park, stumpling on her bowed and wobbly baby legs. It wasn't a good walk. Twice she saw eyes watching her from the shadows of abandoned buildings, and once she heard a feral dog growl at her from a direction she wasn't sure of.

She didn't let herself be scared.

Maybe she should have. If she'd been afraid she would have been more ready for what she found when she reached the park.

Across the wide night-empty street that ran along the north side of Central Park; through the thicket that was supposed to wall off the north edge of the park. Into the trees that seemed in the darkness deep as primordial forest; and the world closed around her like the darkness at the end of life.

The screaming girl screamed from someplace close but impossible to see. The sound of her scream frightened Lisa — terrified her.

I shouldn't be here, Lisa thought. *I should be home in bed where my mama left me.* She felt so stupid, just like she really was a baby all over again, and she hated that so much. . . !

The brush grew thick around her again, and now suddenly it cleared away to show a crowd of two dozen teenagers dancing around a bonfire.

They shouldn't start no fires in the park, Lisa thought. *It's against the law!*

And that was stupid, too, because everybody knows teenagers don't care nothing about the law.

They don't care much about baby girls, either, and Lisa should have thought about that, too. But she didn't. Where she should have turned away and run for her dear life, she crept toward the fire, moving as quiet and as careful as she could. When she got close she realized she could hear someone singing, playing the guitar, and she looked around to see a boy with pitch-dark skin playing music —

Real music. Music like she heard sometimes deep inside her heart when she dreamed about the lady with the sword.

He's beautiful, Lisa thought, but she wasn't sure if the beautiful part was his music or his self. She thought, *I want to hold him,* but she didn't know why. The idea of touching him made her uncomfortable.

The screaming girls stood before the bonfire at the center of the dance. How could they dance so close to the flames? Lisa was certain that the darker girl's hair was going to catch fire, go up in a fury of flame that would burn her till she died. But no matter how Lisa expected it, the girl never caught fire. None of them did. It was like they couldn't burn, but that couldn't be, could it? Everything can burn, people not excepted.

Now the singer's tempo began to pick up, and he slapped the face of his guitar rhythmically to mark the lines of his song.

Lisa found herself caught up in the song, wanting to dance, but she knew that wasn't wise. *They'll see me if I dance,* she thought. *They'll see me if they don't already know I'm here.* And sudden as she had thought she was certain the guitar man knew just where she was. He knew everything about her, Lisa thought, and in his way he loved her even if he meant to see her dead.

They won't kill me, Lisa thought. *I'm not afraid.*

That was a lie; the truth was she was terrified.

But it was too late to be afraid. The music had found its way inside her, and she no longer had a choice: she had to follow the song where it led her, and follow until the music set her free.

She inched toward the fire, still hoping to keep herself out of sight until the bluesman finished his song and she could run. And inched closer and closer until she stood among the dancers, crawling among their legs as the music reached deeper into her, until finally she stood up on her wobbly legs and began to dance wildly, manically, dance on her tiny awkward legs that rolled out from under her and sent her falling toward the fire —

Into the fire and crashing down among the embers. She struggled to get free of the flames as her pajamas smoked and sputtered, searing hot melting sputtering rayon into her skin, but her arms and legs betrayed her — when she tried to stand, to run, to push herself out of the embers all she managed to do was flail among them until she covered herself with char and ember and fiery debris, and Lisa *screamed* —

As the screaming girls saw her flail below them, and forgot their dance to shriek in horror and surprise, and one of them shouted, *It's her, it's her, it's the freak from the window, I told you didn't I, I told you what she'd do!*

And the music stopped and people ran in all directions as Lisa struggled uselessly to push herself out of the fire. She was going to burn to death, why didn't they help her, why didn't they help, did they want her to burn alive? But they didn't help, no help, no help at all and Lisa screamed in fury and frustration as she rolled twice over the hottest part of the fire, crashed over the stones that ringed the fire's edge and came to rest on the far side of the flames.

I'm burned I'm burned I'm going to die, she thought, rolling in the grass among the terrified teenagers. Her clothes were still afire, and her hair smelled like a rat fried on the third rail in the subway, and she could feel the embers clinging to her skin, clinging and burning and she knew her skin was seared and scored and ready to peel away from her flesh and bones —

As she came to an abrupt stop.

At the feet of the bluesman still playing his guitar.

And suddenly everything went quiet, and the world was just Lisa and the bluesman and the music — the music and magic and fire shimmering the air around them.

Lisa sat up, and saw that though her clothes were all but burned away the flames had hardly touched her skin. Even where the embers still clung to her they didn't seem to burn her. She could feel the heat, she could feel the fire burn and blister her, but no matter what she felt she couldn't see it happen.

"I don't understand," Lisa said, and the bluesman smiled at her.

He didn't answer by talking, the way Lisa would have expected. Instead he sang to her: *"You don't have to understand,"* he sang. *"If you knew you would forget."*

"I wouldn't," Lisa said. "I was dead, and I remember all of it — I remember the Lady, and the hallway, and the door that led back into the world. How could anyone forget those things?"

"At the end there are two doors," he sang. *"Nobody knows them both."*

"I know the doors," Lisa said. "I saw them from the hallway. One of them is Heaven. The other one is Hell."

"People go inside, and they don't every come out."

"I think you're wrong," Lisa said. "I heard a story once, and then I had a dream."

"They don't ever come out," the bluesman sang.

Lisa wanted to argue with him, but she knew it wasn't any use. He wouldn't believe her, and no one would believe her, and she hardly believed herself when she heard herself try to contradict him. But how could she help but disagree? In her dream she'd heard Robert Johnson singing *Judgment Day,* and she knew the Gates of Heaven and Hell will open wide one day. And she knew from seeing Robert Johnson, too, because every solitary thing about him spoke of damnation and redemption, and how could both those things be on one man if the doors of Heaven and Hell don't swing both ways?

Lisa heard a sound behind her and whirled around to see the teenagers crowding in around them, watching Lisa and the bluesman. "What do you want?" she demanded, glaring at them, glaring especially at the awful teenage girls who'd screamed outside her window.

No one answered. The bluesman behind her let his song drift away, but he kept playing his guitar — now the melody grew complex, and the rhythm drove hard and beautiful like thunder echoing among the tenements.

"I hate you," Lisa said, still glaring at the girls. "I hate you hate you *hate you.*"

The dark girl laughed. The light girl repeated Lisa's words back at her in a high, squeaky voice, taunting her. *"Hate you hate you hate you!"* the girl said. And then she laughed, too.

And Lisa got so mad.

So mad!

"You stop that, you awful, you, you —"

"*. . .you, you —*"

That was when Lisa lost her temper.

It wasn't good, losing her temper. Losing her temper got Lisa into awful trouble.

As she howled with rage and pushed herself off the ground; lurched toward the girls and caught the dark one by the ankle.

Pushed against the ground with every bit of strength she had in her legs —

And pushed the dark girl off her feet, onto the ground.

"*I hate you!*" she shouted, lunging forward to wrap her hands around the dark girl's throat and *squeeze* as someone screamed and the dark girl's hands flailed uselessly at Lisa, trying to batter her away, but Lisa didn't care, not a bit, she was brave and she was strong even if she was a baby, and nothing any *girl* could do would ever hurt her, Lisa wouldn't let it hurt —

As a boy started shouting from the far edge of the crowd. "Run!" he shouted. "Run, run, the police are coming!"

And the light girl reached under Lisa's arms to pull her away from the dark one still flailing as Lisa tried to strangle her; and Lisa didn't let go so easy, she whipped 'round in the light girl's arms to try to claw her eyes out, but the light girl was too fast for her, she flung Lisa away, away into the air tiny angry blood-hungry baby Lisa flew high through the air until she slammed into the trunk of a tree —

It got confusing after that.

Lisa saw the girls crying in each other's arms, and she saw the teenagers running away, but she never heard the music stop. Maybe it never *did* stop. She thought she could hear it as she saw the Park Police enter the clearing, but how could that be? The bluesman was gone, and if he'd been there the police would have had words for him. Maybe they would have arrested him, even; they sure looked mad enough to arrest somebody when they saw the bonfire burning high enough to singe the leaves and branches up above them.

If they'd heard him the way Lisa heard him, they surely would have gone looking for him.

But they didn't hear, and they didn't look, and as they shoveled dirt into the fire the music began to fade. It ended when they pounded out the embers.

"We need to find the kids who did this," one of the police-men said.

His partner snorted derisively.

"They're miles away by now," he said. "Long gone."

Lisa wasn't gone. She wanted to stand up and say so, but she knew she didn't dare.

"They're always gone," the first cop said. "Damned hood-lums."

His partner sighed. "Just kids dancing, Pete," he said. "You ought to keep it in perspective."

The first cop swore. "Kids my ass," he said. "This is New York." He stepped away from the dead fire, stooped to peer into the woods. "They could've set the park on fire," he said. For a moment he seemed to look right at Lisa, and she thought for certain he'd found her. But then someone screamed some-where east of them, and the policeman turned to look in that direction.

"What do you think that was?"

"I don't know. But I'm going to find out," the first cop said. He pushed through the thicket toward the east; his partner followed a moment behind him.

I'm free, Lisa thought. *I'm saved.*

She wasn't wrong. If she'd got up that moment and hurried home to bed, nothing would have followed her, and maybe she could have had a normal life for a few more weeks before the world descended on her.

But she had to know who'd screamed, and she had to know why, and it wasn't in her to run away just when things began to happen. She pushed herself up off the ground, stumbled across the clearing, and pushed into the thicket on the east —

And saw the Lady with the Sword.

Santa Barbara.

She stood in the clear place just beyond the thicket, waiting for Lisa. The moment Lisa saw her the Lady's sword caught fire and lit the thicket bright as day.

Lisa saw the policemen in the firelight — the policemen and the girls and all the teenagers, too, everyone she'd seen that night except the bluesman: they were all hanging in the bows of a great tall oak, impaled upon the tree's branches like flies run through by an entomologist's nails.

"*Santa,*" Lisa said, and she fell to her knees and began to pray.

The *santa* grabbed her by the shoulder and pulled her back up to her feet.

"Never pray to me, child," the Lady said.

Lisa knew why. It wasn't seemly, praying to a *santa.* She felt terrified, mortified, as though she'd committed some unpardonable sin the Lady could never forgive. "I'm sorry, *santa,*" she said. "I didn't mean —"

The Lady held up a hand to silence her. "Hush, child," she said, and then she gestured at the girls, the policemen, all the half-grown children writhing in the branches of the oak. "Look at them," she said. "What do you see?"

Lisa didn't want to answer, but she knew she had to. "I don't see nothing," Lisa said. "Just what they deserve."

The *santa* frowned.

"You need to learn, child," she said. "You need to tame your rage."

And then the *santa* and the oak and the fire and the sword and the fire were gone, and the light was dark again, shadow-speckle dark as it ever gets in New York City, even up in Harlem. Lisa stood in a clearing surrounded by the dancers, the girls, the policemen — all of them still half-conscious writhing in their agonies.

The light girl and the dark girl lay at her feet; one of them groaned deliriously. When she saw them Lisa got an awful impulse to kick them both right in their faces.

She really did. She almost couldn't stop herself. But she knew she had to, because that was the whole point of why the Lady came to her that night, wasn't it?

Wasn't it?

So Lisa hobbled away from the clearing, out of the park and three blocks north till she got home, and all that way she didn't hurt anybody, not anything, not even the bugs that skittered on the sidewalk as she approached them. But she couldn't stop herself from thinking. And she couldn't stop herself from wishing, or wanting. And oh how Lisa wanted to hurt those girls!

She surely surely did.

•

Lisa didn't have much trouble getting to sleep once she got back up the fire escape and into bed. But even if she slept readily, she couldn't sleep well: all that night she dreamed of the girls and the Lady and her sword and tiny tiny children trying to murder her. In her dream Lisa gave them all as good as she got, and better — she killed everyone who tried to kill her.

But no matter how many she killed there were always more, and as the dream wore on Lisa lost her taste for killing. She wanted to turn and run away; she wanted to wake up and scream for help; she wanted to fall on her knees and pray for salvation and the blessings of the Lord.

But she didn't dare.

Not for a moment.

Because they were that close, and there were that many of them: so many she could never win, no matter how she fought.

•

Lisa was still dreaming that awful dream when her mother woke her early in the morning, before the sun came up. At first Lisa didn't realize who it was or where she was, and she tried to bat her mother's arms away the way she fought off all the ones that tried to kill her.

"I won't let you hurt me," Lisa shouted. "I won't I won't I swear I won't."

Her mother gasped.

"Lisa!" she shouted. "Child, what's got into you?"

Lisa saw her mother, but she confused her waking with her dream. "I won't let you kill me, Mama," Lisa said. "Not even you, I swear!"

"Lisa!"

"I'll kill you!"

"Lisa, *wake up!*" Mama shouted. And then she stepped away. "What kind of a dream are you having, girl?"

As Lisa finally began to see the world around her. To smell the faint stink of her clean sheets; to feel the cool damp summer-morning breeze drifting through her open window.

She tried not to cry, but it wasn't much use. She just couldn't help herself, was all; she saw what she'd tried to do, and she saw the world, and she remembered her dream, and she knew an awful truth about herself — a truth so terrible she didn't dare admit it even in her heart.

And so obvious she couldn't deny it, no matter how she tried.

"I love you, Mama," Lisa said, and she cried and cried. "I surely do."

•

Things should have been so good after Lisa was born again. Emma and Lisa had everything, didn't they? They had their lives, they had their living, they had their place in the world and the opportunity to make it good, and what else can a body ask from God?

We all get our moment in the sun. Emma knew that she and her girl could make the best of theirs.

But it didn't work out. At all. What should have been a new life turned out to be a new kind of nightmare — and no matter how Emma wished she could wake from it, the nightmare went on and on, wearing her away.

It went bad right from the first night of Lisa's new life. Emma woke that morning to find her daughter writhing against her dreams — still asleep but thrashing in bed, twisted in the bedclothes like a hanged man wrapped inside his noose. She said, "Lisa! Lisa, wake up, child, you're having a night-mare!" but Lisa wouldn't wake no matter what Emma said. And when Emma pressed against the girl's shoulder Lisa struck her — hit Emma again and again with those tiny baby hands that were as powerful as the fists of a grown man but sharper and more piercing. Emma wanted to push the girl away and run for her life. But how could she do that? Lisa was her *baby,* for God's sake! A mother can't run away from her own child, not if she has a lick of decency.

So Emma leaned in close as the tiny baby battered her, and she said, "Lisa, Lisa, you're having a bad dream!"

And Lisa said, "I'll kill you, I'll kill you kill you kill you," and there was murder in the child's tiny voice. And no regret at all.

"Lisa!"

"Kill you kill you kill you!"

Emma grabbed the girl by her wrists, and she tried to hold her still. It wasn't much use; the baby was so strong her mother's hands could not contain her.

"I won't let you hurt me," Lisa shouted. "I won't I won't I swear I won't."

"Lisa!" Emma shouted. "Child, what's got into you?"

"I won't let you kill me, Mama," Lisa said. "Not even you, I swear!"

"Lisa!"

"I'll kill you!"

"Lisa, *wake up!*" Emma shouted. "What kind of a dream are you having, girl?"

And finally the girl began to wake, and as she woke she saw what she was doing — and the sight of it seemed to break her heart. She started crying, crying big long deep sobs so sad it made Emma ache to hear them, and *Lord* how she wished she were someplace else, anyplace else; how she wished she could go back to being an ordinary housekeeper who worked an ordinary job in an ordinary hospital; how she wished she could be an ordinary mother with an ordinary little girl who lived an ordinary life like all girls live, she really did, Emma just wished it'd never come to any of the things it came to, and for half a moment she wished she was dead and buried and her life was over so she didn't have to face the awful life ahead of her —

"Time to wake up, baby," Emma said. "We got to take you down to school."

Lisa looked like she wanted to argue with that. For a moment Emma thought it was going to start all over again, the argument over whether or not Lisa was going to go to school — but it didn't. Lisa held her tongue, and she did as Emma asked her to.

•

The day-care center was a Spanish place over on Lexington at 99th called *Escuela Santa Angelica*. Lisa knew enough Spanish to understand exactly what that meant, but she tried not to react to it anyway. What could she do, scream and carry on and stomp her feet? She didn't want to do anything like that.

Every time she thought about getting upset she thought about her dream, and her mama, and how she could've killed her mother if the dream was real. There was a moment as she rose out of her dream when Lisa'd thought she'd murdered her mama. Every time she thought about that she ached so bad she like to die.

Lisa loved her mother, even if the girl was something alive and dead and alive again who might as well have been a demon.

"This is your new school, Lisa," Mama said. "I know you'll like it here. It's a special place! They teach special children, just like you, and they teach them very well."

"Yes, Mama."

Inside the day-care center everything was shabby and run down. There were dust-piles in the corners of the waiting room, behind the chairs. The floor looked like it hadn't ever been mopped.

But Mama didn't even seem to notice those things. "You're going to learn so much," she said. She sounded thrilled — excited out of all proportion to their circumstances. "I talked to these people yesterday. They're *wonderful.*"

Lisa didn't want to think what those people had to say to Mama to make her think this place was *wonderful.* Such a strange idea! Like Mama was suddenly blind or something.

When they got to the waiting-room counter there was no one behind it. Mama tapped on the half-open window, and touched the counter bell, but no one seemed to hear it. After a while she leaned across the counter and called out for help.

For a moment Lisa thought that would go unanswered, too, and Mama would have to take her back home and call in sick to work and stay home with her —

And then the girls came through the door on the far side of the counter.

The dark girl and the light one. The girls from the dance around the fire; the girls who tried to beat Lisa senseless and would have killed her if they could've.

But Mama didn't see that. She greeted the girls warmly, as though she'd known them for years. "I'm Emma Henderson," she said. "This is my daughter Lisa. I spoke to —"

The dark girl smiled. "We've been expecting you," she said.

Lisa tugged three times on her mother's skirt. "I don't want to go here, Mama," she said. "Mama take me home please take me home."

But Mama didn't listen, no more than she listened before.

"You'll be so happy, Lisa," Mama said. "I promise you you will."

"Mama, I'm afraid."

Mama lifted Lisa in her arms and gave her baby such a hug!

"Hush, little darling," Mama said. "There's nothing here to scare you."

And then she set Lisa back down on the ground. And just as quick as *that* she hurried out the door — so fast that she was gone before Lisa had the time to scream in terror for fear of being left alone in the hands of girls who meant to kill her.

"*Mama. . . !*" Lisa screamed, but it was too damn late because Mama was already gone and the door slammed shut behind her. "*MAMA!*"

She bolted for the door, but before she could reach it the dark girl had grabbed her by the arm and stopped her in her tracks.

"Don't try it," the dark girl said. She swung Lisa around and pushed her toward the counter. Lisa tried to catch herself, but she couldn't find her balance, and fell headfirst —

— headfirst into the —

The light girl caught her before she hit her head.

She lifted Lisa in her arms and looked her coldly in the eye.

"We know who you are," the light girl said. "We're watching you. We aren't afraid."

And then she set Lisa down.

Lisa ran, terrified, in the only direction there was to run.

Which was behind the counter, and through the door on the far side of it.

On the far side of the door there was a corridor lined with offices and classrooms; at the far end of it there was a door that opened to the outside. Lisa ran for that door as though her life depended on it, and maybe it did.

But if it did she was lost anyway — because a high smooth wall surrounded the yard on the far side of the door.

Lisa paused as the door closed behind her, looking around

her, trying to find an escape. But there was no escape from that place; nothing at all but the yard and the wall and a woman standing on the far side of the grounds, surrounded by children.

"Oh!" she said. "You're Lisa Henderson, aren't you? — Your mother told us all about you yesterday."

"I'm Lisa," Lisa said, still trying to catch her breath, still looking around and around the walled yard, trying to find a way to escape.

"Why don't you join us here, Lisa, and I'll introduce you to the other children?"

Lisa scowled. "I don't want to," she said. She sulked away from the door, wandered toward the yard's far wall.

"Suit yourself, then, Lisa," the woman said. "We're here when you decide you want company."

Lisa ignored her. Of course she did! She wasn't going to change her mind, not for a minute. Lisa didn't want to be in that awful place, and if there was a way out she was going to find it, and in the meantime she didn't want a part of it if she could help it.

So she found the corner of the yard, and she sat down in it, and she put her head on her knees and covered it with her arms.

After a while she fell asleep. She didn't mean to, but she did.

And for once she slept and there were no dreams — just the blackness of her own heart, suffusing her; and the quiet that comes when the waking world is a million miles away; and somewhere out beyond the endlessness of that distance there were the sounds of children playing in the yard, and the woman calling after them, and now and then a siren sound like you always hear in Harlem in the daytime — maybe it was a police car, or an ambulance, or a fire truck, who could tell when it wasn't right there in the middle of the emergency?

As Lisa slept.

After a while she heard the noise get closer, and then she felt a warm moist hand resting on her shoulder. Someone was trying to wake her, she realized, and for half a moment she thought that meant the day was done and her mama had come back to get her —

Only it wasn't like that at all.

Because it wasn't her mama's face Lisa saw staring at her when she opened her eyes.

Far from it.

It was a boy — he looked like he was what, four, five years old? A little boy who was bigger than Lisa, four or five times bigger than she was. And he had a *stupid* expression on his face, all slack and rolly-eyed, like a brain-damage retard or something.

"You got to wake up," the boy said. "It's not nighttime! Sun's out! You got to wake up!"

The woman should have kept this boy away from her, Lisa thought. And maybe she would have, too, but there were children shouting at each other on the far side of the yard, and she was too busy watching that to even notice how the boy harassed Lisa.

"Go away," Lisa told him. "Leave me alone."

The boy looked stricken. He started bawling. " 'Leave me alone,' " he whined. "I don't like you! Got to get up! Can't sleep all day!"

Lisa didn't have the patience for it. At all. *"Leave me alone,"* she said. *"Right now."*

She didn't bother to see how he'd take that, because she *knew* how he'd take it. She buried her head in her arms and tried to pretend she was a million miles away again —

— and the boy grabbed her by the arm, and pulled Lisa to her feet.

"No *sleep!*" he shouted. "Wake!"

And Lisa just couldn't take it anymore.

Just couldn't take it.

"Get your hands off me," she said, but the boy didn't hear. *"Let me go."*

The retard didn't let go. He shook Lisa like she was a rag doll. "Wake! Wake!"

Lisa managed to get a grip on his t-shirt with her free hand, and pulled herself close to the big stupid child.

Pulled on his shirt with all her strength — pulled so hard she forced the boy to stoop.

That surprised him so bad he lost his grip on her other

arm —

And Lisa couldn't help herself.

She just couldn't help herself. She couldn't think; she couldn't feel; she couldn't hardly see what she was doing. She just started hitting the boy with the fist of her free hand, pounding him over and over again. In her mind's eye his face was a nail and her fist was a hammer, and she had to pound the nail flush with the rest of the world, and she couldn't stop, and she couldn't think, and if she'd stopped to think she would have heard the boy screaming in abject terror, shrieking in shock and rage and agony indignation, pleading for his life as she pounded and pounded him with her tiny fist as hard and mighty as a sledge, pounding and pound —

After a while the woman and the dark girl and the light girl got to her, and pried her off that awful boy. But there was blood everywhere by then, and the boy was all twisty-looking and mewling like a cat half-run over by a truck, and the girls screamed and the woman swore and someone called an ambulance.

Maybe someone called the police. There were a lot of sirens.

Everything got confused after that. Someone forgot to keep an eye on Lisa, and she wandered away from the day-care center. But not for long. She couldn't go long, or far, she realized; she had to be here when Mama got back from work to pick her up.

She went three blocks through the battered parts of Spanish Harlem, and then she went back to *Escuela Santa Angelica*. When she got there there were three ambulances parked in front of the place, and there were people hurrying in every direction, and no one even noticed Lisa.

Lisa didn't care. She didn't want them to notice.

After a while half a dozen medics carried a bloody stretcher out the front door of the school. Lisa didn't watch them. She didn't want to see. She didn't care! That awful boy deserved just what he got, he damn well did, she knew.

But she didn't feel good when she thought that. And maybe it was wrong.

She turned away from the school, and there before her was one of the ambulances, its wide back doors open into shadows so much darker than anyplace should ever be in the daytime. Why was it so dark in there? Lisa stepped up to the edge of the ambulance, peered into the shadows — and saw the Lady cloaked in darkness, waiting for her.

"I didn't mean to hurt him, Lady," Lisa said. "He was just a little boy!"

The Lady didn't say a word. She lifted Lisa in her arms, enfolding the girl in her cloak.

And carried her away.

•

Lisa closed her eyes in the darkness of the Lady's cloak, and she kept them closed for the longest time.

After a while the sounds of the city faded around them, and everything grew still as stone. When the quiet grew deep enough to hurt her ears, Lisa opened her eyes and saw the Lady, carrying her with one arm as she held her bright fiery sword in the other. They were in the corridor, again, the passageway between life and death that led one way to Heaven and the other way to Hell, and the bright sword kept the darkness of that awful place at bay.

It's over now, Lisa thought. *The world is done with me.*

But when she heard herself think those words she knew they weren't true.

"Where are we going?" Lisa asked.

The Lady turned and looked at her, but she didn't answer.

Lisa wondered if she should be scared. What would they do to her, she wondered, after they judged her? — and then she thought about the rolly-eyed boy, and how she hit him so much she put him in the hospital, in the hospital so bad she maybe even killed him. And she knew there was a place for people who do things like that to little retard boys.

And she knew that place was Hell.

I'm going to go to Hell, Lisa thought. And she tried not to be afraid, but part of her was terrified; and part of her just thought it was the right thing because she deserved it. That part wasn't afraid, but it was very sad.

The Lady looked sad, too.

Now they crested an incline, and suddenly the gates of Heaven and Hell appeared before them.

Both gates were closed — bolted home and sealed. Between them there was a fountain, and below that fountain was a reflecting pool.

The pool was glassy-still despite the burbling gush at its center, and it reflected everything around them as clearly as if it were a mirror.

Perhaps even more clearly — for that pool caught the essence of the things around it as no ordinary mirror could; and when Lisa looked at it she knew things about the nature of Heaven and Hell that she didn't want to know.

As if she had a choice!

The Lady carried Lisa to the edge of the pool and set her down beside it — and for the first time Lisa saw her own reflection in that water.

When she looked in that water, Lisa saw herself in perspective. She saw how tiny and insignificant she was — not just among grown adults seven times her size, but before a world infinitely larger than she was, too.

And in the mirror of that water she saw the things about herself she didn't want to see, like the retard-boy's blood that covered her hands, and always would; and as she saw that dried and crusted blood she rubbed her tiny hands against one another, trying to clean them. It was no use, because the boy's blood was a part of her reflection, now, and it always would be, but even so tiny flakes of scabrous matter dusted away from her hands as she rubbed them.

When those flakes touched the water of the pool, Lisa's reflection shimmered, dissolved, and faded away; and then suddenly the water shone as bright as day, driving away the darkness of the hall.

For a moment Lisa thought she'd somehow set the pool afire. But then she saw an image coalesce on the day-bright surface of the pool, and she knew what was to come.

It started like this: she saw an awkward little boy waddling across a yard, watching a baby asleep curled up in a tight little ball.

That's me, Lisa thought. *He's watching me.*

When the boy got close enough to touch the baby, he hesitated a moment — stood hovering above the smaller child, staring at her intently. After a moment he began to drool, but he didn't seem to notice — not even when a long slidey droplet of his drool drizzled down to spatter on the baby's leg.

He spit on me, Lisa thought. *That ugly retard spit on me.*

"Wake up, baby," the boy said. His voice was hardly more than a whisper.

The baby didn't hear him.

"Wake *up,* baby!"

And when the baby still didn't wake, the boy put his warm sticky hand on the baby's shoulder, and began to shake her.

"No!" Lisa shouted. "I don't want to see!"

But the vision continued. As the baby grumbled at the boy, asking to be left alone; as the boy persisted, badgering the baby —

Lisa grabbed the *santa*'s cloak, pulled on it as insistently as she'd yank her mother's skirt. "Make it stop, Lady. *Please?* — I don't want to see again. I can't stand to see it, please?"

The Lady frowned. She didn't answer.

Below them on the water the boy yanked the baby to her feet, and the baby responded by hitting him — again and again and again.

It was so much different, seeing it this way. At first when Lisa'd hit the boy she was just trying to protect herself, and then she sort of lost track of everything. The only time in all of that she really saw him was right at the end, as the teacher grabbed her and pulled her off the boy — for that tiny moment she looked down and saw all that blood, saw the boy looked like something made of pulp, and she ached for him, and she screamed —

Screamed!

But now she saw every moment of it. Every tiny blow the baby's sharp hard fists jabbed the boy. She saw how he first began to bleed the third time the baby hit him in the mouth; how his arm twisted funny when he fell, trying to get away from her; how she hit his nose three times and after that the shape was different.

She heard him scream, and scream again; and then he begged her not to hit him anymore.

The scene transfixed Lisa. She gaped at it; without even

realizing she leaned out over the water to look at it more closely. "Stop it!" she shouted, trembling as the baby battered the soft stupid boy. "I told you, *stop it!*"

But the baby didn't stop. How could the baby ever stop, so far away in time?

"I'm warning you," Lisa said. "I warn you!"

As the baby jabbed and jabbed and jabbed, and now the boy's nose began to gush with blood.

And Lisa just stopped thinking.

Just stopped thinking.

And she lashed out at the image on the water, reached for the baby's throat to tear her away from the boy and throw her out across the hall —

But of course she couldn't do that.

The image on the water was just an image, not the scene itself; Lisa couldn't grab the baby girl who beat and beat and beat the idiot child — because the baby wasn't there. And neither was the boy. All Lisa could do was slap the water, splash the surface; send droplets of that water flying everywhere.

The splashing water spattered all across the pool, but it didn't disturb the stillness of the water. No more than the fountain did.

Lisa didn't care. She hardly even noticed. When her hand came away from the image holding nothing but the droplets of water that clung to it, she struck again and again and again, screaming in rage and frustration, and she felt the same rage consume her that had consumed her as she'd beat the retard half to death, and if she'd been able to get her hands on the baby or the boy that moment she'd have killed them both —

— killed them both —

— and in her rage she forgot herself entirely.

Forgot where she was, forgot what she was doing, and lost her balance.

And tumbled headfirst into the reflecting pool that rests between the gates of Heaven and Hell.

Lisa almost drowned deep down in the stillness of that water. She would've died if anything could die in a place past life and death.

•

This is what Lisa saw as she thrashed and gasped and coughed and choked deep beneath the imperturbable surface of the reflecting pool between the judgment gates:

She saw her mother, worried out of her mind for her missing daughter and the mayhem and the end of their new life;

She saw Robert Johnson, somewhere down in Hell, playing his guitar;

She saw Santa Barbara standing above the pool, watching Lisa, waiting for her to find herself and save her soul from the rage that wanted to drown her;

She saw the open gates of Heaven, and the pearly haze that lay impenetrable to light beyond.

I'm going to drown, Lisa thought. *I'm going to die.*

She tried to remember how to swim, but it was so hard! She was so terrified — panicked by her circumstance, blinded by her rage. And all she knew about swimming was from a few days that summer years ago, when the lifeguard lady at camp taught her how to paddle and when to hold her breath, but she couldn't remember, not for nothing, and everything she did remember didn't work because she'd already breathed in more water than she'd drink in a week.

"Help!" Lisa shouted, trying to get the *santa* to lift her from the pool and save her life. "Help help!"

But her words got lost in the coughing and the choking and the water and the *santa* didn't hear or didn't listen, she stood above the pool as Lisa thrashed and gasped and suddenly lost hold.

Grew weak as a kitten, and tired. As the blackness faded in around her and she died.

•

Lisa didn't really die, of course. No one can die when she stands in that place that's neither life nor death. Instead she lost her grip on where and when she was, and the currents of the world swept the girl away.

When she woke she lay soaked and broken in an abandoned lot three blocks northwest of *Escuela Santa Angelica.*

As she woke she heard the *santa* whisper in her ear.

"You need to let go of your rage, child," the *santa* said. "If you don't let it go it will destroy you."

Lisa turned to face her, to confront her, to accuse the Lady of abandoning her child to the waters that would drown her.

But the Lady was nowhere to be seen.

"Come back!" Lisa shouted. "You come back here!"

"You need to let go of your rage."

Lisa whipped around to face the direction from which the voice had seemed to come — and saw nothing.

"Don't leave me *alone!*" Lisa shouted — and as she said the word *alone* her shout became a wail. Then she was crying, bawling like a baby or sissy or some big soft old retard boy.

"Lisa!" someone called, and for a moment Lisa thought it was the Lady, returned to her, come to save her from her lonely fate in a burned-out lot in Spanish Harlem.

But it wasn't the Lady. It was Lisa's mother, looking frayed and frightened and defeated, like she'd spent the whole afternoon searching for Lisa and thinking the girl was dead.

"Mama," Lisa wailed, and she opened her arms and let her mother lift her from the rubble of the broken lot, and carry her away.

•

Lisa's mama made a telephone call as soon as they got home.

She set Lisa in her chair and picked up the phone and dialed Mama Estrella's number, and when Mama Estrella answered she said, "Mama Estrella? Something terrible has happened. Yes, to Lisa. She, she — yes, please. Come as soon as you can."

Mama Estrella knocked on the door ten minutes later.

"What is it, Emma?" Mama Estrella asked. "What has she done?"

"At the school, Mama Estrella. She hurt a boy, and then she disappeared. When I found her in the field she was — wet. Soaked to the skin with something that, that — look." Lisa's mama gestured at Lisa's clothes, at her own clothes where the water from the reflecting pool had touched them.

The water had bleached Lisa's dress white — not just white but a shade of white so blinding-bright that it hurt Lisa's eyes to look at it. Mama's clothes were white like that, too, everywhere they'd touched Lisa while she was still drying.

"Oh my God," Mama Estrella said. She knelt before Lisa and began to examine her. "Are you burned, Lisa? Your skin, your eyes?"

"No, Mama Estrella," Lisa said.

"What happened to you, girl?"

"I —" Lisa began. And then she stopped. She had to stop, she knew. She didn't dare tell that woman what she'd seen. "Nothing happened, Mama Estrella. I just got lost, that's all."

Mama Estrella scowled.

"You're lying, child. Tell me the truth."

"Tell her the truth, Lisa."

Lisa didn't say a word.

"How did you get wet, Lisa?"

"Wet. . . ?"

Lisa couldn't tell them about the reflecting pool any more than she could tell them about the *santa*. She knew that. She tried to think of a lie to explain the water that'd soaked her, but all the lies that came to her were obviously transparent.

"Don't give her that, young lady. You tell Mama Estrella what happened to you."

Lisa looked down at her feet, pretending not to hear.

"Lisa!"

"It's all right, Emma," Mama Estrella said. She put one hand on Lisa's cheek, ran the other through the girl's hair. Her fingers found an itchy lump near Lisa's hairline and probed it.

"Ouch!"

Bent close to examine it —

— and gasped.

"What is it, Mama Estrella?"

"*Shungó.*" Mama Estrella said that name softer than a whisper, as though she were afraid that speaking it out loud would call the Lady to her. "It's Shungó's hand behind all of this, isn't it?"

Lisa's mama shuddered. "I don't know any Shungó," she said. "And I don't want to know any."

"You've seen her," Mama Estrella said. "The Lady in the grotto behind my store — no, not Mary, the other one. The virgin with the sword."

"Santa Barbara. . . ?"

"Yes, Santa Barbara — *the goddess who repented.*"

"What're you talking about?"

Mama Estrella scowled; she muttered derisively.

Lisa knew why. But she didn't say a word.

"We need to go back to the boneyard," Mama Estrella said. "We need to ask Shungó to take her mark off your daughter's forehead."

Lisa's mama made a frightened little sound, like Mama Estrella had struck her with a rod, or worse. "I won't go back there, Mama Estrella. I won't."

"Emma —"

"Use a little common sense, Mama Estrella Perez. Nothing good ever walks out of a graveyard — not now, not when you woke Lisa, not ever. If I want an exorcist, I'll call a priest."

Mama Estrella started muttering again. It sounded like she was swearing out a curse, but Lisa couldn't hear the words.

"Can you do it here, Mama Estrella? Could you do it downstairs in the grotto?"

Mama Estrella closed her eyes, rubbed her temple. "Let me think," she said. And then she was quiet for a while. Quiet and — faraway-looking. It almost seemed like she was praying.

And maybe she *was* praying. Santeria ladies like Mama Estrella love Jesus as dearly as anyone does, and more dearly than most people do.

"Mama Estrella. . . ?"

Mama Estrella opened her eyes.

"In the morning," she said. "Downstairs in the yard — as soon as the sunlight shines directly on her grotto."

Lisa's mama nodded. "All right, then. If you think it'll help."

Mama Estrella smiled. "It will," she said.

She left without saying another word.

Lisa didn't expect to see her again until the morning, but it didn't work out like that. A couple of hours after dinner, when Lisa and Mama were sitting in the living room watching old movies on TV, there came a knock on the door, and when Lisa's mama answered it she found Mama Estrella waiting for her.

"You'll need me here tonight," Mama Estrella said. "I'll stay on your couch."

Lisa's mama looked a little bit surprised, but she didn't argue. Lisa wished she had; she didn't like Mama Estrella very much. She sure didn't want to spend the night that close to her.

But no one asks little girls about things like company, and Lisa's mama didn't, either. So Mama Estrella Perez stayed with them that night, and when Lisa went to bed she had the strangest dream.

She dreamed the Lady took her hand and led her into an endless night-black wilderness. After a long time they came to a bonfire.

On one side of that fire sat Robert Johnson — she knew him from her other dreams, and she recognized him. On the other side there were six old, old men. They were strange and beautiful old men, and even though Lisa didn't know any of them, she recognized them in her heart, and she loved them.

Of course she knew and loved them! Everyone who has the magic and the music in her heart knows those men when she sees them! They were Kings — old Kings who'd ruled the Mississippi lowlands from New Orleans north to Chicago back before the world broke open. And when they picked at their guitars the sound was beauteous to behold — listen, listen now as Charlie Patton picks his worn guitar, and listen as the strings speak: *"Lord have mercy,"* the guitar says. *"Lord, Lord have mercy. Lord have mercy — pray, brother, pray, save poor me."*

He held the guitar strangely — one hand around its neck, the other all but covering the guitar's open mouth. It was almost as though he were choking the words out of it, Lisa thought, and then she thought that was such a strange idea.

All of it was strange, everything about that dream. Later Lisa decided that she'd only imagined it.

But it was true, every solitary bit: there in the dream that was stranger than the truth she heard Charlie Patton's guitar singing, pleading for mercy.

Then Charlie Patton's guitar went silent, and Lisa realized that the Lady had left her. Robert Johnson stood up on the far side of the fire, and he held out a hand to her.

"Lisa," he said. "Lisa Henderson."

It was the first time in all Lisa's dreams of him that Robert Johnson had addressed her by name.

"I'm afraid," Lisa said, but that was a lie. Lisa was a brave girl! She was never afraid.

Robert Johnson smiled reassuringly. "No one here will ever hurt you," he said. "Remember this place and you'll always have a sanctuary."

"I will," Lisa said. But how could she ever remember? The Lady led her here through the darkness, and Lisa didn't know the way.

"You can always find it in your heart, Lisa, if you know to look for it."

"I knew that," she said. Which was another lie, but Robert Johnson knew and didn't care.

"Come on," he said. "Take my hand, I'll show you something."

Lisa didn't want to go anywhere. She liked the place with the bonfire, and if she could have stayed there for a lifetime, listening to the music and watching Charlie Patton strangle his guitar, she would have done that.

But she couldn't, of course. And she knew that if there was a thing Robert Johnson thought she'd need to see, she'd better go with him and see it.

So she took his hand and followed him away from the fire, out into the darkness and forever and on; it felt like they walked halfway cross the country before they were halfway done.

And now there were trees around them in the darkness, and they were climbing a mountain in the hills of Tennessee.

High above them stood three men with guitars.

"Who are they?" Lisa asked.

Robert Johnson hushed her. "These are the Blind Lords of the Piedmont," he said. "They rule these hills and everything surrounding."

"Blind? — I don't understand."

"Hush."

She tried to make out the words to their song, and then realized there were no words at all — the blind men were humming to one another as clearly as you or I might speak.

When they were close enough to touch the blind men, Robert Johnson knelt to whisper into Lisa's ear. "You need to kneel before them," he whispered, "and ask them for their blessing."

Lisa thought, *I won't!*, but she was wrong. She didn't mean to be, but that was how it happened — something deep inside her knew a more important truth, and when she stood before the Blind Lords it pushed her to her knees and raised her right hand to them, palm down.

"I live to serve you," Lisa said, and she never meant to say that, no more than she meant to kneel.

The black Lord smiled; his white companions folded their arms. "We take your service, child," the black Lord said.

"We take your service, Lisa Henderson," one of his companions repeated. "Bless you, child. Bless your sojourn, and everything that you endeavor."

And then the Blind Lords were gone, and Lisa and Robert Johnson stood alone atop the mountain.

"I never heard a white man who knew about real music," Lisa said, and they both knew she didn't mean just music, but blues music, real blues like the kind that's always got some magic in it, even when the least ones play it.

"You never known nobody from the Piedmont, girl," Robert Johnson said. "Things are different in the mountains."

"What was the song?" Lisa asked. "I know that song. It's like *Judgment Day*, but different."

Robert Johnson looked surprise that she had recognized it. He nodded. "You're right," he said. "It's called *The Eye of the World*, and the Blind Lords will sing it loud and true from their mountaintops after the Kings sing *Judgment Day*."

Lisa bit her lip. "I knew that," she said. "How did I know?"

"It's in the music, Lisa. If you know the music in your heart, you know its deepest secrets."

Far away in the western distance, Lisa could see the great river, and above the river there was a light. "I'm just a girl," Lisa said. "I don't know about things like that."

Robert Johnson laughed.

"You know all sorts of things, child. They're written in your heart. All you have to do is admit them and they're yours."

Now the light above the river grew larger and larger, till it was four times the circumference of the moon, and Lisa could see it was a great wide eye.

The Eye of the World.

"It's beautiful," Lisa said, and it was beautiful, clear and deep and luminescent in a way that made clear everything that shone beneath it.

"Of course it is," Robert Johnson said. "If the world has a soul," he said, "you can see it through the Eye."

And Lisa thought she *could* see the world's soul, deep inside that Eye; not directly, but reflected, the way you see the heart of a woman when you look her in the eye.

"Is it true, Robert Johnson? — Is it true what I heard about you and the Eye of the World?"

Robert Johnson went all slack beside her; he made a sound like the breath of a sigh but defeated, the noise you hear when a vacant body lets go a man's last breath.

"Every word of it is true, Lisa Henderson."

And Lisa could see it was, because now that she thought to look for them she could see the cracks in the Eye's lens; and in her dream she imagined those cracks grew wider and wider till finally the Eye of the World fell open like the petals of a desiccated rose.

"Every word of it is true."

●

Lisa woke crying quietly in the dark. She didn't mean to cry. She didn't want to cry. She hated crying like she did, she really hated it. But it wasn't like she could stop — she knew that because she tried and it didn't do a bit of good.

"Tell me about your dream, Lisa," said a voice in the darkness, and Lisa knew who it was. Of course she did! It was Mama Estrella, poking around in the privatest secretest things that Lisa ever knew.

"I won't," Lisa said.

"You need to tell," said Mama Estrella. "You know you do."

Lisa said, "You're wrong," but she knew the Santeria lady was right. And Mama Estrella did, too; and because she knew she didn't press. She sat in the darkness at the foot of Lisa's bed, waiting and listening, for a time that felt like hours but maybe it was only moments.

And after a while Lisa knew that it was right, and she began to tell. She told Mama Estrella everything, there in the darkness. Told her about the dream with Robert Johnson and the

Blind Lords of the Piedmont; about the reflecting pool outside the gates of Heaven and Hell; about the night she died, when Our Lady of Sorrows appeared to her in the twilight fading of her hospital room.

Mama Estrella took it all in. After a while Lisa began to suspect she'd known parts of it all along.

"Shungó has expectations for you," Mama Estrella said, when Lisa had said everything she knew to say.

"I'm just a girl," Lisa said. "I don't want any *expectations.*"

"I know that, Lisa. That's why I'm trying to *help* you."

Lisa knew when she heard the word *help* that there was terrible trouble caught up around it, but she didn't say anything. What could she say, after all? *Let me alone, Mama Estrella, the Lady knows what's best for me?* Lisa could have said that, maybe, but she was too scared. She loved the Lady and she knew the Lady loved her, but she frightened Lisa all the same, and the dearest part of Lisa's heart just wanted to go back to being an ordinary little girl in ordinary Harlem with her ordinary mama and her everyday school, and she knew that was impossible so long as she went with the Lady.

So she let Mama Estrella wash her and dress her that morning, and when the sun came up Mama Estrella and Mama and Lisa all went down through Mama Estrella's store, into the grotto in the back yard.

And Mama Estrella made a candle from three kinds of sacred oil and a water that made the flame sputter pungent smoke, and she made Lisa kneel before the Lady's statue in the grotto.

And she said a prayer in a language Lisa didn't know, but three times she recognized the name *Shungó*, and twice she heard *Barbara.*

When Mama Estrella finished her prayer, the statue at the center of the grotto began to move. It moved as easily as a Lady made of flesh and blood, but it still looked like stone.

"*Santa,*" said Mama Estrella. "*Santa,* we beseech you —"

— as now the statue's sword caught fire as the Lady raised it high above her head, to strike —

"— beseech you to set our daughter free."

As the sword swung hard and fast and bright to cut the Santeria lady in two.

•

They got Mama Estrella to the hospital in time for the doctors to reattach her arm, but only barely. She spent seven hours in surgery, and all that while she was half awake and murmuring, no matter how they drugged her.

She woke the moment they wheeled her into the recovery room, and demanded to speak to Emma Henderson. The nurses tried to reassure her back to sleep, but she refused to let them, and persisted in her demand until they relented.

"You need to find the Seventh King," Mama Estrella said when they brought Emma to her. She was sickly-looking — sweaty and wide-eyed from the drugs, pale and shriveled from the trauma of her wound. "Take my car. Go to Greenville — Greenville, Mississippi. Take Highway 82 through town. Three miles south of Greenville you'll see three tall pines that cross themselves. There's a dirt road between two of those trees. It leads through a pinewoods toward a bluff.

"Follow the road until you know you should stop, and look south — you'll see a shack. The last of the Seven Kings lives there. Knock on his door and he'll find you, even if he isn't there."

Hell
Timeless

There are a thousand stories about John Henry, and a thousand thousand variations on those tales. Some of the stories are literally true; some of them are figuratively true; some of them are wrong. That's the nature of stories, isn't it? They show us all the highlights of the world, but they never leave us certain we can trust the things we know. We listen because they delight us, and mind them as much as they illuminate our hearts; but no one with a lick of sense ever trusts a tale he can't verify himself.

There's no way at all to be certain where John Henry is concerned. All the tales about him are echoes of one another; and perhaps John Henry himself was only an echo of them all. Who's to say whether we should believe the stories about his songs, his deeds, his sermons? Even the events recounted in ballad that describes his competition with the engine are uncertain, and those events are so well known most people take them for the gospel truth.

But there is no gospel truth where John Henry is concerned. His birth, his death, his marriage and his sons — all of them are mysteries clouded by a history of uncertain times.

One story says he was born in Africa in the 1830s to a great songster and his beautiful frail wife. His mother died the day she named him (but no story ever tells the name she gave him), and his father died when he was ten. When both his folks were gone his drunkard uncle sold him for a slave.

The slavers took him north and west, smuggling him into Georgia, where they sold him to the cruelest masters they could find. Those masters — avaricious planters — beat the boy, abused him, and battered him to break his spirit. They would have succeeded, too, if they'd never given him the Good Word of the Lord.

The moment that that child heard of God he knew Him and he loved Him, and he took the hymns the planters taught him and twisted them around the music in his heart until he made a song greater than any hymn the planters ever knew.

The planters never heard him sing his song, but they heard it all the same: he made a song that every black man sang to Praise the Lord, and when the white folks heard it they sang too, even if they only kept the music in their hearts.

John Henry's faith and his song and the nature of his song all grew mighty and most fine, and his faith was a treasure more valuable than gold. It guided him as he learned to sing and work and struggle, and it taught him how work and perseverance make us strong even when they serve our oppressors. When the war killed his masters and the soldiers in blue uniforms wrecked their plantation, John Henry took up arms and fought alongside the best of them.

When the war was over he traveled far and wide, working his way from one end of the country to the other and back again. As he grew old his music grew deep and rich and wise, and in his time he passed away and died.

No one knows exactly where he's buried, but there are those who will tell you his grave is on the side of a great mountain high above the Mississippi, where the great man looks down upon the river and the land and the nation that he loved. His ghost watches all of us, they say, loving us and guiding us as no other spirit could.

Near St. Marys, Missouri
Easter 1949

Robert Johnson and Peetie Wheatstraw got off the train at St. Marys early in the morning Easter Sunday. They tried to find a hire car to take them to the Mountain, but because of the holiday there were none to be had. That left them with no option but to make the trip on foot.

In some ways that was for the best. The people of St. Marys knew about the Mountain in those years, and they suspected it mightily; lots of busy minds would have taken note if two unearthly men like Peetie Wheatstraw and Robert Johnson had hired a car to take them to the Mountain.

Whether it was for the best or not, it wasn't an easy walk. The countryside gets rough and uneven along the river north of St. Marys, and the weather was terrible. Terrible! Easter came early in 1949, and the winter that year was a rough one besides. Even in a mild year the mountainous parts of Missouri get real winters, and on Easter 1949 the winter was very real indeed. It snowed on and off all day that Easter, and when it wasn't snowing the temperature went just high enough to thaw a little of the thick snow already on the ground and turn it into slush. That bitter melting cold burned Robert Johnson as it never could have burned him when he was still truly a deadman.

Or maybe not. By the time they'd walked the fifteen miles from St. Marys station to the foot of the Mountain, even dead Peetie Wheatstraw had took himself a chill.

"I don't like this cold," he said, pausing for a moment to look at the trail that led from the riverside up to the summit of the mountain. "It aches me grievously."

Robert Johnson had started shivering two miles back, but he didn't let that intimidate him. "What's the matter," he said. "Can't you take a little cold?" And then he laughed bravely till he realized that laughing let the cold run down deep into his lungs.

"Don't give me that," Peetie Wheatstraw said. "You going

to catch yourself another pneumonia if we don't get you to a fire."

Robert Johnson shrugged. "I ain't scared of no pneumonia," he said, even though the whole idea of pneumonia scared him something terrible. "They got a pill they call penicillin, now. Pneumonia don't kill nobody who finds themself a doctor."

Peetie Wheatstraw looked at him like he was out of his mind. Which maybe he was, or maybe they both were, or maybe every soul upon that Mountain was out of his mind. "You watch out for those city doctors," he said. "They kill a lot more than they save. Always have, always will." He gestured at the trail. "C'mon, Robert Johnson. Get a move on. Charlie Patton has a shack half a mile up the Mountain; he always keeps a fire there."

The trail up was easier going than the trip from St. Marys had been, because life is always milder on the Mountain than it is in the world outside. If the world is cold then the cold upon the Mountain is less bitter; if it snows upon that Mountain then the snow is light and airy, too soft and dry to seep through a hiker's boots. When the thaw comes it comes all at once, in one warm afternoon, and the runoff flows into the springs and streams without ever muddying a trail.

But the mildness wasn't much help for Robert Johnson. He'd already took his chill, and there wasn't a fire in the world that could warm it quickly out of him.

When they reached the shack Peetie Wheatstraw put his hand on Robert Johnson's arm. "Wait here," he said. "I'll have to tell Charlie Patton that I've brought you."

Robert Johnson nodded to show he understood, but Peetie Wheatstraw didn't see. He was already opening the door of the shack, greeting Charlie Patton, speaking to him too quietly for Robert Johnson to hear. After a while — a long while, longer than Robert Johnson expected — Peetie Wheatstraw leaned out the door of the shack and told him to come in.

He didn't look happy when he said it. He looked — worried. Which is a very strange expression to see on the face of a man who calls himself the Devil's Son-in-Law.

It only took Robert Johnson a moment after he got in the shack to realize why Peetie Wheatstraw looked that way: the reason was Charlie Patton.

Charlie Patton was angry — spitting angry, and angrier still when Robert Johnson held out his hand to introduce himself.

"You keep that to yourself," Charlie Patton said. "You're a stranger to me, Robert Johnson, and I'd just as soon see it stayed that way."

Now there were deep connections between Robert Johnson and Charlie Patton. Patton, after all, was the man who taught Son House blues, and Son House was Robert Johnson's teacher. The two men weren't even strangers; Charlie Patton had worked the plantation where Robert Johnson grew up, and lots of nights when he was a boy Robert Johnson sat at the fireside with the other children, listening to Charlie Patton play.

Back when he was alive the first time, Robert Johnson would have took exception to talk like that from a man who might as well have been his kin, but in his new life he was a God-fearing man, and he loved God, too, and because he feared and loved the Lord he turned the other cheek when he was able. When Charlie Patton refused to shake his hand Robert Johnson took the insult with good humor and a measure of grace; he said "All right, then," and clasped his hands before him to show he didn't plan to take offense.

"Show a little courtesy, Charlie Patton," Peetie Wheatstraw said. "This man is our guest. He isn't here to ask a favor from the Mountain King; he's here because John Henry sent for him."

Charlie Patton spat into the fire.

"I saw him sing, twelve years ago. I know who Robert Johnson is."

Robert Johnson winced. He stared at his shoes.

"You don't know nothing, Charlie Patton. I've been watching this man for months. I know him like I knew my brother. He ain't the person who he was."

Charlie Patton scowled. "I saw him," he said. "I saw the Eye."

"I know you did."

"There are things for which a man can never be forgiven," Charlie Patton said. "There are gifts so fine that vain men don't deserve them."

Peetie Wheatstraw didn't answer that right away. Instead he spent a long moment looking at the fire through the open door of the shack's woodstove, looking like he was weighing his words and trying to decide how much he ought to say.

"I want to show you something, Charlie Patton," he said at last. "You say you saw the Eye, twelve years ago? I've seen the Eye — four, five dozen times these last few months. It hangs above the river watching him for hours on end.

"It doesn't hate him, Charlie Patton. Just the opposite, in fact — I'd swear I see it watch him full of adoration." He stepped to the door of the shack, and opened it. A cold wind gusted through the aperture. "See it for yourself," he said. "It's watching now, just as I thought it would be."

And sure enough, the Eye hung above the river, staring at them.

Staring at Robert Johnson. *Watching* him, lovingly.

Then suddenly the wind reversed itself, and the door slammed shut with a terrible bang.

"I don't believe you," Charlie Patton murmured, but that just wasn't true. He turned away from Peetie Wheatstraw and Robert Johnson and began tidying his shack. After a moment he went to the cookstove to stir the beans simmering atop it. "Sit down," he said. "Be comfortable."

Later when they all were warm Charlie Patton served them beans and rice, and after that he found his guitar. "I haven't played in a long time," he said. "I don't play much these days."

Everyone who knew the Mountain knew that was true. There was a reason Charlie Patton lived so low on the Mountain, instead of near the summit with the other Kings.

"I didn't play for a long time," Robert Johnson said. "But these days I play more than I used to."

Charlie Patton eyed him carefully, measuring the man. "Is that a fact?" he asked.

"It is."

Charlie Patton nodded. "I know a song," he said. "I bet you never heard it."

Peetie Wheatstraw raised an eyebrow. "And what song would that be?"

They all knew what he was asking about.

"Nothing that ought to make you fret, Bill Bunch." Bill Bunch — *William* Bunch, more rightly — was Peetie Wheatstraw's born name, but he never used it when he no longer was alive. "Just a little song I know. You ought to hear it, too." Charlie Patton gripped the guitar strangely — one hand around its neck, the other all but covering the guitar's open mouth. And as his hands moved, the guitar seemed to speak. *"Lord have mercy,"* the guitar said. *"Lord, Lord have mercy. Lord have mercy — pray, brother, pray, save poor me."*

Robert Johnson laughed. "John Henry can make his hammer ring like a bell," he said. "But you got yours talking like a lady."

Even Peetie Wheatstraw had to laugh at that. "I never met that lady," he said. "Maybe Charlie Patton ought to introduce me."

And they laughed.

When the laughter died, Charlie Patton said, "This here is a song about a man who lived and died and lived again, and instead of him going on to his damnation — or reward! — he found himself back on earth being somebody he never ought to be, something nobody ever ought to be — something dead and alive at the same time, a body not alive enough to feel and not dead enough to go still and decay. I know a man who's like this song, and there are days I feel for him, I tell you."

And then he sang.

His song was a four-four ballad with loose, uneven rhymes; it was long and sad and sometimes beautiful; but it was also a little on the maudlin side, and there were places where it dripped with self-pity. It was the story of Charlie Patton's reawakening as his music charmed him out the gates of Hell. It told how he'd traveled three weeks on his own after he came back from Hell, curing the sick and straightening the lame, enlightening the ignorant and teaching miserable people to rejoice. When those three weeks were over he came to a crossroads, and there at the crossroads was John Henry, singing.

John Henry made his hammer ring like a bell.

Charlie Patton played along with him — played his guitar for the first time since he'd come back to the world of man and woman. As they played, the magic in their music transported them, and when their song was done the two deadmen stood upon the great Mountain above the great river.

Charlie Patton never meant to climb that Mountain, but his music took him to it anyway. When the song was over and they stood together on the Mountain, John Henry told Charlie Patton who he was and why he was and what his role was in the scheme of things, but Charlie Patton didn't like that. Not at all.

So he came down from the mountain and went back to his vocation among the people, whispering songs that cured the sick and straightened the lame. He could have done that for a lifetime, because he loved the work. But it isn't in human nature to take a gift and let it go at that, and the day came when a rich farmer demanded Charlie Patton raise his dead daughter from the ground.

Charlie Patton didn't have it in him to raise nobody from the dead. Sure, he'd walked out of Hell himself, but that didn't mean he could walk out of Hell for a little girl who'd already spent three years moldering in her grave.

Charlie Patton told that farmer there was nothing he could do. But the farmer wouldn't take that for an answer. He put his shotgun to Charlie Patton's head and told him he was going to sing. Then he built a bonfire beside the little girl's grave, exhumed her, and called people from thirty miles 'round to witness his daughter's resurrection.

Charlie Patton did as he was told. What else could he do, with a shotgun to his head? But no matter what he did, he couldn't raise the dead. He sang to the child's bones, and did everything he could to tease them back to life. But all he managed to do was make the dry bones dance.

They danced to his song for as long as he could sing it, and when the song was over they collapsed. The farmer cocked his gun and told Charlie Patton "Boy, you going to sing, I warn you," and Charlie Patton sang, of course, and by and by the bones began to dance again. But no man can sing forever, not even a hoodoo man, not even a King who ruled by moral right as Charlie Patton did. Somewhere after midnight his voice gave way and his guitar strings snapped and Charlie Patton collapsed in an exhausted heap.

The bones collapsed beside him.

And the farmer, good to his word, blasted Charlie Patton's skull with both barrels of his shotgun.

Now, you can't kill a deadman, and the lead that tore the top off Charlie Patton's skull didn't send him back to Hell. But the blast most surely startled him, and it scared him, too. When he saw he was still a living deadman he shrieked in fear, grabbed his guitar and three big pieces of his broken skull, and ran.

It must've been a funny thing to see, old Charlie Patton running like his life depended on it (which, of course, it couldn't), carrying his guitar in one hand and most of his head in the other.

Or maybe it wasn't. Surely the townsfolk didn't take it in good humor; but then Charlie Patton's egress took him directly through the center of the crowd. He ran into and over half a dozen of them, and what is a mob like that supposed to do when some bloody gruesome monster deadman barrels into them?

They did the only thing they could do, of course.

They tore Charlie Patton to pieces.

•

When the song was over they were all quiet for the longest time — Charlie Patton quiet because he'd said his piece and played his blues, and he thought that said it all; Peetie Wheatstraw quiet because he'd heard it all before; Robert Johnson quiet because there are some things you just can't tell a man, no matter how clear you see them.

It was Robert Johnson who finally broke the silence.

"How the *hell* did you ever get yourself back together?"

Charlie Patton shrugged. "Deadman's body got a draw to itself. Like a magnet, but different. One day I woke upon the Mountain, and I knew this life was meant for me."

The way he said it there was no mistaking that he wasn't any too happy about the life that was meant for him. And deeper under that there was something else — like he was scared, or something. Robert Johnson thought maybe he was scared to face the world again after the terror that ripped him limb from limb, and maybe that was the reason he didn't go back out into the world or up onto the mountain with the other hoodoo men, but there's no way to know a thing like that — a secret that a man keeps in his heart — for sure.

●

An hour after noon Robert Johnson finally had got rid of his chill, and by then the woodstove had dried their boots. Peetie Wheatstraw said, "The day ain't getting no younger," and the other men both allowed as it was so.

"I'm ready," Robert Johnson said. He held out his hand to Charlie Patton once again, and this time the King took it.

"I'm glad I know you, Robert Johnson," he said. "God bless you, and see you on your way."

"I know He will," Robert Johnson told him as he put on his coat. "His hand guides us all."

Charlie Patton nodded. He patted Robert Johnson on the back as he saw him to the door.

Outside the door was the Eye of the World, still hanging in the sky above the river, watching Robert Johnson.

Hell
Timeless

When he was young the King who was a slave took God from his masters and came to know Him as no slaver ever could, and he Loved Him and worshiped Him so well that the white man took a lesson. (Anyone who cares to know just what that lesson was should compare the practice of worship in the rural South with the ministries back in England. The men who came from Africa taught their masters powerful lessons, and in the end their wisdom flourishes everywhere it reaches.)

Later, the story says, he grew as crude and rough as any man. In those years he was just a man — a man like men everywhere, who lived his life and cursed his lot and made the best of a hard life of toil and frustration. Some say he repented just before he died in 1912, but others say he was too proud to repent. These people say he went to Hell, but Hell could not contain him — they say he stood before the inviolable door that leads out to the world, and he sang.

Sang so true and powerful and intense that the door could not deny him, and opened up to set him free.

Others say he survived the contest with the engine, and lived three more years before dying at a party on Juneteenth — they say he sang that night as he sat dying before the Juneteenth bonfire, and he sang so true and powerful and intense that he never even noticed that he died, and the Devil could not touch him. By the time the night was over, they say, Hell had forgot it owned him.

But there's no disagreement about the blues. The great king went to Hell after he died, and when he'd seen the Devil he walked up out of Hell into the world, and as he came he brought the blues back with him.

He brought hoodoo with him, too, but wary people don't tell that part out loud.

Near Johnson City, Tennessee
The Present

Lisa and her mama got to Tennessee three and a half days after they left New York. It hadn't been an eventful trip to that point — not really. The only weird part of all of it from the time they left Mama Estrella's bedside at the hospital to the time they got to Johnson City was the hitchhiker. And even if she looked weird with her big watery eyes and funny ears, she didn't do anything weird. Just hitched a ride in Pennsylvania, got out the car at the first rest stop.

Mama got all tired-looking after the hitchhiker left. She said, "I need coffee." Ten minutes later she pulled off the highway on the outskirts of Johnson City.

Half a mile later they were pulling into the parking lot of the place with the big KRISPY KREME DONUTS sign.

"Donuts, Mama!" Lisa said. "Can I have donuts?"

"I'm just stopping for coffee, Lisa. It's too early for donuts, don't you think?"

*"Ma*ma! I want *d*onuts, *m*ama!"

Mama sighed. "All right, Lisa. All right. Just one."

"I want *lots* of donuts, Mama."

"We'll see. Come along."

There were three blind men in the donut shop. Lisa hardly noticed them at first. Of course she hardly noticed them! Mama was buying donuts at the counter, and then they were sitting at their table, eating those airy-cremey donuts unlike anything Lisa'd ever had in all her years in Spanish Harlem. And how could a girl like Lisa notice three old men sitting around a table when there were donuts to be eaten?

Well, there was no way, of course. No way at all.

But then the donuts were gone, and time went on forever as Mama sipped from her great tumbler of coffee. And Lisa got so bored.

Wouldn't anybody?

She watched the cars go by out on the road until she got so sick of seeing them. She watched the donut ladies tidying the store front, wiping the counters and bringing out new donuts; she counted strip-mall stores along the road through Johnson City; she looked at the round and woody Appalachian mountains that hung above the city.

And then she saw the old men.

They were dirty old men, wrinkly smelly vagabonds dressed in worn-out clothes and black taped-together glasses. They were blind men, she realized, and two of them were white and one of them was black, and there were guitar cases resting at their feet.

I know those men! Lisa thought, and she remembered the blind men in her dream, and she felt she knew their names but she couldn't remember.

She pushed out of her seat and crossed the room to look at them more closely. Mama didn't even notice — she was too busy with her coffee.

"I know you," Lisa said.

And of course she did: everybody who's ever heard the song knows these men when she sees them. For they are the Blind Lords of the Piedmont, and their nature is implicit in the contour of the land.

The black man turned and smiled at her. He seemed to recognize her, but of course he couldn't see.

"And we know you, Lisa Henderson," he said. He reached out to her, and for a moment Lisa thought he would take her in his filthy vagabond arms, but he didn't. He didn't touch her at all, in fact.

Instead he gave her a gift.

"What is it?" Lisa asked, taking the gift from the vagabond's palm. It looked like a whistle — but different. Lisa had never seen a whistle anything like it.

"It's an instrument," the black vagabond said. "A kazoo — the simplest instrument there is. You hum in it. It makes a sound you'll want to hear."

"I don't understand," Lisa said. "Why are you giving this to me?"

"You'll need it," the vagabond said. "God speed you on your way."

"Lisa. . . ? Where are you, child?"

Lisa looked over her shoulder to see her mother. "Right here, Mama. Talking to the men."

"There you are! What men? What're you talking about, girl?"

"Right here, Mama," Lisa said, and she gestured at the three blind vagabonds —

But they were gone.

There were no vagabonds.

There was no one in the store at all, in fact — no one but Lisa and her mama and two donut ladies scurrying back and forth behind the counter.

"No one, Mama," Lisa said. "I'm just playing a game, that's all."

For the longest time Lisa really thought that was so — she thought she'd imagined the blind men like a daydream that picked up where the dream three nights ago left off.

And then in the car as Mama drove the car back onto the highway, Lisa looked down into her hand.

And saw the kazoo, waiting to teach her secrets that she did not want to know.

Los Angeles, California
The Present

Dan Alvarez heard her before he saw her, but he knew that she was there for a long time before she made a sound. She had that kind of presence — thick and palpable, electric as a thunderstorm about to break. It was late July, and Dan Alvarez lay in his bed awake and uneasy, as unable to sleep as he'd been every night for months.

Three big gusts of wind pressed against the window across the room, rattling the panes, the edges of the frame. It would rain soon, Dan thought — that was why he felt the storm about to happen. That was all it was.

Dan Alvarez almost managed to believe it, too.

His life was always like that, he thought: he was a storm waiting to happen, never breaking loose. Any day now, any damn day real soon one or another of the half-dozen bands he played with would take off, and he'd have a career, a real honest-to-God rock 'n' roll legend career and tell the bar gigs and the temp agencies to put it where none of them would ever see it again.

Of course he felt the tension in the air — he was a tension waiting to happen, a legend waiting to be told.

Like hell.

Even in his worst moments Dan knew better — no matter how he wanted to believe, he knew too damn well that it just wasn't so. He wasn't going anywhere, and every day that went by he had a little less heart for bashing his head against the walls that surrounded him.

And then it finally came: a great flash of lighting so bright like the sun suddenly come to earth beside him — that close, so close that thunder burst right with it. No delay, not even a beat. Like it hit a block away, maybe closer.

He rolled over onto his side. Pulled the blanket tight.

And heard the scratching tapping at his window pane.

Someone was out there in the thunder and the rain. Some-one who wanted his attention.

Who the hell. . . ?

But he didn't want to know who it was. He was scared out of his mind, and if he'd had the nerve he would have pushed away the blankets and run for his life — but he didn't have the nerve, didn't have any nerve at all too scared to move to speak to look who the hell in the storm it was thundering out there.

Too damned scared to move, let alone run.

Too scared to look, too, but his eyes opened in spite of themselves.

And that was how he first saw her: watching him through the glass.

Our Lady of Sorrows, Santa Barbara.

It didn't matter that he'd never seen her before. He'd known her all his life. Seen her shrines and grottoes outside dozens of houses back home in Union City; smelled the potion that bore her name hot summer afternoons when his mother came from the *botanica*; shivered when he saw the painting of her in the bar where wrinkled superstitious Cuban grandfathers smoked fat cigars as they sipped at their *cervezas*.

Santa Barbara: the virgin with the burning sword, blood-hungry and terrible.

Dan Alvarez sat on the edge of his bed, shivering with fear. He wanted to run. Wanted to look away from the *santa*. And if he couldn't run or look away he wanted to ask her why she'd come for him. She meant to kill him — he knew that. Couldn't help knowing! Look at her, so beautiful and angry in the flickering chiaroscuro light from her burning sword — look at her! Blood-red eyes, long soft coils of black hair piled high and cascading from her head; skin white as ash. Whiter than any living thing ever ought to be. Dan saw her and knew she was all terror of the dark distilled and made tangible; knew she was the wrath of the Lord set out upon the world to do his bidding — or worse!

She wants me to let her in.

But he knew he didn't dare.

I've got to open the window.

Because she was his fate, come to him. Come *for* him. There was no way he could avoid or delay what she had for him — only deny it, and denying the inevitable wasn't a thing Dan ever managed to do.

When he finally stood and crossed the room, it was as involuntary, as unconscious as when he'd opened his eyes.

Just like a fate, he thought.

"Santa," he said when the window was open. "I live to serve you." He felt stupid to say those words — like some *guajiro* hick in a story of his grandfather's. And he wasn't any damned hick! He was American, an honest to God rock 'n' roll American boy with talent nobody ever bothered to abuse, and the day was going to come really soon when they'd all regret they'd missed their opportunity!

They were, Dan swore they were.

The *santa* smiled. When she spoke her voice was a whisper through the open window, throaty and hungry as desire. "I hear," she said. "I have come."

"Why are you here for me, Virgin?" Dan Alvarez tried to keep the fear out of his voice, but it wasn't any use. "I know I am unworthy."

The *santa* ignored his question. She reached through the window to touch his face, and for a moment it was a tender gesture that cast a warm light on Dan's life — fulfilled him, made him whole enough to die happy and content. And then the touch changed. Not so dramatically that anybody watching would have noticed, but Dan felt it, and there was no way she could have touched him like that without meaning to. Her fingers pressed hard against him, hard as though she were trying to probe the bone of his skull right through his skin. Maybe that was the point, he thought; maybe she pressed him the way a butcher probes a sow he means to buy to slaughter.

Maybe.

Dan tried to protest. *"Santa —"* he said, but she waved to silence him before he could say another word.

"Do you accept me?" she asked.

He didn't understand, but he knew in his heart that he didn't dare say anything but *yes*.

"I do, *santa.*"

And all hell of thunder broke loose above him — lightning struck the roof, shattering the building's wood frame. Sundering the roof and walls; setting the sundered bits afire.

> *Among the Saint Francois Mountains*
> *Of Southeastern Missouri*
> *Easter 1949*

The snow was dry and powdery out on the Mountain, the same way it always is on winter afternoons; as Robert Johnson walked through it as he climbed the Mountain the stuff puffed and billowed like airy dust all around his boots. It was cold snow, he knew. It had to be cold. But it was so dry he hardly felt the coldness.

"The Mountain is beautiful," he told Peetie Wheatstraw

when they'd been hiking for an hour. "I wish I never had to leave."

Peetie Wheatstraw smiled.

"Then stay," he said. "The Hoodoo Doctors will surely make you welcome."

Robert Johnson frowned. "I know they will," he said. And he wanted to say, *But I can't stay with them,* but even though he knew in his heart that he couldn't stay, he wasn't sure yet why that was.

"Don't put your mind at worry," Peetie Wheatstraw said. "There's plenty of time before you leave. And if you leave you're always welcome to return."

Peetie Wheatstraw wasn't telling any lie, but Robert Johnson knew that he was wrong. He dreaded to learn why.

"I'm serious, Robert Johnson. There's a place for you here. It's yours when you want it."

Robert Johnson frowned. "I know there is," he said. "I appreciate it."

Neither one of them said much after that. Maybe because the Mountain was steep and tall and they needed to save their breath for the climb — and maybe because there was nothing left that either one of them wanted to say out loud.

Either way, it made their climb go faster. A few minutes before three o'clock they rounded the last bend before the hollow, and they could see the village with its thatch and wood and bake-mud houses, its swept yards and its two great common houses.

Ma Rainey met them at the edge of that village.

Now Ma Rainey wasn't just any Hoodoo Doctor; she was one of the Seven Kings (though at that date there still weren't yet seven), no matter how she was a Queen and not a King. She was secondest of all the Kings, and she answered to no one, not even John Henry his own self. In some respects she was his master, and some folks said she was his mistress. But they didn't live together. John Henry lived in his mansion high on the summit of the Mountain; Ma Rainey kept a humble swept-yard shack in the village of the Doctors, and she didn't live no way that anyone could criticize.

Ma Rainey smiled and she opened her arms to Robert

Johnson. "Give me your hands," she said, and she smiled as warm as sunshine in the spring. "I've wanted to know you for a long time, Robert Johnson. I've heard the most amazing things about you."

Ma Rainey, she was so intense — Robert Johnson got bashful as a schoolboy when she looked at him that way.

"I can imagine what you've heard," Robert Johnson said. "And I imagine it ain't altogether good."

Ma Rainey laughed, and her laugh was the sound of new leaves fluttering in the May breeze.

"And not altogether bad, neither, young man." She looked into his eyes and she smiled again, and Robert Johnson knew she saw him all the way deep down into his core, and loved him faults and all. It made him feel so naked, the way she looked at him! Naked and exposed and *touched*, too, like something intimate had passed between them and he didn't even realize as it happened.

Robert Johnson felt his cheeks flush, and not for the first time he found himself glad that his skin was so dark it didn't show how red he felt.

"You're a gracious lady, Ma Rainey. I'm pleased I have the chance to know you."

Ma Rainey seemed to glow. "Why, thank you, Robert Johnson." She let go of one of his hands and turned to lead him into the village. "You're just in time for dinner," she said. "Let me show you to the common house."

Dinner was beans and greens and barbecue pig meat like you ain't never had, no sir, nobody off the Mountain ever eats like that.

On the Road in Eastern Tennessee
The Present

Some people say a kazoo ain't nothing but a toy for children. Some ways they're right, of course. Kazoo ain't got much for range, and when you compare it with a real horn that old kazoo is kind of sad.

But it's wrong, too. Music is what you make of it, however you go about it; and there aren't many places where you'd use harmonica that a kazoo can't serve you adequately well.

And even more than that, the kazoo is so simple and straightforward that it ain't like other instruments. Most kinds of music measure craft as well as talent, but the toy kazoo is so simple that it measures talent plainly.

Lisa played and played that toy kazoo all the way her mama drove from Johnson City west and south to Greenville. As she played her natural talent bloomed, and by and by the strangest consequences happened on the roads around them.

> *Among the Saint Francois Mountains*
> *Of Southeastern Missouri*
> *Easter 1949*

For Robert Johnson, the strangest thing about dinner in the common house of the village on the Mountain was meeting up with Sonny Boy Williamson again. He hadn't seen Sonny Boy since that awful awful morning on the bluff over Greenville, but the time they'd spent together before that morning had left a mark on Robert Johnson, and he thought of Sonny Boy most kindly and quite often. When he saw him as a deadman Hoodoo Doctor (and at an age so young!) he mourned a little. But the striking thing about Sonny Boy wasn't his metamorphosis past death, nor even the frightful tale he told when he described the night a robber murdered him in Chicago.

The most frightful thing was the look in Sonny Boy's eyes.

He looked haunted — burned and tortured to his core, as though he'd spent a thousand lives of torment in the cruelest parts of Hell.

"Sonny Boy," Robert Johnson asked, "what the hell has happened to you?"

Sonny Boy pretended like he didn't understand that question; he just retold the story of his murder, and how his partner Big Joe Williams gave up music after Sonny died.

"I heard that," Peetie Wheatstraw said, and he sounded very sad.

Big Joe Williams was in the car with Peetie Wheatstraw when Peetie died in that car wreck, and because there were no next of kin Big Joe inherited Peetie's guitar. He took it north with him when he went to Chicago.

Chicago was where Big Joe got hooked up with Sonny Boy Williamson. Big Joe played Peetie Wheatstraw's guitar and Sonny Boy played the harmonica he'd took to when his guitar began to give him fits, and together they played the clubs and juke-joints. Three times they recorded, but none of those recordings ever saw the light of day.

God willing, no one alive will ever hear a record pressed from those recordings.

Because strange things *happened* in those sessions, and the happenings left their record on the tape. The folks who've heard the master say the music itself is haunted — they say hoodoo comes afire when that record plays aloud, just as it burned when Big Joe and Sonny Boy played live in those last years of Sonny's life.

But where the live sessions were fantastically haunted, eerie and seductive, the haunting on the tape is a horror that torments all who hear it.

"Big Joe going to be okay, Peetie," Sonny Boy Williamson said. "I know he is."

Peetie Wheatstraw nodded. "I hope you're right."

Robert Johnson cleared his throat. "You still haven't told me, Sonny," he said. "How come you look so — haunted?"

For the longest time the whole damn table went so quiet you could hear the sound of snowflakes on the wind — and then finally Sonny Boy broke the silence.

"That's right," he said. "And I ain't going to tell you, either."

Ma Rainey — who sat at the far end of the table — cleared her throat. "I hear you've retaken to performing, Robert Johnson," she said.

Robert Johnson pushed his plate away. "I play now and then," he said. "It hasn't caused me any problem."

"I heard him," Peetie Wheatstraw said. "His gift has grown in the years since he was alive."

"Is that so?" Ma Rainey asked.

Robert Johnson shrugged. "You're very kind," he said to Peetie Wheatstraw. "I try to get along."

Ma Rainey smiled. "I heard a tale from Furry Lewis," she said, "himself a talent of no small measure. You know he sweeps the streets of Memphis? He's heard you many times,

Robert Johnson. He recognized you the day you reached that town."

"I know a street sweeper," Robert Johnson said, "and I noticed he had a *gift* about him. But I never heard him play."

"Someday you will, I think. His *gift* is very fine."

"If you say it, Ma Rainey, then it surely must be so."

Ma Rainey laughed, and her laugh was a song that Robert Johnson wanted to hear forever. "Robert Johnson!" she said. "I hope your faith in me won't turn out to be mistaken."

"I know it's not."

She laughed again, and Robert Johnson realized that he'd begun to fall in love with her. He wondered if that was wise, or even appropriate.

"I want to hear you play, Robert Johnson. Peetie Wheatstraw and Furry Lewis have spoke of you so highly! I have to hear you for myself."

"I'll do that, if you like," Robert Johnson said.

"It would please me," Ma Rainey said.

When dinner was over and the table was clear Ma Rainey built a great fire in the potbelly stove at the center of the common house, and half a dozen Hoodoo Doctors brought out their guitars. But they didn't play themselves. Instead they waited for Robert Johnson.

Robert Johnson didn't hurry. He spent a long time tuning his guitar, and then he just held the guitar for the longest time, warming his hands to the strings. When he finally played he played good God-fearing tunes, and that surely made three Hoodoo Men discomfortable. He played "When the Saints Come Marching In," and "Go Tell It on the Mountain," fast like blues, not gospel-slow the way most people play it. When those were done he thought a long time before he played "Let Your Light Shine on Me," which most people know rewritten and abused as "Midnight Special," even though it's really a hymn about the light from God's lighthouse. Robert Johnson didn't play it exactly the way Blind Willie played it on the back side of the same record that had "God Don't Never Change," but he played a lot more like Blind Willie than he'd played when he was alive.

When he was halfway through "Let Your Light Shine on

Me," Sonny Boy Williamson took up his harmonica and began to accompany him; when he got to the next chorus three of the hoodoo men jumped in to play backup with their guitars.

"Shine on," Robert Johnson sang, *"shine on! Let the light / from the lighthouse / shine on me!"*

And then the room went quiet, and Robert Johnson realized that the place was all-but-glowing; the air around them was dense and warm, pure and Godly with the presence of the Lord.

The silence lasted for the longest while. It was Sonny Boy Williamson who finally broke it. "You've grown, Robert Johnson," he said. "You've grown in ways I can't begin to measure."

Someone said *yeah,* and someone else said, *it's true, it's true.* "I thought the *giftie* was going to speak to us," Ma Rainey said, and Robert Johnson blushed again, and he felt very shy.

•

Robert Johnson and Peetie Wheatstraw spent that night in guest rooms at the common house. Up until the small hours of the morning Robert Johnson slept as well as he ever did in all his days. Of course he slept that well! That Mountain was a special place, and the village was a special place upon it. The common house was more special still, for it held the warmth and good will that all common houses hold. If there is a place in all the world where a body can sleep secure and well-assured, it is that house upon that Mountain.

But three hours after midnight someone screamed, shattering the silent night, transforming the dreamy village of the doctors into a nightmarish place.

"What is it?" Robert Johnson shouted as the sound of the scream woke him. He threw off his covers, found his boots beside the nightstand, and pushed them on.

No one answered his question, and for a long moment he began to think he'd dreamed the sound. But then he heard another scream. This scream was nothing like the first — nothing at all like the first. Robert Johnson recognized it, even though he'd hardly spent a day in Hell: it was a demon's scream, shrill and piercing, inhuman and bizarre.

It ain't fit for no living man to go challenging a devil, but Robert Johnson didn't think far enough ahead to be scared.

Even if he had thought he probably would have done the same thing he did that night — throw on his coat, hurry out the door of the common house, into the village square.

When he got to the square he saw fiery lights burning in Sonny Boy Williamson's shack, and went to investigate them. He could have guessed what he'd find, and maybe a part of him did guess — he'd never heard about the devils who'd tormented Sonny since that morning over Greenville, but it was of such a cloth with Robert Johnson's life that the knowledge was very near a part of him.

The door to the shack was open when Robert Johnson got to it, and there were half a dozen people standing by the entrance. Inside there was a hellfire burning all around Sonny's bed, and Sonny his own self was on fire. Three devils danced in and all around that fire, tormenting Sonny like he'd chose his lot to be eternal pain among the damned.

"They shouldn't be here," Robert Johnson said. "Devils can't go walking in the world of men."

The hoodoo lady who stood beside him scowled. "You cracked the Eye of the World, Robert Johnson. The Lady pressed the pieces back together, but every day the devils try to cut the bonds she tied around it."

"He broke the Eye of the World?"

"No, he hasn't broke it, yet. But the cracks are wide enough to let demons slip onto the Mountain."

Robert Johnson pushed his way through the crowd by the door, walked across the shack to stand beside the burning bed.

"Get on with you," he said to the devils. "You've got no business in this world."

The devils jeered; one of them spat grey crud into Robert Johnson's eye.

"*Damn* you," Robert Johnson shouted. "Damn you to Hell." He grabbed the spitting demon by the throat, planning to lift it off its feet and throttle it —

And the most amazing thing happened.

Where Robert Johnson touched the devil its foul flesh seared — boiled and broiled and burned away like putrid fat when you drop it in a vat of acid.

Those devils should have known to run the moment that

they saw Robert Johnson. No devil can ever stand against a man who's found salvation, and they all cower before the ones who've been redeemed. Robert Johnson had stood before the Pearly Gates of Heaven, and he'd touched them with his good right arm.

But devils lose their sense in the heat of the moment, and those creatures were no exceptions. Three of them tormented Sonny Boy as the fourth, burning in Robert Johnson's grip, thrashed and screamed. Robert Johnson lifted it into the air, and the creature tried to plead for mercy, but the words burned away before anyone could hear them.

"I said, 'Get on with you,' devil. And I meant it." Robert Johnson hefted back and threw the awful creature with all the force he could muster; the devil went sailing across the shack. It would have hit the south wall if it hadn't vanished in midair.

The three tormenting Sonny vanished only a moment after the first.

When they were gone the only sound in the shack was Sonny Boy gasping for air, still trying to find his breath — deadmen don't need air, but the reflex to breathe persists in many of them, and commands them in some moments of extremis.

And then a woman said, "I told you he could exorcise them," and Robert Johnson looked up to see it was Ma Rainey speaking about him. She smiled when she saw he had his eye, and something in her smile made Robert Johnson feel as silly as a schoolboy.

Greenville, Mississippi
The Present

Emma could feel the Lady close and looming, almost as though she was in the car with her and Lisa. Emma had felt the presence watching them angrily all the way from New York, and it didn't go away when they got to Mississippi. She kept expecting Shungó to appear before them on the road and warn Emma away from her destination, but she never did.

They got to Greenville early in the afternoon, and Emma thought their journey was over — but it wasn't. Mama Estrella's directions turned out to be useless. Emma couldn't find any dirt roads at all off highway 82 — and all the roads that led west from 82 led west into pinewoods toward a bluff.

At first Emma thought that had to be her own error, so she drove back up 82, watching all the side roads from the opposite direction.

And still found nothing.

So she went into town and found a pay phone to ring Mama Estrella at the hospital — but all the phones were out of order.

Every solitary phone in town, it seemed.

At half past two she pulled into the convenience store parking lot for the third time (she'd been there twice already, trying to get the out-of-order pay phones in front of the store to work) to ask the clerk if he knew what was the matter.

Inside the store was cool and air-conditioned, startling in contrast with the torpid Mississippi heat outside. The clerk behind the counter was a dark-skinned man with short white hair. He looked to be about as old as time.

Despite the heat he wore a red bandanna around his throat.

"I need to make a long-distance phone call," Emma told the clerk, "but all the pay phones in this town are out of order."

The clerk nodded. "I know they are," he said. "We had a thunderstorm two nights ago. That there —" he nodded at the old beige phone on the wall behind the counter "— is about the only working phone on this end of Greenville."

Emma wanted to scream. She was exhausted from her trip, addled from the heat, and confused from driving back and forth over unfamiliar roads. She wanted to find a place to rest — a place where she could hide beneath a blanket and pretend the world went on without her. She wanted to get a hotel room and spend three days recovering from the trip.

But there just wasn't time. She knew that, deep inside her heart: things had begun to happen quickly and in ways she couldn't afford to ignore.

"Lord Almighty," Emma said. "How far will I have to drive to find a phone that works?"

The clerk shrugged. "I haven't heard that much of the news," he said. "Far as I know phones are out for miles all around."

"Damn. Damn damn damn damn," Emma said — and then she did begin to cry. It was all too much, just too too too damn much.

"Ain't no need to cry, ma'am," the clerk said. "Use my phone if you have to. But if it's got to be long distance, make it brief, please."

The offer surprised Emma, and a part of her regarded it suspiciously. But she took it all the same. She stepped behind the counter, dialed the hospital's number (from memory – Mama Estrella was in the same hospital where Emma had worked the last twelve years of her life), and asked for Estrella Perez.

When she told Mama Estrella about the trouble, Mama told her to go to the first crossroads south of Greenville and burn an offering.

"Say what?" Emma asked her.

"Buy a new pack of cigarettes," Mama Estrella said. "Go to the crossroads, open the pack, and smoke one – just one cigarette. When you're done, put the pack to the center of the crossroads and leave it there. Get in the car and drive the way you'll know you have to go."

"That's crazy," Emma said. "What do you think I am, some kind of a witch?"

"I don't think anything about you, Emma. But I know how to help you find the road you need."

Emma sighed. "Thanks, Mama," she said. "I'll be in touch."

Mama said goodbye, and Emma hung up her phone. "Can I leave you a couple dollars for the call?" she asked the clerk.

The clerk shook his head. "You weren't on for long," he said. "I'll take care of it." He smiled, and even though his smile was beautiful it chilled Emma to the bone. "Anything I can get you?"

The way he asked that question made Emma's chill start all over again – for a moment she almost thought he'd heard Mama Estrella's instructions.

"Yes," she said. "There is. I need a pack of Marlboros – no, two packs. – Yes, the red ones, thanks."

She paid the clerk and left without saying another word.

Los Angeles, California
The Present

Dan Alvarez was never sure what happened to him after the

thunder. Later he could remember running blindly through the raining dark, stumbling, battering himself again and again. But he could never remember how he escaped the burning wreck of his apartment.

Never remembered what happened to the *santa,* or what she meant for him when he *accepted* her.

The thing he remembered clearest was waking in a ditch in an abandoned industrial park. Sitting up and looking around to see the city of Los Angeles dark and fiery all around him — the power was out everywhere for miles, no electric lights anywhere he could see in every direction. But there was light. Plenty of light — the whole damned city was on fire.

If he'd had any sense he would have counted his blessings and crawled back into the ditch. It wasn't safe, wandering around with the city burning. But he wasn't thinking at all, let alone thinking sensibly. In the dark and the thunder and the rain Dan Alvarez was a creature of his frightened heart, and when his heart screamed at him and told him to run for his life, he *ran.*

Ran.

And it was good he did, because there were flash floods in Los Angeles that night. Twenty minutes after Dan Alvarez ran terrified from that ditch a storm of white water and hard debris roared through it, and if Dan Alvarez hadn't run he would have died a horrible death of batterment and drowning.

As it was he almost died anyway — when he wandered too close to the broken walls of the Los Angeles County Reformatory and the riot and the looting that came when its prisoners ran wild. The prison was ten blocks southeast from the ditch, and Dan's run took him directly toward it.

I've got to run, a small voice whispered deep inside his skull, *I've got to go home.*

He tried to run home, but the truth was that he never could. His apartment was gone, blasted by thunder and burned to the ground, and there was nothing but nothing for him to run home to, and all he could do was run and run and run forever in the night until he dropped from exhaustion —

He was a block and a half from the prison when he stumbled as he moved out into the center of the street, trying to get around a tractor-trailer parked along the shoulder. He tried to catch his balance, but the road was too slick and he was moving too fast and he was too winded. One foot caught on the back of the other, and came down sideways and out of kilter; his ankle gave way and he dove face-first into the asphalt —

— face-first into the asphalt as lightning struck the lightless prison gates and the walls came tumbling down. Someone screamed, and gunfire exploded brightly in the darkness, and Dan knew he had to run.

Had to get up and run for his life, or he was going to die.

Run run run! said the voice in his head, but he couldn't run — he couldn't even move. For the longest moment he lay paralyzed on the dark rain-wet road as people screamed and guns blasted and now a mob of people stampeded through the broken prison walls and out into the city. Dan damn near got trampled by the crowd that ran toward him — if he hadn't roused himself enough to roll under the semi rig the throng would have trampled him to death.

When the crowd was gone there were more flashes of gunfire, and the sound of shots exploding not too far away. Dan knew he couldn't stay where he was. He knew he had to run. So he pushed himself back onto his feet, and he forced himself back into motion.

But he was too numb, too exhausted to run. When he tried to run all he managed was a slow trot, a run so slow he could've walked more quickly in the day in the sunshine when the world was decent and alive.

After a while the trot went away entirely, and Dan Alvarez found himself skulking through the shadows, creeping around the edges of the firelight as the city burned.

Here there were looters, and storefronts shattered and set afire; here there were rioters taunting a homeowner as the poor man tried to hold them at bay with a shotgun; here three policemen stood guarding half a dozen people they'd bound in handcuffs and leg irons.

In his mind he was an animal, prowling warily, ready to turn at any moment and struggle for his life. Now gradually he realized he was hungry, and when he saw the broken storefront he didn't think how it's looting when you rummage through a broken store. He was hungry, and he knew there was food inside; he went in and he ate.

He found cold cuts behind the shattered doors of the store's cooler; deli ham and Genoa salami, still wrapped in their tough plastic wrappers. Dan peeled the backing of the ham package, and he ate hungrily, shoving big fistfuls of cured meat into his mouth, hardly even bothering to chew.

When the ham was done he threw the wrapper on the floor and closed his eyes, savoring the fullness. He felt like a predator, walking away from the rent carcass of his prey; he wanted to raise his head and howl at the moon.

And then he did howl, long and low and sad.

It was the wrong thing to do.

Wrong wrong wrong.

Because there were police out on the street, and they heard him. One of them turned to face Dan and shone a flashlight in at him. Dan tried to hide from the beam, but he wasn't fast enough; the policeman saw him clearly before he had the chance to duck.

"You there! What're you doing in that store?"

Dan didn't say a word. He didn't even breathe; he kept low and still and prayed the police would go away.

His prayer went unanswered. Of course it did! Police don't just walk away when they find young men looting stores in the middle of riots! They go in and arrest the ones they find, even when they've only looted for the food they need to eat.

"Answer, damn you. You want us to have to come in there and get you?"

Dan wanted to taunt them. *Go ahead,* he wanted to say. *Go ahead, I'm not afraid.*

But it would have been a lie. He was terrified and he didn't dare taunt the cops, because he knew they'd kill him if they had to.

One of the policemen swore; the other one said, "I'll move toward him from the right side. You take the left." His partner grunted, nodded, turned on his flashlight, and started moving toward Dan.

They're going to kill me, Dan thought. He heard something hard and metallic snap into place, and thought he saw gun-metal glint in the scattered light. *I've got to run,* he thought, but when he looked around he saw that there was nowhere to run.

"Put up your hands and step out of the shadows. Don't make any sudden moves."

They were getting close, now — too close. Dan eased away from the cooler, crawled toward the cartons that lined the store's back wall. Pressed himself into the shadows.

But it didn't do him a bit of good. Not one damn bit.

Because the first cop came around the aisle on Dan's right, and as he did his flashlight caught Dan squarely, dragging him out of the shadows —

And Dan screamed.

"Don't move!" the second cop shouted, and his partner froze. But Dan didn't freeze. He couldn't freeze; he was too terrified. Instead he bolted into the light, bolted at the first cop who shot his gun three times *bam bam BAM* at point-blank range and that should have cut Dan to shreds — should have left him a pile of wrecked and bloody meat leaking blood on the filthy floor. But didn't, somehow. None of the bullets hit Dan, or if they hit they passed right through him, doing no damage at all. Dan ran into the cop; his shoulder caught the barrel of the gun, and Dan just kept going. Into the cop, knocking him over as the cop screamed and his partner swore, bellowing threats he couldn't make good without shooting his partner, too. The cop went down, knocking over a display of canned dog food; Dan kept going, stepping over the cop and on him, one foot came down on the cop's face, and something crunched underneath it. Dan didn't look back to see what it was. There wasn't time for that. Wasn't time to do anything but run.

Run!

Through the fiery streets, through the night, into forever.

When Dan stopped running he was in a trainyard, surrounded by boxcars. He saw an open car and knew that he could hide there through the night; he climbed in and found a corner so dark that he felt lost inside it.

And hid.

After a long while he drifted off to sleep.

Somewhere in his sleep he heard the car bang into another and felt it lurch. A while after that there came the music that

train wheels make as they roll along the smooth Pacific rails —
rhythmic and mild, gentle and compelling.

The music reassured Dan in his rest, and soothed him deeper
and deeper into his sleep. By the time he woke California was
a place as distant as his dreams.

Greenville, Mississippi
The Present

The ritual at the crossroads worked just as Mama Estrella
had promised it would. Emma parked a few yards from the
intersection, opened the pack of Marlboros, and smoked one.
When she was done she carried the open pack to the middle
of the intersection, set it on the pavement, and returned to her
car.

And drove away.

Half a mile later she saw a dirt road she hadn't noticed
before, and turned onto it; followed the dirt road for ten
minutes before she saw a weathered wooden shack in the
pinewoods off to her left.

That's it, Emma thought. There wasn't any doubt about that
in her heart; this was the place she'd crossed half a continent
to find.

Lisa was asleep in the car seat, just as she had been since early
that morning.

"We're here," Emma said, rubbing Lisa's shoulder. "Time to
wake up, baby."

"Leave me alone," Lisa said. "Wanna sleep!"

Emma bit her lip. The girl had such a temper these days —
Emma was more than half afraid to cross her.

"You want to wait here in the car, child? — Maybe I won't
be there long, I hope."

And suddenly the girl's eyes opened wide.

"Be where?" she asked. "Where are we?"

Emma eased the car onto the grassy side-path that led toward
the shack, slowly, slowly pushing the car through the brush.
"This is the place Mama Estrella told me about. There's someone here who can help you, she said."

"I don't want any help," Lisa said. "Just leave me alone!"

"I told you that I would already," Emma said, stopping the

car a few yards from the shack, putting the transmission into park. Cutting the ignition and opening the door. "You want to stay here, Lisa, that's your concern."

Lisa mumbled belligerently — Emma couldn't quite make out the words, but she knew she wouldn't have liked them if she'd heard them.

"Are you coming?" Emma asked as she got out of the car. Lisa didn't answer, but she climbed out of her car seat and followed Emma out the driver's side door. She followed Emma along the last few yards of the path, stood beside her as Emma knocked on the rickety wood door.

A soft familiar voice told them to come in. It was very familiar — intimately familiar, though for the life of her Emma couldn't think how it was she knew it.

"Hello. . . ?"

Emma pressed on the door, and it swung open as easily as the door to a pantry.

"Hello, Emma Henderson. Good afternoon, Lisa."

Inside the shack it was dark as dusk, and Emma could scarcely see a thing. There were shadows that looked like furniture, and she could see the silhouette of a man on the far side of the room, but all the details were opaque. Emma took her daughter's hand and stepped carefully through the threshold, uncertain of her footsteps.

"I know you," Emma said. "Where do I know you from?"

The silhouette laughed. "I've known you all your life, woman. But we only met this afternoon."

The man from the store, Emma thought. And as she realized him the room brightened to reveal the details she remembered — the short, snow-white hair; the dark, leathery-creased skin; the scarf he wore around his neck despite the fact that it was high summer in Mississippi.

His name was Leadbelly, or maybe it was Huddie Ledbetter, depending whether a born name or a taken name is the true measure of a man, and he was neither dead nor alive. He was seventh of the Seven Kings, the only King surviving, and in his way he was like her daughter Lisa.

He was a rogue and a scoundrel, but he was gifted like no other; he was the man who'd tried to kill Robert Johnson, after that man's rebirth and redemption; he was a murderer so cruel that twice the judges put him away for life, and so gifted that twice he'd sung his way to freedom, for his songs so charmed the men who imprisoned him that they could not help but set him free.

He wore his scarf to hide the scar that marked him: somewhere late in life he lost a barroom brawl, and when his rival finished with him he slit Leadbelly's throat and left him for a corpse. But Huddie Ledbetter didn't die — he walked away and healed without ever going to a doctor. All his life and all his death he wore red scarves around his throat to hide the bright white slash that marked him for who he was. But he could not hide his nature, and the scar was just the most obvious bit of that.

"You can call me Huddie Ledbetter, if you like," he said.

Emma's eyes went wide. "I know who you are," she said. "You died before I was born."

Leadbelly laughed, and his laugh was the music of the world. "I've heard that said," he told her. "Do I look dead to you?"

Emma laughed at the question, because he'd asked it so good-natured there was no way to answer it.

That was when Lisa let go of her mother's hand and stepped toward the deadman. "You can't fool me," the child said. "I know who you are. I can see it!"

Leadbelly laughed again. "Is that so?"

"It is," Lisa said. "You've been to Hell, I know. The devil-mark is all over you."

Leadbelly went quiet for a moment. And he looked so old! Older than he'd looked back at the store, and sadder, too. He knelt to look Lisa in the eye; held her head in his hands. When he kissed her forehead Lisa tried to squirm away from him, but she couldn't.

"You *can* see the marks, can't you, child?" he asked. "I should have known you would." He eased away, watching Lisa as carefully as a necromancer reads his offal. "Don't let those marks concern you, child. I don't mean you any harm, and I don't mean to lead you toward temptation."

There was something in his voice when he talked about the marks — Emma thought it sounded like regret, but she wasn't any surer of that than she was of anything else.

"Something's wrong with my little girl, Mr. Ledbetter," Emma said. "She's been through things — I can't begin to tell you."

The old man looked at Emma quizzically. "Tell me what you please," he said. "I'll listen if you like."

"Two days ago she almost killed a little boy," Emma said. "There's something terrible got into her."

The old man looked — alarmed. Unsettled, too. "What happened?" he asked.

Emma told what she'd learned from the nursery attendants — how Lisa had beaten the boy to within an inch of his life and then disappeared from the school; about the water that covered Lisa when Emma found her — water that had bleached everything it touched without burning the way ordinary bleach would. She even told him about Mama Estrella and the ritual in the garden, and how the shrine had come to life and nearly murdered Mama.

"Down here we call her the Lady," he said when she told him about the horror in the shrine. "But you know that, don't you?" He stared away into the darkness, looking worried.

Emma nodded.

Leadbelly got to his feet, crossed the room, and began to search among the shadows; when he finally stepped out of the darkness he held a beautiful old guitar.

Emma knew that instrument the moment she set eyes on it — it was Leadbelly's battered twelve-string guitar. When she looked at it she was certain she could feel the hoodoo seeping from it. "Follow me," Leadbelly said. He stood by the door of the shack, waiting for Emma.

Emma put her arms around her daughter, holding the girl protectively. "I won't let you hurt my baby."

Leadbelly scowled. "I wouldn't ever harm her," he said.

Lisa put her hand on Emma's arm and pressed just hard enough to get her mother's attention. "I'm not afraid, Mama," she said. "The old King doesn't mean me any harm."

Emma wanted to say, *Child, what're you talking about, what do you mean, "old King,"* but the girl pushed Emma's arms away before her mother could say a word.

"Lisa. . . ?"

"It's all right, Mama," Lisa said. She was crossing the room, heading toward the door, and now she met him in the doorway, took his hand, and followed him into the pinewoods.

Emma wanted to shout at her — *What do you think you're doing, child?* — but it was too late, because they were gone into the woods and the girl wasn't going to pay any attention anyway. So she swore under her breath and threw up her hands and sighed.

And followed her daughter and the hoodoo man into the west, through the woods and the tall grass and the palmettos, up the gentle rise until they stood on the bluff that overlooked the Mississippi River.

Right around dusk Leadbelly led them to a ring of big rocks up on the bluff; in the center of the ring there was a black scar of char and ashes from an old bonfire. "Help me find some wood," he said, and Emma looked around to see that there were fallen branches all around them, lying in the grass and among the palmettos.

Emma stooped, pulled a branch half the size of a sapling out of a palmetto thicket. "Looks like a hurricane came through here," she said.

Leadbelly shrugged. "I don't know about any hurricane," he said. "But there was a big storm three weeks ago."

He took the branch from Emma, hefted it, and broke it cleanly over his knee. Folded the two halves together and broke them as a pair.

"You need more?" Emma asked.

The old man shrugged. "Small stuff," he said. "Get me kindling — there, see that branch of twigs?"

Emma grabbed the branch he pointed at, shook away the pinestraw that still clung to it, and handed it to him.

Leadbelly broke the twigs up into kindling, arranged it around the big wood, and lit the fire with an old Zippo lighter.

Lisa lifted Leadbelly's guitar out of the grass. "I like your guitar," she said. She let it rest on her knees as she ran her finger up and down the strings. "It's very beautiful."

The old man turned around, swearing as he did. "You put that down," he said. "I never told you you could touch my hammer."

For half a moment Lisa almost looked afraid. "You never said I couldn't," she said. And then she set the guitar gently on the grass beside the old man.

"Lisa!" Emma said. "Don't you be fresh!"

The old man shrugged. "Let her say anything she pleases," he said. "It don't bother me."

He took the guitar by the neck and lifted it off the ground. Carried it to the far side of the fire and began to play.

As he played he sang. He sang a song with no words at all, but he didn't need words, because he wasn't singing to Emma or Lisa. He was singing to the fire, and as he sang the fire roared to life.

So beautiful, that fire. It had a very special beauty, because it was enchanted, and not just enchanted but revealed — for as Leadbelly sang the fire grew not only greater but truer, and by and by its truth grew ultimately revealing. Truer and clearer and more beautiful, and now the light it cast showed things not shadowy as firelight but true as sunshine.

"I saw a fire like this lots of times," Lisa said at last, but she wouldn't say no more than that, no matter how her mother prompted her.

"Is that so, child?" the old man asked.

But Lisa wouldn't answer him, either.

Now the fire grew so true that its light began to suffuse them. For a moment Leadbelly looked transparent as a ghost — Emma could see the river through his heart, and she knew the magic in the music had consumed them all; consumed them all as it grew truer and truer, so true that now it showed the deepest secret truth about each of them.

Emma could even see the ghost of her own truth, surrounding her: it was the specter of courage, for she was a woman with backbone who would never flinch from any terror if it meant the welfare of her child.

The true light showed Leadbelly for the angry mean-tempered scoundrel that he was — but it showed the splendor of his *gift*, too, and it showed he knew something true and important about the nature of the world. Listening to him in that light Emma knew that he sang songs that God whispered in his ear.

And then she looked at Lisa.

Lisa looked dreadful in the true light from the fire: her skin was venous, mottled, and leathery as the surface of the cancer that bore her. And the look in her eye was so bloodthirsty! — And standing behind her with a hand on Lisa's shoulder was Santa Barbara with her burning sword.

On a Railway in the Southwest
The Present

Somewhere in the night it came to Dan Alvarez that he had to go to New Orleans, but he never learned why. He had an intuition, and it went like this — he dreamed that he was made of music, and as the music sounded it rang out of the Mississippi Delta, just like the blues when men first sang it. Blues grew so beautiful as it flowered from the misery of the Delta, because hardship, poverty, and oppression are gifts in their own awful way.

They're gifts because they bring the greatness out of all of us, no matter how they grieve us.

I want to be a hobo bluesman, Dan thought in his dream. *I want to move from town to town like a no-account bum, and I want to play those songs so laced with magic that they change everything that hears them.*

Dan had heard lots of songs like that on scratchy old records — old recordings full of mystery and magic, and something higher and more beautiful, something — something magic in those blues. Dan loved those blues. It was the ghost of their beauty that drove him into rock 'n' roll, but he never found the ghost in rock, no matter how he looked for it.

And maybe that's the nature of the beast. Maybe that's what it is — magic. Maybe, Dan thought, the blues aren't just music.

Maybe they're magic.

Then he was dreaming again, and he dreamed an awful weirdling dream where cruel gods walked the earth —

No, not gods, these weren't gods but something less, they were petty godlets that run and hide when they see the shadow of the One True Lord —

And now in his dream it was 1952, and Dan stood among

a crowd of great musicians on a high bluff outside Nashville, Tennessee, and all the bluesmen all the true bluesmen and women *sang. . . !*

Among the Saint Francois Mountains
Of Southeastern Missouri
Easter 1949

When the demons were gone everybody wandered back toward their rooms and bed, but Robert Johnson wasn't tired anymore.

Not tired at all. How could he be tired, as frightened as he was? He wandered back toward the common house, and into its kitchen. He found the kettle and the tea, and he put a pot on to brew, and sat looking out the window at the night and the river and high among the stars the watchful Eye of the World.

Ma Rainey found him there a little while after he poured the tea. She took a seat not far from him and asked him what was the matter. It wasn't a real question — just a way to start a conversation. Ma Rainey knew how he would answer long before she asked.

"I don't know," Robert Johnson told her. It wasn't a lie, exactly, but it could have been more true. "Just unsettled, I guess." He sighed, gestured at the teapot. "Pour you a cup?"

"Please," Ma Rainey said.

Robert Johnson poured the tea. Leaned back in his chair to stare out the window at the Eye.

"It's breaking again," she said. "Did they tell you that?"

Robert Johnson felt a chill despite the warmth of the room.

"I'm not sure," he said. "But I knew it in my heart."

And that was true, too: he could feel the fissures in the lens of the Eye of the World as though they were flaws in his own heart separating from one another. He'd been able to feel them for longer than he could remember. Since the night Leadbelly tried to murder him? From the night he stood before the Pearly Gates, when he first knew redemption? Maybe he'd been able to feel the Eye in his heart from the day he first sang *Judgment Day* — it could have been that long, growing in him like a passion for the nature of the world.

"If you look closely at the Eye, you can see the cracks. Look, look Robert Johnson — they look like tears, don't they?"

Robert Johnson looked, and he saw, and he told Ma Rainey that he did.

"You know," Ma Rainey said, "that's only one side of the Eye that watches over the river. The inside of the Eye is a portal that watches the world from Hell."

Robert Johnson had heard that story when he was a boy. He said that to Ma Rainey.

"If you look directly at the lens and as closely as you can," Ma Rainey said, "you can see Lucifer's great throne room in the Mansion called Defiance. Every night ten thousand devils come to that room to batter on the Eye. One night will come, and they'll break it through."

" 'And Hell will rain upon the Mississippi River, as the walls come tumbling down,' " Robert Johnson said, quoting a phrase from the secret Book of the River (whose words are written on the heart of each and every bluesman who ever lived to die and sing again).

Ma Rainey smiled. She reached across the kitchen table to rest her hand on Robert Johnson's hand. "We need you here, Robert Johnson," she said.

Robert Johnson didn't know what he could say. What he thought was, *You know I can't*, but he didn't understand why he thought those words, and how could he say such a thing when he didn't understand the reason why?

"You don't need *me* here," Robert Johnson said. "John Henry lives up on this Mountain."

Ma Rainey looked so sad.

"I wish that you were right," she said. "But awful times are on us."

Robert Johnson shook his head. "John Henry sang down the walls of damnation," he said. "A man like that don't need no help from me."

Ma Rainey set her tea cup on the table, then turned to stare into the darkness. She was quiet for a long while; Robert Johnson knew she was weighing her words, measuring out what she could say to him.

"Last fall," she said, "two beggars found their way onto the

Mountain. They were dressed in humble clothes, and looked for all the world to be the kind of vagabond thieves you find skulking in the rail yards. But Charlie Patton saw them as they climbed past his shack, and he knew them when he saw them. Of course he knew them! Any deadman gonna know those two when he see them, because they were Dismas and Gestas, and those two were the thieves who died on crosses to the Right and Left Hands of the Lord.

"Charlie Patton saw them, and he called to them, but Dismas and Gestas ignored him. They do those things, you know — they wander about the world in strange and mysterious ways, doing the Lord's own work. For as they died the Right and Left Hands of the Lord so they continue: they are His Hands from Kingdom Come, and they serve Him without hesitation.

"Charlie Patton did the only thing he could think to do: he sang a song he knew the King would hear, and in that song he told John Henry who was on the Mountain.

"John Henry sent me down to meet Dismas and Gestas. For all the good it did! They very near ignored me! I opened my arms to greet them, and they took my hands — and led me back up the Mountain to John Henry.

"They carried me up the steep side of the Mountain, past the village without a pause. When they got to John Henry's mansion the doors opened spontaneously. All the doors in that place opened before them, and nothing anyone could do would cause a moment's hesitation. Peetie and Blind Lemon tried to bar the door to John Henry's sanctum, but the bars all fell away as quickly as anyone could lay them in place.

"Dismas and Gestas carried me into John Henry's den, where the King sat in his great leather chair before his roaring fire, and when he looked up at them with his wide startled eyes Dismas held up a hand to silence him.

" 'Tonight we stood before the Pearly Gates,' Dismas (who is also known as the Right Hand) said. 'As we watched Robert Johnson's transubstantiation.'

" 'That great sinner's heart redeemed him,' the Left Hand said. 'He saw his error and repented, and his redemption carried him to the bosom of the Lord.' "

Ma Rainey just stopped there, as though she'd told the whole story and Robert Johnson was supposed to understand. But he didn't understand at all. He was more confused, in fact, than he'd been before she started.

When he told Ma Rainey that he was confused, she sighed long and slow, as if she were disappointed in him. "I don't understand," Robert Johnson said. "Why would they tell you, tell you — ?" He tried and tried to finish that sentence, but he couldn't because his moment at the Pearly Gate was a dear and secret thing to him, and it made him ache to try to speak of it out loud.

"Robert Johnson," Ma Rainey said, "in all creation there were only six times where a soul has come back to this world from redemption. When Saint Peter persuaded you to return, he did it for a mighty purpose."

Robert Johnson couldn't argue with that — not least because he didn't understand what Saint Peter did, or why, and he didn't know what this world meant for him. "I guess," he said.

"John Henry needs you, Robert Johnson. That's what the Right Hand of the Lord told him: 'This man has seven Mysteries,' he said, 'he has a gift unlike all others, and he has his redemption. The time will come when you will need him, and his nature is so changed you may not find him. You must call him now or you will never find him.'

"John Henry climbed out of his great leather chair, and he knelt before the Hands of the Lord. He thanked them for their guidance and begged them to enjoy his hospitality — but before he could finish they were gone."

"Gone where?"

Ma Rainey shrugged. "Disappeared," she said. "Vanished as suddenly as they'd first appeared below Charlie Patton's shack." She reached into her bag and brought out a pack of Kool Filter cigarettes; took one from the pack, lit it, and drew from it so hard the ember tip glowed bright with fire.

She let the smoke sift away from her in a long and billowy sigh.

"That smells so good," Robert Johnson said.

Ma Rainey smiled.

"Share it with me, Robert Johnson," she said.

Somewhere out on the Mountain the mockingbirds began

to sing.

Greenville, Mississippi
The Present

Emma screamed when she saw the *santa* standing behind her little girl, and she screamed even louder when she looked down at Lisa and saw the dreadful apparition of the girl herself. Leadbelly dropped his guitar and kicked sand into the fire — kicked and kicked until the fire subsided and the darkness of the bluff enfolded them.

"Be very still," Leadbelly said. "Don't let them know if you're afraid."

Emma forced herself to stop screaming, and she tried to be still. But she was terrified — so frightened that she couldn't stop trembling entirely.

"Don't be afraid," Leadbelly said. "I've got a light. I'm about to turn it on."

"Please," Emma said. "Please please."

She heard a click, and now fluorescent light flickered from the tube of Leadbelly's pocket lantern, on and off and on and steady now as the pinewoods filled with that pale blue fluorescent glow. . . .

"It's all right," Leadbelly said with a voice as soothing as good brown mash. "Ain't no call to be afraid."

As Emma looked around and around the woods, at the sky, at the river, at the shadowy pines, at the smoldering dead fire.

At Leadbelly.

And then she turned to look her daughter in the eye —

But her daughter was gone.

"Lisa!"

Gone, gone, gone, gone beyond the dark side of the moon. And no matter how they looked for her she stayed gone, too.

On a Railway in the Southwest
The Present

In Dan Alvarez's dream it was September 1952 on a ridge above Nashville, Tennessee. Half a thousand men and women stood on that ridge beneath the moon and thunderheads. Some of them had guitars, some of them played harmonicas. Some of them played other instruments — some of them just sang.

A cloud roiled up to cover the moon, and now in the darkness the greatest of them all began to *sing.*

Oh how he sang! He sang a song they all knew in their hearts, a song Dan Alvarez knew in his heart, but no matter how they knew it not a one of them could have lined out a solitary verse.

Until they heard *him* sing.

Now the choir joined the King in song, and the ridge shuddered to hear them all.

As they sang the sky folded, roiled, and thundered, stormed and raged against the night. When the storm had shaken itself to dissipation Dan Alvarez could see the Eye of the World high in the clouds above the ridge, and when he stared into the Eye he saw Hell and the demon loa press against the lens from deep inside.

Dan Alvarez knew that tune. He thought, *That's* Judgment Day, even though he'd never heard the name of that tune, because no matter what he didn't know the song was in his heart just like it's in the heart of every man woman and child who ever sang the blues.

But the song wasn't *Judgment Day.* Dan knew that in his heart almost the moment he thought the words *Judgment Day.* It was a song as great and as deep and as powerful as that apocalyptic strain, but where *Judgment Day* is fire and brimstone calling up the end, this song was joy and redemption and the divine promise of a better world to come.

And then finally Dan recognized the song he heard in his dream.

"The Ode to Joy"! he thought, and he was exactly right. It was "The Ode to Joy" he heard, rebroken, syncopated, twisted, and remade into blues, but it was still Beethoven's melody, beautiful as it was the morning that the master wrote it.

Now in Dan's dream the moon rose high, and the sky began to close — and suddenly there came a great explosion, a powerful shattering of the night that sent electric fire in every direction.

When it was clear the sky had closed again, and the great ones lay scattered and broken across the bluff.

Just before Dan woke he saw a white boy come wandering

through the carnage, and he recognized that boy. The boy's name was Elvis Presley, and even if he had just a mediocre *gift* he was a figure charged with destiny.

Young Elvis Presley wandered among the strange unearthly fires still flickering on the ridge until he reached the centermost summit where the great King once had stood.

And there among those terrible unholy embers Elvis Aron Presley found the hammer that once rang like a bell.

He grabbed it and he ran — stealing a heritage that was neither his by right nor by legitimate assumption.

And then he ran for his life.

As well he might.

Among the Saint Francois Mountains
Of Southeastern Missouri
Easter 1949

That next day it was springtime on the Mountain, and Robert Johnson drew it in as deeply as he could. It was spring, and there were new buds on the trees, and as Robert Johnson climbed the final bends of the trail that led to John Henry's mansion at the summit, he thought the Mountain could be any mountain anywhere in the south, any mountain anywhere at all. Just a beautiful green mountain covered with trees and brambles and wildflowers blooming in the spring. But it was special, too — Robert Johnson could feel how special it was. There was something *extraordinary* about that place, something tremendous and triumphant. As he climbed the last steps up the Mountain he felt as though he were ascending the steps of the mansion in the sky, up beyond the Pearly Gates.

When he reached the mansion gates they opened to admit him of their own accord, just as they'd opened for the Hands of God in the tale Ma Rainey told. Robert Johnson walked into the mansion's great hall, and his feet carried him inward as though they had minds of their own. In through the hall as it grew deep and dark, down inside the Mountain; past the pillars of damnation; through three stations and their attendant chapels; into the bowels of the Mountain.

To the doors of John Henry's sanctum, where the great King sat before a roaring fire in his deep leather chair.

John Henry was a great dark mountain of a man — taller, broader, and more gentle-eyed than Robert Johnson ever expected to find him.

He wore a crystal talisman on a leather thong around his neck — a great jewel cut in the shape and image of the Eye of the World. Some say that pendant was no jewel but a tiny mirror always fixed upon the Eye, and when the Eye was shut, the pendant was shut too, and when the Eye gaped open it did too.

The Lady gave his pendant to him, everyone knows that. Some say the Lady is his consort, and that may be true.

"Huddie Ledbetter tried to kill me last fall," Robert Johnson told the great King. "That's something I think you ought to know."

John Henry frowned. The expression was a frightful thing on his broad dark face; it gave Robert Johnson a chill as bad as any he'd felt in his new life. "That man worries me," he said. He didn't say another word about the subject, but Robert Johnson hadn't expected him to.

"He worries me, too," Robert Johnson said. Of course he worried Robert Johnson! He'd drugged Robert Johnson with *spirit liquor*, slit his throat, and left him for dead, bleeding into the river. If the river and the Eye hadn't held him in their hearts, Robert Johnson would have died for certain.

"I didn't call you here to talk about no Huddie Ledbetter," John Henry said with his voice as deep and sonorous as a hot wind from the mountains. "I called you here to see you — and to show you something."

The great King lifted his amulet off his chest, pulling the heavy leather thong that held it over his head. Held the amulet out to show Robert Johnson —

And as he looked at it Robert Johnson knew that he was looking into the Eye of the World, honest and true, and no matter how it was just a jewel John Henry wore around his neck, no matter how the Eye of the World still and always hung in the sky above the river, watching the land; no matter what else was real and true this was still the Eye. Robert Johnson looked deep into it and he saw that mighty lens, cracked and patched and battered once again. He saw through the lens into

Lucifer's great chamber in the Mansion called Defiance, where ten thousand demons pressed and beat the cracks unceasingly.

"It's breaking, Robert Johnson," John Henry said. "But you can see that, can't you?"

Robert Johnson nodded. "I see the devils down in Hell," he said. "They're going to smash it through."

John Henry said, "You see it all, then."

He set the Eye on the table that he kept beside his leather chair and turned away from Robert Johnson. For the longest while he stood facing the fire, looking into the flames as though he expected to find the same sort of revelation there that Robert Johnson saw when he looked into the Eye.

John Henry said, "Every day those devils get that much closer. Last month they made it onto the Mountain where the Mountain stands between Hell and the world. Now every night they come for Sonny Boy Williamson."

"I saw them last night," Robert Johnson said. "I don't think those devils will be back."

John Henry laughed, deep and melodious. "That's what I heard," he said. "More power to you."

Robert Johnson shrugged. "I was there," he said. "I do what I can."

The great King wheeled around to face him, turning away from the fire. "There's an awful confrontation coming," John Henry said. He sounded — terrified. More frightened than Robert Johnson ever imagined any King could be. "We're going to need you, Robert Johnson."

Robert Johnson nodded. "Call me," he said. "Call me and I'm yours."

The King nodded. "You know I will," he said. He lifted the Eye off the table, pulled its thong over his head, and let the jewel fall back to its place beneath his throat. "I want you here," he said. "Stay here on the Mountain. Stay here in my mansion if you like."

Robert Johnson wanted to take the hospitality the great King offered. He truly did. But before he even took a moment to think about the question, his heart told him that he never could. Robert Johnson spoke the words his heart told him to because he knew he had to; it was only later that he understood what they meant and why he had to say them.

"You know I can't," Robert Johnson said. "The Mountain ain't no place for a man alive."

John Henry nodded and allowed as it was so.

"And there's something back in Memphis — something that I've got to do. I don't know what it is, but I can feel it in my heart."

The King blinked; for half a moment he looked surprised. Then he nodded sadly. "If that's what you hear, you need to listen to it, Robert Johnson. You'd be a comfort to me here — but that's not as urgent as the music in your heart." He sighed. "Be ready for me," he said. "I know I'll need you soon."

•

Robert Johnson left the Mountain two hours before sundown without stopping to tell anyone goodbye. Maybe that was for the best.

For when he reached the foot of the Mountain, half an hour after moonrise, he looked back at the summit and saw a great fire on the Mountain.

And he knew that fire was no place for the living.

He hiked back to St. Marys, and in the morning he caught the southbound train to ride it back to Memphis and his life as Hinky Tom.

And waited for the King to call him to his service.

It was a long wait — much longer than he ever would have guessed as he stood in the King's sanctum talking before the roaring fire. Six months went by, and then a year; and now Robert Johnson found himself in love. Such a crazy thing, to fall in love when he was no ordinary man, when he didn't dare make any commitment for fear the King would call him to a fate so grave it frightened a man with shoulders broad enough to shield the world.

But it wasn't like he had a choice. Robert Johnson met Virginia Henderson, and the moment that he knew her he loved her against all common sense; and because his heart commanded him beyond the possibility of denial, he married her, and they made a cozy home not far from the river.

Six months later Huddie Ledbetter died, and Robert Johnson felt it when he rose back from Hell to be seventh of the Seven Kings.

A few weeks after that Robert Johnson's wife turned up pregnant with their daughter. When she was born Robert and Virginia named their daughter Emma.

Robert Johnson loved his daughter Emma more dearly than anything else he'd ever known in the world; in Hell; he loved her more dearly than he loved the Pearly Gates of Salvation.

But he hardly had the chance to know her.

Because the King called him three days after Emma's birth. Robert Johnson answered the call, just as he'd promised he would. And though he returned from it, that return was only for a moment before he was lost forever to the ones he loved.

Greenville, Mississippi
The Present

Emma and Leadbelly spent hours searching the woods by the pale blue light of Leadbelly's fluorescent lantern. That light was bright enough to let them see for miles in thin pinewoods on the bluff, but even so it did them little good. No matter how they looked, no matter which way they shone the light, there was no sign of anyone — no sign of anything alive. Nor were there any tracks: Leadbelly searched and searched the ground for spoor, but he found none.

When the sun was high and bright Leadbelly said "Enough of this. Follow me. We need to try something different." And he led her to his musty cottage in the deep deep woods. He made coffee and served it with sectioned oranges, and sat with Emma near the dark hearth still dusty with ashes from last winter's fires.

And began to play his melodious twelve-string guitar. Softly, softly, picking and strumming no recognizable tune but an endless half-melody — a melody from a jam session, but how could anyone call something so quiet and gentle a jam?

After a while he seemed to doze, but he played on and on. Till now the music drifted away, and Emma faded asleep still sitting in the wide-armed chair beside the hearth.

The last thing she heard was Leadbelly, snoring.

Los Angeles, California
The Present

Dan Alvarez woke panting, gasping for air. It was pitch night in the boxcar, he was as alone as alone gets, and now the train rounded a bend and moonlight flooded in through the open boxcar door.

And in the moonlight he saw that terrible thing that followed him out of his dream, beautiful and ominous and powerful as it was the day John Henry carved it from the wood: the great guitar that Elvis Presley stole.

Memphis, Tennessee
September 1952

Robert Johnson climbed the Memphis ridge to search for Blind Willie one final time before he answered John Henry's call. This time he found the hardest path, and he followed it against the grain until it led him to Blind Willie's shack.

When he reached the door he found Blind Willie waiting for him, as though the gospel songster who became a King had known that he was coming.

And perhaps he did.

"I owe you something dear, Blind Willie," Robert Johnson said.

Blind Willie tried to say there was no debt between them, but Robert Johnson cut him off before he could finish speaking.

"It doesn't matter if you hold me to account," Robert Johnson said. "I hold myself accountable."

And then he gave Blind Willie the seven Mysteries he'd kept hidden in his heart for years.

When he was done Blind Willie thanked him, and invited him in to sit a spell.

Robert Johnson hesitated to accept that invitation. It was nearly dusk, and the great King's call was still in his ear. But then Blind Willie said, "There's something that I need to tell you, Robert Johnson," and Robert Johnson knew he had to hear the word.

"All right, then," he said, and he followed Blind Willie into the darkness of the shack.

Blind Willie poured two cups of sassafras tisane from the brew-pot on the stove, and carried them to the table. "There's sugar in the covered bowl if you like it sweet," he said, pointing at the bowl in the center of the table.

Robert Johnson thanked him, stirred in half a spoon of sugar, and sipped his brew as he sat back in his chair.

"The Lady came to me last night," Blind Willie said. "In a dream she came and talked to me."

Robert Johnson snorted. "I thought you were a man who didn't go around talking to no Ladies," he said.

Blind Willie cleared his throat. "She came to me," he said. "I don't go looking for her."

"I always thought you didn't have no truck with any Caribbean devils," Robert Johnson said. He was partly sardonic when he asked that, but he meant the question, too. Blind Willie was a strictly righteous man.

"I saw her, and I bade her get away from me, devil, yes, yes I did. But then she knelt before me and began to pray. I heard her pray for forgiveness, Robert Johnson, and I know from the way she said that prayer that she's prayed it every night for a million years. If a devil speak a prayer like that, his words surely would catch fire, or he would go to his redemption, one; and the cataclysm from either act is a thing no deadman could mistake. I looked at her again, and I could see she wasn't just a fallen angel, but a repentant one. Repentance leaves a mark upon a body, Robert Johnson. You of all men ought to know about that."

Robert Johnson shrugged. "I don't see nothing when I look into the mirror. But if you tell me you can see it, I believe you."

"When her prayer was done she got up off her knees and sang to me. Three songs, she sang — one of them was *Judgment Day,* and another was 'The Ode to Joy.' The third song was 'When the Saints Come Marching In,' but the words she sang were strange to me. I never heard no one sing those words before, and I swear to you, Robert Johnson, if I never hear those words again it won't be a day too soon.

"She said those words were a calling, and when you sing them — *you,* Robert Johnson — you will call the tumult down upon the devils out of Hell."

And then he said the words he didn't dare to sing. I won't recount them here for the same reason Blind Willie spoke them where he could have sang them. No one ever sings those words, no matter how clear they remember them — when bluesmen sing that version of the song they hum out the most important passages, or slap the syllables on their guitars, or hide them in cacophonies of music.

It isn't *Judgment Day*, that song, but it's powerful juju even so.

"She said you'd know when you had to sing," Blind Willie said. "She told me other things, too, but I've got to face those things myself."

Robert Johnson frowned. "Tell me," he said. "Tell me everything you know."

Blind Willie looked away. He looked so sad, Robert Johnson thought — like a man in mourning for the loss of everything he loved.

"You need to tell me," Robert Johnson said. "I need to know before I go to face the fire on the ridge."

After a while Blind Willie looked up and allowed that Robert Johnson had a point. And he told him all of the most terrible things the Lady had divined to him — how the day was close upon them when Our Lady of Sorrows would descend into Hell to seize the inside of the Eye from the place it hung in the great receiving room of the Mansion called Defiance; how the Eye would fall to pieces when she lifted it — and if the hoodoo men and Robert Johnson didn't sing to give her cover the demon horde would rend her limb from limb as they tried to storm the aperture between this world and the next.

How before her work was done Blind Willie, John Henry and all the Kings, all the hoodoo men and Robert Johnson, too — they all would face the hordes of Hell, and hold them with their song.

And then Blind Willie told him how each of them would pay a terrible price. When the song was done every solitary one who stood against the hordes of Hell of them would be gone, and there would be no deadmen in the Delta Kingdom.

And Robert Johnson would be dead and gone to Hell, no matter how he once had tasted the sweet wine that is redemption.

Lisa woke alone and confused in an alley in New Orleans' French Quarter.

It was hours after midnight, so late that even the nightside streets were deserted — but Lisa was a world away from the nightside streets. The alley where she lay was surrounded by old wooden houses that had all but collapsed upon themselves, and as they crumbled the houses had filled the alley with rotting verminous debris. Lisa could feel it throbbing, thriving as she woke to push herself out of the filth and shake away the roaches that crawled upon her.

"Mama. . . ?" she called, but there was no one near enough to hear her. *"Mama!"* she screamed, but no one heard that, either. She hurried out of the alley, into the tourist streets where beggars slept oblivious along the sidewalks, calling and calling and screaming for her mother everywhere she went.

But no matter how she ran, the only ones who answered her were the bums who told her to be quiet.

Now she came to the docklands, and saw a great sign that said WELCOME TO THE CITY OF NEW ORLEANS!. When she saw that she knew that something awful had carried her away, and that her mother was miles and miles from her, upstream on the river.

She walked more slowly after that, and she didn't bother shouting. Because she realized something when she saw the river — she realized that she had to be calm, and walk as quiet as she could, or the awful things would find her when she couldn't hear them come for her.

Maybe she was right, too. Lisa was right about a lot of things that day, and she regretted all of them.

Lisa followed the riverfront road south through the docklands. The Port of New Orleans was a dying enterprise, and Lisa saw it dying as she traveled south. Every block she went the docklands grew seedier and more abandoned, till finally a mile south of the French Quarter she realized she was walking in a ghost town. Here the docks and factories lay crumbling in ruins; even the river seemed to fester and boil as it ran along the ghost-town shore.

Somewhere along her way she made a turn to follow river-wise that only people who've been *touched* can make, and her way took her out of the mundane collapse of southeastern New Orleans, into a place where only the damned, the unlucky, and those with special *gifts* can go. Some people call that secret place the Devil's Quarter of New Orleans, but wise people don't call it anything at all.

Because the evil in that place knows when people speak of it, and it watches them quite closely.

Lisa had a sense about that — a sense, almost, of where she was. She thought, *I should turn back,* and she meant to do that. But then she heard a vague cacophony somewhere in the distance, and she followed it step by step by step into the east as the river bent south.

When Lisa came around the bend she saw the mansion, and the distant cacophony became an unsettling din, and she knew she'd found the fate that had carried her downriver to New Orleans.

And because she knew she'd found it, she faced it, no matter how it scared her worse than anything alive.

The mansion was a frightful old place, battered and aban-doned-looking — but it wasn't abandoned at all. Just the oppo-site, in fact: there were lights in all the windows, and when she got close enough to see the night-dark lawn Lisa saw that the mansion's grounds were littered with the unconscious bodies of drunken revelers. There was a party in that place, but it wasn't a party that anyone with any sense would ever visit.

Unless they absolutely had to.

Unless something in their hearts told them there was a destiny inside that place that they could not avoid. Lisa knew that kind of destiny when she stood at the edge of the drive that led to the mansion. She knew she could turn and run away, and maybe if she did she could have a life, a good life and a decent life and maybe someday she could find her mother again and she and Mama could drive back north to Harlem and their life and Lisa could grow old enough for school, real school like where they really teach you something instead of chasing you out onto a tarmac where the retard boys could pick at you, yes, yes, Lisa knew what there was for her if she turned around and ran.

And a part of her wanted to run back to that, and try to make it good.

But the biggest truest most honest chamber in her heart told her that something terrible had caught her, long ago, and that she'd never be free of it until she faced it and conquered it, and that was destiny.

And Lisa met it.

She wound her way along the drive, stepping gingerly and around the drunken derelicts until she reached the mansion's great front stoop. There by the door with the doorknob too far above her head to open, Lisa had one last moment of trepidation. She was only Lisa! She was only a baby! The world was too big for her, and too terrible, and she didn't dare to face it —

And then she saw the open door at the far end of the stoop, and she knew she had to face her fate no matter what it was.

It wasn't bad at first.

No one at the party in the mansion even noticed Lisa for the longest time — their drugs, their obsessions, their conversations absorbed those people too thoroughly for any of them to see a child walk among their knees. Lisa used her invisibility for all that it was worth — here she stood in the shadows near a coatroom and listened to three ladies whisper conspiratorially among themselves about the end of the world; and when that conversation faded she wandered deeper into the party where the men dressed freakishly and all the women seemed enchanted; and now she forgot herself entirely as she gawked at the red-eyed whisperer who looked partly like a woman and partly like a man — and felt every hair on her body stand on end as she realized that the people around her weren't people at all. They were — things, *outré* things that somehow had that knack of seeming like people, and once she realized there was a difference to distinguish she saw that none of them were people, none of them at all anywhere in the mansion were alive were human were born of man and woman *people* —

That was when Lisa knew she had to leave. It didn't matter

what destiny there was for her inside that place; it didn't matter if she didn't have the nerve to face her fate; it didn't matter if she had to spend all her living days trapped in a lie that bent over and over on herself, Lisa had to go *now now now* —

But there was no way to leave.

Because every door she found was closed and locked, and even if she'd had a key to open one Lisa wasn't tall enough to reach the handle.

All of the doors were closed! All of them!

All of them but one.

And that was the door that led to the basement.

Lisa knew better than to go into that basement.

Of course she did! She could smell that awful smell that wafted out the door, that smell like sulfur-rotten eggs, and she could hear the faint and distant screams of agony every time she passed near it.

That basement was the worst place she could go. The worst place in the world, and maybe in the next world, too.

And then the freaky man-woman shouted, and Lisa whirled around to see him pointing at her, shouting and pointing and screaming for someone to *grab that brat before she gets away*, and Lisa knew she didn't have a choice.

No choice at all.

She had to run or she was lost, and there was only one way to go.

Into the basement.

Into the underground and down down down.

Like Orpheus.

To Hell.

> *Somewhere in America*
> *Traveling by Rail*
> *The Present*

Dan Alvarez cradled the dream guitar in his arms for the longest time — sat leaning against the boxcar wall, pressing silent chords against the frets, fingering the strings so carefully that he made no sound.

He was so careful not to make a sound. So careful! That guitar was a periapt — a charm like a talisman but large as life.

It was the great King's guitar; it was Elvis's guitar. It was the music of the spheres made material and true. Dan Alvarez was a brave man, but he wasn't brave enough to play that instrument alone.

After a long long while he fell asleep with the guitar still cradled in his arms. In his sleep he began to dream again, and now in his dreams he was a black hobo songster. In that dream it was half a century ago, and the blues were alive and thriving — not that awful crap you hear in city juke-joints but *blues*, vital and alive and as real as the fate that waits to welcome each of us to his grave. In that dream he hoboed from town to town across the countryside, making his meager livelihood with his sonorous guitar, and times were hard and folks were poor and Dan scarcely made it from one meal to the next, and if he didn't know his licks so effing well he wouldn't eat at all.

But he did eat, every day. And some days he ate damn well.

In his dream he pushed the plate away from him and pulled his guitar over his shoulder, and he sang. Before he realized what he was doing he began to play that periapt guitar.

The world shook as he picked its strings, and as it shook the *santa* came to hear him.

When Dan Alvarez saw Our Lady of Sorrows the dream melted away to leave him back on the train rolling and rolling somewhere in America. On the train he was just nobody half-talent Dan Alvarez again — but even if he was just a would-be musician who made his living as a fry-cook at Denny's, he sang the music of the world and played the chords that only the great ones master.

The *santa* smiled on him, and Dan Alvarez supplicated himself before her. She was so beautiful, he thought. More beautiful than he could bear to see.

"Lady," Dan Alvarez said, letting the guitar slide out of his hands, onto the boxcar floor, "*santa.*"

The Lady smiled again, so beautiful. And now she pointed out the boxcar door — at the town lights that appeared on the horizon.

Dan knew what she meant. She wanted him to go to that place, wherever it was. That was the place she'd been prompting him all along — from the moment he'd first seen her outside his apartment window she'd been pushing him toward this place, this time, this moment.

Dan felt a sinking dread in the low part of his gut. He felt sweat beading up on his forehead despite the cool wind rushing through the open boxcar door.

"I'm afraid," he said. "It scares me, *santa.*"

The *santa* watched him steadily, evenly; nothing in her expression shifted as Dan told her of his fear.

"I don't want to go there, Lady," Dan said.

But the *santa* never heard him.

Because she was already gone.

The Devil's Quarter of New Orleans
The Present

The scariest part of Lisa's descent into Hell was the loneliness.

Loneliness.

The moment she set foot on the stairway the party and the noise disappeared behind her in a haze of damnable possibility. It was as quiet and as empty on that stair as it was in the corridor that led to the fountain and the Gates of Judgment at the reflecting pool before Heaven and Hell, and lonelier, too, because each time she'd been to that hall the *santa* had held her hand.

But there was no *santa* here. No one followed her away from the party; no one greeted her on the basement stair to Hell; no one spoke or sang or called to her — until she reached the basement.

When Lisa rounded the last steps of the stairway she found Robert Johnson waiting in that basement anteroom of Hell. He sat in a folding chair on the far side of the room; a cheap tin lamp hung from the ceiling above him, shining on him like a spotlight. When he saw her he lifted his guitar onto his lap and began to caress its strings.

He was so beautiful, that Robert Johnson — his pretty pinstripe suit; his wide white-toothed smile so bright against that face as dark as pitch; his slender, nimble hands coaxing Grace from the strings of his guitar. He began to play, and his song was the most amazing thing — and the rhythm and just the whisper of a chance hiding in the melody, and Lisa stood listening transfixed agape, lost and away from everything she knew.

It didn't matter anymore, she realized. It didn't matter if this was Hell or New Orleans or a terrible memory from her first infancy; what mattered was the magic and the music and the whisper of a chance, and if that meant she had to follow Robert Johnson down to Hell, then that was what it meant, and even if Lisa was afraid she didn't hesitate, not for a moment.

"Follow me down," Robert Johnson sang, "Follow me down to Hell."

And Lisa did.

Somewhere in America
Traveling by Rail
The Present

Dan Alvarez climbed out of the boxcar when the train came to a stop. It was dawn by then, but even in the daylight it took him a long while to figure out where he was. He kept expecting to be somewhere in the South — in Memphis, maybe, or even in New Orleans — but the farther he went the clearer it became that he was a long way from either of those places. The dirt was wrong, for one, and the odd trees in the rubble were all wrong for the South.

Then he saw the water tower at the far end of the rail yard, and there on the side of it was the word DETROIT in big blocky letters.

Dan thought, *Detroit? What on God's earth would she want me to do in Detroit?* But even as he thought it something in his gut began to guess her purpose.

He didn't like it. Not one bit.

As Dan passed the water tower the trainyard opened out into a wicked slum — a city built of paint-peeling wooden houses and run-down brick-face stores and uncertain structures falling in on their foundations. Even in the cloudless-bright summer morning there was a dankness about the place, a night-quiet foreboding that hung above the city, promising collapse.

When he'd gone a few blocks Dan began to think he should

turn back, find himself another train, and hobo south to find a more inviting city. A few blocks after that he was sure he should turn back, and twice he stopped and turned around — and hesitated. And thought of the Lady, and remembered what she needed from him. And turned back around to walk deeper and deeper into the crumbling city.

Three miles from the trainyard Dan Alvarez saw the Lady standing in the shadows of a dead-end alley, beckoning to him. Dan didn't hesitate an instant. He ran to her, ran to throw himself before her, promise her his service, beg her for her mercy.

But she disappeared again before he reached her.

And where she'd stood a vagabond lay death-still and wheezing half-covered with garbage from the overturned barrel beside him.

"Man," Dan Alvarez said. "Oh man."

He knew what the Lady meant him to do. Of course he knew! It was as obvious as obvious gets — no matter how disgusting it was.

Too damn gross. Too damn gross to think about, let alone to do.

"Mister?" Dan called to the bum. "You've got to wake up, mister."

The drunk didn't answer. Didn't even stir. He was too far gone — drugged or drunk or deep asleep or something, Dan didn't want to know, didn't even want to think about it.

He stooped, leaned in close to whisper into the man's ear. *"Mister!"*

But that didn't wake the man, no more than shouting at him had. Dan put his hands on the man's shoulders and shook him, but that didn't wake him either.

"Damn. Damn damn damn."

Is he dead? Dan wondered. *Why would she send me after a dead man?*

He couldn't imagine. Couldn't begin to imagine.

Unless she meant him to take the body to a morgue?

No, he wasn't dead, couldn't be dead — there, listen, he was wheezing again. *Dead men don't wheeze, do they?*

Dan knew they didn't, knew they couldn't possibly. But he

didn't find the knowledge reassuring.

He put his hands under the man's shoulders, lifted his stinking vomitous body to carry him over his shoulder.

Damn!

And carried him out of the shadowy alley, into the day.

In the light of day with the clean summer breeze carrying away the stink, Dan noticed how cold the body was, as if it really were the body of a dead man. And he was so light, too — he was a full-grown man, and not a young one, either, but he weighed no heavier than a child on Dan's shoulder.

Maybe he is *dead,* Dan thought — and then the vagabond began to mumble half-intelligibly.

What was he saying? Dan could almost make out the words — almost, not quite, and he said "What's that?" but the derelict didn't answer. The moment he heard Dan speak to him the man went silent.

Dan carried the man four blocks before he spotted the dive hotel. It was a broke-down sleazy motel place with a big sign out front that said this was the Dew Tell Motel, and God that place was gross, but if they hadn't been so gross they never would have let Dan check in with that stinking vomitous drunk man weighing on his shoulder.

But they were what they were, and they took Dan's money, and he thanked God for them.

Dan hauled the drunk across the parking lot to his room, room 5C. It wasn't clean in there, but it was lots cleaner than Dan or the vagabond, so he carried the man straight into the bathroom and set him in the tub instead of setting him on the bed.

Took the guitar off his other shoulder, and set it carefully in the back corner of the closet. Closed the closet door to hide the guitar, and went back to the bathroom to look at the derelict.

He's filthy, Dan thought. *I've got to clean him, give him a shave, get some clean clothes on him.*

The drunk farted loudly, and his gas made an emphatic, almost derisive sound against the tub. It almost made Dan think he was responding to Dan's thoughts.

"Fart all you want," Dan said. "I'm going to clean you up.

If I've got to have anything to do with you, I'm going to get rid of that damned stink."

He went to the tub, lifted the man's slack body, and undressed him. He was even lighter and colder than he'd seemed when Dan had carried him — so cold and empty that if he wasn't dead he was seriously ill, and maybe Dan ought to get him to the hospital. . . .

. . . .shit-smeared shorts; skin everywhere crusted with flaky scunge. . . .

Well, maybe he had to get the man to a doctor. But first he was going to get him clean enough to touch. Dan tossed the last of the man's clothes onto the bathroom floor and turned on the hot water tap; pushed the faucet upward to engage the shower head.

Stepped away and let the streaming water begin to wash the vagabond clean.

It didn't go very fast. Some of that crud was so thick it'd take hours for the water to wear it away.

He glanced at the pile of filth-encrusted clothes, trying to figure out how he was going to get them clean. And realized there was just no way. Even if he'd had a laundry to wash them in, they were so filthy that he could wash them over and over a dozen times and the things would still show stains, and maybe they'd just fall apart. *He's going to need new clothes,* Dan thought. He looked at his own shirt and slacks, which were ragged and filthy from the fire in his apartment, from the run through burning Los Angeles, from the days-long journey by boxcar. *I need clothes, too.* There was a rummage store a couple blocks back — he remembered passing it just a few moments after he'd carried the derelict out of the alley. *But I can't leave him here, can I?*

The derelict lay unconscious in the tub, oblivious to Dan, to the steamy water streaming down on him, oblivious to the world.

He isn't going anywhere, Dan thought. And he was right, too.

But even so he hurried. Out the motel-room door; across the sun-warm blacktop of the motel parking lot; a block and a half down the street to the secondhand store.

He found shirts and shorts in the rag bin — they were stained and tattered, but cheap as they could be, because the store sold rags by the pound. Slacks were harder, because he had to guess the derelict's size more carefully — he spent a couple minutes looking through the stacks of work pants before he realized there was no way he could guess a 37" 29" from a 35" 30". And gave up, and grabbed a pair that looked more-or-less right and a pair of suspenders to make the difference work.

Carried the clothes to the counter, still rushing, grabbed a couple of disposable razors from a bin beside the register. As he worried about the passed-out bum soaking in the water, and what if he drowned?, and Dan knew he had to hurry. . . .

Until he got to the counter and saw the old woman.

There was something remarkable about that woman. Something — divine. Oh, you couldn't see it by the way she looked. When Dan first saw her he thought she was a bag lady like a thousand other bag ladies he'd seen across the years — filthy, old, and worn; eyes that glittered crazy like she'd missed her medication three days running; there was a tiny drop of spittle leaking out the left corner of her mouth.

But no matter what he saw when he looked at her, when Dan stood before her at the counter he could feel the same majesty and grace he felt when the *santa* came to him.

He set his purchases on the counter before her with the same supplication that a worshiper offers up a sacrifice, and waited for her to respond.

But she didn't respond. She stood at the counter staring at him, weighing him as the *santa* had weighed him.

After a while she smiled at him, and Dan thought he would cry.

"You're an angel, aren't you?" Dan asked.

He knew the truth before she even began to answer him: he could see through to her heart, no matter how she looked at first. It didn't matter that she wore the strangest smile on her worn and filthy face; that her skin was blotched and mottled with sickly-looking blemishes; that there were wide dark gaps in her mouth where three teeth should have been.

Nothing could disguise her from him. Not even the stinking, filthy overcoat, six months out of season.

"If you need those things, Dan Alvarez," the angel said,

"they're yours. Go with God. Follow your heart."

And then Dan stood alone in an empty, abandoned shop. All the secondhand store goods were gone, and the windows were boarded over, and if it weren't for the door ripped half off its hinges Dan never would have got himself out of that place.

•

When he got back to the hotel room Dan Alvarez found the tub clogged with grit. There was filthy water spilling out all over the bathroom floor, and if it hadn't been for the extra drain in the center of the floor there would have been an awful mess to mop.

But there was a drain, and the floor wasn't any problem, not really. The real problem was the vagabond — he was bobbing around in the water like a drowned man when Dan got to him, and the water was up over his face sometimes and sometimes not, and he'd took a lot of water down his lungs, to judge the way he coughed when Dan pulled him up out of the water.

So much water down his lungs. Coughing and coughing it up as Dan pounded on his back. But the coughing didn't seem to wake him, and the pounding didn't either, and Dan began to think the poor sot would've drowned without even noticing he was about to die, and then he thought *ha ha what if he's already dead, you can't drown 'em when they're already dead,* and he almost started to laugh at that till he realized there was something very wrong, something very very wrong. Because the guy just coughed up more water than anyone could breathe in and survive, and what the hell was going on?

What the hell?

Crazy, all of it was crazy. Dan couldn't make any sense of it. How could anybody. . . ?

Dan couldn't figure. There wasn't any way to figure, and no point trying when the business at hand was so awful — the filth, the matted hair everywhere on his body, and Dan pulled three big clots of filth away from the drain but the tub still clogged again.

Cleared the drain again, got the soap and a washcloth, and began to try to scrub the derelict clean.

Hard, disgusting work. Damn near hopeless work, but Dan

kept at it, and slowly, slowly the derelict came clean.

Soaped down the man's hair, rinsed it, soaped and rinsed it again. Pushed it back, out of the way; grabbed one of the disposable razors from the place he'd left it by the sink.

Soaped the face and scraped away the bristly beard, bit by bit by bit.

When he was halfway done shaving the man, he had an awful laugh.

He looks like Elvis, Dan thought. Imagine that! Like something from the headlines on a supermarket tabloid, I Found Elvis — *Miracle in Detroit*, and Dan had another laugh. What a joke, I Found Elvis. Ha ha.

Scraping and scraping with the razor, and two, maybe three times Dan thought he cut the man, but he never bled. When he was done Dan soaped and cleaned the man's face one final time, then turned off the water and let the tub drain. When it was empty he patted the man dry with a towel, lifted him out of the tub, and carried him to the chair on the far side of the hotel room.

He did his best to dress the man. But it wasn't easy — he was all slack and wobbly, and putting clothes on him was like trying to shovel air into a sack.

Shirt over his head; shorts, slacks —

And something in all that pushing and pulling must've shaken the man more than half-drowning in the tub, because suddenly his eyes were open.

"What they hell you trying to do to me?" the man asked.

And Dan gasped.

"I said, 'What you doing?'"

And gasped again.

"Huh? What are you, some kind of a pervert?"

"Just getting you dressed, that's all."

Because Dan knew that voice, and he could never ever ever mistake it.

"You ought to show a little respect."

The voice was Elvis's voice, and no matter how impossible that was — no matter how Elvis was twenty years and more dead and buried on the grounds of his Graceland mansion, it was Elvis and no other who spoke to Dan.

"Elvis. . . ?"

The man's eyes brightened for a moment — and then suddenly his expression became querulous and uncertain.

"Who are you?" he asked. "What do you want?"

Dan blinked. "I don't want nothing," he said. "I just found you passed out in an alley, that's all. I figured I ought to help."

"I bet you want to help," the deadman said. He snorted derisively. "You and everybody else."

Memphis, Tennessee
September 1952

Robert Johnson never got back to the Mountain. He never got farther than the West Memphis train station, in fact — he climbed off the bus from Memphis just as the southbound train was getting in, and before he got from the ticket counter to the train the whole damn station went thick with hoodoo, and Robert Johnson turned around to see the deadmen climbing off the train — hundreds of them. Hoodoo Doctors, Kings, Ma Rainey, even ordinary bluesmen, every solitary one of them from up and down the Mississippi valley — all of them all of them climbing off the southbound train.

Robert Johnson wandered away from the ticket window, staring at the hoodoo men, watching them intently to try to understand. . . .

Wandered down the platform, still staring, as dozens of Hoodoo Doctors hurried past him.

John Henry was the last one off the last car of the train. He was carrying his own bags, acting like anybody, anybody alive or dead anybody at all, and you'd never know he was the wellspring of ten thousand legends, but Robert Johnson knew him.

He could never forget that man. Never. He knew the sight of him as well as he knew the shadow of his own heart.

The great King saw Robert Johnson, too. He nodded to him as he climbed down the train steps, and greeted him when he got close.

"Let me carry that," Robert Johnson said, because it was a burden he knew he had to share.

The great King shook his head. "I carry for myself," he said.

"I wouldn't ask no one to tote for me."

Robert Johnson nodded. "That's right," he said. "Of course."

Ma Rainey spoke up from somewhere behind him.

"You know it is," she said. "Just like the Bible's right."

"Blind Willie give you the song?" the great King said.

Robert Johnson nodded. "He did," he said. Somewhere deep inside him he wondered how the King knew he'd gone to see Blind Willie, but deeper still he knew the reason why: the King was in his heart, and Robert Johnson in the King's, and there's a natural sort of knowledge that goes with that kind of sharing.

"Good," the King said. "I knew I could count on you."

And then he started down the platform, hurrying toward a place and a destiny Robert Johnson couldn't imagine. When he was gone thirty yards he turned back to face Robert Johnson and Ma Rainey, and called to them.

"Come on," he said. "Ain't no time to waste."

And then he turned to start away so quickly Robert Johnson had to run to stay with him.

Detroit, Michigan
The Present

The deadman Elvis got quiet after Dan figured out who he was. He straightened out his shirt and folded his arms and sat there in the chair glowering at Dan for the longest time, and after a while Dan realized that he wasn't going to say another word. So he left the deadman sitting in the hotel-room chair and went to the bathroom for his shower.

Took a long damn while to get clean. He wasn't as deep-down filthy as the deadman had been, but he was dirtier than he'd ever been before.

That happens to men who ride the rails by boxcar — the land gets into them, and they have to scrub and scrub if they ever want to get it out.

He never did get completely clean, but he got close enough — clean enough not to stink in polite company. When he was done he put on the clothes he'd found at the secondhand store and left the bathroom wondering if the derelict would still be there.

He was, of course.

When Dan got out of the bathroom he found the deadman sitting on the edge of the hotel bed. In his arms he held the dream guitar — the magic hammer that the Lady brought to Dan as he slept in the boxcar two nights before.

The deadman looked up at Dan as Dan approached him.

"Hell of an instrument," he said.

He picked at the strings with his cold, dry hands.

"It is," Dan said.

"I always loved it," the deadman said.

Dan nodded. "I can see why," he said. "She had me bring that for you, didn't she?"

The deadman shook his head. "No, no — she took it from me years and years ago. It's been a long time since I've held it."

He was picking "Love Me Tender," and Dan half expected him to croon, but he didn't, thank God. Bad enough he had to play a song like that on the great King's guitar; Dan knew he couldn't bear to hear him sing as well.

"Play something real," Dan said. "Play — I don't know. — Play 'Jailhouse Rock.' Play something boogie-woogie."

The deadman's hands went slack, and his shoulders sagged; he looked up at Dan with an expression — like someone had hit him, or worse. "Damn you," he said. "Damn your eyes."

And then he took hold of that guitar like he meant it, and he began to *sing*.

Sing!

And God that man could boogie-woogie, even if half the songs he ever sang were things that made him sound like some third-rate Bing Crosby from the sticks. He played "Jailhouse Rock" like a man who understood what boogie-woogie meant, and like he'd lived a wear-you-down life to show him what it was all about, and the beat consumed the hotel room with its syncopated rhythm, and *God God God* that man could sing, he sang like when he was alive but deeper and truer and with the grace and vision that come to those who've been to Hell and clawed their way back into the light of day; he sang the song like jail was Hell and his eternity, and the song was his life and his passport and his manumission, and before he was done Dan knew in his heart every solitary fact about the damnation of Elvis Presley, no matter if he could not articulate a word of it.

When the room was quiet Dan said, "That's why they call you King."

But the deadman shook his head. "No," he said, "I seen the King. I heard him play his truest song that night on the bluff over Memphis. And I seen him lately, too — I seen his ghost at the Lake of Fire, where the shore meets Hell near the delta of the River Styx. And even if he's only a ghost too faint to kiss a fire, he's still the King. On my finest day I'll never hold a candle to him."

Part of Dan wanted to allow as that was so, because it was. But another part wanted to argue with it, because he'd heard the song, and he knew the deadman had a terrible bright gift, and just that moment he thought that the man was King because he was born to be, and not just because he'd stole the great King's hammer.

"You got your licks," Dan said. "I heard you. You can make that hammer ring."

The deadman shrugged. Let the guitar fall onto the bed beside him; got up and started for the door.

"Where are you going?"

"I don't know," he said. "I'll be back."

It was hours before Dan saw him again.

Memphis, Tennessee
September 1952

When they got to the station's parking lot there was a car waiting to drive the King away. At first Robert Johnson didn't realize that he was supposed to ride there with him — when they got to the car he stepped back and watched as first Ma Rainey and then the King climbed into the back seat, and then he closed the door for them and waved to wish them well.

Such a silly man, that Robert Johnson. He was so confused and so reluctant to face the fate that waited for him that he didn't even realize why the King had found him, and what he was supposed to do, and how critical he was to the great song above the river.

But that was Robert Johnson for you, in that short but

righteous second life of his: he was a man so meek and unassuming that he never guessed the measure of his destiny.

As Robert Johnson waved the great King rolled down his window and called to him.

"Robert Johnson," he said, "you ain't getting done with this that easy," and then he laughed. "You take the shotgun seat — ride up front with Furry Lewis."

Robert Johnson blinked and blinked, trying to find himself in the confusion of his circumstance.

"Shotgun. . . ?" he asked, and as he spoke that word he saw a shotgun in his mind's eye. And as he saw it red deamonous hands grabbed that rifle by its stock and trigger, cocked the gun, and blew them all to kingdom come.

As Robert Johnson began to understand the vision and his circumstance and destiny, and maybe that moment if he'd turned and run he could have saved himself from the fate that waited for him.

And maybe not.

Because even if his circumstances and his nature damned him as certainly as they possibly could, it would not have saved him to turn tail and run. For cowardice is damnable, and the pits in Hell reserved for cowards are crueler and more inescapable than all the others taken as a whole.

●

Furry Lewis drove them up the Memphis ridge and through the forest just below it; along the hard road less traveled by until they passed Blind Willie's shack, and beyond that to a clearing near the high point over Memphis.

They were the last to get there, damn near — but that was just as well, all in all, since it meant the food was already cooking.

Lots and lots of food, and good company, too — because the singing that night started in the way it always does, with barbecue and pot-luck food and jugs of good corn liquor — special stuff made carefully to keep it free from *spirit liquor* and the awful fate of deadmen.

Some people call gatherings like that one hoe-downs, and some of them call them barbecues or jubilees or parties. If you go far enough afield the music changes and the people say carnival or festival, but the reason for the celebration never changes. The food and the drink and the company are all a part of a ritual that's older than the continent, and dearer, too. The music is the natural end of it — not so much a fragment as it is the solvent that disintegrates the night.

It dissolved that night entirely. Some nights it changed forever, in a way.

Detroit, Michigan
The Present

The deadman came back to Dan's hotel room at three-thirty in the morning. He didn't bother to knock, and he didn't need to use a key to get in, no matter how Dan had locked the door and switched the deadbolt home.

Dan sat bolt upright when he heard the door open. He opened his eyes to see the deadman standing in the darkness, silhouetted against the streetlight streaming through the open door.

"We can leave when you're ready," the deadman said.

He'd cast away his rags and dressed himself in a white silk suit — coat, vest, shirt and jacket brilliant and shimmering the color of pearls. Dan couldn't imagine where he'd found clothes like that here in the hard slums of Detroit.

Dan tried to rub the sleep from his eyes.

"Leave for where?" he asked. "I don't understand."

The deadman turned to glance out the open door; as he did his face caught in the chiaroscuro, and Dan saw that he was frowning.

"The Lady sent you for me," he said. "She didn't tell you why?"

"No," Dan told him. "She didn't even tell me who you were."

The deadman nodded.

"We're going down the river," he said. "I found a boat today."

When Dan heard him say "the river" he heard "the Mississippi," but he was wrong.

"But the river is so far from here," he said. "You can't get a boat there from Detroit, can you?"

The deadman laughed, and his laugh was a thing that chilled

Dan to the bone, no matter how there was no malice in it. "The river's everywhere," he said. "If you know how to sail, you can find it any time you want."

And Dan thought, *That's wrong, that's wrong, you can't get onto the Mississippi unless you're sailing on a river in the Mississippi basin,* and he was right, as far as that goes, excepting that there are canals here and there and if you know how to work them you can get a boat a lot of places people never realize. But he was wrong, too, because the deadman wasn't talking about the Mississippi.

He was talking about the River Styx, and what he said was true: the river is the soul of every stream, and its current is our destiny, waiting for the day when we will sail.

"Give me a minute," Dan said. "I've got to get my boots on."

His shoes, his ragged slacks; Dan looked around the hotel room to see if there was anything else he needed to gather before he left that place behind. Filthy clothes — too dirty to clean, let alone to carry with them.

And the guitar, leaning against the wall beside the night-stand.

They couldn't leave the guitar — though there was a part of Dan's heart that wanted to leave that instrument behind and never look at it again.

Dan lifted it with both hands and held it out for the deadman to take.

"Don't look at me," the deadman said. "I died to get away from that thing. You've got to carry it now."

Dan pulled the guitar strap over his shoulder.

And followed the deadman out onto the hard streets of Detroit in the small hours of the morning.

Past prostitutes and drunkards; past a gang of weird-eyed teenage boys howling oaths at one another as their leaders contemplated murder; past a knoll where eight police cars were gathered, face to face to face, and patrolmen sat idly on the hoods of their cars, sipping coffee and smoking fat cigars as they whispered fearfully to one another; through six blocks of dockyard buildings so abandoned Dan thought he'd lived to see the last days of the world; down to the riverside, and here there was a boat.

It wasn't a special-looking boat or anything like that, but the deadman must've paid a pretty penny for it all the same. Boats don't come cheap, after all, and though that boat was a small one it wasn't the smallest size by far. It had two bunks and a closet down below the deck, and sailboats with bunks and pantries are yacht-toys for the idle rich.

"I don't know how to sail," Dan said. "I won't be much help."

The deadman shrugged.

"Damnation isn't hard to find," he said. "All rivers run to it. The current will drag us there sooner or later — and then the boat will find its own way."

Dan didn't like the sound of that, but he didn't want to argue. He followed the deadman onto the boat and sat in the spot where the deadman told him to. He didn't object when the deadman unlashed the ropes that held them to the dock and pushed them away from the shore, and he didn't say how much it frightened him when a south wind blew suddenly from nowhere to fill their sails and theirs alone.

It pushed them north, toward Lake Huron, which is wider than an inland sea. Before the night was done they were on water away away from everywhere, on water that could be anyplace because there was no land in sight, only the water and the sky and here and there a gull that found the air above them and hovered there, glaring at them with hard red eyes that spoke volumes that no ordinary bird could ever say.

In the morning the wind went hot and bitter, sulfury, and Dan knew they'd left the world behind. Now they came upon an outlet from the inland sea, a river where the current drained away from them, and that current drew them down no matter how the wind went still.

That was when Dan finally asked the question whose answer he didn't want to know. "Where are we?" he asked.

The deadman smiled. "We're on the river," he said. "You know that."

That was true, no matter whether Dan wanted to admit it to himself or not.

"I don't understand," he said. "Explain yourself."

The deadman laughed.

"We're on the River Styx," he said. "We're sailing past damnation, and there before us lies the Lake of Fire."

And he laughed and laughed.

"You're shitting me," Dan said. "We're heading toward the Mississippi, right?"

The deadman shook his head, still laughing.

"We're not," he said. "This river is the Styx."

"I don't believe you."

The deadman stopped laughing. Shrugged.

"Believe it or don't," he said. "You can see it for yourself, any time you want."

"Huh?"

"Look into the water," the deadman said. "The bottom's thick with those who tried to rob the ferryman."

Dan didn't want to look. He didn't want to see what he knew was waiting for him, waiting in the water —

But he couldn't stop himself.

He looked over the edge of the boat, and saw them, hundreds and thousands of them, dead and lifeless on the bottom of the river but writhing in the agony of their damnation, wide eyes pleading with him, arms outstretched as they begged for succor, lips moving silently as each of them begged him for their freedom. Some of them had coins, and others only outstretched palms, and when Dan looked at them he knew he had to help —

"We've got to save them," Dan said. "We've got to help them find their way ashore."

Deadman Elvis shrugged. "You can try," he said. "It won't do them any good."

Dan wanted to scream. "How can you say that? Don't you have any compassion?"

The deadman sighed and shook his head.

"You just don't get it, do you?" he asked. "Everybody tries to save them. Of course they do! Who could stand to see another man so damned and helpless without offering a hand?"

"Make sense," Dan said. "You contradict yourself."

"No," the deadman said, "I don't."

"I swear you do," Dan said. "You're heartless."

"I'm not."

"You are."

The deadman trimmed the sail. "I can moor here, if you want. You can throw them a rope, and try to help them come ashore. I tried it once — I did. The first time I was here."

"You did?"

"Of course I did! What do you think I am, an animal?"

"What happened?"

The deadman sighed again. "The same thing that always happens. They tried to drag me down and force me to replace them."

"But why?"

"Because they think their damnation is a fate somebody put on them, and they figure they can get out of it if they give it to somebody else. But they're wrong. The ones they drag down there always get away, just like I did, and the ones who try to do the drowning never find their way ashore — just like they never did when they tried to drown me."

Dan didn't say anything right away. Part of him knew that the deadman was right, because he'd seen the self-defeat in the eyes of the damned below him. But another part, maybe the biggest part, could never walk away from folks so terribly in need.

"You want me to moor the boat?"

Dan nodded.

The deadman shrugged, shifted the sail until the wind began to push them ashore. "It's your funeral," he said.

"You're wrong," Dan said. "You're just wrong, that's all."

"If you say so," dead Elvis said, laughing. "You know how they get there? It happens when they try to rob the ferryman. It's not like they say about him, you know. He takes folks across whether they got the coin to pay him or they don't. The ones that got the money, they pay him, and the ones that don't, he takes them over and they owe him. If they can pay later, then they do, but it ain't like the ferryman has got a collection agency. Hell, he even takes the ones who got the coin but lie to him they don't. What's he care? It ain't like he hasn't got enough.

"But for some people, that just ain't enough. They get out in the middle of the river, and there's that purse hanging from the ferryman's belt, and they just can't help themselves — they try to take it from him, because they figure this is Hell and they're all damned and what does it matter?

"But they're wrong. So wrong! When they try to take his purse the ferryman disappears for them, and his boat goes, too, and there they are in the middle of the river with nothing to hold them dry. And down they go. It isn't anybody else who damns them; it's them what damns themselves. If any of them ever repented, the Love of God would whisk them away in a moment, but no, no, the damned never repent, hell no, they got their pride, and even if they gave it up they'd still think they'd done the only reasonable thing under their circumstance. Same thing with them trying to get out — no matter how you try to save them, the things they do will damn them all over again. They'll try to damn you, too, but it never works that way."

"You're wrong," Dan said. "You're blaming the victims for their own fate."

Elvis shook his head. "Not this time, I'm not."

The bow of the sailboat brushed against the shore, and Elvis threw a line ashore to the firmament of damnation. It struck a withered ash tree, and wrapped around its trunk.

"I'll show you," Dan said. "I swear I will."

"Be careful," Elvis told him. "False oaths pave a quick road to damnation."

Dan stepped over the edge of the boat, onto the shore. "I'm already here," Dan said. "What've I got to be afraid of?"

Elvis grinned. "Be careful or you'll find out."

Dan huffed at him. "Toss me a rope," he said.

Elvis shook his head. "I won't," he said. "I never gave nobody the rope to hang himself. I ain't going to do that now, either."

"Well, to hell with you, then," Dan said. He leaned over the edge of the boat, spotted a coil of rope on the deck; grabbed it and stepped back ashore.

Walked a few yards downstream; held one end of the rope firm as he tossed the line to the damned throng in the river.

The response was immediate and dramatic — there was a pull

on the line so strong and sudden that the first jerk like to drag Dan off his feet.

But Dan was stronger than that. He wasn't any saint, but there was too much virtue in his heart for the first sudden tug of damnation to pull him off his feet.

The first tug didn't drag Dan down, and the second and the third didn't, either. But the fourth time the line drew taut it moved harder and faster than any attraction had ever come to Dan; and his strength, his weight, his inertia, and his character were nothing before it.

The damned ones pulled Dan Alvarez into the River Styx and drowned him in their venom and their hate. When he was down they planted his steadfast form in the muddy river bottom and climbed him like a ladder to the surface of damnation.

But it didn't work, just as the deadman said it wouldn't; and every time the damned ones clawed their way to the surface, the surface rose above them, and every time they flailed through it the bottom drew them down again.

Then things got crazy as the damned fought among themselves, crowding one another away as each of them tried to press the other out of the way so she could have Dan to herself — and now Dan floated to the surface like a bloated corpse.

He tried to swim ashore, but when he tried to move his muscles refused him. He was paralyzed, he realized, and probably as damned as the ferry-thieves bickering down there on the murky bottom —

And then someone grabbed him by the collar and began to drag him ashore.

At first Dan thought it was the deadman come to save him from the fate he'd already once tried to warn Dan away from, but no, no, it was a woman, Dan saw, a beautiful frail girl who lifted him from the water, onto the damned shore; turned him over, dragged him away from the water, and began to force the water from his lungs.

"You're sick, Dan Alvarez," she said. "Your sins have festered down inside your spirit."

Now she placed her lips on his, to draw more water from

him; and when the water all was gone she breathed into him, forcing air to fill his lungs. Dan felt — strange. Sensually aroused, almost, but in a way that only seemed erotic.

This is what it's like to be in love, he thought. And maybe that was right, or maybe it was just desire obscuring his imagination.

She breathed into him three times, each breath more intense and dearer than the next, and then Dan felt his paralysis give way.

"What did you do?" he asked, reaching up to touch her cheek. As he touched her he realized that he had no business touching her, that no matter how he felt they weren't lovers and there was no intimacy between them, no love but the love we each have for the ones we see in need. He pulled away. "I'm sorry," he said. "I didn't mean —"

She shook her head, and took his hand, and pressed it back against her cheek. "Hush," she said.

And that was all the words between them.

For the longest while.

And then after that long while, Dan realized that the deadman Elvis was standing a few feet from them, watching them, waiting for them. He looked up to face the deadman and he felt so ashamed, so naked and embarrassed, but what could he do?

"Elvis," Dan said. "I didn't know you were here."

The deadman's frown deepened. "Don't call me that," he said. "Especially not here."

"Don't call you what?" the woman asked. "I don't understand."

The deadman just shook his head. "We've got to go," he said. "We're wasting time."

Dan wiped the water away from his eyes. "All right," he said. "I'm ready."

The deadman turned to the woman. "You're coming with us, aren't you?"

"I —" she said, "I —"

Elvis knelt beside her, touched her shoulder, looked her in the eye. "It's going to be all right," he said. "Come with us. You'll be fine."

And then she cried and cried and cried, and Dan wanted to take her in his arms and comfort her, because he ached to hear her in such pain.

But he couldn't.

Because she was in the deadman's arms, and those were all the arms she needed.

•

There was no wind when Dan climbed into the boat, but that didn't seem to worry the deadman. He untied them from the withered ash, pushed their boat away from the shore, and opened up the sail. As soon as he did the hot wind found them, and the boat sped downstream more quickly than Dan ever imagined that it could.

He took his seat by the boat's stern, and watched the shore. He tried not to think about the damned ones below him in the water, and he tried even harder not to think about the girl.

It wasn't much use. He knew the damned were down there, and the girl — he still hurt every time he caught a glimpse of her. He didn't want to know why. He didn't want to imagine!

But he knew, and his imagination ran away with him, and away, and away. It brought him awful things that left Dan shivering and ill.

That was just the water, Dan tried to think. He'd took too much water in his lungs, and it wasn't just water but the damnable water of the River Styx, and of course it gave him vapors. Of course!

But Dan knew better.

A while after dark he felt sick and very tired, and he went belowdeck to find his bunk and rest.

After a while he slept, and as he slept nightmares came to him. But no matter how bad those nightmares were, they were better than the troubles that plagued his waking mind.

Somewhere in the night the girl came to him — he woke to feel her slip beneath the sheets beside him, and now she pressed herself against him as close as close could be.

Dan thought, no, no, *I can't do this, I can't go sleeping with some other guy's woman,* and he tried to tell her that he couldn't but the words wouldn't come to him. And then it didn't matter whether she was his or Dan's or nobody's woman but her own, because she touched him and he wanted her and the desire was on him intense beyond thinking, and Dan was lost.

Lost inside desire and away away in Hell.

He wanted her more than anything or anyone he'd ever wanted in his life, and he was sure, and he knew in his heart that if he could marry her that moment he would.

When he thought that thunder pealed long and slow somewhere a thousand miles away, and Dan knew he'd plighted himself.

"I love you," he said, and she said she loved him too, and she kissed his lips so gentle and so intimate and true, and God he wanted her, and loved her, and needed her as dearly as he need life itself.

There was something very different, now. Dan could feel it. Different about them, about their surroundings, about the world and damnation and everything that surrounded them.

"Take me," she said, and he did.

A long time after they were done Dan looked up from their bed, looked out through the door swinging freely on its hinge, and saw that they'd left the river.

He knew that the moment that he looked up, because there was fire everywhere all around them, fire and light and the embers of damnation, and they were sailing on the Lake of Fire toward the Bosphorus of Hell.

Memphis, Tennessee
September 1952

The celebration on the ridgeline over Memphis was a party no one ever could forget. The food was better than it could be; barbecue more pungent, spicy, and intense; the companionship dearer and more lively than any other fellowship of man.

But it didn't do anything for Robert Johnson.

All he could think about was his wife, and his darling daughter not even three days old, and how the hell could destiny take him now from a life that he'd only just come to prize. . . ?

But it did. It always works that way, doesn't it? The things we lose before we come to love them are things we might just as well have never owned; but when life leaves us without the things we love we mourn them till we rail against their loss.

Furry Lewis saw him alone and mourning in the shadow of three pines, and he asked him what was wrong.

"I miss my little girl, is all," he said. "I hardly even know her."

Furry Lewis frowned and nodded. Furry Lewis wasn't any deadman. He was alive — he was one of maybe seven dozen living bluesmen who'd come to play that song upon the ridge. He didn't have a family himself, but he could see the ghost of Robert Johnson's loss. "I take you down," he said. "I take you down, if that's what you want. We got a little time."

"To Memphis. . . ?"

"If that's what you want." He kicked a stone, and sent it rolling down; it could have rolled forever down that ridge for all that Robert Johnson saw.

"All right, then. You say we got the time, let's go."

Greenville, Mississippi
The Present

Emma woke jittery and covered with sweat late in the warm Greenville afternoon. When she woke she saw Leadbelly still sat in the seat across from her — he was deep asleep, but he was still holding his guitar, and his fingers still rested on the strings, caressing faint and beautiful music from them.

"I saw her," Emma said. "I saw my baby in my dream. She was in New Orleans, scared and lost and all alone."

The deadman's eyes flickered open drowsily. "You dreamed your child?" he asked. "I knew you would."

"I've got to go to her," Emma said. "My darling needs me."

The deadman nodded. "Yes," he said. "She needs us both."

"Us both. . . ?"

The deadman nodded. "I'm coming with you," he said. "I know the Mansion in New Orleans."

And Emma should have known then, she really should have. Because she hadn't mentioned the Mansion, and till that moment hadn't realized what to call it.

But she didn't realize, and she didn't think too clearly, because after all she was still half asleep. "Okay," she said. "Let's go."

Leadbelly stood up, slung his guitar over his shoulder, and started toward the door. "I'm already waiting," he said.

And then he was gone.

When Emma got out to her car she found him waiting for her in the front passenger seat, no matter how she had the keys, no matter how she'd locked things tight when she'd got out of the car the day before.

Five minutes later they were on the road, rolling south toward New Orleans as quickly as Emma could drive. Three times that night she was sure she'd get pulled over for a ticket, but every time the deadman sang and the policeman faded away with the distance in the night.

They got to New Orleans three hours before sunrise that next morning — but it was a long while before they found Lisa.

Memphis, Tennessee
September 1952

Robert Johnson felt like a burglar as he opened the door to his own home. He'd only been gone for hours, but that little wooden house down by the Memphis waterfront was already strange to him, and he felt like a trespasser to walk in without knocking.

"Ginny. . . ?" he called. "Baby, I got company, all right?"

His wife was upstairs with the baby. She was in bed as she'd been abed three days now, recovering from her labor.

"Is that you, Tom?" Robert Johnson's wife called him Tom because that was how she knew him, as Hinky Tom.

"Yes, baby, it's me. Are you decent for company? I got a friend here wants to meet you and baby Emma."

"Come on up, Tom," she said. "I'm pleased to meet your friend."

Robert Johnson nodded to Furry Lewis, who was still out by the car, waiting to see if he were welcome. "It's all right, Furry," Johnson said. "C'mon on up. Door ain't locked." And then he hurried up the stairs to see his woman and his daughter, not bothering to look back and see if the other man followed him.

His wife Virginia smiled when she saw him — but only for a moment. Because it only took a moment to see the expression on her husband's face. And that expression was a mask of fear and dread — the kind of countenance that passes from one love to another as though it were wildfire; as though it were some plague as contagious as the cough.

"What's wrong, Tom?" Virginia asked, already half as frightened as her man.

"It's come to something awful, Ginny," he told her. "I come back to say goodbye."

"Oh *Tom*," Virginia said, and now she was a woman made of tears where before she'd been an angel made of gossamer and gold. *"Tom."*

And what could Robert Johnson do? He went to her and wrapped his arms around her, and he told her that he always loved her and that he'd be back for her, no matter if the maw of Hell should devour him.

He didn't mean it badly, but that oath was as false as it was sincere, profanely false, and it damned him as surely as the trueness of his song. Because it grew naturally from his love for his wife and child, it was a grave oath and a precious one; he loved his family too dearly ever to repent it.

Then like out of nowhere there came the sound of a throat clearing just behind them, and Robert Johnson whirled around to face the intrusion —

Which was Furry Lewis, come to call on them just as he'd been invited.

"You folks need some time alone? — I can wait in the car, if you like."

Virginia raised a hand and eased her husband just far enough aside that she could look the visitor in the eye. "Don't be silly," she said. "I want you to know my daughter."

And then she lifted her sleeping infant in her arms and lifted her high enough for everyone to see. "Her name is Emma," Virginia said. "She's precious as the stars."

Greenville, Mississippi
The Present

When Emma and Leadbelly got to New Orleans the deadman told her they had to get a hotel room.

"I don't understand," Emma said. "What do we need with

a hotel room? — I'm here to find my little girl, not to visit."

"Your baby's at the Mansion," Leadbelly told her. "If you going to get yourself presented at the Mansion, you got to make yourself presentable."

Presented? Presentable? — those were words that made no sense to Emma. "I saw a mansion in my dream," Emma said. "I didn't see no presentation."

"Trust me," Leadbelly said. And Emma shrugged and sighed and worried some, but she didn't see how she had any choice but to do like he said.

So she trusted him.

Which was something that she never ever ever should have done.

They found a cheap and sleazy rendezvous motel a mile and a half south of New Orleans, and Emma checked them in as Mr. and Mrs. Smith. That was a mistake, just like the others, but it wasn't the worst mistake she made that day — not by half.

There were two double beds in the room; Leadbelly went to the nearer one as soon as he got in the door. He sprawled himself out in the center and folded his arms behind his head and smiled like the cat who caught a jaybird.

"We might as well get some rest," he said, still smiling. "They won't have us down to the Mansion till after midnight."

"Midnight," Emma said. "Is that so?"

"It's a natural fact."

"I see," Emma said. She pursed her lips. "Well, you go ahead and get some rest, then. I'm going to get myself a shower while I can."

She carried her suitcase into the bathroom, turned on the hot water, and closed and locked the door behind her.

She took as long and hot a shower as she could bear to, but no matter how she washed herself she couldn't scrub away the greasy gritty feeling all those days of travel had pressed into her skin.

I need to soak, she thought, and decided that she might as well. Pressed the drain lever and closed the shower valve to let hot water stream out the faucet into the tub, then eased her aching body down and put her tired feet up on the rim of the tub.

And rested soaking in the steamy water for hours till the bath went cool. Maybe she slept that way, or maybe she only rested numbly half awake; later on she was never sure.

When the water was cool enough to chill her, Emma lifted herself from the tub, dried herself and dressed in her warm flannel nightgown.

Gathered up her dirty clothes and left the bathroom to tuck herself beneath the warm soft blankets on the empty bed —

Only it didn't work out like that. Because the moment she stepped out the bathroom door the deadman was all over her like a lover, touching her and whispering in her ear and making promises he never meant to keep.

"What are you doing?" Emma asked. "What do you think you're doing?"

"Baby," Leadbelly said. "Oh baby. . . !"

Emma kneed him, *hard*. The deadman groaned and went limp.

Fell to the floor, holding himself. Where he made the saddest sound, a piteous sound, almost — as if he weren't the man who'd just damn near tried to force himself on her, but some poor mistreated child.

Emma ignored him. She stepped away, crossed the room to find her bed —

As the deadman glared up at her with eyes that glinted wildly, so full of lust and rage and indignation —

"You want me," he said. "You know you do."

Emma shook her head. "I don't."

He looked — like a predator about to leap. Like he was about to attack her, to grab her and rip off her clothes and have her whether she wanted him or not —

And then the promise of violence in his eyes began to fade. "Baby. . . ."

"Don't you 'baby' me," Emma said.

"You want me to help you find your little girl or not?" Leadbelly asked.

Emma scowled at him. "Of course I want your help," she said. "But I want you to keep your hands to yourself, too. If that means you won't help me, then I'll help myself."

Leadbelly swore under his breath, but he didn't raise a hand to her. He just sat there on the floor, glaring at Emma as she tucked herself beneath the covers and tried to settle off to sleep.

After a while he sulked away to his bed. When she heard him move Emma thought *What am I doing here? I got no business sleeping in a room with a man like that.* That was right, wasn't it? She needed to get up and go out to the car, lock the doors and put the seat back and try to pretend she was someplace safe — but every time she got up to move she found herself still lying abed in the hotel room, and it was like she was in a dream, and then she realized that it was a dream, and she'd only got up and left that place a dreaming, not for real, and she got up and left only to discover that was a dream too, and on, and on. . . .

After a while the deadman seemed to sleep, and Emma thought that maybe it was safe here after all. But even as he slept Emma could feel his anger — all seething and bitter like the vapor from a man who's met an insult he can't deny or answer.

And maybe he was insulted, and maybe he was enraged. But whether he was or not he didn't say or do anything to her.

In some ways that scared Emma most of all — because she could feel how mad he was, and she knew he meant to do something, and the more he waited to retaliate the worse it had to be.

Or maybe not. Maybe he just forgot. Emma waited and waited for him to come to her and ravish her in her sleep, but he never did; and when he woke he treated her well enough, no matter how he wasn't friendly.

The deadman yawned, sat up in his bed. "Wake up," he said. "We got to take you downtown for a presentation."

Emma shivered as she rubbed her eyes. "I still don't understand," she said. "I come down here looking for my little girl. What the devil has that got to do with presentation?"

Leadbelly rolled his eyes. "It's got everything, that's what," he said. "Your baby went down to the Mansion. If you want her back that's where you've got to go."

"I don't like it," Emma said. "Not one solitary bit."

But she went to the bathroom and put on the best dress in her suitcase all the same. When she was done she left the bathroom and asked Leadbelly what he thought, and the dead-man smiled at her hungrily.

"You look fine," Leadbelly said. "You look mighty fine."

"That's good," Emma said. "But don't go looking at me like that, you hear?"

Leadbelly scowled and muttered something cruel, but he looked away all the same.

"Let's go," he said. "It's getting late."

Emma shrugged. "If you say it is, it is," she said. And followed him out the motel-room door.

When they got into the car the deadman started giving her all kinds of strange directions — first into downtown New Orleans and the French Quarter by a roundabout approach, then south along the river road where the French Quarter gave way to a maze of rotted houses, burned-down warehouses, and collapsing docks.

Into a part of the city you can't find by accident, unless you're touched and marked, or guided by a soul who knows the Devil.

The ones who know that place call it the Devil's Quarter of New Orleans. The Devil doesn't go there often nowadays, because he doesn't have to — the world has changed across the years, and now it does the Devil's handiwork without him. These days the Devil's Quarter is a shriveled deadland, all but empty and abandoned — all of it but the Mansion. The Mansion never died. It never could, and never would, no matter what.

"That's the place," Leadbelly said, but Emma already knew. She recognized that place from her Lisa dream back up in Greenville. She remembered every detail of that dream, and she never would forget a mite of it. "You can pull right on up the drive. Valet will park the car for you."

Emma never had much use for valets; she liked to park her own car. "That's all right," she said. "I'll park out here on the road."

"Suit yourself," the deadman said — and then he smiled, bright and wide. "It ain't going to matter in the end."

But he was wrong. Just once that night, he was wrong; and after all the terrible mistakes Emma made those days in Green-

ville and New Orleans, it was an act just as seemingly inconse-
quential that saved her: the place she parked her car.

But it makes sense, in a way — because the tiny things that
led her down the damnable path were honest mistakes, and the
thing that saved her was an honest virtue, almost equal. What
saved her was her nature and the nature of her heart.

Memphis, Tennessee
September 1952

They visited three hours with Robert Johnson's wife and
daughter, and then he kissed his wife goodbye.

"I'll miss you, darling," he said before he left. "I swear I will
return."

Virginia smiled sadly and tried hard not to cry. She didn't
say the truth that ached her heart.

"I love you, Tom," she said. "Your daughter loves you too."

"I know she does," said Robert Johnson, and he kissed
Emma on the forehead and promised her the stars.

And then he left without looking back, because he knew that
if he did he'd break his heart.

Furry Lewis was already in the car, waiting for him. "Running late," old Furry said. "Looks like we better hurry."

He drove his car fast and a little reckless — he hardly stopped
at stop signs, and he didn't read no speed signs, and twice he
rolled through stoplights before they changed to favor him.
Robert Johnson was certain some policeman was going to pull
them over for a ticket, but none ever did. They made damn
good time, in fact — five minutes after they pulled away from
Robert Johnson's driveway they were starting up the ridge-road
where the moon was waiting for them —

And then that big black Cadillac came round the bend ahead
of them.

And swerved hard like it was out of control, back and forth
across both lanes, and when it stopped it stopped but good,
cutting them off. If Furry Lewis hadn't had some incredible
kind of reflexes he would've plowed right into it, killing them
both for certain —

And Robert Johnson looked up, and he saw who it was
behind the wheel of that car.

Which was Leadbelly.

Smiling at them hungrily from behind the wheel, and right there while they looked at him he reached over onto the passenger seat to get something, and when he came up again there was a short-barrel shotgun in his arms, and suddenly he was blasting —

— *blasting!* —

Shooting at them with that goddamn thing, and if Furry Lewis hadn't already had that car of his into fast reverse winding down that bluff they would have gone to meet the Maker, there and then.

Upon the Lake of Fire
Approaching the Bosphorus of Hell
Timeless

On toward midday they sighted land, and for a moment Dan thought they'd found their destination.

"We're here," he said. "Where the hell are we?"

Dead Elvis just laughed. "We're in Hell, all right," he said. "But this isn't where we're going."

"Oh," Dan said. "What is that?"

The deadman pointed at a wide gap in the wall of granite rising up before them. "That's the Bosphorus of Hell," he said. "Beyond it lie the fallen city Firgard and the Sea of Fire and Ice."

"We're going to Firgard, then?"

Elvis shook his head. "No. We're going past it — through the Sea of Fire and Ice; past the Infernal Hellespont; into the Bay of Ages and across it to the Mansion called Defiance."

"That sounds like a long way," Dan said.

Elvis shrugged. "The Lake of Fire goes on forever if you let it," he said. "It stretches farther than anyone could sail. Next to that Defiance is as close as it could be."

As Dan watched the boat drew down into the passage, and now the granite cliffs surrounded them, and the fire that they sailed upon suffused the air around them with heat and ash and foul vapors. In places great waves of flame rose up beneath them, threatening to smash them into one cliff or the other; and once they passed a fiery whirlpool vortex, a fire-spout tornado that promised to consume them — but Elvis pulled hard on the ropes that tended their sails, and now a hot wind blew them clear.

"That was close," Dan said. "It would have been the end of us, if that fire spout had touched us."

Dead Elvis shrugged. "Maybe," he said. "Maybe not." He gestured at the bunk. "You ought to wake her," he said. "We're going to need her soon."

"The girl, you mean?"

Elvis laughed. "That girl of yours is a woman, boy. Her name is Polly Ann."

"Polly Ann. . . ? You know her?"

Elvis hummed a few bars, and then he sang a half-verse from "John Henry": " 'Polly could drive steel just like a man, yes, yes, sweet Polly could drive steel just like a man.' " And then he laughed and laughed, but Dan didn't think it was so funny.

"You ought to show a little respect," he said. "You really should."

Elvis laughed again. "Believe me, son," he said, "I couldn't regard that lady more highly than I do."

Memphis, Tennessee
September 1952

Furry Lewis backed them up behind the bend and parked here, out of the line of Huddie Ledbetter's shotgun fire.

"What're we going to do?" Robert Johnson asked.

"I ain't got the first idea," Furry Lewis told him. "Maybe get around him somehow?"

Robert Johnson snorted. "How we going to do that with him shooting at us?"

Furry Lewis looked thoughtful, and then his face brightened, and he started to answer — but he never got to finish.

Because that was when that big black Cadillac came roaring round the bend, and old Leadbelly had his shotgun hanging out the window, braced against the doorjamb, and when he saw the car with Robert Johnson and Furry Lewis he started shooting.

Damned near got them, too — as it was he took out one of the windows in the back.

Furry Lewis didn't take the time to think, or if there was any thinking he'd done it all already — because as soon as the Cadillac come around the corner he got that Buick of his into gear and stomped on the gas pedal.

And put that vehicle in motion.

Only there wasn't no place to go. Down the road was a long straightaway that went from there to Memphis, and uproad was Leadbelly with his shotgun, trying to blast them both to Hell. Left off the road was a sheer drop right off the bluff — and right was a forty-degree grade over rough terrain.

Straight up to the bluff.

And Furry did the only thing he could.

He went right, the hard way, up a grade so steep that the dirt damn near flew out from under them, and all behind them went big avalanche clusters of sandstone rocks and loose red dust, and that poor old Buick hardly had the engine for it.

Leadbelly would have got them, easy, if it hadn't been for the looseness of the dirt. Because even though it took him a while to get the Caddy turned around and headed up the incline, he had a hell of a lot more engine for the task than that old Buick did, and he would have caught them in a second if he hadn't had to eat their dust.

Halfway up the bluff he caught them, and tried to blast them off the side of it, and would have, too, except his gun was clean of shells by then. Robert Johnson looked back just then to see him pulling the trigger over and over when it didn't do no good, and now he swore and rammed the back end of the Buick with his Cadillac —

That was a mistake.

Because even though it sent the Buick reeling off to the left, it did a damn sight worse to the Caddy. Leadbelly bumped into the Buick, and the traction went loose underneath his tires, and suddenly he was sliding downhill with his tires spinning out of touch with the dirt, sliding sideways downhill till now his car went end over end down the hill —

And they were safe.

And there was nothing to do but roll back up onto the road and drive the rest of the way to the top of the bluff.

Right? Right. . . ?

Only it didn't work out that way. Oh, Furry Lewis found the road just over the rise, and he drove on it like he meant to. But Leadbelly wasn't any more gone than a deadman's curse. They hadn't gone more than a quarter-mile when the Cadillac roared around a bend behind them, and there he was, just like Robert Johnson knew he'd be, and what else do you expect from a deadman like Huddie Ledbetter, seventh of the Seven Kings?

"Damn," said Furry Lewis. "Damn damn damn."

"You better hurry," Robert Johnson said. "He's catching up with us right quick."

Furry Lewis pressed the accelerator harder, but it didn't make no never mind. "This old Buick ain't going to go no faster," he said. "We got all the fast it's going to give."

It was true, too — the Buick's engine wasn't any match for the big V-8 underneath the Cadillac's hood.

"What the hell you going to do?"

Furry Lewis sighed. "Only thing I can do," he said. "Drive harder and smarter than he can."

Hard left off the road again, and now they were roaring up the bluff face, slipping and sliding and half the time their tires weren't in any kind of contact with the soil, and now they stalled and slipped five feet back down the hillside before they slammed into a big rock and found their purchase once again.

"Christ almighty," Robert Johnson said, so scared he didn't even think of how he'd spoken so profane. He didn't have no chance to think, neither, because just then there came another three blasts from Huddie Ledbetter's shotgun, blam! BLAM! *BLAM!*, and one of the explosions took out the Buick's rear window, pointy spray-shards of glass went flying everywhere, through their clothes, slivers of the stuff into their skin like needles, bad, bad, automobile windows were like that back before they started using that glass that busts up into cubes.

"Damn," said Furry, and he jammed down on the accelerator, but the Buick didn't go no faster. Worse, it lost traction again, and now they were sliding down the incline —

"He's going to get us," Robert Johnson said. "Won't take him but a minute to get here."

Furry Lewis stole a glance back over his shoulder. "No," he

said. "Look — he's going up to catch us at the next rise."

Robert Johnson made an exasperated sound, and then he swore. "Can't win for losing," he said. "Got us either way we go."

Furry Lewis looked back and forth and back again, and then he said, "Hell with that."

And turned that car around, and got the Buick moving down that ridge road about as fast as it could go.

By the time Leadbelly figured out they weren't going up to meet him, that Buick was *long* gone.

When they were far enough down the road for Robert Johnson to stop expecting Leadbelly's shotgun to blast him to kingdom come, it finally occurred to him that running away wasn't going to get them up the ridge. "What you doing, man?" he asked. "They need us up there."

Furry Lewis grinned. "I got an idea," he said. "I'm going to take this thing south past the Mississippi line, then come round back the east way."

And he did exactly that, no matter how long it took — drove south along the river road through Memphis, south and south past the Mississippi line; now east along the old cow trail that ran from Nashville to the Mississippi. Twenty minutes down that, then a hard left onto a dirt road that would lead them to the Memphis bluff.

And all that way they never saw a solitary sign of Huddie Ledbetter. When they saw the bluff rise up before them Robert Johnson came to think they'd actually done it — slipped past that murderous deadman to make it up the ridge —

And then they came round the last bend before the bluff, and there was Huddie's Cadillac, parked square across the narrow dirt road.

"Aw hell," said Robert Johnson. But Furry Lewis didn't look disturbed.

"It's okay," he said. "I saw this coming. I got a way around it."

"What?"

"Get down," he said. "I'm going to gun this thing."

And he slammed down on the Buick's accelerator so hard it made the valve-heads rattle. Bore right down on Leadbelly, who was still trying to get his shotgun cocked and aimed at them, but they were moving too fast, there wasn't time, and Furry's Buick hit the rear panel of the Caddy as Furry drove into the shoulder, knocked the Cadillac spinning, damn near drove the Buick into the ditch on the far side of the shoulder, but no, no, they were pulling through, bounce and slam and Robert Johnson damn near went flying through the windshield, then wham back down into his seat, and there's the Cadillac behind them where Leadbelly's still trying to get that in gear, but it don't do him no good, no good at all, because he's sidewise now and where he goes when he puts the car in gear is straight into that damn ditch, Christ on a crutch look at him swear.

"Whoa," said Robert Johnson. "Nice job."

"Don't get excited," Furry Lewis told him. "He's going to be back in a minute."

"Then hurry," Robert Johnson said. "We ain't got that far to go."

Furry Lewis sighed. "I do my best," he said. "I can't make no promises."

Now the road pulled along another cutaway, zagging here and zigging there as it followed the contour of the rise up the back end of the bluff. Once they nearly went sailing off the edge of a hairpin turn, one wheel over and spinning wild over the cliff edge, and it was going to fall, they were going to fall, it was over over over — no. The Buick found its traction again, and the off wheel found dirt, and they were alive, they were going to live thank God — Furry slowed the car when they came to the next hairpin, less they damn near fall all over again, and Furry said "He's right behind us, damn damn damn, get your guitar this is the bluff get your guitar —"

As they roared around a hairpin turn —

— as Leadbelly's Cadillac slammed into the back end of the Buick —

— as Robert Johnson, puzzled, reached into the back seat to fetch his guitar —

— and Furry Lewis screamed, *"Out!"* as he reached across Robert Johnson's lap to open the passenger door, pulled back and gave him a good hard shove on the shoulder —

— and Robert Johnson went flying.

Out the door, onto the road, into the cliff wall opposite.

As Furry Lewis slammed on his brakes and pulled the Buick's steering wheel hard to the left. The Cadillac slammed into the Buick's side, and the momentum of the impact carried both cars over the edge of the bluff.

For the longest time Robert Johnson lay beaten and broken and disoriented in the place where the bluff met the road.

And then he began to hear the music.

Up on the bluff.

So beautiful, that music. It was the number Blind Willie played that morning he first met Robert Johnson in the cabin on the bluff — "The Ode to Joy," recut and remade and syncopated into blues, and it was intensely beautiful. Beautiful that morning in the cabin, and infinitely more beautiful now as two hundred *giftie* bluesmen live and dead played the melody in rounds.

Beautiful so beautiful Robert Johnson cried to hear it.

And slung his battered guitar over his aching back.

And clawed his way to the summit of the bluff.

●

When Robert Johnson reached the summit someone gasped and three dozen voices said "He's here!" and the great King — there beside him at the summit — nodded and whispered that he'd known Robert Johnson would arrive. A murmur washed back and forth across the crowd, and when it subsided the rounding ode reached a new intensity.

Robert Johnson brushed his hands against one another, trying to clean the grit that'd ground itself into his skin as he'd climbed the bluff, but it didn't do much good. He pulled his guitar around, and found its strings, caressed its frets.

And waited for the song to come to him.

Now he stole a glance at the great King, and saw that the Lady stood beside him. She looked — like a doting wife, almost. Such a strange thing for a Lady such as her! An angel from on high, standing by John Henry loving him like a bride!

But then John Henry was the King, and when Robert Johnson watched him play he saw that same magnificence he felt when he stood before the Lady.

"*Santa,*" Robert Johnson said, and she turned for a moment to smile on him, and Robert Johnson was complete.

•

After a while the Eye of the World appeared in the sky above the bluff, and Robert Johnson knew the end was coming for them.

It was so crazed, that Eye. Battered in a thousand thousand fragments that only held to one another because the Lady loved them so. When he looked at it Robert Johnson knew that soon, too soon that love would no longer contain the Eye, and when it flew asunder the end would be upon them.

And in a measure as great as any measure could be, that end would be his fault.

Robert Johnson felt so sad.

He stole another glance at the Lady, and he saw her kiss the great King and step away into the sky.

Into the sky and across it, till now she stood before the widening Eye — which opened like a portal to show the great receiving hall in the Mansion called Defiance.

After a moment she stepped through the open portal.

Inside that hall ten thousand devils set upon her, as if they meant to tear her limb from limb —

And Robert Johnson knew that it was time for him to sing.

As "The Ode to Joy" faded all around him, and Robert Johnson sang the words that Blind Willie gave him.

The tune was the tune we all know as "When the Saints Come Marching In," and the first three verses were verses of that song.

But the third verse was something else entirely, and I can't recount it here entirely, for the words should burn this paper. But they began like this:

> Now when the moon
>   Go down in blood
> Now when the moon
>   Go down in blood

You can hear that much on some recordings, if you look far and wide enough. But you will never ever hear the whole entire.

As Robert Johnson sang, the Eye of the World went red as

fire; and now slowly slowly it descended toward the bluff. As it fell the cracks grew wider and wider still, like bloodshot veins widening until the blood consumed it all, and the moon came down in blood, just as Robert Johnson sang.

> Now when the Crown
>   The Lord was off
> Now when the Crown
>   The Lord was off

And Robert Johnson saw that crown, now, though he'd never seen it once before: the *giftie's* dearest gift, and it sat upon the great King's head. It was beautiful and glorious, brilliant as ten thousand jewels, and as the Eye fell to earth the crown tumbled from John Henry's head and clattered down the bluff, splintering in jewelry as it fell.

Robert Johnson expected the Eye to fall asunder, but it never did, not even as the devils dragged the Lady down to beat her bloody, no, no, that was the magic of the song that Blind Willie gave him: it was music made of magic, precious of the good Love of the Lord, and where it held the air no foul thing could ever triumph entirely.

But after two more verses the song was done.

And when his song was done the Eye of the World burst asunder, till now a great fiery vortex consumed it — engulfing every living thing around it.

But no matter how the fire could consume him, the great King didn't yield to it. "Sing!" he shouted, and he played the remade "Ode to Joy."

And as his song rose out of the maelstrom, it touched everything and everyone that heard it, and his host sang with him, now, the throng of Kings and bluesmen and Doctors sang and played that song whose heart is God's dear love for man, and the fire burned everywhere but in their hearts.

When the devils in the vortex that once had been the Eye heard that song, they ran for the sake of all that they held dear, for no evil thing can survive unchanged if it knows the Love of the Lord, and now the Lady lay alone and broken in the Great Hall of the Mansion.

The great King, still singing, nodded to Robert Johnson, and now that bluesman picked up the melody in round, and stepped into the vortex to bring the Lady to her feet.

"Lady, Lady," Robert Johnson said, "it's over now, the devils all are gone."

In the distance through the vortex Eye Robert Johnson could still hear the song that was God's Love, and it made him strong to bear the sight of one so beautiful so horribly abused, for the Lady was a bloody ruin.

"It's over now," he said, and then he cried, because he hurt so bad to see her.

And now finally the Lady roused from her unconsciousness. She looked up, and saw Robert Johnson and the Great Hall and the shattered remnants of the Eye. And she said, "No, no, no, it isn't done."

And she gathered the broken fragments of the Eye, and fit them into one another as though they were a puzzle. She tried to fuse them back to one another as she had so many years before, but the pieces were alien to one another now, and nothing she could do would make them bond to one another.

As the legions of the damned returned to Lucifer's great hall, and made ready to devour them once and for all.

"Sing," she said, "and your song will hold them all at bay."

And then she led him down the corridors of Hell.

Miles and miles, until they reached that only sacred glade in all damnation — the place where Our Lady of Sorrows met with her Repentance, and found Salvation there; the glade in Blue Hell that once had stood upon the most beautiful isle in all the earthly world; the place that once contained the earthly facet of the Eye of the World, back when the Eye still looked on Heaven. There in that glade beneath the water of her sacred stream she set the broken pieces of the Eye, and the cool clean water surrounded the disparate fragments that were the Eye. They held it true because it covered them, joining them, but it could not weld them whole.

When she was done, the singers on the bluff collapsed from exhaustion, and the fiery vortex consumed them all.

When it was done there was not a ghost among them, live or otherwise. The vapors of the hoodoo Kings were pale gasses that could hardly influence a dream, much less walk the earth; and when they were gone the great halls of the Mountain Kings collapsed in ruin, and an awful pestilence fell down upon the people.

An awful, awful, awful pestilence.

A pestilence where things that seem fair were always foul, where people who get their dearest wishes have those wishes destroy them; a pestilence where love and compassion destroy people they never meant to hurt.

In the years that followed the people came into every gift they'd ever dreamed.

And then those gifts destroyed them.

Robert Johnson cried out in agony and loss when he saw the hoodoo masters die. When he cried the song that kept the damned away from him fell still, and in a moment they were on him. He died in an instant, and would have gone to his reward.

But how could he, when he'd sung that song? He knew that it was true, and he loved it as he'd loved his life. In time he came to have regrets, but no regret could ever mask the truth inside that song — and what repentance ever comes from those who know that they're right?

•

As the fire died, as the earthly facet of the Eye rose (still cracked and crazed, but held together by the only Godly water in all damnation), young Elvis Presley — who'd come to the wooded ridge a-hunting squirrels, and stumbled into destiny — wandered through the ashes and the vapors, gaping at the fading carnage. Here in a moment some great bluesman's bones grew dry and dusty, aging in a moment as though they'd seen ten thousand days and nights of storm and wind; there upon the summit the vaporous ghosts of Kings dispersed into the wind.

Now it began to rain, and the bones and the ashes and the vapors washed away into the river as though they'd never been.

As though no King had ever ruled the river delta, and the land were some petty province of politicians and presidents and barons of foul industry.

But in all that death and devastation, one relic did remain:

the great King's guitar. It lived because the Lady lived. It was she who'd made the hammer that rang like a bell, and as she survived it did as well.

And young Elvis Presley, stunned and astounded and agog as he wandered through the ruin, found it there.

And picked it up.

Carried it away, into his destiny.

Within the Bosphorus of Hell
Timeless

When they'd traveled ninety miles through the Bosphorus of Hell the maelstrom's intensity redoubled, and here the tiny boat was racked — tossed and tumbled in the fiery channel. A windstorm blew into the canyonlike passage, and with the wind came wet rain that steamed and sparked and spattered hot droplets as it touched the fiery sea, till now the rain became a hot steam fog that hid the rocks and hazards from them.

"Sing!" Elvis shouted. "You know the song!"

The boat rocked, and Dan tightened his grip on the rungs beside his seat. It didn't do him any good. The boat's keel hit something hard, so hard it damn near shattered. The impact sent Dan reeling across the deck, smashing his head into the starboard side.

"Not me," Dan said, pushing himself dizzily off the deck. He was dizzy, and he wanted to puke but knew he didn't dare, and he wanted to cry like a baby and maybe he did, who can say what a man does in a fog too thick to see? "You're the King," Dan said. "You know that song."

And that was true, but Dan knew it, too — when he said *that song* he knew the tune, and he knew he had to sing it no matter what he said.

Polly Ann began to hum.

"Don't be afraid," she sang, *"the storm's a song / song's a lover / love's a tempest / raging in your heart."*

Dan had never heard that song before, but he knew it all his life. And Hell knew it, too, for as she sang the steamy mist coalesced in droplets all around them.

"You're right," Dan said, and then joined her in the chorus.

As the maelstrom eased and the wind blew clear to drive

them south toward the meridian of Hell.

The Devil's Quarter of New Orleans
The Present

When Emma and Leadbelly reached the great front door of the Devil's Mansion, an elegant figure — Emma almost thought it was a gentleman, but after she looked him in the eye she knew that couldn't be — an elegant figure stepped out to receive them.

"My name is Emma Henderson," Emma said. "My mother was Virginia. This was once a man name of Huddie Ledbetter, but lately folks have called him Leadbelly."

As she spoke Leadbelly grinned, ear to ear; when she was done he took a bow.

The devil in the tux-and-tails — Emma knew he was a devil because his eyes were slitty snake-eyes, even if the rest of him looked human — the devil in the tux-and-tails nodded, turned sharply, and stepped back into the Mansion. When he was gone Emma asked Leadbelly who he was.

"I don't know his name," Leadbelly said. He smiled wickedly, and Emma knew he was about to lie. "I don't know much about this place. I only get here now and then."

Emma scowled. "I bet you don't," she said.

"I don't!" Leadbelly said. "I wouldn't lie to you."

His words rang so hollow that there wasn't any pretending about them. Emma huffed; Leadbelly didn't try to contradict her.

And then it didn't matter, because the devil with the fancy clothes reopened the door. He greeted them dryly, and showed them to the parlor.

"Wait here," the devil said, "until the Master calls for you. Find the hospitality of his house if that please you."

Emma thanked him; Leadbelly rubbed his hands.

"C'mon," he said when the devil was gone. "We going to roll the bones."

Emma gave him a cross look. "I'm not doing anything of the sort," she said. "I don't gamble with the Devil."

Leadbelly shook his head. "Ain't no call to gamble with the Devil," he said. "Remember, luck's a Lady."

Emma frowned again. "Don't fool yourself," she said. "This ain't no Lady's Mansion."

"Get on with you," Leadbelly said. "You coming or you not?"

Emma hesitated — and felt suddenly afraid. "You ain't leaving me alone here," she said. "What kind of fool you think I am?"

Leadbelly chuckled; he had a smug and greasy expression on his face. "My favorite kind," he said. "My very favorite one."

He wandered down a corridor lit bright with candelabras, to vanish through a door of beads that glittered bright as jewels. Emma hurried after him, because no matter how she dreaded to see that man gamble with the Devil, she dreaded aloneness in that place much worse.

Inside the glittering door was a casino, just as Emma had expected; she found Leadbelly standing at the roulette wheel, watching it hungrily.

"Give me a number," Leadbelly said.

"I won't give you nothing," Emma said.

"I said, 'Give me a number,' damn it. And I meant it."

Emma scowled. "And I said I wouldn't give you nothing, and I still won't give you nothing."

The wheelman grinned wide and hungry. "Double zero?" he asked.

Leadbelly grinned back at him. "That's what she gave me, all right," he said, and then he placed his bet.

Which lost — so badly that it cost him double to stay in.

When he saw that Leadbelly grabbed Emma by the wrist and looked her in the eye so angry, so enraged! "What kind of Lady are you?" he asked. "You ain't got no kind of luck."

"I wouldn't give you nothing," Emma said. "I said that and I meant it."

The deadman swore. "Woman," he said, but before he could go farther Emma cut him off.

"You said my little girl was here," she said. "You take me to her, Huddie Ledbetter. You take me to her now!"

Leadbelly swore under his breath, but he seemed to acquiesce. "Okay," he said. "Follow me down."

"What?"

"Follow me down," Leadbelly said, and he held out his hand to lead her away —

But before they could go a second step the doorman found them.

He tapped Leadbelly on the shoulder, and cleared his throat, and the dead hoodoo man whirled around as though he'd been challenged — to see the doorman standing behind him, watching coolly, almost imperiously.

"Oh," Leadbelly said, suddenly humble as a child. "Sir."

"The Master will see you now," the doorman said. "He's anxious that you hurry."

Within the Bosphorus of Hell
Approaching the Fallen City Firgard
Timeless

The calm lasted as long as they sang, but no one could sing forever. When his voice grew tired Dan tugged Elvis's sleeve to urge him on. *"You too,"* Dan sang. *"You too. You have to sing!"*

But the deadman only scowled and turned away.

"Damn you!" Dan shouted — and when he swore his song was broken. Polly's shattered too, just a moment later as she gaped at him.

And then the maelstrom had them. It rose up out of nowhere and in a moment, so powerful and intense that the first blast of it threw them half across the strait.

The second threw Dan into the bulkhead, knocking him senseless.

The third tore their sails from the rigging.

"Sing!" Elvis shouted — but by then it was too late.

Much, much too late.

For the gale that dashed them on the rocks was already in the air around them, and no song could have stopped it, no matter how pure or true. As Dan tried to find his voice it lifted them out of the fiery sea, carried them in air across the channel, and broke them on the rocks.

Damning them forever at the inner sphincter of the Bosphorus of Hell, by the Fallen City called Firgard.

An age ago the angels cast that city from the precipice of Heaven, and now where once it was an exalted Jewel of Heaven it is a ruin in Hell that writhes with the animate corpses of the damned. It lies on the south bank of the Hellish Bosphorus where that perilous channel meets the Sea of Fire and Ice.

"Swim!" Elvis shouted, pointing toward the shore. As he shouted the wrecking impact threw Dan off the deck, into the fiery sea —

Where he sank deep beneath the hot bright waves, and damn near drowned down in the blazing brine. The whiteness of the heat down there stunned and frightened him, and burned him, too, and for a long hard moment Dan could not tell which way was the surface and which way was deeper, hotter water, and he would have drowned, he surely surely would have drowned gasping and gagging on the fiery white plasm if Polly hadn't saved him.

She found him in the deep, as she'd found him in the River Styx, and saved him as she'd saved him there. Grabbed his collar, dragged him to the surface; pulled him through the burning brine and up onto the rocks that were the shore.

Pressed his diaphragm, easing the fiery water out his lungs; kissed him, drawing air.

Dan came around slowly. At first he hardly breathed at all without assistance, but now breath by breath he came back among the living, and he saw her, and he loved her, and he couldn't bear to ask her why she saved him because he was afraid to hear the answer.

"I love you," Dan said. His voice was weak — so weak he hardly heard himself. "I want to hold you here forever."

Polly smiled. "I love you too, Dan Alvarez," she said. Dan didn't understand, and he still didn't want to. He took her love as she gave it to him, without questioning it, and maybe that was the best thing all in all.

"We need help," Elvis said. Dan looked up to see that the deadman's white suit was filthy, soaked with ashy water, speckled with glowing and sputtering bits of emberous debris. "We have to go to the city."

He pointed at the rocks above them, and Dan looked up to see the city known as Firgard for the first time.

It's a dreadful place, Firgard. A city of broken splendor and horrific love; a place where foul things seem fair and fair things foul, where death and life, salvation and damnation twist around one another until no stranger can pare one from the other.

"You're out of your mind," Dan said.

Polly shook her head. "He's not," she said. "It isn't just the boat. There is an errand here we need to realize."

As she spoke she helped Dan to his feet. When he tried to answer her with protests she pressed a finger to her lips and shook her head.

"There isn't any other way," she said. "We've got to go."

The Devil's Quarter of New Orleans
The Present

The Devil's doorman led Emma and Leadbelly out the back door of the casino, into a great wide glass-ceilinged room. The room was bright with moonlight shining down upon them through the glass, and brighter with the light of a thousand crystal chandeliers. In its center was a wide spiral stairway — a rich, wide stair, wide enough for an army to descend walking side by side by side. Its marble steps were carpeted with red velvet; its banisters were bright polished gold.

Such ostentation, Emma thought. *You'd think the Devil had no shame.*

"This way," the doorman said, leading them down the stair.

The stairway went down on and on forever, so deep that Emma came to think they'd already descended to the center of the other, and then it still continued.

"Don't you get tired of these stairs?" Emma asked the doorman when she thought she couldn't go another step. "Got to be a time when even the Devil's too tired to go on."

The doorman only smiled. "The damned are all beyond despair," he said. "It isn't that much farther."

Outside the Fallen City Firgard
Hell
Timeless

Before they reached the ruined city they came upon a campfire.

Six ghosts and the shadow of a deadman sat around that

fire, each of them holding a guitar. The ghosts sat apart from the deadman's shadow — they seemed to shun him, in fact.

And perhaps they did shun him.

"That's Leadbelly," dead Elvis said, pointing at the shadow. "He isn't really here. But his shadow always follows the ghosts of the six Kings — because he was the seventh."

Dan felt as if every hair on his hide stood on end, but of course they didn't. It was just a chill, and chills like that are only natural in Hell. "The Seven Kings," he said. He'd never heard that phrase before, but he knew it in his heart, just as he'd always known the Kings themselves, no matter how he'd never thought of them as rulers.

"That ghost was Ma Rainey," Elvis said, and then he nodded at each of the ghostly Kings in turn. "That was Charlie Patton — Blind Lemon Jefferson — Blind Willie Johnson — Peetie Wheatstraw — and there, near the fire, that was once the great King himself, John Henry."

Dan frowned. "I thought 'John Henry' was just a song," he said. "A song about a man and a machine."

Elvis scowled. "John Henry was a lot of things," he said. "'He could make that hammer ring like a bell.'"

"I heard that said," Dan told him. "Lots of times. But I haven't ever heard any hammer ring like a bell."

"I bet you ain't heard it," dead Elvis said. "If you'd ever heard you wouldn't doubt, not for a moment."

Dan shook his head. "Of course I never heard," he said. "I wasn't born till twenty years after you stole that guitar off the bluff."

The air around them went very still for a moment, and Dan could feel the deadman seethe with anger —

And then he wheeled around and grabbed Dan by the collar, lifted him clear off his feet.

Started shouting.

"What the hell you mean by that, huh, boy? What the hell you mean, 'stole that guitar off the bluff'? Who the hell you think you're talking to? What the hell you think you're saying? Stole? *Stole?"*

"You stole it," Dan said. "I know you did. I saw you in my dream."

"I found it," Elvis said. "In the ashes. I didn't steal nothing, you hear me?"

"It wasn't rightfully yours," Dan said. "You know it wasn't."

"Shit," dead Elvis said. "You think it's rightly yours now?"

"Oh no," Dan said. "Not me. I brought it back to you. I'd bring it back to him," he said, nodding at vaporous John Henry, "if he was anything but a ghost."

"You're wrong," dead Elvis said, lowering Dan to the ground. "The Lady put it on you, just the same as she put it on me. It's yours no matter if you want it or you don't."

Dan backed away. "It's not," he said. "You aren't any ghost. That guitar's yours — you ought to take it. You got a problem with responsibility?"

The deadman swore and grabbed for Dan's collar again, but this time Dan had the sense to get out of his way. "I died to get away from that goddamn thing," he said. "I ain't about to let you put it on me, hear?"

Now Polly Ann had missed this altercation, because she'd waded back out among the rocks to get a few things (like the dead King's guitar) off their broken boat. She'd also missed the sight of Leadbelly's shadow — and of the ghostly Kings.

It was a hard thing when she did see them. Polly came up over the rise from the shore, and saw the fire and the shadow and the ghosts, and then she saw John Henry, and she screamed.

It was horrible, that scream. Horrible as anything Dan had seen or heard since they'd gone to Hell. Half of it was terror, but the other half was grief, and the fear and the sadness coiled 'round one another till they made Dan ache to hear them, and she dropped everything onto the rocks as though she didn't even realize what she had, and she ran to the ghostly King's side —

— ran to him —

— ran to him and wrapped her arms around him, and Dan felt jealousy cut through him like a knife, so hard, so sharp, so cruel, and now she wailed again entirely in anguish as she tumbled through the great King's ghostly arms.

Sobbed and sobbed and sobbed so sad, Dan almost felt for her through the curtain of his jealousy, and now one of the ghosts took up his guitar and sang, sang so beautiful so clear and true Dan could almost hear them Lord the song so beautiful so faint as the others joined him and the shadow of Leadbelly looked on resentfully. . . .

"What are they singing?" Dan asked. "I can't make out the words."

Elvis turned to look at him coldly. "I can't hear anything at all," he said. "That's what I been trying to tell you."

But Dan remembered "Jailhouse Rock" the way the deadman sang it in the motel room in Detroit, and he knew that was a lie. "Like hell," he said. "I bet you're hearing every word."

The deadman didn't answer. And then there wasn't time to answer, as a sudden storm blew up through the Bosphorus — hard and wild, a hailstorm cut with cold cold rain that stung them everywhere it touched.

"We'd better find shelter," dead Elvis shouted — and even though he shouted from almost close enough to touch, the storm beat so hard and loud that Dan could hardly hear him. "You get the girl. I'll get her stuff."

Dan didn't even think about what that meant — the moment was too hard and cold and frightening. He ran to Polly, who still lay sobbing among the rocks, lifted her to carry her away — and saw they were alone now, that the rain had killed the bonfire and driven the ghosts and their shadow away. He wanted to ask where they were gone and why they'd appeared before them, but they were gone, and there was no one to ask, and Polly sobbed and sobbed as Dan lifted her onto his shoulder and hurried toward the city of the damned.

Blue Hell
Timeless

Lisa and Robert Johnson wandered through Hell for hours and hours. All that time Lisa kept thinking that she should have been scared, and she should have been howling for her mother, but what she felt was — fascinated. And hungry, too, the way you feel hungry for something when you want to see more and more and more.

She should have been scared, she knew. The only reason she wouldn't feel scared was if she was a frightful thing herself, and she wasn't any horror, she was Lisa! Little baby Lisa, that's all!

Only that wasn't all she was, and she knew it.

Where they started out — in the tunnel that led down from the basement — everything was all fire and brimstone, just like in the picture books when somebody draws Hell.

But it didn't stay that way.

Step by step the walls around them grew darker and more fetid, till now Lisa could smell something dank and earthy as rotting humus and jungle earth —

— and now they came upon a wide mahogany door, and Robert Johnson freed the bolt and let it open wide.

He stepped through and stood on the far side, waiting for her. Lisa followed him gingerly. She was certain in her heart that she was following Robert Johnson into a trap. A trap, a trap, a real trap, she could feel the waiting lurking malevolence in that place, and Robert Johnson ought to feel it, too, if he had any sense he wouldn't go in there what kind of an idiot was he, anyway?

"This is Blue Hell," Robert Johnson said. "It used to be an island on the world."

As he spoke the mahogany door slammed shut of its own accord behind them, and Lisa heard the bolt on the far side of the door bang home.

And they were trapped.

Trapped in a fetid jungle blooming thick with dark blue foliage.

So blue, that place. Everything about it was blue — the leaves, the grass, the trees, the light, so blue, so blue, was it a trick of the blue light that surrounded them or was everything really so blue. . . ?

She looked at Robert Johnson, to see if the light would make him blue, but his complexion was too dark to take on color; she looked at her hands and saw that the light and the reflections cast her just-so-slightly blue, but nowhere near as blue as her surroundings.

"I don't understand," Lisa said. "What do you mean, it used to be an island? Why do they call it Blue Hell?"

Robert Johnson only answered her second question. "Just the color," he said. "Nothing else."

Lisa waited for him to answer the other part for the longest time, but he never did.

She followed Robert Johnson into the thriving Hellish dark. As the air around them grew thick and humid, till now it began to smell like a disease, the lurking presence that she'd felt intensified. She could feel demonic eyes watching them from somewhere deep inside the crowding leaves and branches — skulking in the jungle shadows, staring through the thick blue dark.

"You feel them, don't you?" Robert Johnson asked, pausing in a clearing, looking back at her over his shoulder.

"Who?" Lisa asked — too quickly, too frightenedly, and the falseness of the question was obvious.

"The loa," Robert Johnson said. "That's who those demons are."

Lisa bit her lip. She said, "Oh," and she looked down at her feet.

"It's better not to look them in the eye," Robert Johnson said. "If you stare at them they take it as a challenge."

He led her half an hour through the jungle, deeper and deeper into the fetid blue flora, till now Lisa thought she could hear a trickle of running water. And on as the sound of water grew stronger and closer, and now the lurking devils seemed farther and farther away —

And suddenly the jungle parted, and they stood in the most beautiful place Lisa had ever seen.

At its center was a shrine, and on both sides of the shrine there was water — water from a cool, misty brook ran through that clearing. Where the water came back together on the far side of the shrine, there was a deep pool of the clearest coolest water Lisa had ever seen.

So beautiful, that pool. When Lisa saw it she wanted to wade in and let the water wash away every awful thing she'd ever done — every awful thing that'd ever happened to her.

But there was no time.

No time at all.

Because the loa came for them the moment that they entered the clearing — came out of the edges of the clearing and stood there, glaring at them hatefully, blocking their passage.

"They're going to kill us," Lisa said.

Robert Johnson shook his head.

"They can't," he said. "Not here. They can't even come any closer while there's water in the shrine."

Now the water in the pool began to roil, and Lisa wanted to say, *You're wrong, see, see? They're coming at us from the water* —

But then she saw who it was in the water, and she knew she was wrong.

Because it was the *santa* in that water, Santa Barbara, and Lisa thought, *We're saved, we're saved, a saint has come to save us from the horrors of damnation!*

But she could feel how false those words were as soon as she thought them. There was no salvation in that place, unless it came from down inside; no one could save them unless they could save themselves.

Still, the loa kept their distance. None of them would dare to speak to the *santa*, much less challenge her. As she rose out of the water they melted into the jungle.

And Santa Barbara beckoned to Lisa and Robert Johnson, urging them toward the brook.

"She'll tell you," Robert Johnson said. "She can tell you things I can't pretend to know."

The Mansion Called Defiance
Hell
Timeless

The doorman led them down the stair, into the Mansion called Defiance; through the great receiving room where ten thousand demons waited, watching hungrily as Emma, Leadbelly, and the Devil's butler passed.

Through the receiving room to the Devil's Sanctum where the Prince of Lies awaited.

Huddie Ledbetter smiled all slick and greasy as a politician when he saw the Devil.

"Master," he said, and when Emma heard that word she felt so ill, not just because she knew he meant to betray her but because no living man nor woman should ever call the Devil *Master.* "I've brought a bride for you, Master — someone precious enough to settle our account."

The Prince of Lies laughed wickedly. *"Ledbetter, you're a gambler,"* the Devil said. *"But you know you always lose."*

Emma heard Leadbelly swear under his breath, but she didn't pay much attention. She was too busy looking every which way, trying to figure out how the hell she was going to get herself out of that place. And not finding anything at all.

"You're wrong," Leadbelly said. "This is the girl's mother," he said. "She's Robert Johnson's daughter, too."

The Devil hissed. *"You think I don't know who she is?"*

Leadbelly flinched.

Emma saw curtains along the walls on either side of the Devil's throne. There had to be doors behind those curtains, didn't there? That was the only hope she had — she had to find a moment to make her break, and run for the door, and pray nobody caught her.

It was almost no hope at all.

"I'm sorry, Master," Leadbelly said. He spoke humbly, but Emma could see how the words humiliated him — he looked so angry! Like a rock that hisses at the edge of a fire just before it shatters. "I only wanted to settle my debt, Master. I owe you more than I want to owe anybody."

The Devil laughed and laughed and laughed, so wicked and so cruel. *"Gambling debts!"* he said derisively. *"You think I only own your debts? — you're wrong, little man. I own you. Don't you realize? Everything you do, I own; everything you think you think for me. Every breath you breathe is mine. Because* you *are mine."*

Now they stood at the foot of the Devil's throne, almost close enough to touch the Devil.

"Yes, Master," Leadbelly said — and Emma saw that he was trembling, literally shaking with rage.

"Kneel before me," the Devil said. "Supplicate yourselves."

Emma said, "I won't," but she didn't really have a choice. It wasn't a request; it was a command, and as the Devil spoke it Emma felt herself stoop and kneel involuntarily —

As Leadbelly swore —

And snapped.

"Damn you!" Leadbelly shouted. "Who the hell do you think you are?"

As the Devil laughed at the presumption of the question,

and Leadbelly's knees buckled beneath him, and —

And Leadbelly forced his knees to straighten, and stood to face the Devil, and raised his hands against him.

"I'm going to kill you," Leadbelly whispered, still trembling as his knees shook and shivered underneath him — "I swear I am."

That was when Emma saw he had a razor in his hand, just before Leadbelly stepped onto the dais of the Devil's throne and slit that fallen angel's throat as if he were a hog for slaughter.

Memphis, Tennessee
September 1952

When the last fire burned itself cold on the ridge over Memphis, the blues were all but dead. Oh, there were still talents scattered here and there across the land — but there was no one on the Mountain, and there was no order, and there was no rule to guide the people's spirit. They were terrible days, those last weeks of September 1952.

Like a winter of the spirit where there was neither magic nor music.

Oh, there was white Elvis Presley, half a talent laboring under the burden of the great King's guitar; and there was Furry Lewis, six months convalescing in the hospital after his automobile wreck. And there were tiny lights whose talents grew in the vacuum — grew and grew to fill the void, grew until their gifts exceeded the ability of their hearts to contain them.

The magic overtook those bluesmen. It haunted them, and ruined most of them. Many turned to drugs or *spirit liquor,* trying to tamp the music and the magic that haunted them; so many of them came to bad ends.

Like Tampa Red.

It isn't hard to hear what happened to Tampa Red, even from a distance of years, listening to recordings. The difference between the sides he cut in his youth and those he produced after his retirement is dramatic. When he was young he sang dance blues, snappy and glib, music you can listen to for years and never notice. But his later work is unmistakable. There's an eerie, haunting quality about it that no one ever could mistake; hear it once and you never will forget it.

Red quit recording after the death of his wife, in the early fifties, just after the horrible events above Memphis. He quit because something had changed — in the music, in the world, and in himself. Grief had put something deep and compelling in his blues (which till then had been light and facile, easy music from an easy talent, pretty but callow). And as he and the world and his music changed in concert, things began to *happen* when he played.

The hoodoo was in him, then. But he — like Elvis and so many others after the fall of the Seven Kings — didn't want to face it. He was a musician, not a hoodoo man; he wanted to sing, not make songs to charm the dead out of their graves.

But the magic was in him, whether he wanted it or not.

So Tampa Red did the hardest thing he ever did in his life: he set his guitar aside. He took his savings home to Tampa, bought him a little place in a neighborhood only lately gone to hell, and lived the same life every other retired person lives in Florida: quiet and peaceable and mundane.

No hoodoo in that life, nor ever ought there be. Tampa Red liked it mighty fine, no matter how sad it made him not to play.

Then one night he met three people in a bar — three men who knew his lifework, and loved it out of all proportion to the resonance he'd carried in those days. When he was deep in his cups he told them who he was, and told them he still knew his licks.

I could record tomorrow, he said, and the three men laughed, and after a while Red laughed along with them.

Then the third man said, "You know, I believe you," and Red sang three haunting choruses of "Tight Like That," and they all knew how true it was.

"We'll rent a studio tomorrow," the second one said. Tampa wasn't any music town, but any place the size of Tampa has a place where local businesses record their radio advertisements, and they rented that.

And Red set that place on fire.

He truly did. All three of the men and the engineers they hired saw the brilliant flames that burned around him as he played — but later they decided they imagined it among them, because the photos that they took showed nothing but an old old man, picking his guitar.

Not that it matters. Because the fire was the least of what took place in that studio: the most of it was music, alive and magical, full of hoodoo sorcery and things no man could describe; and if the magic lost itself in that room, the music found its way to tape, and anyone who listens to that album knows the reason Red retired.

Because his talent grew too great for him, and (for all the saltiness of his early songs) he was a Godly man who never would abide that.

•

Red made one more album, a year after his comeback. The scene that grew up from his singing that time was a terrible, terrible thing, and does not bear recounting. The sight of it frightened him so dearly that he never sang again.

•

It was like that for Washboard Sam, too. He'd given up the music back in 1946 — quit playing and recording blues, set his guitar down, and spent the rest of his life as a policeman, raising a family, trying to be an ordinary man.

But the music came for him, all the same. It came to him in his dreams, starting in the early fifties, and haunted him till finally he knew he had to play.

He played in public three times after his retirement: recording dates in 1953 and 1954, and during a European tour in 1964. He died in 1966 of heart failure.

But some folks say he never died.

They say that Sam became a deadman, just as if he were one of the seven lost forgotten Kings, and if you know the place and the password and the right day of the year, you can find him to this day, playing songs that cleanse the hearts of wicked men and teach the lame to heal.

•

There are other names, too. Stevie Ray Vaughn was a bluesman who came to a strange untimely end, and now they whisper his unlikely name in the strangest, most unlikely times and places.

Furry Lewis died in 1983 at the age of ninety. The records he recorded in the last days of his life are amazing things.

Elvis was the King, but everyone who knows him knows he never meant to be.

The Shrine of the Repentance of Shungó
Blue Hell
Timeless

For the longest time Lisa sat on the sandy bank of the stream beside Robert Johnson, waiting for the Lady to speak. As she sat, she listened — to the Hellish jungle all around them; to the wind in the infernal blue sky; to the sound of poor damned Robert Johnson breathing lifelessly.

But most of all she listened to the stream. It sounded so beautiful, that stream — the sound of the brook was the strumming of a guitar, gently pressing four-four time.

The whisper of the leaves on the breeze as they stood beside the water was the song that was the motion of the world.

Some of those who've heard the music of the shrine say it's lonely, ponderous, and sad; blues music like you hear when you get up in the morning and the blues are there to greet you.

But other people say that it isn't sad or happy, but beautiful and intense as the music that is the sum of all our lives.

•

Robert Johnson pointed at the water that ran through the shrine. "The Eye of the World is down there," he said. "I helped the Lady bring it there in 1952. It cost me everything I loved, and it cost me my salvation. But I don't regret it for a moment."

Lisa frowned. "That can't be," she said. "I saw it, hanging high above the river. How can it be here and there?"

Robert Johnson shook his head. "You don't understand," he said. "The Eye has two faces. One of them hangs above the river, waiting for Judgment Day. The other one is here in Hell, waiting to carry the damned to the world and Armageddon and their Judgment."

•

Hell.

The brook that strums, the jungle forest that whispers secret histories of all our days, the basin that holds the lens that

Hoodoo Doctors call the Eye of the World — there's no way anyone who witnessed any of those things could mistake that they're touched divine and sacrosanct. And people ask how ever there could be such a holy shrine in the bluest pit of Hell.

Sensibly enough.

But the sense in that misses Hell's true nature. For it's a place not only for the damned but for the damned and unrepentant. Who among us, after all, hasn't once or another time sinned enough to damn him straight to Hell? The God Who loves us knows our weaknesses, and He loves us even so. Hell isn't a place of Holy Wrath and Retribution; it's a place to separate the pious from the unrepentant.

It's not a pretty place. Just the opposite, in fact: Hellish means just what it does because the Pits are Awful. But that Hellishness reflects not Divine Judgment but the nature of the occupants. And there are those among the unrepentant with greatness, love, and beauty in them, no matter how they sin.

The *santa* told Lisa these things as the girl sat on the shore of her stream.

And she told her so much more.

She told her history a thousand thousand years untold, history unknown not because it's secret but because the living have forgot it. She told how, long before man came to the western hemisphere, another island shimmered in the sea that now surrounds great Hispaniola — a rich blue thriving place that bloomed with a thousand thousand flowers.

In a glen near the center of the island there was a shrine. There was a window in that shrine, and the window looked at heaven from the world.

The loa — a class of Higher Beings (angels, almost, but very different) — the loa built the Eye to celebrate their love for the Lord. They built a thousand other wonders, too — like their great mountainesque sculptures that stretched miles into the heavens. They took great pride in their accomplishments, and after a while they grew to hold themselves in high regard.

They grew so vain, in fact, that when man arrived in the Americas, the loa built temples that man might worship them. They were gods, they told the men who found them. They demanded to be worshiped. They demanded sacrifice — *human* sacrifice. And taught the Mayans, who taught the Aztec. . . .

When the blood began to stain the sea the Lord could abide no more. He walked upon the earth to cast the loa and their paradise into Hell, removing them forever from the living world. This was just a moment after the great revolt of angels, in the hours after God cast Lucifer and his confederates from Heaven; the two events were linked directly. The great isle of the loa slammed into the firmament of Hell only moments after Firgard smashed to Hell beside the sphincter of the damned Bosphorus.

For a moment, then, the Eye of the World — which only moments before had rested at one portal in the second Paradise of earth and at the other atop a glittering tower high above Firgard, the greatest Jewel in Heaven — for a moment, then, the Eye of the World rested with both antipodes in Hell. One of them in the most beautiful glade in Blue Hell; the other one atop the broken tower.

But that circumstance only lasted for a moment. For the Devil saw the comely jewel where it rested above the tower, and took it for his own; and seven angels, seeing the other about to fall into his foul hands, fought their way down into Hell to retrieve the second facet of the Eye.

The angels set the Eye they saved high above the Mississippi River, where now it watches us lovingly, waiting for the Last Days and the Destiny assigned to it. The Devil took the facet that once had looked on Heaven and hung it in the great receiving hall of the Mansion called Defiance, and for a time it was his dearest prize.

Those who've got the *gift* can see the Eye where it hangs above the river; on days when it shines clearly they can see through it, directly into Hell. Those who have that *gift* call it the Eye of the World, and they know it waits for Judgment Day.

●

Ten thousand years after the Lord cast the loa into Hell, Shungó — greatest among them — returned to the glade that once held the aperture toward Heaven. When she sat in that glade her mind's eye looked back on the heights from which she'd fallen, and saw in reverie the glorious sight of Heaven viewed from earth.

As she remembered the Glory of the Lord, humility came to her, and she saw the error of her ways.

Seeing, she repented.

I was wrong, Shungó thought. *So wrong.* Her heart filled with regret, and she mourned every sin she'd ever made —

Then the Hands of the Lord appeared to her, and took her arms to carry her to Heaven and redemption. There the Lord took her to His bosom as He takes all angels to Him.

And kissed her, and sent her out into the world to be his ears and eyes upon the earth. He called her Santa Barbara, and He loved as dear as He loves all His pious children.

•

"Something's wrong," Robert Johnson said. He pointed at the place where the stream split to feed into the basin, and Lisa saw the water slowing to a trickle. "That water shouldn't ever be that slow."

The Lady looked uneasy, but she didn't look surprised.

"This is why we're here, isn't it?" Lisa asked. "You saw this, didn't you?"

As the water slowed Lisa waited and waited and waited for an answer, but the Lady never gave one.

The Fallen City Firgard
Hell
Timeless

Dan carried Polly into the ruined city, looking for shelter. But all the houses that he found were broken, crumbling, ceilings collapsed among their walls, and for a moment that stretched on and on Dan thought he'd find nothing but debris —

And then he found the tower.

The tower was nearly as ruined as every other thing in the Fallen City — nearly, but not quite. It had three walls, and the stone stair at its center was still intact; three of its seven floors still stood unbroken, and at its top the tower keep stood sound as it had the day the angels made it. Dan saw that place, and he saw shelter; he hurried to the refuge of the stair without thinking how the hair on his arms stood on end as he passed

through what once was an inviolable door; didn't think about
the music that rang in his ears, the flickers of light just outside
his vision, the promise of something, something —

But it didn't matter what, because Dan didn't even notice.

Maybe that was just as well.

Because if he'd realized where he was, Dan would have gaped
in wonder. He would have marveled at the fallen majesty
around him, and he might have lost his presence of mind. . . .

But he didn't. How could he notice any of those things, with
Polly sobbing on his shoulder, *sob sob sob* broken little sobs like
the sight of ghost John Henry had broken something deep
down in her spirit?

He couldn't, of course. It wasn't in him to notice anything
with her in such awful pain, and that's as it should be.

He sat on the last steps of the stair, and he held Polly in his
arms, and he cooed into her ear. He said, "I love you, Polly,"
and he really meant he did, no matter how guilty strange he
felt when he said those words.

Polly looked up at him with wide mournful tearful eyes, and
she told him that she loved him, too.

And she kissed him like a lover, and Dan felt his heart fill
with desire too intense to deny —

And heard music, so beautiful, so powerful that music, he
thought the wings of angels carried him away —

But no. No, it wasn't angels, Dan looked up and saw dead
Elvis come to join them, carrying their bags, and not just their
bags but the guitar.

He had the guitar in his hands, and he was playing, God
that man could play, listen to him listen to him Dan had near
forgot the power of his music in the days since they'd sailed
out of Detroit.

Then he paused, and looked up to see Dan and Polly
watching him, and looked — abashed.

"You swore you'd never play again," Dan said.

"I know I did," dead Elvis said. "I meant it, too." And he
held the guitar out to Dan, waited for him to take it.

But Dan never did.

"It's yours," he said. "Ain't no sense in you denying."

Elvis frowned and shook his head, but that didn't change a

thing. After a while he rolled his eyes and shrugged and slung the guitar over his shoulder.

"Let's go," he said. "We haven't got much time."

"What? Where?" Dan asked, but Elvis didn't answer. Instead he led them out into the dying rain, through the Fallen City.

Miles and miles through the Fallen City, until they came upon the fountainhead of a clear beautiful spring.

When Dan stood at the foot of that spring and looked into its depths, he saw another fountain and another pool on the far side of its depths, and beyond that pool were two great doors, and those were the gate of Heaven and the gate of Hell, the Gates of Judgment we all come to one way or another.

At the far end of the spring the water led away into a subterranean stream — or tried to. There was rubble and debris fallen all around the aperture where the water went to ground, and Dan saw that a great amphitheater had only just collapsed into that end of the fountain.

"The Lady told me that he'd send that storm," dead Elvis said. "She said he meant to block the stream. She told me that we had to reopen the passage if we could."

"I don't understand," Dan said. "What do you mean? Who sent the storm?"

Elvis sighed. "The Devil sent it," he said. "Who else you think gives weather down in Hell?"

The Mansion Called Defiance
Hell
Timeless

Now Leadbelly was a man of mediocre scruple, and he'd been in league with the Devil for so long as he'd had gambling chits in Hell. Which was all his death and a big snatch of his life as well.

But even if he was a damnable man, he was a brave one, and a fellow with a temper, too. When the Devil made a monkey of him, Huddie Ledbetter didn't take it, not for a solitary moment. He stood up to Old Scratch, no matter if the Devil want him to kneel like some Master's Boy, and when the Devil pressed him Leadbelly took after him with the razor in his hip pocket.

So brave, that Huddie Ledbetter. Brave and venal and foolish, all those things at once. He sliced the Devil's throat, and kept on cutting; tore his Devil head clean off, so it rolled onto the floor, and picked the thrashing body off the Devil throne and heaved it half across the room.

Someone screamed, and someone else screamed, and Leadbelly said to Emma Henderson "Girl we better run," and Emma took it kindly because even if she wasn't any girl she liked it when a body thought she was one.

"This way," Emma said. "I saw a door behind that curtain."

The Fallen City Firgard
Hell
Timeless

"We need to clear the passage," dead Elvis said. "This water feeds into the shrine that holds the Eye of the World. The Eye got broken years ago; it's the water that holds its lens together."

Dan stared at him blankly.

"The lens is all that separates Hell from the world. If the basin goes dry, the Eye is broken again — and God only knows what will happen."

As he spoke Elvis waded into the water and began shoveling great handfuls of mud and debris away from the aperture. After a moment Polly waded in after him, and started shoveling, too.

"C'mon, Dan Alvarez," Polly said, "we need you here. You have to help."

And what could Dan do? He waded into the spring and started hauling broken stones out of the water.

It went quickly, with three of them working; in a few moments they'd all but cleared the aperture.

"I need some help with this one," Elvis said. He was braced against the boulder that half-blocked the aperture, trying to lift it and not having any luck.

"All right," Dan said — and he stooped to press against the boulder, heaved —

And Polly screamed.

"Not that way!" Elvis shouted as Dan heaved the great stone, rolling it up and over the aperture —

Elvis tried to stop him.

He really did.

But by the time he did it was too late. The great stone already rested on the aperture, and now there came the sound of twisting roots and collapsing soil as the great stone's weight crushed the stream passage, blocking it entirely.

As spring water roiled up to flood the square.

As the sky went dark and the Hellstones screamed and night collapsed into the day.

The Shrine of the Repentance of Shungó
Blue Hell
Timeless

Lisa stood at the edge of the brook that cut across Blue Hell, staring into the water. Staring at the basin as the water that fed it slowed and slowed now to a trickle.

Stared at the lens that was the Eye of the World.

For a moment, now, the Eye swirled open, and Lisa could see through it — it looked out onto a bluff in Tennessee, and Lisa knew that bluff, but she couldn't remember where she knew it from, maybe from a dream. When she looked close she could see the lens was broken, and that the water held it whole.

But every moment that passed the water was lower, lower, till now it hardly covered the Eye of the World.

"Fifty years ago," Robert Johnson said, "I sang to the Eye of the World. I broke it, damn near. It would have broke, too — but the *santa* heard me sing, and she went to the Eye and held it whole.

"She held the shards in place, but she couldn't mend them back together. When the Devil broke it again, she hid it here in the water where no evil thing can go. But the water's drying, now, and the Devil knows. Every devil in Hell knows. They're waiting, out there in the brush — waiting for the stream to dry."

Lisa turned to the *santa*. "What can we do?" she asked. "We've got to stop them, don't we? That's why you came for me, isn't it?"

The *santa* frowned. She looked very sad.

"No, child," she said. "There's nothing we can do to contain them."

As the last trickle of water in the stream ran dry.

And the loa descended upon them.

The Fallen City Firgard
Hell
Timeless

Polly screamed as Dan and Elvis scrambled, trying to push the stone away from the collapsing passage, and now the sky flickered dark and white and blue and bright as Hell came tumbling down around them, and the city metamorphosed, and somewhere so so close an infant child screamed in mortal terror for her life.

As Hell came true to the world, and the barrier that pares damnation from the toil of mankind collapsed around them.

"Sweet Jesus," Elvis swore, "oh Sweet Jesus we're too late."

As Hell became New Orleans.

The Mansion Called Defiance
As Hell Becomes New Orleans
The Present

The whole Mansion started shaking as Emma and Leadbelly ran for the door. It was an earthquake, Emma thought, but everybody knows you don't get earthquakes in New Orleans, and you don't get them in Hell, either, do you?

But the walls shook and the floors shook and great pillars tottered all around them as Emma pulled the curtain away from the side door and ran like hell.

Ran like hell.

Down a long, musty corridor, and now she realized this was the Mansion's basement, there, that door was the Mansion's wine vault and now ahead of her the root cellar, and Emma said "What the hell are we going to do?"

And Leadbelly said "We're going to run, that's what," as he pushed past her into the root cellar all dark and musty, and everything here smelled of dust and soil —

"It's too dark in here," Emma shouted, stumbling through a pile of something soft and wet and unidentifiable.

"Come *on*, damn it," Leadbelly said, rushing through the dark as though he knew where he was going.

As thunder blasted and blasted all around the Mansion.

"I can't," Emma insisted. "I can't see where I'm going!" And as she said that she ran smack into a post, bruising her face, damn near knocking her off her feet. Maybe she started crying then, or maybe not; later on she wasn't sure when the crying started.

"You've got to get up," Leadbelly shouted. "The stairs are over here. You coming or aren't you?"

As a dozen voices screamed in the hall behind them.

"I'm coming!" Emma shouted, trying to find her balance, trying to disentangle herself from the post, trying to figure out which way through the dark —

As the latch Leadbelly was pounding on broke free and hinges screeched and Leadbelly threw open the cellar door.

And sunlight flooded the root cellar.

"This way," Leadbelly shouted.

But he didn't need to say so. Nobody had to tell Emma Henderson twice — not once she'd seen the light.

The Fallen City Tumbling to Earth
In Arabi, Louisiana
Near the New Orleans City Line
The Present

As they worked, trying to reopen the stream, the Fallen City metamorphosed around them. Dan was working so hard trying to open up the aperture that he hardly saw it happening around him — but he felt it, all the same. The fetid Hellish air gusted away to be replaced by the blustery wet wind that roils through New Orleans just before a storm; and now it began to rain fat wet tropical droplets like you get every afternoon along the Gulf of Mexico. Gulls cawed in the air around them, and Dan knew it was too late — he knew that no matter what happened to the stream, the transformation was complete, and nothing he could do would ever change it.

"I need help again," dead Elvis said.

Dan looked up to see the deadman braced against a great slab of rock — it looked as though it'd once been the roof of the passage, but now it was fallen into the water.

"From me?"

The deadman nodded. "Be careful this time," he said. "We

need to wedge it from *here,*" he pointed at the edge of the slab that was nearest to his feet, "and roll it there."

Dan did as the deadman asked him — bent, heaved, lifted as dead Elvis pushed and guided the stone —

And something went wrong.

So wrong.

Where Dan had expected the resurgence of the stream to push the shadow of the world away, it did the opposite — every solitary thing around them transformed as the water burst through the reopened passage. The Fallen City disappeared around them, as though they'd never stood inside it, and Hell subsided as though they'd never sailed the River Styx to reach the Lake of Fire.

Where a moment before they'd stood in the ruins of an enchanted fountain, now they stood in the wash from a broken fire hydrant, staring down into the pipes of a crumbling sewer.

"Something's wrong," Dan said. "This isn't Hell anymore. It's, it's — where is this?"

But he knew where he was.

Just as he'd known where he was going all along, from the moment he first climbed hobolike onto the boxcar, and there was the sign, right there beside the dusty weather-beaten road:

WELCOME TO THE CITY OF NEW ORLEANS

The Devil's Quarter of New Orleans
The Present

They'd run half a mile before it came to Emma that they were back where they'd started that day — in the Devil's Quarter of New Orleans. It was an understandable mistake, some ways; this part of the city had collapsed on itself years before. The houses and the shops were gone, rotted to mulch or razed by fire, and even the streets were sandy and overgrown with brush.

She stopped, set a hand on Leadbelly's shoulder, and asked him to wait.

But Leadbelly wasn't having none of that. "What do you mean, woman?" he asked her. "They right behind us, don't you know? You better watch out. They kill you if they can."

Emma looked over her shoulder at the Mansion half a mile back. She didn't see anyone or anything coming after them, but she could feel it, all right — something big and terrible, not just something, not just one, but — hundreds.

"What are they?"

"The loa," Leadbelly said. "Devils. Come on! They're getting closer." He pulled her wrist — but Emma stood her ground, and pulled him back.

"We need to get the car," Emma said. "We can't run far enough or fast enough to get away from the Devil. But maybe we can drive."

Leadbelly scowled, and for a moment he looked like he was about to argue with her — and then there came the sound of footsteps from exactly the direction he was about to run toward, and Emma screamed and they both stopped thinking. They just ran, was all, ran for their lives as some hungry *thing* chased them, roaring, fetid rotting breath so close Emma could smell it, so intense the smell like to make her ill, and Emma *screamed*.

Not thinking, not planning, not doing anything at all but running for their lives, but they couldn't have run better if they'd tried, because there was the car, the battered old Buick waiting for them like the answer to a prayer.

"Get in the car," Leadbelly shouted. "Get the engine running."

And then he did the bravest thing Emma ever saw.

He turned to face the thing that hunted them.

Hauled his fist back and struck the awful thing that Emma couldn't see, but when he struck it it bled profusely, and the blood was plain to see.

Blood everywhere on the demon, covering its reptilian hide like paint that spattered everywhere, and everywhere it touched the ground it burst afire.

For three long moments as Emma hurried toward the car, the demon reeled from the blow Leadbelly struck it. But then it found its legs, and lunged at the hoodoo King —

But by the time it reached him Leadbelly was gone, running for his life down along the river road.

Emma found her keys and jammed them into the door; unlocked it, climbed behind the wheel, started the ignition, and got that vehicle in motion.

I'll catch up with them, Emma thought. *Let him jump onto the hood and drive us both away.*

Only it didn't work out like that, and it never works out like that, because it never does, nobody can jump onto the hood of a moving car without stumbling and getting run over by the tires, and Emma saw that as she got close behind them. It just wasn't going to work, and no matter how long she followed in the car it wasn't going to work, and if she didn't do something real fast the devil would have its hands around Leadbelly's throat, and it'd rip him limb from limb from limb —

And Emma did the only thing she could think of doing.

She stepped on the gas, and crushed the devil under the heavy chrome-plate bumper of her battered Buick.

It made the most disgusting sound. Hideous — a nightmare screaming sound as the Buick crushed its unearthly flesh and bones, and great ugly sulfurous clouds rose up from under the Buick, and Emma thought she'd set the car afire but no, no, it was running fine as she could please, and then tumble tumble crunch the devil corpse passed under the car, and Emma hit the brakes, put the Buick in reverse, and rolled back over the smoking carcass for good measure.

When it was passed back under the front Emma stopped the car again, and spent the longest moment staring at the *thing* she'd killed, feeling dirty, foul as a murderer, awful, awful, how could she kill like that?

Leadbelly climbed into the passenger seat.

After a while he whispered, "We better go," and Emma knew he was right, because there had to be more like that coming for them now, any moment now descending on them —

And she put the car in gear, and drove back toward New Orleans.

After a while Leadbelly said, "We shouldn't be here."

That took a while to sink through. But when it finally did it scared the hell out of Emma.

"What do you mean?" she asked.

"That cellar door doesn't lead back to the world," he said. "It comes out in the garden of the Mansion — the one that looks over the Lake of Fire."

The Fallen City Come to Earth
Arabi, Louisiana
Near the New Orleans City Line
The Present

Dead Elvis took a flashlight from the pocket of his vest and gestured at the open sewer. "We've got to follow it," he said. "No matter what it is."

Dan looked at the deadman and the sewer and back at the deadman again, and he wanted to say *You're out of your mind.* He almost said it, too. But there was something in Elvis's voice that told him not to argue, and told him that the deadman was right.

"Where are we going?" Dan asked.

Polly put her hand on Dan's shoulder. "The shrine," she said.

Dan turned to face her, confused. "Shrine? I don't understand."

Polly blinked; she looked — dumbfounded. But why would that question confound her?

After a moment Elvis cleared his throat. *"The Shrine of the Repentance of Shungó."*

"The *Lady,*" Polly said. "We've got to go to the Lady's place."

Dead Elvis was already halfway down the sewer hole.

"Ain't no Lady in that sewer," Dan said. But even as he said it he knew that he was wrong.

Polly grimaced. "Be quiet, Dan," she said. "This ain't the time to argue."

As she climbed down the stinking hole after the deadman, Dan shouted after her — "Come back," he shouted. "Come back, damn it!"

But she didn't pay him any mind, and maybe that was for the best. Because there wasn't anything real in Dan's reaction. The whole notion of crawling through the sewers disgusted him, and he was afraid of what he'd find there, and, and —

— and he kicked the dirt and cursed and shouted five long

minutes after his companions disappeared into the sewer. But when he heard a scream from somewhere deep down in the earth, Dan Alvarez didn't hesitate.

Not for an instant.

He went down the manhole ladder faster than he could have fallen, and kept running, running like a devil through the slog and the shit and the filth that grew all along the sewer walls, ran so far so fast that he was sure he'd gone a wrong turn, sure he had to turn back the way he came and run in the opposite direction —

And then Polly screamed again, so close Dan could almost taste the sound of her, and Dan rounded a corner to find her, to find them both, Polly and dead Elvis beset by devils and all but overrun, big powerful devils who towered above them like carnivorous giants, slashing with great razorous claws and fangs, and it was bad, so bad, blood and battery everywhere, Polly and Elvis had nothing to fight back with but their bare hands and the flashlight swinging back and forth across the tunnel, light arcing back and forth to graze the blood and the horrors glinting red and hateful in the broken dark —

Their hands, the flashlight, and their song.

No, not *their* song — Polly's song. Elvis wasn't singing, and no matter how they needed him to sing he wouldn't, but Polly sang so fine, sang "John Henry" right and true with all the words and verses nobody can record, and her words and her music were so powerful and true that they set the devils away from her, and near kept them at bay.

When she came to the chorus Dan joined her, and as he did the pathetic flashlight in Elvis's hands became a saber made of light, so brilliant and bright it lit the sewer damn near white as day, and brighter than that now as the devil caught inside the light screamed in burning agony and tried to run but couldn't run, the sword-light burned its legs away in great sulfur-fuming clouds of smoke, Dan choked and damn near started hacking when it rushed into his face, but he held the cough back no matter how it hurt because he knew he didn't dare stop singing and the burning demon screamed hideously in agony, screamed a nightmare sound that haunted Dan for all his life and on into eternity that sound so hideous to hear went on and on as the other demons broke and ran. . . .

The demon screamed for a long long time, smoking and burning all the while. Then finally it burned down into the sewage, and if it screamed in that filth there was no way to hear it anyhow, but it thrashed and thrashed in the filth and even if they didn't hear the screaming they heard the sound of devil stumps splattering filthy water everywhere for a long time.

"Follow me," Elvis said. "Keep singing."

Dan followed and he sang, at least partly because he was too scared to do anything else. Polly followed, too, and she sang so beautiful, like an angel, Dan thought, but if she was an angel she was his angel out of Hell.

Elvis led them for miles through the reeking dark — through sewage and runoff and awful things growing in the dark, and now Dan smelled sulfur and he knew there were devils watching him, waiting in the dark to tear them limb from limb, and he sang hard and loud to keep them in the shadows, and they stayed there. . . .

Deeper and deeper into the filth and the dark till Dan thought they were crawling back down into Hell or maybe they'd never left Hell in the first place, and they were heading toward the fate that always waited for them —

— and then suddenly there was daylight at the far end of the sewer, pure true daylight like the most beautiful sunny day you ever saw, and Dan almost cried for joy but he didn't dare, he didn't dare stop singing because he knew the end was on them if he did.

When the light was almost close enough to touch, Elvis said, "It's okay now," and then, "We're safe. You can stop."

But the things Dan saw as they stepped out into the light didn't make him feel safe at all.

Just the opposite, in fact.

One moment they were in the darkness where sunlight barely filtered around the last bend of the tunnel, and then they stepped around that final brilliant corner and saw the carnage just ahead of them where the sewer emptied out into a bayou.

The bayou was an unholy wreck. Its water ran brilliant red with blood, and the swamp forest all around hung torn to shreds of leaf and wood and vine.

In the center of it all was the desecrated shrine.

The bayou and the shrine scared him worse than any thing had scared him since that last night in LA, scared him worse than Detroit or the Lady or anything he ever saw in Hell, not just because of the destruction, not just because of the fuming stinking devil carcasses strewn across the scene, the thing that scared him worst of all was the desecration. It was a holy place, that shrine, something beautiful and glorious and true that spoke about the nature of creation, and something vast and powerful had harnessed great energies to destroy it.

At the center of the destruction lay three bodies Dan recognized before he even saw them. The tall, dark man was Robert Johnson. The bloody disfigured woman beside him was Our Lady of Sorrows, Santa Barbara.

And before them both was the body of an infant child.

Dan ached worst of all to see the murdered child. It was beaten and battered and bruised, cut from end to end and covered in blood. What hideous beast would stoop to murdering children, Dan wondered — and then he saw the blood wasn't the child's blood at all, it was the yellow pus-thick blood that seeps from the corpses of demons, and it wasn't leaking from the child's wounds but covering her hands.

"I think she's still alive," Polly said.

"They're all alive," dead Elvis said. "They'll recover, anyway. Robert Johnson and the baby both died before. The *santa* is an angel."

Dan glanced at the *santa* and he thought *Elvis is out of his mind,* because the Lady wasn't just dead, she was a bloody mass of dismembered parts, sinews and arteries and long strings of torn gut strewn quivering in every direction. "Are you sure?" Dan asked.

"Watch closely," Elvis said. "Even in its desecration, this is still her shrine. If you watch carefully enough you'll see its manna knit her back together."

Dan didn't believe that for a moment, but he didn't bother to argue. There wasn't time. Because the mangled baby had begun to come around, and as she woke Dan took her in his arms to hold her, to comfort her —

To try, anyway. Only it didn't work out like he meant, not at all. Because something shifted in the baby's gut-wound as Dan lifted her, and the baby *screamed!* in agony and started flailing —

— and then she swore.

Swore like a truck driver, or worse than that, and for a long hard moment Dan thought he'd took a devil in his arms to comfort, and he like to scream but he was too scared. As the baby flailed and writhed and hit Dan upside the head, so strong, her tiny fists as cruel as rail spikes driven by the hammer that rang like a bell, Dan lifted the child in his arms, lifted it above his head to hold it at arms' length, and the tiny baby screamed at him all outrage and frustration, "Put me down, God damn you," she swore, "put me down or I'll hurt you like you never hurt before."

And what could Dan do? He set the baby down as Polly and the deadman watched him, and they laughed ha ha ha oh what a joke and Dan wanted to ask them what was so damn funny but he was afraid that if he did it'd get the baby started on him all over again.

"I'm sorry," Dan said. "I didn't mean you any harm."

The baby made a derisive noise. "Keep your big hands to yourself," she said. "If I want you acting like my mama, I'll ask you for your help."

Robert Johnson groaned on the far side of the shrine. Dan looked up to see him moving, twitching, almost, almost as though he were alive no matter how his spine was twisted backward on itself.

"The Eye," someone whispered, and Dan thought that was Robert Johnson but it wasn't, it wasn't him at all, it was a woman's voice, not Polly someone else and then Dan realized that the voice came from the quivering heap of twisted flesh that once had been the *santa. "You need to gather up the fragments of the Eye. Quickly! There's only an hour of daylight left. They can't touch you here while the sun still shines. But the night belongs to Hell."*

"I'll find them," the baby said. She didn't hesitate a moment; she waded out through the running sewage, into the bayou jungle. As she waded through the filth dirty water ran through her open wounds, and Dan wanted to say, *Little girl, be careful, that water there is filthy you're going to get a terrible infection,* and he might have done it, too, but Polly put her hand on Dan's arm and shook her head.

"You've got to let her show you," Polly said. "She saw it all. She knows what to look for."

Polly was right about that, too. The baby tromped purposely into the broken thicket, stooped, and spent a moment sifting through the debris — and when she stood again she held in her hands the most fabulous jewel Dan had ever seen.

More beautiful than anything he'd ever imagined; more forbidding than his most frightful nightmare.

"The Eye of the World," Polly said.

Dead Elvis fell to his knees and began to pray.

"That's it?" Dan asked. "That's the Eye of the World?"

Polly shook her head. "Only a fragment," she said. "You'd know it if you saw the whole."

"We need to help her find the rest, don't we? — that's what the Lady said, we had to find it all before dark."

Polly shook her head. "The girl knows," she said. "Stand away and let her work."

As Polly spoke the girl carried the glittering jewel through the sewer, and set it before the Lady's still-quivering remains. When the girl had trudged back into the sewage Polly crossed herself.

Elvis kept praying. Prayed so hard and clear and true that for a moment Dan thought he'd repented the things that damned him to the world and Hell — but maybe not, because no salvation ever came for him.

Or maybe salvation did come for poor dead Elvis Presley. But if it did it came for all of them. And it was a long long time coming.

The French Quarter of New Orleans
The Present

When they got past the French Quarter Emma saw big clouds of smoke off to her right, and she got a dreadful feeling. Part of her didn't want to confirm it, but another part — the part she could never deny — had to know for certain. She didn't have a choice, not really; she took a right, a left, and then a right again, and there they were, just as she'd dreaded — fire trucks all crowded up in front of New Orleans City Hall.

"What you doing, woman?" dead Leadbelly asked, huffing angrily. But he knew — Emma could tell.

"That isn't any accident," Emma said.

Leadbelly frowned, and looked away — and as Emma followed the line of his gaze she saw that there were fires starting everywhere around them, everywhere. Flickering flames here, there, half the buildings in the Quarter starting to catch fire. . . .

"We better get out of here," Leadbelly said. "This whole damn Quarter's going up."

It was easier to say that than it was to do it. Traffic was stopped dead by City Hall, and backed up even worse down the one way to their left.

But there wasn't any traffic at all coming toward them on the one-way. So Emma did the only thing she could — downshifted as she slammed her foot down on the gas and banked hard right, trying to run the one-way before some fool could turn head-on into them, but it didn't work. They didn't get halfway down the block before Emma heard the siren and saw the flashes of light from the fire truck's strobe; before she had time to react the truck was turning to barrel down on them, head-on, slam, crash, it was going to run them down —

And Emma panicked.

Where she should have tried to drive the Buick into a driveway or up onto the sidewalk, her leg twitched almost involuntarily, pushing her foot all the way down onto the accelerator and there was nowhere to go with the Buick's engine roaring to life, nowhere but into the tiny gap of road between the truck's left fender and the left edge of the road, but there wasn't room that way, no room at all, no room for an old full-size car like the Buick —

— no room —

But they made it, somehow. Maybe the gap was wider than it looked, or maybe the Grace of God found them for a reason, or maybe, maybe, maybe God knew what, but they made it through, just barely. Just before they finished passing the truck the Buick's left side scraped the back end of the fire truck and sent them rebounding into the curb so hard it was a wonder their tires didn't separate from their rims —

And then they were out on the street, past the truck, hanging a hard right away from City Hall, and never mind the sparks that rose up off the tire rims, trying to set the car afire; if Emma let those worry her she would have gone hysterical.

Four blocks back toward the river with fires breaking out all around them in the Quarter, and then right again for an eight-block dash to the Pontchartrain Expressway.

Up on the highway, and they were safe running for their lives.

They would have made it, too.

Would have got themselves clear of New Orleans and the Hell descending all around it, but something went so wrong.

So wrong!

Before they got halfway to Metairie, they came to barricades, and half an army of National Guards enforcing them with tanks and half-tracks and APCs, like to blow them off the road, Emma thought, and if their guns hadn't glittered oh so bright Emma would have tried to run the barricade, she really wanted out of there that bad.

But she didn't run, because she knew it wasn't any use. Even if she'd managed to jam the Buick past the Guards and the big guns and the tanks and armored cars, she would have run headlong into the fire consuming the highway half a mile down the road — it was serious, serious stuff, that fire, a military convoy that'd wrecked and caught fire, burning wild and out of control, and if she could have run the fire the toxic fumes from the smoke would have killed her anyway. Serious stuff, that fire, and it wasn't getting anything but worse.

And even if Emma couldn't know what lay ahead of that road, she knew trouble when she saw it, and she knew what to avoid; when the National Guardswoman with the bright red armbands waved her off the highway, Emma went where she was directed.

Into an awful traffic jam of local streets, and she tried and tried to figure how she was going to run for her life, but there were too damn many cars all around them and the fire was on them, too, there were hints of fire everywhere and any second now the whole damn place was going up.

Any second.

There was nowhere to go. No way to get there, anyhow. But Emma didn't stop trying, because she knew she didn't dare. She had to, she had to — she had to think, that was what it was. She had to pull the car off the road and look at the map in the glove box and *think.*

Think.

Off the road and out of the traffic that was hardly moving anyway, into the parking lot of a weathered-looking Kmart. She found a parking spot up near the front, parked, cut the engine, and sighed.

Her hands were trembling, she realized. She wasn't sure how long they'd been like that — so long she couldn't remember when it started.

"What you doing?" Leadbelly asked.

"Trying to figure where we going to go," Emma told him. "I got to look at the map. You want to hand it to me? It's in the glove."

The deadman popped the glove-compartment latch and handed her the map. Emma took it, opened it — spread it out and tried to figure where they were.

Where they were was lost, damn near.

"Late afternoon," Leadbelly said. "You want to get back on the road. We don't get out of here before the sun goes down, we ain't getting out of here at all."

Emma bit her lip. "I'm not leaving this town till we find my little girl," she said.

Leadbelly scowled. "Your little girl is done for," he said. "Ain't nothing you can do for her."

Emma swore. "You're wrong," she said. "Just wrong, is all."

"Then you better find her before sundown. Or you ain't never going to find her at all."

Emma looked back and forth across the map, trying to figure where she had to go. Out on the left end of the map were the new suburbs, places like Kenner and Metairie, and the New Orleans International Airport. On the right — east by southeast along the river — was Arabi, the run-down little town where they'd spent that night in the motel. . . .

Someone shouted, and Emma looked up to see a couple bickering near the entrance to the store.

"They're here," Leadbelly said. "They're everywhere."

"What do you mean?"

"Keep watching. You'll see."

He was right, too. For as Emma watched the couple their bickering intensified, till now the woman reached into her shopping bag, drew out a gleaming brass curtain rod, and struck her husband with it.

Emma gasped. Leadbelly just laughed, and Emma thought that was the cruelest thing. "Mind your humor," Emma said. "She's going to put that poor man in the hospital." She opened the car door, and started to get out to rush to the man's side to pull his wife away and stop things before somebody got themself killed, but before she could get halfway out of the car the deadman took her arm and held her back. She looked back over her shoulder to see him shake his head at her.

"You don't want to get involved," he said. "This is devil-work. That man is lucky — the metal stick his wife has got is hollow. Look, look — it's broke in half already, and he ain't so much the worse for it."

Emma started to object, but Leadbelly took his hand off her arm and held it up to silence her. Pointed at the couple, and Emma saw the woman looking stunned and appalled at her own behavior, look how her jaw hung slack, look how her husband looked so dumbstruck. . . .

"You think it would've gone any better with you there in the middle of things? I swear to you it wouldn't."

The South Side of Chicago
The Present

That evening dead Stevie Ray Vaughan called Furry Lewis in Chicago.

"Did you see the news?" Vaughan asked. "New Orleans."

"I don't need no TV news," Furry Lewis told him. "I can feel it in my bones."

Vaughan didn't answer right away. He never did, where it came to knowing things you can't set eyes upon, but that was Vaughan for you. "You want me to call Red?"

"Red knows," Furry Lewis said. "He's going to meet me here this evening."

Another silence that went on and on. "You need me?"

Furry Lewis sighed. "You know I do, Stevie Ray."

"Okay," Vaughan said. And then, because the silence got so large he felt it himself, he added, "I had to ask."

Furry Lewis laughed real gentle, not derisory at all. "You always think you do, Stevie Ray. But it isn't so. You ought to learn to listen to your heart."

Vaughan didn't like that kind of talk — he never did, not when he was alive nor after he had died. He answered as directly as he could. "I don't want to hear about it," he said. "I'll catch the next bus out of here."

Bayou Country
Near Arabi, Louisiana
The Present

The baby gathered seven interlocking jewels and set them each in turn before the carcass of the Lady. It took a long, long time — hours, it seemed like, but maybe that was just the way it seemed. Dan wanted to wade out into the filth and help the child search, but every time he even thought about it Polly frowned at him and shook her head. Dan hated that. Bad enough she wanted to stop him, but did she have to know him even when he only thought about things like that? Sometimes she even seemed to know before he did himself, and she'd take his hand and squeeze it and shake her head just so slightly, and Dan would realize she was right, and he was about to step out from the shrine on an impulse he didn't even realize, and he had to stop — he didn't know why. Maybe there was something in him? There were devils all around them, he could tell, and maybe some of them were called temptation.

When baby Lisa retrieved the seventh jewel Dan saw how each of the gems was a mate among the others, and when they all came together they'd be a treasure infinitely greater than the sum of their individuality, and more than that, too, because the Eye was alive in a way, and its life was God's Love for the World and All Mankind made tangible to see, and when he saw that he understood why Elvis prayed, and he fell to his knees —

But only for a moment. Because the moment he began to pray a voice spoke to him. "There isn't time, Dan Alvarez," the voice said, and Dan knew that voice — as surely as he knew the rhythm of his own heart. "Stand and face me, all of you."

It was the *santa* returned to life, and everyone who heard her did as she instructed. Polly, Dan, and Elvis climbed to their feet; Robert Johnson straightened out his twisted back and stood as best he could. Baby Lisa stood crying beside the *santa*, tugging at her skirts.

"You came back," Lisa said. "Lady Lady you came back." And the relief and wonder in the baby's voice were so intense they were contagious, and Dan like to cry himself, glory glory glory to stand before Our Lady of Sorrows and beg her for her blessing, Dan would have repented there and then if he'd had an idea what his sins were — but he didn't, not for a moment. Pride is like that for everyone, isn't it? It hides our foibles from us till their omnipresence consumes us, and then it fades away. . . .

"The night is falling," Santa Barbara said. "When it comes they will surround us once again."

Baby Lisa's eyes went wide, and Dan saw the whole notion terrified her. "Make them stop, Lady," Lisa said. "Don't let them hurt us again, please please don't let them."

The Lady started to answer — and then she stopped. At first Dan didn't understand why, but then he saw the Lady look at the deadman Elvis, and when she nodded to him, ever so slightly — so small a nod that no one who'd missed the glance could have known it — when she nodded to the deadman Dan knew the fix was in.

Elvis cleared his throat and crouched to look the baby in the eye as he spoke to her.

"We've got to walk back into the city, Lisa," he said, and that was news to Dan as much as it was to the child. "There's a tower there that's the shadow of a tower down in Hell. We've got to take the Eye there and reforge it." He looked away, and Dan knew that the next thing he said would be the hardest news, because it was bad enough to scare a deadman. "Every devil out of Hell will try to stop us when they see us, and when it's dark they'll be as real as you and me. Because without the Eye the world is Hell, and Hell is the world, too. There are songs our friends can sing to keep the damned away, but they won't work forever."

Lisa had her arms wrapped around the Lady's leg; she looked terrified. "I don't want to go back to the city," Lisa said. "I'm too scared to go."

The Lady frowned, and her frown was more beautiful that the smile of a beauty queen. "We need you, Lisa," Santa Barbara said.

"I won't go," Lisa said. "I won't I won't."

The Lady nodded; after a moment she turned away and started out of the bayou. Dan Alvarez, Robert Johnson, dead Elvis, and Polly Ann all followed her, one by one by one. When they were almost disappeared into the bayou jungle, Lisa gathered up the glittering jewels that were the Eye and hurried away to join them.

As the night came down upon them all.

Western New Orleans
The Present

Things didn't work out for the fighting couple like Emma hoped they would. Oh, they kissed and made up, all right, and weren't they sweet like that, isn't forgiveness the bounty of our hearts? But it didn't last. Because just the moment after they kissed, store security came bounding out the front door of that Kmart and arrested the poor lady. And who could argue with them? Her husband tried, but it wasn't like he really had a case — his wife had assaulted him with a metal rod, and that's serious criminal stuff, and where there are three dozen witnesses it doesn't matter whether the victim testifies or not, because the crime is the crime and there's plenty of evidence.

Jury might feel different when it got to court, but there's a long way between arrest and the jury.

"Get your hands off my wife," the man told the security guard — and that wasn't any security guard at all, Emma realized, it was a real policeman with a gun and everything, and look how he took the handcuffs off his belt and put them on the lady. . . . "Did you hear me, mister? I told you, 'Get your hands off my wife.' "

As they spoke a crowd gathered around them, pressing close to fill some morbid curiosity. "This woman assaulted a customer," the policeman said. He said it like he worked for the store, not the police. Maybe he was moonlighting — yes, Emma thought, that made a kind of sense, the man was such a crab because he was working double hours for the city and the store. "Store policy — she goes downtown to the lockup. We let her go and she hits somebody else, the store could get sued."

"But she's my wife!"

"You want to bail her out, that's your business."

The man was beet-red, furious; when he put his hand on the policeman's shoulder there was no mistaking that he meant it as a threat. "I'm not going to let you take my wife away," the man said. "I don't care what you think she's done."

And then the policeman did the thing that made everyone who saw him choose his side or the other.

He pulled his gun and aimed it at the man's head, right between his eyes.

Cocked it, and stood there still as stone, half a millisecond away from death and blood and thunder. "Don't touch me," he said. "You shouldn't ever touch an officer of the law."

And he was right, so far as that went, even if everything about the way he said it was so wrong.

Not that it mattered, right and wrong and all. Because there was something demoniac in the air, and it was in the policeman and husband just as it'd been in the wife, and when the beet-red husband heard the policeman say *don't touch me* he didn't think the way any rational person would; he thought, *That bastard is going to hurt my wife,* and there wasn't a gun in the world that would have scared him, no matter if it was pointed at his head or not. He looked the policeman in the eye, and he smiled, and fast as lightning his arm went up to knock away the policeman's gun hand, and Lord he was fast, it really was some devil in the air to make a body move that fast, and of course the policeman fired but it was too late, he missed the man and his shot went wild —

His shot went wild into the crowd and struck a child.

It got crazy after that. The cop lost hold of his gun, and the irate husband tried to beat him to a pulp, but the cop wasn't that easy to take down, and there was the same demoniac hand guiding him that guided the husband, and the child's mother wailed as she screamed for an ambulance, and half the people in the crowd tried ungently to pull the husband and the cop apart, and the other half tried to help the fight on one side or the other, and suddenly Emma realized that everyone was fighting.

Everyone but the wounded child and the handcuffed woman.

The child was going to die if somebody didn't do something. She really really was.

The handcuffed woman had it damn near as bad, because in the violence and the confusion she'd lost her balance and got knocked over, and without her hands she had a hard time getting to her feet, and Emma saw her getting trampled. . . .

As darkness settled on the city.

And in the darkness Emma saw the most amazing sight: she saw the devils that worked the mob, fomenting hate and ugliness, pounding and beating on the people who they whispered to, driving them to breed the evil in their hearts.

The South Side of Chicago
The Present

When Stevie Ray Vaughan got to Furry Lewis's place on the south side of Chicago, he found Tampa Red on the dead bluesman's couch. There was a White Sox game on the TV, and Red was watching it intently, as though the fate of the world hinged on its outcome. Any maybe it did; Red had a feel for things most other people can't imagine.

Furry Lewis was in the kitchen, drinking coffee; he wasn't much for television. He owned one, but he didn't really watch the thing.

Vaughan didn't knock. He'd had the run of Furry Lewis's place ever since that morning Furry found him wandering the cemetery. He opened the door with his key, saw Red and the game, nodded, and headed for the kitchen. "What time's the bus?" he asked, because that's the way hoodoo men are, they take the bus even when they're heading halfway across the continent.

Busses keep them closer to the land.

"Ain't got no time to take the bus," Furry said. "Ain't got no time at all. Whole City of New Orleans is on fire, riots all over town. Louisiana governor just called out the National Guard."

"You want to fly?" Vaughan asked, incredulous. Furry Lewis had never set foot inside an airplane, so far as Vaughan knew; never as a deadman, surely.

"I want you to call those folk you used to know, back when. I want you to rent us a plane. A charter, don't they call it?"

Vaughan laughed. "I wouldn't call anyone I knew," He said. "They'd think I was a ghost, or worse. And maybe they'd be right."

"You can't do it, Stevie Ray?"

Vaughan held up a hand, shook his head. "Oh, I'll do it, all right. If we've got the money I can find a way to get a plane."

"There's always money," Furry Lewis said. He didn't need to say another word; Vaughan knew he had access to money as he wanted it, same as Vaughan did. There's magic in a deadman's song, and money draws to that magic as surely as the rain draws toward the soil. This would be significant if the dead had any use for the stuff, but generally they don't — Furry Lewis could have lived in splendor on John Henry's forgotten Mountain if it pleased him. But the Mountain is a lonely place these days, populated chiefly by the vapors of those the world has very near forgotten, and Furry Lewis didn't need that kind of emptiness, no matter whether he was dead or alive. He could have kept a Mansion; he could have kept a city thrall to serve him if that had pleased his heart — but it didn't. Furry Lewis kept a simple upright home on the South Side, not far from where the projects face Lake Michigan and Gary, Indiana. It suited him precisely.

"Okay, then," Vaughan said. "You got a phone book here? I thought you did. Give me a few minutes with the phone. I ought to be able to get us something."

Bayou Country
Pushing toward New Orleans
The Present

When the sun came down and the moon went up the Devil's henchmen were everywhere like beggars on the streets, watching them hungrily with eyes that spoke demands they never put to words, and now there were more of them and more still till the bayou jungle grew thick with devils like a plague foretold in the scripture.

Dan Alvarez didn't like it. At all. The moment that he saw the first of them he was certain the devils meant to set upon them — and he was right. But for the longest time they hung back from Dan and Polly, Robert Johnson and the *santa*, dead Elvis and the baby trailing after them.

"The Devil never comes when you expect him," Polly said. "He never could."

Dan stole a glance at the fiery specters hiding everywhere around them in the bayou jungle, and he was sure Polly had to be wrong. "This is Hell," he said. "Everything you see is here because the Devil abides it."

And Polly looked at Dan as though he were *so stupid.* "You're wrong," she said.

Dan waited for her to go on, but she didn't. When he got tired of waiting he made a derisive sound and asked her what she meant.

"I mean that Hell is the kingdom of the damned — you can't go to Heaven if you can't get right with God, and if you can't get to Heaven then you're going to go to Hell. But that ain't the Devil's fault, no matter where you go."

Dan wanted to argue with her, because everybody knows Old Scratch is the Prince of Lies and Darkness. But he didn't know where to start, not least because he knew that she was right.

"Devil's just as damned as everybody else," she said, "but worse."

"No," Dan said, "the Devil is temptation."

Polly laughed. "He likes company. But he can't damn you. You got to damn yourself."

"Not me," Dan said. "If I go wrong I'll repent."

She laughed again. "Everybody always says that. But the things that damn us all are the ones we're sure are right — things we love, things we're proud of. Things that we accomplish! It's easier to say 'I repent!' than it is to do it."

Dan gestured at a set of eyes, peering at them through the thickness of the jungle brush. "You think they're waiting for us to repent?" he asked, and then he laughed — too hard, too long, too mean.

It was late dusk, now, and the devils seemed closer than they'd been before — much closer. Threateningly close. Dan looked up to measure daylight by the darkening of the sky, and saw that there were only moments left to them.

But it didn't matter if the sun went down, did it? The moon was already up, full and bright — bright red, tonight, deep bright red like a blood moon.

Dan heard the music in his head, clear as though Furry Lewis sang it for him: *Now when the moon / come down in blood. . . .*

Dan shivered at the sight.

"There isn't time to stop and stare," Polly said. "We have to hurry."

"*The sun is gone,*" Santa Barbara said. "*Sing!*"

And Polly sang. After a moment Dan joined her; and then Robert Johnson sang, too, and when Dan heard that voice his own song felt so thin. But he sang anyway, because he knew he had to keep the night at bay.

Suburban New Orleans
The Present

"You better get that engine started," Leadbelly said. "Crowd's about to run a rage."

"What?" Emma asked. She hardly even heard him speak; she was too engrossed, watching the crowd, watching the devils that sifted through it — all but invisibly. Emma could see them, now that the sun was down, and the people in the crowd walked and moved as though they saw the ones who walked among them. But they didn't seem to *see* — they acted like the devils in their midst were just their neighbors, just ordinary people whispering to them, chiding them and needling them to lure them toward damnation. . . .

"I said you better get a move on," Leadbelly said. "I think there's going to be a riot."

Emma laughed nervously. "That's silly," she said. "This isn't any riot —"

But she was wrong. Just plain wrong. Because the moment that she spoke a second security policeman came out of the Kmart, carrying a shotgun and a bullhorn.

And he used them both.

Bullhorn first, raising it to his mouth, and shouting into it: "Put your hands in the air, all of you," he shouted through the amplifier. "Put your hands in the air and stand perfectly still. Or I'll shoot you all."

The crowd didn't really react until he threatened to shoot — and then it reacted in about the worst way it possibly could, surging toward the officer, roaring in unison like a pack of blood-crazed predators.

The policeman reacted the only way he could — he started shooting. *BLAM BLAM BLAM BLAM* round after round out of the shotgun, and now there were blood and bodies everywhere, people screaming in agony people dying people cut to ribbons dead and oh by the way there weren't any devils anywhere to be seen once the shooting started.

As Emma started the Buick's engine and put the car in gear; as the blood-mad mob kept coming, surging into the shotgun fire, *BLAM BLAM BLAM BLAM* more and more dead people everywhere but they didn't stop, and now they were pouring out of the store, hundreds of them coming down on the policeman from every direction to tear him limb from limb. . . .

The last thing Emma saw as she tore across the parking lot was the sight of the second policeman's decapitated head flying into the air, trailing blood and brains and entrails as the mob shrieked and screamed in ecstasy.

Meigs Field, Chicago
The Present

Vaughan didn't have any trouble finding them a plane. At all. Forty minutes after he picked up the telephone receiver they were out at Meigs Field, getting on a twin-engine turbo-

prop Vaughan had chartered. Twice as they crossed the field
people looked at Vaughan like they'd seen a ghost, but nothing
came of either of those sightings — partly because Vaughan
caught their eyes as they saw him, smiled, shrugged, and said,
"People say I look like him, it's funny, isn't it?"

And it ended there, both times. Of course it did! Everybody
knew Stevie Ray Vaughan was a dead man, and no sensible
people ever think they've talked to ghosts.

Red and Furry Lewis looked uncomfortable as sin getting
on that plane. Vaughan didn't understand why, at first — didn't
understand until they were in the air, soaring through the sky,
and the trouble came on him.

So hard.

Vaughan was a *giftie* bluesman, and he was a deadman, and
when he sang amazing things would happen, because of who
and what he was — but he was also a city boy, and he didn't
know his lore.

Didn't know a lot of things he should have known, in fact.

"What the *hell*. . . ?"

"The soil," Furry Lewis said. He looked quivery and ill, like
a man about to die of some terrible disease. What he meant
was, there's a connection between a deadman and the soil, and
a deadman soaring through the air is a man severed from his
subsistence. Vaughan didn't get all that, but he got enough
from the two words Furry Lewis said to understand the trouble.
He reached forward to tap the pilot's shoulder with a trembling
hand, and he said, "Fly low. Low as you can."

The pilot started to argue with that — with good cause, since
it went counter to their flight plan and their instructions from
the air-control tower — but Vaughan held up a hand to silence
him. And then he whispered a verse from Sister O. M. Terrell's
take on "Swing Low, Sweet Chariot," which is about as hip and
bluesy as a gospel number can be.

And the pilot swung low, just as Vaughan's song commanded.

It got a little better after that. The deathliness and the cold
receded, and the song that deadmen call the music of the world
came back to them, or nearly did, at least. It never got comfortable while they were in the air, but so long as they flew low

Vaughan didn't feel as though he would expire.

Not that he felt good. Just the opposite, in fact — the flight was miserable, even agonizing. When air-control directed them to land a hundred miles early, outside Baton Rouge, it almost came as a relief.

The pilot peered back at them, cleared his throat. "The tower said Lakefront Airport is closed," he said. "New Orleans International, too. Closest open field is Baton Rouge."

Vaughan nodded. Furry Lewis groaned, and it looked like he wanted to say something, but the words never came.

"All right, then," Vaughan said. "Get us as close as you can."

The pilot nodded; banked the plane and started the descent toward Baton Rouge.

"We'll have to rent a car," Vaughan said. "It's a drive from Baton Rouge to New Orleans. Not a long drive, though." Furry Lewis nodded weakly; Tampa Red didn't even seem to hear. Red didn't look like he was hearing anything, in fact — he looked dead. Corpse-dead, as though he'd gone back to his damnation or on to his reward.

As the plane swung wide, banked again, leveled, straightened, and touched the runway.

And the aching stopped, and the music of the world became a song large enough to consume them, to propel and define them, and Red whimpered like a man released from agony.

"Praise God," Furry Lewis said. "I've never known a longer hour."

Slower, now, and slower still as they approached the terminal and the plane eased to a halt. The pilot secured the brakes and opened the hatch to let them climb out of the cabin.

Vaughan got dizzy trying to stand up; Furry Lewis left his seat unsteadily. But Red was worse than either of them — by a lot. He stumbled as he left his seat, and then stumbled again on the stairs, and Vaughan began to think he'd never find his legs. Vaughan took his arm, and helped him down onto the runway.

"You going to be okay, Red?" he asked.

Red nodded, but he didn't look good. He didn't look good at all, in fact.

"You want some help?" Vaughan asked, and when the other

deadman didn't answer Vaughan put his arm over Red's shoulder, and steadied him for the walk across the tarmac. As they entered the terminal Red seemed to find his legs, and Vaughan released him — but he kept close to Red, watching him carefully.

"Where from here, Stevie Ray?" Furry Lewis asked.

"Car-rental counter. Up ahead and to the left."

Just before they got to the car-rental counter, Red stumbled again. Vaughan barely caught him in time to save him from collapsing to the floor, and when he tried to steady the deadman Red's legs went to jelly underneath him.

"Red. . . ?"

"I'm okay," Red said. "I just took a little faint, that's all."

"Yeah," Vaughan said. But he didn't think so, not for a moment. "Think you can make it to the counter? Car's right past the counter, by the door."

"I'll be fine," Red said. "You know I will."

And he waited for Vaughan and Furry Lewis to reassure him, but neither of them did.

"Why don't you take a seat, Red?" Furry Lewis asked. "Wait with him, Stevie Ray. I'll rent the car."

Vaughan nodded. "I'll do that, if you like," he said. "It wouldn't take a minute."

"No trouble," Furry Lewis said. "You think I don't know how to rent a car?"

The truth was that he didn't know, because he hadn't had a need to rent one in the years since he'd passed on, and while he'd rented cars for the great King back in the early fifties, the car-rental business has changed dramatically across the decades. But it ain't like doing business with Hertz takes rocket science; and anyway Furry Lewis had charm enough to fake the parts he didn't know.

"All right," Vaughan said. "Let me know if you need help."

Furry Lewis allowed as he would, but he didn't have a solitary intention of asking for help. And he didn't need it, either.

"I'd like to rent a car," he told the rent-a-car clerk.

"Would you like a midsize or a compact, sir?"

Furry Lewis grinned. "I'd like a Cadillac," he said. He'd seen those pricey Japanese and German cars around, but he didn't think much of them. His idea of a *car* was the same as it'd always been — wide seats, big motor, whitewall tires.

The clerk smiled. "We've got one," he said. "I'll need your license and the credit card you'd like to put this on."

Furry Lewis reached for his wallet. "I'd just as soon pay cash," he said.

The clerk frowned. "That can be arranged," he said. "But I'll need a credit card to secure the rental."

Now Furry Lewis was a deadman, and he didn't have no credit cards. He could have had some if he'd put an effort to it — Stevie Ray Vaughan had — but it wouldn't be a simple undertaking, and Furry Lewis had never gone to the effort of making the requisite arrangements.

He didn't have a current driver's license, either, though he had the one he'd died with back home in a drawer full of memorabilia.

So when the clerk asked him for a credit card and a driver's license, Furry Lewis put a spell on him. Oh, it wasn't any evil spell, but it was a deceitful one: he hummed a little tune as he reached into his wallet and brought out two smooth strips of plastic, and as he hummed he smiled very wide.

"That'll be great," the clerk said, running one of the strips through a device that would have took an impression from it if it'd been a credit card; copying nonexistent numbers from the surface of the other. When he was done he asked Furry Lewis how long he'd need the car.

"I'll take it for a week," Furry Lewis said. A week was longer than he figured he would need the car, but it was better to be sure.

"Insurance?"

"Yes, please."

"Great. And you wanted to pay for that in cash?"

"I do."

The clerk pushed a contract toward the deadman; at the bottom there was a dollar amount, circled in red ink. Furry Lewis took the money from his wallet and pushed it toward the clerk.

The clerk handed him the keys along with his change.

"Right out that door," he said. "Third car on the left — you can't miss it."

Ten minutes later they were on I-10, heading toward New Orleans. They made good time at first. It wasn't hard; all the traffic was moving in the opposite direction.

Furry Lewis did the driving; Vaughan rode shotgun. Red took the back seat — both sides of it. He sprawled out across the length of it, sort of resting, sort of stretching out, but not as relaxed or comfortable as either of those things. More like a man writhing in the dirt someplace, maybe suffering a little, maybe suffering a lot, but without the stamina to wail. . . .

He seemed to get a little better as they drove the Caddy east-southeast toward New Orleans.

But not much better.

"What's wrong with him, Furry?" Vaughan asked as they passed a sign that said La Place — 10 Miles. As he asked that question Red groaned from the back seat, long and low all haunting-like, so unearthly that even dead Stevie Ray Vaughan shivered at the sound. "I don't like the sound of that at all."

Furry Lewis didn't take his eyes off the road, but he nodded. "I don't like it, either. I don't know what's got into him. He ought to be vivacious as he ever is."

Vaughan leaned back to get a glance at the prone deadman. "Red? Hey, Red, is there anything we can do for you?"

Tampa Red shook his head — so slightly that Vaughan almost didn't see it. "I'm fine," he said. "I just don't feel so good, that's all."

Now the sign before them said La Place — Next Exit 2 Miles, and Vaughan reached into the glove box to check the map to see how far they had left to go. He could have saved himself the effort — because suddenly there were red traffic-control cones lined up all along the highway, shunting them toward the exit, and the sign said Road Closed — All Traffic Exit Right.

Two dozen heavily armed men and women in National Guard uniforms stood on either side of the sign, enforcing the closure.

"What the hell. . . ?" Vaughan asked.

Furry Lewis swore profanely.

When they were halfway off the exit it finally came to

Vaughan that they'd come across. "They've closed the city down," he said. "All the way the hell out to here."

Furry Lewis nodded.

Vaughan looked at his map, trying to figure out how they were going to get into the city. It wasn't much use; the New Orleans detail map gave out long before La Place, and the state map only showed two roads along the route — I-10 and US-61. They knew I-10 was closed, and it was an easy bet that US-61 was, too. Too easy; there wasn't a chance they'd miss it if they closed I-10.

No way to go around to the north — Lake Pontchartrain was in the way.

But it was different to the south. Because south of New Orleans is Cajun country, and there are more tiny roads through the swamps than anyone can count — lots more than the National Guard can close in a few hours.

"We ought to be able to get through if we travel along the south bank," Vaughan said. "We need to turn back — the nearest bridge goes across the river about ten miles back."

Furry Lewis nodded. Turned left under the Interstate, then left again to get back on it going in the opposite direction. Twenty minutes later they crossed the river by Vacherie and turned right onto SR-18, which is what the maps call that part of the river road that follows the south bank of the Mississippi from Baton Rouge to New Orleans.

SR-18 took them all the way into the outlying suburbs of New Orleans before they found another National Guard road-block at the junction with Interstate 310.

Just before they got to the roadblock Red sat up in the back seat and groaned. He was breathing, Vaughan could hear — breathing laboriously and unsteady. Vaughan looked back and saw that Red was covered with sickly sweat like he'd never seen on a deadman.

"Turn right," Red told them. "Right here, into the dirt."

Furry Lewis didn't argue with him; he did exactly as Red asked. Vaughan, now, he would have argued — he did argue, in fact. Not that it mattered.

"There isn't any road here," Vaughan said. "What're you going to do, plow through that hedge?"

Furry Lewis laughed, because that was exactly what he meant to do.

Through the hedge; crosswise over some farmer's driveway; through a barbed-wire fence on the far side of it.

"It's going to cost you a piece," Vaughan said, "when you pay for what you just did to this Cadillac's grille."

Furry Lewis shrugged as the Cadillac surged into the pasture. "I'm good for it," he said.

Vaughan laughed. "I know you are," he said.

As half a dozen head of cattle scattered across the field, trying to get out of their way.

"Bear left," Red whispered. "You'll find a dirt road not far from the southeast end of the field."

Cow-pats spattered off the tires, and here and there the Caddy's tires spun wild in the mud. When they were halfway across, the farmer came out of his farmhouse and started waving a shotgun at them.

Furry Lewis didn't pay him any mind, except to laugh a little at the sight of the man in such hysteria.

Kept laughing, too, even when the farmer raised his gun and started shooting.

Maybe because the farmer missed, or maybe because Furry Lewis was a deadman not susceptible to murder, or maybe because the whole experience struck a chord with him — who can say?

Who can say indeed.

As they reached the field's southeast corner, and the Cadillac plowed over the corner fencepost.

"When you get to the road, turn straight," Red said, which made no damn sense at all until they got to the road and came onto it where it bent, and to their right it was more-or-less west and straight ahead mostly south.

A long, smooth dirt road that looked like it went on forever into bayou country. It wasn't on the map — not either one, not the state map nor the detail map of New Orleans.

"I bet the Guard doesn't even know about this road," Vaughan said. "I think we're going to make it."

Furry Lewis didn't look convinced. "I wouldn't worry about the Guard," he said. "But I'm not looking forward to what's ahead of us."

That brought back the things Vaughan saw on the news that afternoon, and reminded him of the dread he felt in his heart when he'd seen it.

Sobered him considerably.

"Look for yourself, Stevie Ray," he said. "There, in the swamp-woods off to your left. Let your heart look through your eyes, and you'll see them."

It was dusk, almost the end of dusk — but when Vaughan looked into the woods he saw them clearly as he'd see in the brightest part of day.

Clearer, maybe. For the things he saw were minor loa — swamp devils like you'd conjure in the tropics to curse the children of the wetlands. And hellish things like those are clearer in the night than they can be in the day.

"It's Hell, Stevie Ray. All around us, here — Hell has fallen up to earth."

Stevie Ray Vaughan wanted to argue, because he didn't want to believe that such a thing could happen. But even as he did he knew that he was wrong.

He knew where he was.

Of course he did. All deadmen know the winds of Hell. They taste those winds for hours when they're gone, before they sing the Hell-door open and walk back among the pathways of the living.

"Five miles down along this way," Red said. He sounded stronger, now — almost hale and whole. "And then you'll find a crossroads. There will be a fire, there, and the ruins of a boneyard. The bones will tell you which turn to take."

Vaughan understood that better than he was comfortable with. Furry Lewis said, "Of course," and gave a little nod like that was the obvious thing.

Suburban New Orleans
The Present

Emma didn't pay much attention which way she went as she tore out of the Kmart parking lot. That was a terrible mistake, because her turns took her exactly where she didn't want to go — back into the old heart of the city, where the hardest part of Hell had fallen up to earth.

A terrible, terrible mistake.

The first clue she had that she'd stumbled into something bad was when the streetlights went dark all around her, as power failed throughout the city suddenly lit only by the brilliance of the blood-red moon — and just as suddenly dead-end barricades appeared before her on the road.

"Oh my God," Emma whispered, slamming down on the brake pedal. The Buick's tires screamed and skidded long and hard before the car came to a stop.

Backed the car up; put it back in gear. Rolled back onto the road.

When she came to the next intersection Emma saw light off in the distance to the right, and she thought that light had to be a way out of this awful place.

But she was wrong.

When she followed the light it led her to the worst thing she'd come upon in a day full of terrible discoveries: it led her into the midst of a battle where a legion of the damned did battle with the Louisiana National Guard.

She screamed again when she saw that.

"We've got to get out of here," Emma said. She did a U-turn, drove a few blocks back away from the battlefield. Turned into what looked to be a quiet alley; pulled the car over, switched on the dome light, found her map, and tried to figure out how the hell they were going to get out of there.

As she read the map she felt a hand on her leg, sliding upward — it damn near scared her to death. When she saw it was Leadbelly making a pass at her she grabbed the hand by the wrist and pushed it away from her.

She wasn't gentle. At all.

"What's the matter, baby?" Leadbelly asked. "You don't like me?"

"You tried to sell me to the Devil," Emma said. "You thought I'd pay a gambling debt! Keep your foul hands to yourself."

"Oh," he said. "Oh, Emma Henderson, it wasn't really like that. You know it wasn't! You got to understand what I was trying to accomplish!"

"I bet you were," she told him. "I hate to think what it would have come to if the Devil would have took me."

"I wouldn't let him do that," Leadbelly said. "I would have took you back, woman. I promise that I would!"

That was half a lie, at least. But Emma wasn't certain which half was which.

But it wasn't like she had a chance to consider the question. Because suddenly there was heavy breathing too damn close, and Emma tried to push dead Leadbelly away from her — only Leadbelly wasn't there.

When Emma tried to fend him off all she pushed against was air.

Because Leadbelly wasn't anywhere near her.

He was on the far side of the car, leaning against his window, staring into space, and the breathing wasn't coming from his direction anyway.

It was coming from outside the car.

Emma didn't have to think to realize they were in some awful kind of trouble; she reached for the keys to start the ignition, turned, turned and the car's engine rolled over but it didn't catch. Stole a glance over her shoulder as she pumped the gas pedal, one, two, three, and dear God sweet Jesus there were eyes out there staring at her, wide enormous eyes the size of plates and bloodshot yellow. Emma screamed she tried to start the car but it wouldn't start, wouldn't effing start, the engine was flooding oh God no no no —

As the glass beside her shattered, and some awful thing dragged her from her seat.

Through the shattered window as shards of glass shredded her blouse, gouged her arms, her breasts, but she hardly felt it, she screamed, flailed wild with her fists as she saw teeth like carving knives glitter in the moonlight —

And she knew she was going to die, and she knew that there was no hope in the world, and she could have gone limp defeated as the awful thing devoured her but that wasn't Emma, she tried to fight so long as she could —

— *kicked* —

— and hit.

Something.

Hit something soft and wet.

The toe of her right shoe, oh Christ her foot was in it up to the ankle what was that stuff no, no, no, no —

— as the devil roared, doubled over, dropped her —

Emma tried to run.

She really tried.

But it wasn't that easy. Her foot was stuck in, in, she didn't know what. She didn't want to know, and then it was free, but it was, it felt, oh God she was on fire, wasn't she?

And all she managed to do was stumble a few hysterical steps as the *thing* came up looking for her with a vengeance.

It got her, too.

And it killed her, long and slow and painfully. . . .

Caught her by the back collar of her dress as Emma tried to run, raised her high above its grinding jaws teeth gleaming like a thousand sabers, vapor rising up like the stink of death dear Lord that was its breath as it lowered Emma into the crushing maw —

As the talons that held Emma released her, and she dropped into the pit —

No.

No no no no.

It didn't happen like that, no matter how Emma thought it did.

Oh, the talons released her, and Emma fell screaming to her death, but something went wrong on the way down, and suddenly she was on the ground, hitting the pavement *hard* shoulders first, and suddenly a mountain of fetid meat fell beside her, and she looked up disoriented to see Leadbelly. He had his switchblade out again, and it was gleaming in the moonlight, awful ichorous stuff drizzling along the edge, from the point —

"*Leadbelly,*" she said. She was crying, wasn't she? Yes, she was sobbing, trembling. . . .

"I told you I'd do right by you. You believe me now, Emma Henderson?"

Emma didn't have an answer. She didn't have words, didn't have — didn't have the presence of mind to comprehend the question.

"Come on," he said, taking her arm, helping her to her feet. "We got to get out of here before another boogie man can find us."

Bayou Country, Jefferson Parish
The Present

There were boneyard vapors at the crossroads, directing them to the left, and they almost went that way. But before they did Furry Lewis pulled over to the edge of the road and parked the car and cut the engine. Got out of his seat and left the car to approach the crossroads on foot.

There he faced the ghosts, and held them to an interlocution; and when he did he learned they meant him ill.

He came back to the car shaking his head.

"They're trying to direct us into a trap," Furry Lewis said. "I don't know what it is, but I don't like it. I'm going the other way."

Vaughan frowned. He gestured at the map. "That's going to take us a long way from New Orleans," he said. "Maybe hours away."

Furry Lewis hesitated. "Maybe," he said. "Maybe we ought to run the trap."

Red opened his eyes again when he heard that. And spoke very softly, but with a sureness that chilled Vaughan to the bone. "No," he said. "That's wrong. Bear left, here. Follow the road with your heart."

And who could argue with that? Furry Lewis said, "If you're sure, Red, that's what we'll do." Vaughan shook his head, but he didn't say a word.

The swamp road led them southeast among the bayous, in the general direction of the river's outlet to the sea. A couple times Vaughan wanted to say, Wait, this is wrong, we're going way the hell out of our way, but he knew that was wrong, because it was only sense, and the real path was a thing like Red told them — it was a thing you had to follow through your heart.

Swamps and bayous on both sides of the road, and now and then murky-looking pinewoods. And then suddenly there was a big abandoned pepper plantation off to their left, and

Vaughan saw a man in a uniform, and the moment that he saw that man his heart knew of him.

"Pull over," he said, "You've got to pull into that farm on the left."

"I see him," Furry Lewis said. "You think I could miss a man like that?"

But that was a question that wasn't what it seemed, because the truth was that till that moment Furry Lewis had failed to notice him entirely; and that was strange, and partly frightful, too.

"I dreamed about him in the air," Red said. "That's Robert Brown — known generally as Washboard Sam — flesh and bone."

"I know it is," Furry Lewis said. "You think I don't know Sam?" As he asked that question he pulled into the plantation's driveway, and followed the driveway's left branch back toward the place where Washboard Sam stood guard.

Nobody answered the question. They all knew the answer.

When they got to there they found Washboard Sam leaning on a fencepost. His uniform was a security guard uniform, and he was the law in that place as much as there was one.

There was Magic all around him, buzzing in the air with a strange electric intensity. When he looked Stevie Ray Vaughan in the eye the deadman's lifeless heart began to beat.

"I never heard you, Sam," Furry Lewis said. He looked — amazed. Stunned. And it only makes sense that he'd be amazed, after all; for all the years since the great King died, he was the one who kept the tradition; first when he was alive and then after he passed on. After Elvis died refusing the burden and the legacy, Furry Lewis came upon the Dominion his own self. If the world were upright Furry Lewis would have heard the music anytime a deadman sang it in the river kingdom.

But it wasn't right. And that wasn't news; it hadn't been right in a long, long time.

"It's in the nature of the times," Washboard Sam said. "The music doesn't carry like it should."

Furry Lewis allowed as that was so.

That was when Red opened the back door and pushed himself out of the Cadillac. Stood beside it on uncertain legs, leaning against the side of the car to steady himself.

"The Lady sang to me, Sam," he said. "All the way down in Hell, she was, and she sang to me as I lay deathly in the air."

Washboard Sam didn't say a word. He didn't look pleased to listen, either.

"She told me where to find you, Sam. And she told me to bring you with us."

Vaughan wanted to ask what else she'd told him, but he knew it was the wrong moment.

"Is that so?" Sam asked.

"It's a fact," Red said. He held up a trembling hand, as though he were taking an oath. "I swear it is."

"Where she sending you?"

"New Orleans," Furry Lewis said.

Vaughan shook his head. "Hell," he said, and he didn't mean it as an expletive.

Washboard Sam laughed. "That's wrong," he said. "You can't go anyplace you already are."

And that was exactly true, Vaughan realized when he looked around him — the pepper, the woods, the swamps, everything around there took a demonic cast, and when he looked closely at the plantation around him he began to wonder if it was a place dragged up from Hell, or a worldly place possessed.

And then he thought, *It's not a worldly farm at all, it's something from damnation* — but he wasn't sure as he should be.

"You'll help us?" Vaughan asked. "We need you if you can."

Sam frowned. "I will," he said.

The Devil's Quarter of New Orleans
The Present

The way back into the city led through the Devil's Quarter, and that was a frightful thing. Under the light of the blood-red moon what should have been the ruins of the worst part of the city were ruins of another place entirely — Dan Alvarez recognized them as the Lady led them out of the bayous.

They were the ruins of the Fallen City, and Dan had walked among them before — just hours ago, when he and Polly and dead Elvis had crawled out of the fiery waters of the Bosphorus of Hell.

"I'm afraid," Dan whispered into Polly's ear. "There are devils everywhere."

Polly took his hand and squeezed it. She said, "Sing," but she didn't sound reassuring.

At least partly because she couldn't be. Oh, the devils kept their distance as Robert Johnson sang and played his guitar; as the baby Lisa played her toy kazoo; and when Dan sang with them they stayed even farther back. But Dan knew it couldn't be that easy to disarm the Legions of the Damned, and he was right.

For as they crossed the Devil's Quarter, the damned grew thicker and thicker around them, till now as they reached the Devil's Mansion a vast and seething mob surrounded them, and if their song had paused a moment the horde would have consumed them in a moment.

Robert Johnson sang "Let Your Light Shine on Me," just as Blind Willie sang it, and the mob gave way again and again — until they reached the great lawn before the Mansion.

When they reached that place the mob stood its ground, and for a long moment Dan Alvarez thought they'd reached their end. There were so many of them! Thousands and thousands of them, devils and damned men and women with hearts as black as the starless sky, and every moment a thousand more welled up through the doors and windows of the Mansion, and soon the thick of them would press in upon them. . . .

"*Make way,*" the Lady demanded. "*Make way or I will make it through you.*"

But the damned horde did not yield.

Not even when the Lady drew her great fiery sword, and leveled it; not even as great flowers of fire bloomed out of it, piercing the night.

Instead of yielding the mob surged toward them —

For Lisa it was like this:

One moment she was standing terrified behind the Lady, half certain that the *santa* could protect her no matter what might come, half convinced that it was hopeless, and the demonic bloody hungry mob would overrun them in a moment, tearing them limb from limb from limb, and now the great red-eyed doglike thing thundered out of the crowd, bearing down on her, and she screamed. and screamed again as its shoulder slammed into Dan Alvarez, throwing the poor man half a dozen yards, and now the demon's great black-taloned left arm shot toward her like a club made out of hard sulfurous flesh, grabbing her by the hair to lift her off her feet, and she thought her scalp would tear away from her skull, and it hurt, hurt, and tiny baby Lisa who wasn't any baby down inside tiny baby Lisa *screamed* as the demon swung her 'round and 'round its canine head —

And suddenly there was fire all around her, and Lisa fell hard on her back. At first she thought she was about to die, she *knew* she was about to die, the dog demon was going to kill her look the shadow the show of the devil plummeting toward her —

No.

Collapsing on her.

As Lisa found the presence of mind to roll out of the way, and saw the demon drop headless to the ground beside her —

— as its head rolled and rolled through the air, hit ground, bounced, and came to rest before her feet.

And Lisa looked up to see the Lady standing above her, smiling hungrily. Black demon blood sputtered and fumed as it drizzled from her sword.

"*Santa,*" Lisa said.

The Lady said nothing.

Not a solitary word.

Instead she stepped into the thick of the demonic throng — and began to cut a path of blood and butchery, leading them to war.

Downtown New Orleans
The Present

There was another National Guard roadblock when they got to the Greater New Orleans Bridge — the one that crosses from Jefferson Parish into downtown New Orleans — but this one was a shambles. There were splintered barricades and the corpses of three dozen Guardsmen, and off the sides of the bridge ramp were the burned-out hulks of overturned humvees.

Stevie Ray Vaughan said, "Grim," and somebody else, maybe

Red, grunted in assent. Furry Lewis didn't say a word; he kept his eyes on the dark surface of the road and tried to avoid the obstacles that littered their way.

When they got to the far side of the bridge they could see fires scattered all across the city, but there was no other light. Vaughan wondered how long the power had been out, and how much was left of the burning city, and he found an answer in his gut but he didn't want to admit it, not even to himself.

The nearest of the fires was City Hall, burning spectacularly a few blocks to their right. There were wrecked fire trucks all around it and demons dancing through the flames, and other devils gnawing on the bones of firemen. When Vaughan saw that, he ached, and turned away before he could see anything else.

But there was no escaping it. Because that was where Furry Lewis pulled over to the side of the road, got out of the car, and walked to the rail at the edge of the bridge ramp.

And watched.

"Look," he said, and Stevie Ray Vaughan looked because he knew he had to.

Terrible, terrible fire. Roaring out of control. He got out of the Cadillac a moment after Red and Sam, and joined Furry Lewis at the rail.

"As bad as it could be," Red said, and he pointed. Vaughan thought he was pointing at the brigade of Louisiana National Guard moving up Loyola toward City Hall. *Imagine that,* Vaughan thought, *the Louisiana National Guard thinks it can meet the Legions of the Damned with a brigade of weekend warriors,* and he wanted to laugh at the thought but he wanted to cry, too, because he knew they were good brave and loyal men and women, and he knew they were doomed. . . .

"Not the soldiers," Red said. "Look inside the fire."

Vaughan gasped when he saw what Red was pointing at. Because he saw a great tower in that fire, a place as dear and doomed as any place that ever was or ever will be.

For inside the fire that was City Hall stood the great ruin of the tower of the Fallen City, and every bluesman knows that place in his heart. That tower (in its greatest days, before angels cast it out of Heaven) was where three angels forged the Eye of the World.

"That's where we're going," Furry Lewis said. He sounded surer than Vaughan had ever heard him sound.

"Through that fire?" Vaughan asked. "That place is overrun with — things from Hell. I wouldn't want to try to get through either one of them."

Furry Lewis shrugged. "Let the Guard do its job," he said. "They're good at what they do."

"They aren't any match —"

Furry Lewis cut him off. "You're wrong," he said.

And then he began to play.

After a moment Red and Sam joined him, and Vaughan found the song inside him, too.

As their song slowly slowly filled the night. It reached the Guard in wisps and phrases, like a rumor of a chance, and buoyed them as the most terrible enemies in creation set upon them. As Vaughan watched good men died, and others struggled, but bit by bit they drove the Enemies of the World away.

By ten o'clock the battle was two blocks away from City Hall, which maybe didn't matter since the fire had entirely consumed that place. Furry Lewis told them to keep singing, and led them into the city on foot.

It wasn't as short a walk as it seemed to be when they stood on the bridge. Not at all. It was a long half mile off the bridge ramp, and the way was so dark — with the power out and all the streetlamps dark, with no light at all but the burning city and the blood-red moon — so dark that they had to move slowly, carefully through the night and menace closed in all around them. It was almost eleven before they got to the steps of City Hall, and by then there was nothing left of that place but ashes and dust and cool embers of what once had been a fire.

Ashes, dust, embers — and the ghostly ruins of a tower that once had commanded the Cliffs of Heaven, and not long ago had abided on the shores of Hell.

"It's beautiful," Vaughan said, because the music was in his heart, and he could hear the song of Heaven when he saw that place.

"It is," said Furry Lewis. He climbed the blackened stone

steps that not long ago had led to New Orleans City Hall, stumbled through the drifty ashes to stand before the tower —

And a cool wind roiled from the east, and somewhere in the nearest distance a mockingbird cawed four and four, syncopated — as the Blind Lords of the Piedmont appeared in New Orleans.

— In the City of New Orleans, far, far from the kingdom where they rule.

Two of them were white and one was black, or maybe one of them was white and two were black, or maybe they were all black, the paintbrush touches us all in its way, doesn't it? We are a nation made at the crossroads where two things meet, and the consequences of that meeting make us all the people who we are.

The Blind Lords appeared in a mist of vagabond dust, and Furry Lewis smiled at them — no matter that they were uninvited trespassers in his Delta Kingdom.

He called them by name (they have the names of angels, and maybe they've taken them or maybe they were born with them) and they smiled like they'd met a brother at reunion, and as they did some great rift in the nation's heart began to heal as it never could before.

"I love you," Furry Lewis said. "You are my brothers and I love you."

The Blind Lords didn't answer, and long as the four Kings of the Delta waited they never answered, but their silence neither embraced nor denied the love the King proclaimed.

Two of them were white, now, and one was black. These things change from time to time, depending on the circumstance and the context. They aren't nearly so important as they seem.

Because we are the nation that the crossroads built, and after that what else matters?

"You've come at a fine moment," Furry Lewis said. "You come to help?"

The Blind Lords didn't answer. No one who saw them could be exactly sure what that meant.

"We aren't here," the darkest of the Blind Lords said, "but only seem to be."

That was true, of course. The Blind Lords of the Piedmont may neither tread in Hell nor upon the Mississippi Delta; it's a consequence of their nature, just as they are a consequence of ours.

"I don't get it," Vaughan said. "If you aren't here to help, what are you doing?"

And the Blind Lords smiled. And the first of them (or was he the third?) struck an unmasterable chord as his companions touched the fallen tower —

Which exploded in a palisade of light and sound like an explosion, but musical and fundamental manifest: and when the light went dim every solitary fact about their circumstance had changed.

Where a moment previous the broken citadel had towered, now there stood a gleaming structure as glorious as it had been the day the angels erected it, and where grey ashes had sifted in the wind now there was a mist as beautiful and pure as the cloudy wisps that decorate the heavens, and where the cacophony of battle had permeated the air now there was a music like the ringing of the spheres.

"Lord, Lord," said Washboard Sam.

As Red fell to his knees and began to pray.

A moment later Furry Lewis joined him. Vaughan and Sam just a moment later still.

When their prayer was done Vaughan looked around him and saw a crowd was gathering.

"Where are they?" he asked. Furry Lewis cocked an eyebrow to ask him what he meant. "The blind men, the Lords, where are they?"

Furry Lewis shrugged.

"Gone," he said. "As if they never were."

"But we need them!"

Furry Lewis shook his head. "No," he said. "They've done everything they can."

•

Leadbelly's directions only ended up getting them more lost. When they'd driven ten minutes through the chiaroscuro of the dark and burning city Emma realized that they were back where they'd started, on Loyola, not far from the French Quarter.

And then she saw it, gleaming glorious as an icon through the Hellish dark and burning: the Tower.

So beautiful, that Tower. Beautiful and Godly in the midst of the awfulness of that night where the world had turned to Hell, and the moment that she saw it she knew it was their salvation.

She pulled the car over, got out of it, and walked toward the Tower. Leadbelly called after her. "What the Hell you think you're doing, woman? Where do you think you are?" But Emma ignored him. Which was just as well; half a moment after he asked those questions he got out of the car, slammed his door, and ran to catch up with her.

And followed Emma to the edge of the Revival.

•

Vaughan stood on the steps, looking out at the crowd. He tried to pick out faces, pick out people, sort the living from the dead — but it wasn't easy. Some of them damned, come up from Hell, and some were the living breathing people of New Orleans. None of them repentant, but none of the damned among them were damned beyond all hope of salvation — no one who was damned through and through could abide the sight of the Tower as it stood in Heaven, he thought. When they saw the light it drew them, and that attraction marked the decency inside them.

Then someone whispered, *It's the Jubilee,* and a murmur went back and forth through the crowd, and Vaughan felt it begin to happen all around him. . . .

There is a thing some people call the Carnival and some people call Mardi Gras, and other people call the Jubilee; some of them celebrate it at the Easter season and other people observe it in high summer. Evangelicals call it a *revival,* and that's as true a name as anyone could give it. They call it any time it comes to them, and it came to them that night when Hell became New Orleans.

Washboard Sam, still wearing his uniform of authority, knew it in his heart. Because he knew it he directed it. He stood on what were once the steps of City Hall — they faced south from the Tower — and sent Furry Lewis south before him. He sent Tampa Red east and Stevie Ray Vaughan west.

"Sing it out," he said. "Sing it to the people of the city — let them hear the Good Word of the Lord."

"Sing what?" Stevie Ray Vaughan asked. "I don't understand, what do you want me to sing? And why?"

Washboard Sam smiled, and he said, "There's a song inside your heart, Stevie Ray Vaughan. Find it and sing it, and that song will show the way."

And then he began to sing himself.

Inside the four points of that compass, there before the steps that led toward the gleaming Tower, their song made a place where no wholly evil thing could walk, a place that drew men and women with the shadow of Salvation in their hearts as surely as a light will draw the firefly, and when they came they stood mystified before the gleaming Tower that once was the Blessed Jewel of Heaven.

●

When Emma and Leadbelly got to the corner of Loyola and Perdido they found a throng of people crowding around the Tower, so many of them pressed so thick that there was hardly room to pass. Leadbelly stopped at the back edge of the crowd to peer at the Tower, at the crowd, at the bluesman singing endlessly hypnotic jam somewhere just out of sight — and when he got a good look he started to back away.

"What's the matter?" Emma asked him. "Don't just stand there — we've got to go inside."

Leadbelly scowled. "No, woman," he said. "Woman that ain't the place for men like me."

Emma looked at him crossways. "You're wrong," she said. "I know you are."

"I'm not," Leadbelly told her, but Emma wasn't having none of that. She grabbed his wrist and pulled him half off-balance into the crowd, and when he resisted they both stumbled and ended up falling forward as the crowd gave way —

— gave way —

Gave way to reveal the singing deadman, and that was Furry Lewis.

Now Leadbelly and Furry Lewis had some history between them, and it wasn't pleasant stuff. But there was no way Emma could know that. When Emma saw that man her knees like to collapse beneath her, because she knew he was a man who'd heard the Lord's voice whisper in his ear, and that voice carried through his song as truly as a night gives way to day, and day to night thereafter.

But Leadbelly didn't see him till he got up from his stumble and found himself face to face with the man who was first among the Kings.

"Come on," Emma said, pulling Leadbelly past the bluesman. But her pulling was no use, because there was a barrier where Furry Lewis sang, and that barrier was hard as steel so far as Leadbelly was concerned, no matter how nobody there could see it.

"I can't, Emma Henderson. Like I said, that place is not for me."

He turned away from Furry Lewis. And where he might in some other circumstance have pulled a knife on the deadman, or threatened him, or sneered at him and walked away, in that moment in that place on that night Huddie Ledbetter, known most commonly as Leadbelly — Huddie Ledbetter felt himself ashamed.

And in his moment of shame Emma pulled his wrist again, and now he fell through the barrier as surely as though he had never stood before him in the first place.

●

It took the *santa* and her party most of an hour and a half to cut their way through the demon horde. Dan sang until his throat grew hoarse, and he kept singing, because he knew that the moment that his song should fail the horde would be upon them, tearing them limb from limb. . . .

They all sang, even dead Elvis — all of them but the *santa*. Maybe she had no song inside her heart, or maybe there was no room for song inside her as she cut the path before them with her great fiery sword that flared and sputtered each time it drew the ichor of a demon, and the fire and the chary bits of demon-hide were everywhere, filling the air like an unholy rain, spattering their clothes, their skin. Caustic on Dan's skin, acrid where he breathed the vapors from it, and now as Dan looked at the grue that covered him he wanted to scream — scream and turn and run for his life and his sanity.

Run for the hills! he thought, but there are no hills around New Orleans, and anyway he'd be torn to ribbons the moment that his song should end. Despair tried again and again to consume him, but he didn't stop singing. Not even for the time it would take to breathe. He didn't dare, and he knew it; his fear was greater than any despair could ever be.

And then they came around a corner onto Loyola, and there in the distance was the Tower.

So beautiful, that Tower! From where Dan stood it seemed to be made of pure white light, and it spoke to his heart of hope and the promise of Redemption. Filled his song with hope and joy, and now as they heard the sound of machine-gun fire the *santa*'s sword cut hard and fast through the horde, and the horde opened up before them to reveal a battlefield.

Someone in the distance shouted, "Don't shoot! They're on our side!" and Dan couldn't begin to imagine how they knew such a thing, but he was glad they did.

As the *santa* raised her sword before them to light the way, and now they passed unchallenged through the lines of the Louisiana National Guard.

●

Come midnight the crowd inside the songsters' compass huddled close before the Tower, and the revival started of its own accord. Washboard Sam, standing on the steps that once led to New Orleans City Hall, let his song drift away, and he addressed the crowd before him as though he were a revivalist and the stair-steps were his platform.

"My friends," Washboard Sam the revivalist said, "my friends, I have called you here tonight so that we may all behold the testimony of three sinners!"

And the crowd roared in response, repeating his refrain: *"Testimony of the sinners!"*

"Three people whose acts and deeds in the course of their mortal lives and their damnation have condemned them to tarnation, and given them the cruelest fate a body may endure. But all of these sinners have heard the Glory of the Word of the Lord, and that word is God! Yes, yes, my friends, yes it is!"

And the crowd roared, *"Yes it is!"*

The revivalist stepped out onto the front edge of his plat-

form, and he picked out one of the damned residents of New
Orleans, seemingly at random. But there was nothing random
in his choice — nothing at all.

For the woman he chose was the worst of sinners. Her name
was Rebecca, and she was the owner-lady of the Greenville bar —
the woman who'd spent a week in a state of assignation with
Robert Johnson as her jealous husband looked on; the same
woman who'd given him the succor and the strength to shatter
the Eye of the World.

The woman stood when the revivalist pointed to her, and
started toward the platform. She trembled as she walked toward
it, and trembled worse as she climbed onto it.

"Before you stands Rebecca Carter," the revivalist said. "In
her day she was a good woman and a bad woman, too; she fell
into temptation, and in the end that sin consumed her.

"But there's more to Rebecca Carter than the sin. There's
the light inside her, too, the light in every one of us who's
heard the Good Word of the Lord —

"Good Word of the Lord!" the crowd roared.

"— and it shines through her sin as gloriously as it shines
inside that Tower!"

The owner-lady wept as the revivalist described her.

"My name is Rebecca Carter," the owner-lady said, "and I
have sinned."

"Sinned!"

As she spoke, as the crowd roared, a torch-bearing procession
made its way through the crowd, and the torch its captain held
was no torch but a burning sword. Somewhere in the crowd
Emma Henderson saw the procession and the people in it and
shouted, "That's my baby! My baby Lisa!" and she tried to run
to embrace her child. But the sinister man beside her took her
arm and held her back, and he said, "No, Emma, you can't —
she's got a special place this evening," and after a moment the
frantic mother relented.

As the procession passed through the crowd, climbed the
platform, and continued past it, into the glorious Tower made
of light.

"My first sin was adultery," Rebecca Carter said. "I loved my
husband, but I saw another and I took him as though he were

my own."

A murmur passed through the crowd. Someone repeated the last line of her confession, as though it were a refrain: *"As though he were your own."*

"He wasn't mine, and I knew it. And even worse I took him in the plain sight of my husband. And that drove his heart insane." She paused, as though she expected a response, but there was none. "My husband tried to kill my lover, and he beat me half to death. When the beating was over, I tried to save my lover, and I very nearly did it. But he died — partly because his death was foregone, partly because his vanity consumed him in a hail of fire and brimstone."

"His vanity consumed him," the crowd responded, but softly, softly, as though the words consumed them, too.

"I didn't return to my husband when my lover was gone, but took up in a boardinghouse, and kept to myself while my heart recovered from my loss and my body recovered from the beating he gave me.

"And then one night, three months to the day after the beating, I put a pistol in my purse to ensure my self-protection, and I went to my husband's new tavern, intending to give that awful man a piece of my mind.

"I found him in a dark corner of the tavern, writhing in a barmaid's arms. And there and then a thing came over me that I never imagined I could know: I felt a jealous rage consume me!"

"A jealous rage consumed her!"

"I saw him, that man I reviled and the wanton girl, and where a moment before I'd despised that man now I knew I owned him, and could not bear to see him with another. In that moment I forgot myself. I took that pistol from my purse and shot them both, and then I shot again and again, for the rage in my heart demanded I make certain they were dead. And then I ran from that place, and my life, and all my worldly goods, into a life of poverty and misery and terror of the law.

"But from that day to this, no matter what the misery that found me, I never regretted. Not for a moment. That rage consumed me until this evening, when I saw the Tower and the light. And now as I look upon it I know the error of my ways, as light dispels the darkness of the heart!"

Now Rebecca Carter wailed, and her cry was a sound of torment as like to anguish the damned. Her face became a mask of grief and regret, and as her wail trailed off she began to sob piteously.

"I was wrong," she shouted. "He was a dirty bastard, but he was mine, and I loved him, and he's gone. And I killed him, Lord Lord, Lord, I killed him."

"Lord, Lord, Lord."

•

Lisa didn't stop playing her kazoo until the Lady led them into the Tower made of light. And even then she kept it in her hand where she could get it in a moment if the darkness pressed on them again — but it didn't press. There was no dark inside that Tower, no dark and no possibility of darkness. It was the only homely place Lisa had been since, since, since so long she couldn't remember anymore.

So beautiful. So wonderful. So safe. Lisa felt as though someone had taken an enormous weight off of her back.

As the Lady led them through the base of the Tower, onto a winding stair that seemed to rise endlessly into the sky. They climbed that stair forever before they finally reached the top of it — where a great wood-and-iron door opened into the most amazing room Lisa had ever seen.

Inside that room there was a forge — like the blacksmith's forge in a movie Lisa saw when she was six, but cleaner and brighter and more beautiful.

The Lady piled seven logs into the forge's hearth, drew her sword, and set them afire. In a moment the fire was roaring, and the Lady took a bellows from the wall to stoke the flames hotter, brighter — and now the whole room glowed with the fire's heat.

All that while Robert Johnson, dead Elvis Presley, and the man and the woman who'd come with him stood watching the Lady intently, as though the fate of the world hinged on the fire she was building.

And maybe it did — Lisa could feel something great and important weighing on them, and every moment the weight grew more intense, till suddenly Lisa's shoulders could no longer support it. Then she felt so tired, and she thought, *What if I crawl away into the corner of the room and drift off to sleep. . . ?*

That was such a crazy idea, Lisa thought. But the lethargy consumed her, and she knew that if she didn't give in to it she'd stumble off her feet and collapse to the floor. Besides, no one would notice. They didn't really need her, did they?

But she knew they did, because the Lady told her so.

She kept thinking that as she sat in the corner, trying not to drift away: *They need me need me need me need me how can I sleep when the world has broken open?* — And then her dream began, and Lisa knew why sleep had overtaken her.

In her dream there were seven Kings, the old Kings who've only walked the world and Hell as vaporous phantoms since the battle on the ridge in Tennessee. The Kings stood around a forge, stoking the fire inside its hearth, and they were solider and more real than Lisa had seen them in any other dream. As Lisa approached the forge, one of the Kings — the one they call Blind Willie — turned to face her. He knelt to look her in the eye, and whispered to her.

What he whispered was a song: "Jesu Joy of Man's Desiring," recast and recut as blues. When the song was done he said, "Remember that, Lisa — it's important."

And Lisa said, "I don't understand. Why is it important?"

Blind Willie frowned, and hesitated. "When the Lady forges the Eye," he said, "You need to sing that song. There's a fire in that song, and the Eye needs a fire like that. The King will sing it with you. If he doesn't, you've got to make him sing."

And then she woke, as suddenly and wakeful as though she'd never slept at all.

•

As Rebecca Carter sobbed and shivered on the platform, a man approached her from the crowd. He was a horribly disfigured deadman with the scars of six pistol shots in his skull. When Rebecca Carter saw him, she gasped. And shouted, *"Fred!"* as she ran to embrace him, sobbing and wailing and shivering all the while, and after a while he led her away from the stage.

And maybe they shared a good eternity in damnation together, or maybe they were each other's damnation, and that was always meant to be. Or maybe they found that other thing that came upon the City of New Orleans late that night — who can say for sure? People hurt each other when they love each other. It's wrong and it's destructive, and maybe the cure is to run away and never look back — but maybe there's a time and place where people who've hurt one another can learn to live in love and peace, respectfully and Godfully, and maybe Fred and Rebecca Carter found that for each other.

Who can know? Who can say? Some days, some times, the only thing that we can do is pray.

•

When Lisa woke she saw the Lady taking the shattered Eye of the World from her carry-bag. So beautiful, those fragments — like jewels, but brighter and more glorious. One by one the Lady took them from her bag and placed them in the forge, till now the furnace hearth inside that place made the glittering fragments shine like tiny suns.

Lisa went to dead Elvis and tugged on his sleeve. "I had a dream," she said. "Blind Willie says you have to sing."

The deadman yanked his arm away from her. He had an expression on his face like she'd bit him hard enough to draw blood; he swore profanely under his breath.

"Get away from me, girl," he said. "I ain't got no business with Blind Willie."

"You're wrong," Lisa said. "He told me! He said, 'The King will sing it with you. If he doesn't, you've got to make him sing.'"

Dead Elvis scowled. "You've got the wrong man," he said. "The King you're looking for is Furry Lewis, out at the revival."

"No it isn't. I know who is the King, and I know you when I see you. You've got to sing."

•

When Rebecca and Fred Carter had disappeared into the crowd, Washboard Sam returned to the platform and peered again out into the crowd. This time he chose one of the greatest among the fallen — Sister O. M. Terrell.

When he saw her and pointed at her, the Sister stood unsteadily. The revivalist said, "Behold before you, sinners, Sister O. M. Terrell, who heard the sweet word of the Lord, and sang it to us all!"

"Sang it to us all!"

"She heard the good word, but she sinned. And that sin carries her to this day."

The crowd gasped, and there was a quiet hush — a hush so sad it like to break the Devil's heart, because he heard it where he sat upon his throne in his Mansion called Defiance, still aching from the cut Leadbelly gave him. Of course he heard it! When the Devil listens he hears everything in Hell, and that night he listened intently.

"Let her sing," the revivalist shouted, and the crowd roared, *"Let her sing!"*

And Sister O. M. Terrell staggered half-drunkenly to the edge of the platform, then climbed up onto it in a clumsy and unladylike fashion. When she was on the platform the crowd saw that she was holding her beautiful guitar, and no matter what else had become of her she still had the majesty and the poise that marked her as a *giftie* songster.

She strummed three chords, and the crowd murmured with awe.

"I lived a hard life, my friends. And it led me to this sorry state they call damnation."

Someone whispered *damnation.* A child in the back began to cry.

"I was a good woman, and an honest one; I took the *gifts* the good Lord gave me and made His handiwork my life work. And I did it well! But in my declining years I fell from that blessed state of Grace we call Salvation, and I found two demons."

"Two demons!" the crowd shouted back at her.

And Sister O. M. Terrell said, "Yes, yes, yes, I found two demons. One of them was smoke and one of them was drink, and they burned a fire in me that fed upon itself — and me."

"Burned afire!" the crowd repeated. The child wailed, now, shrieking piteously. She was so loud that for a moment she became the focus of the revival, and the Sister tried to comfort her from the platform.

"Do not weep for me, young lady," she said. "I am my own woman, and the mistakes I took to damn me are my very own.

They are indeed."

The crowd said, *"They are indeed,"* and the child calmed — just a little.

•

When the Lady took the smithy tongs from their place above the hearth and drew the glowing fragments of the Eye from the forge, Lisa lifted her kazoo to her lips and began the "Jesu" Blind Willie taught her in the dream.

The Lady smiled at her, because she knew the melody and knew what it would do — and then she beckoned.

"The Hammer," she said, and Lisa knew what she meant. Because she knew the Hammer that rings like a bell in her heart — and she'd recognized it when Dan Alvarez had carried it toward them through the bayou. The Hammer you use in the forge where you cast the Eye is John Henry's guitar, the Hammer that rings like a bell, the same Hammer the great King took from its place on the door of Hell. When it sat on the Black Door it was a sounding chime, and when the great King plied it open with the song in his heart it metamorphosed in his hands until it was the guitar that Elvis Presley stole. But underneath it all it was still the Hammer that three angels used to forge the Eye of the World an eternity ago.

And as Lisa played "Jesu Joy of Man's Desiring" on her toy kazoo, the melody resonated inside the Hammer's sounding box where it lay slung over Dan Alvarez's shoulder. The sound and the resonance surprised Dan Alvarez, and it seemed to frighten him, too. He took the guitar off his shoulder, held it out before him like it was some dreadful beast that set upon him. And he gaped.

For the longest time as Lisa played, he gaped.

"The Hammer," Santa Barbara repeated, more urgently this time.

And Dan Alvarez looked back and forth across the room, terrified and panic-stricken. Back and forth and back again, until his eye settled on dead Elvis.

Dan crossed the room toward him.

"It's yours," Dan Alvarez said, looking the deadman in the eye. Lisa nodded, carefully because she knew she didn't dare to interrupt her song.

"I told you," dead Elvis said, "and I'll tell you again — that Hammer ain't none of mine. I took it once, and that was a terrible mistake. But I don't take it anymore, you understand?"

But Dan Alvarez ignored him. He kept moving, slowly, steadily, carefully across the room until he stood just inches from the protesting deadman.

And then he put it on him. Not listening to the protests, not letting dead Elvis push it back on him.

As the guitar began to play, almost of its own accord.

Now, dead Elvis could have turned and run. He could have dropped the Hammer on the floor and said that was the end of it. He could have made his protests good a dozen different ways — but he didn't.

He couldn't, in the end. Everybody knows that. When the music's got inside a body there's no way he can avoid it; when the Hammer that rings like a bell takes you, it's got you, and there's no way to deny it.

Dead Elvis took John Henry's periapt guitar, and he *played*.

Played the melody Lisa drew for him, because it's a melody nobody can deny; and in the end that song consumed them all.

•

When Sister O. M. Terrell finished her testimony, she broke out into song, and the crowd sang with her. She sang "Let Your Light Shine on Me," which some people know (with its uplifting verses made coarse and ungodly) as "Midnight Special," and then she sang "You Know the Bible's Right," and when she was done the crowd was full of the clear pure spiritual joy that comes when plain folks find salvation.

Then the revivalist stepped back onto the platform and chose another sinner from the crowd.

He chose the worst man inside the compass, and some people would've said he found a man who never could repent. Maybe they were right, and maybe they weren't, but when Washboard Sam was revivalist the third sinner whose testimony he took was Huddie Ledbetter.

"Huddie Ledbetter," he said, pointing. "Huddie Ledbetter, I call you to testify before us!"

And Leadbelly swore a foul foul oath. "I won't," he said, and he meant it — but Emma Henderson pushed him forward, just as she'd pulled him into the revival's compass, and before he realized what was about the whole crowd was pushing him forward, from one to another to another, and it made no difference how he tried to resist, because the revival had took him and it was determined.

When he stood on the platform he glowered at the crowd. He wasn't pleased at all.

"You want you a sinner? All right, then, you got me."

"A sinner," the crowd repeated, all serious and grim.

"Yes, I'm a sinner. I like to drink, and I like to gamble, too. I turned on friends as bad as I turned on enemies, and I never took a shame of it, not when I could avoid it. I tried to kill a man who trusted me, and I tried to sell a woman to the Devil. But I never bowed to no man, and I don't bow to nobody else, either. You want me to say I was wrong? Maybe I was. Maybe I'm sorry. But if you want a man to kneel and pray, you better find another man."

A hush descended on the crowd. Leadbelly began to leave the platform, but then he stopped. Suddenly, abruptly. As a woman stood — far, far in the back, a woman stood, and she said, "You're lying, Huddie Ledbetter. I heard you sing, and I know you heard the sweet music of the Lord. You can't hear that song without you ever feel repentance in your heart."

Huddie Ledbetter swore profanely.

"Lady, what do you think you know?" he asked. "What do you know about what I heard or didn't hear? You never lived my life. It's mine."

The woman was still standing. "I know you, Huddie Ledbetter. I heard you sing, and I know you for everything you are. And you ain't as bad as all of that."

"You're wrong," the deadman said. "I can't begin to say how wrong you are, lady."

But even as he said those words, something shifted in his heart, and every congregant saw it. The woman said, "I'm not," and Huddie Ledbetter looked ashamed, as though he were a virgin and her words had stripped him naked on the stage.

"I'll tell you what's so wrong," he said. And then he sang the song that was his testimony, and when it was done his heart was bare, and every one among them knew his sins.

But even more important, he knew those sins himself. And who can look honestly upon his own worst deeds and not bemoan them? That night at the revival Huddie Ledbetter repented, and in repenting changed the nature of the world.

●

As Elvis played he sang wordlessly, and the Crown that was the Kingship he'd denied descended on him. Furry Lewis felt it happen from his place out on the south point of the compass, and when he did he hooted with delight and took up the song that reverberated from the Tower.

As the bluesman, the hoodoo man, and the Kings all sang rounds that shaped and molded the furnacebright substance of the Eye —

That was when the terrible presence descended on the Tower. It came as contrast, heralded by darkness visible streaming rays among the Light. Everyone who saw that darkling shine knew it in her heart even before Scratch emerged into the Tower.

Lisa shuddered, and she almost lost her song. Dead King Elvis swore, and the darkness shone more brightly.

"Lucifer," the Lady said. "You've come."

Her voice was full of sadness, but it held no fear.

"I have," the Devil told her. *"You knew I would, didn't you? I come to claim the treasure of my kingdom."*

The Lady shook her head. "You have no business here, Morning Star. Leave us be."

The Devil laughed as he stepped forward to seize the molten substance of the Eye from its place within the forge. The Lady raised her hand, warning him away, but Lucifer ignored her.

He tried to, anyway.

Shouldered Santa Barbara aside, reached into the furnace —

— as the Lady shouted, drawing her fiery sword. "Your guard, Scratch," she shouted.

Now the Devil may be arrogant enough to try pushing Our Lady of Sorrows out of his way, but he isn't stupid. When she called him out he reeled around to face her, and though he had no weapon on him but his hands, he was a match for her. When the Devil sets himself to face a challenge his hands are stronger than damnation and his claws as fierce as fire on the sun; when he turned to face the Lady he was terrible and strong. Parrying her sword with his bare hands; meeting her blows so powerfully that he all but struck it from her hands —

Parried, parried again, and now he got both hands around the blade, and slowly surely began to pry it away from her. The Lady met that by twisting the blade and rushing toward him — the one to try severing his fingers, the other meant to run him through. But neither of those strategies did her any good. The Devil's grip was too severe to break and his fingers were too cruel to rend, and now he lifted the great fiery blade until he pulled the Lady off her feet — and brought it down again so hard so fast she lost her grace and tumbled to the floor.

The Devil didn't hesitate an instant when that advantage came to him. He saw her off her guard and leapt upon her.

Wrung his hands around her throat, and strangled her to death.

So slow, so long — the Lady died hard and bitter, all the while pounding at him with her sword. She gouged him grievously, but the Devil didn't let that stop him. No matter how he bled, no matter that great geysers of his ichorous black blood sprayed across the room, he didn't loose his grip.

When Dan Alvarez saw how she was dying, he started toward her, intent to rip the Devil off of her or die trying. But when he made to move the woman whom he loved touched his arm so gently, caught his eye, and shook her head.

"Let her be," Polly sang, improvising to force the tune onto her words. "This is how the Devil would distract you — and you must never lose the song."

Lisa heard that, and she thought, *That's right* — but only for a moment. For when she looked back at the Lady and the Devil and the horror happening before her, she knew a terrible truth: she knew that Dan and Polly both were right, and that the Devil was trying to distract them and he was trying to kill the Lady, too, and if he could do either one then everything was lost.

And then she thought about her dream, and she thought about Blind Willie, and she knew an inspiration.

It came to her like this: she was walking toward the Devil all black-bloody and destructive, toward the Lady dying as he strangled her, and Lisa moved slowly slow and careful all focused on her song. Closer, now, and closer, till she realized she was close enough to touch the Prince of Lies, so frightful, all the hate in the world crystallized into a single form, and then she knew she still had to get closer. Softening her music till it wasn't much more than a whisper, and playing close below his dreadful horns, almost directly in the Devil's ear.

Played and played as the Devil now began to tremble. The music hurt him, didn't it? And Lisa knew that made a kind of sense, because the music Blind Willie gave her was the most beautiful thing she'd ever found in all the world or Hell, and the Devil was all awful ugliness made tangible to see. But it still amazed her — look, look how he grew pale, how the hard crimson of his skin faded toward lavender. He was getting weaker, wasn't he?

As the Lady trembled and went still.

When Lisa saw that she forgot about her song.

"Lady!" she cried, and she didn't even notice how her kazoo clattered onto the floor —

As the Devil cast the fallen Lady away and turned to strike Lisa, hard. The back of his great hand caught the tiny girl no bigger than a baby — caught her in the soft center of her belly and slammed up, up into her till Lisa went flying across the room.

Hit the wall and dropped like a rock till she smacked face-first into the floor, and oh she hurt, hurt so bad she couldn't even cry she didn't have the wind her breath she couldn't breathe she was dying Lisa realized and the Devil still came at her, oh God oh God he lifted her by the collar lifted her high with one arm as he hauled back to bludgeon her with the other —

As something bright and fiery filled the room, and a streak of black and silver flashed through the air behind the Prince of Lies —

— and suddenly as anyone could imagine the Devil's head tumbled from his shoulders.

His body went all slack, collapsing to the floor, and Lisa fell hard beside it but she didn't care, she was alive, she hurt she was alive and there behind the fallen Devil was her Lady, Santa

Barbara, standing broken and abused but never beaten.

"Come," she said, grabbing the Devil's severed head and hurling it through the window. "There is no time. Find your song before it fades again." As she spoke she gestured at Lisa's kazoo, which rested on the floor just inches from the Devil's leaking carcass. She didn't wait for Lisa to respond before she turned, sheathed her sword, and crossed the room, returning to her place before the fire.

She didn't have to, either. Even as the Lady spoke Lisa scrambled to her feet, no matter how her aching stomach made her want to curl up into a ball and die. Scrambled to her feet, found her instrument, and found her song.

When she looked up she saw the *santa* beginning to weave the Eye into the music with her tongs.

As she wove it the ghosts of the old Kings came to walk among them.

Vaporous old men and Ma Rainey condensing into people as touchable and real as you and I.

As the old Kings joined the song to hammer the Eye in the forge that fell from Heaven.

•

As the Kings sang, as the deadmen sang, as the bluesmen sang, as Huddie Ledbetter testified his sins, the Legions of the Damned found a desperate new strength, and in their desperation they found the courage that let them overrun the Louisiana National Guard and storm the revival compass.

But by then it was no use.

For as they approached the compass the whole revival took up in song, singing "Jesu," and the joy and the melody and the deliverance that rose up from that song and the penitence of the revival were so intense that they called the Pearly Gates of Heaven down into the Hell that was New Orleans.

The Right and Left Hands of the Lord stepped out of the revival crowd, and opened the gates so beautiful and wide, and what Legion of the Damned can abide the clear pure sight of Heaven?

None can, and that's a natural fact. The damned ran, screaming in agony for Mercy, never knowing that Mercy itself was what they ran from.

As the Saints went Marching In.

When they were gone the Damned too were gone from the City of New Orleans, and Hell itself had peeled away from our mortal plane, for neither that damnable place nor its denizens can abide the Gates of Heaven, which stand always by their nature in a state of Profound Grace.

•

When "Jesu" reached its seventh chorus at the forge-hearth the Eye took shape inside the song, and the Tower began to dissolve around Lisa, the *santa*, the deadmen, and the bluesman.

When the Tower was gone they stood atop the old ruined tower down in Hell, still singing; and now the Eye rose up into the infernal sky, where to this day it watches the damned and reminds them of their last hope for salvation.

As the song faded away, the *santa* pointed at the Sea of Fire and Ice. There was a boat beached along its shore — an ancient Roman galley, waiting for them.

Lisa said, "She means that it's for us," and she started down the weathered Tower stairs. After a while the others followed her.

They went to the boat and sailed it out across the Sea of Fire and Ice — all of them but the *santa*, who disappeared somewhere in the ruins of the Fallen City.

That galley carried them in a state of Grace through all the worst parts of Hell. Through the Sea of Fire and Ice, that great flaming arm of the Lake of Fire where shards of ice (and even icebergs) float among the embers, promising the fire and ice that will someday end the world; past the Infernal Hellespont and beyond that the fiery Bay of Ages, and out among the abysmal islands that speckle that arm of the Lake of Fire. Nestled among them lies the Damned Peloponesis, and there the galley grounded on the shore of the Lake of Fire where it looks upon the Mansion called Defiance.

Dead Elvis led them through the Mansion, and up the endless winding stair that leads to the Devil's Mansion in New Orleans.

That Mansion was an ashen ruin, and the entrance to it from the stair lay blocked with ash and hot debris. It took them hours to clear the way, and they might never have cleared it at all if Lisa's mother and the new Kings hadn't stood on the far side of the ruin, digging down toward them from the world.

When they finally broke through to see the light of day, Lisa and her mother cried for joy at the sight of one another, and the Kings faced one another and the place the world had made for them.

Some say they went upriver from there, to the old Kings' forgotten Mansion on the Mountain. But that's speculation, like as not; no living person knows the ways of those who really rule the Delta.

Alan Rodgers is the author of *Pandora*, *Fire*, *Night*, *Blood of the Children*, and *New Life for the Dead*. *Blood of the Children* was a nominee for the Horror Writers of America Bram Stoker award; his first story (actually a novelette), "The Boy Who Came Back from the Dead," won a Stoker and lost a World Fantasy Award. During the mid-eighties he edited the fondly-remembered horror digest, *Night Cry*. He lives in Manhattan with his wife, Amy Stout, and his two daughters, Alexandra and Andrea.

Those who would like to reach the author by electronic mail can write to him on Genie at the address "ALAN.RODGERS". (Stated as an Internet address, that's "alan.rodgers@genie.geis.com".)

ALSO BY ALAN RODGERS . . .

PANDORA
FIRE
NIGHT
BLOOD OF THE CHILDREN
NEW LIFE FOR THE DEAD

If you enjoyed this Longmeadow Press Edition you may want to add the following titles to your collection:

ITEM No.	TITLE	PRICE
0-681-00525-4	New Eves SCIENCE FICTION ABOUT THE EXTRAORDINARY WOMEN OF TODAY AND TOMORROW	14.95
0-681-00693-5	Bloodlines	19.95
0-681-41598-3	The Book of Webster's	17.95
0-681-00754-0	The Official Fan's Guide to The Fugitive	12.95
0-681-00729-X	The Works of H. G. Wells	19.95
0-681-00753-2	Silver Screams: Murder Goes Hollywood	8.95

Ordering is easy and convenient.
Order by phone with Visa, MasterCard, American Express or Discover:
☎ **1-800-322-2000,** Dept. 706
or send your order to:
Longmeadow Press, Order/Dept. 706,
P.O. Box 305188, Nashville, TN 37230-5188

Name _____

Address _____

City _____ State _____ Zip _____

Item No.	Title	Qty	Total

Check or Money Order enclosed Payable to Longmeadow Press	Subtotal	
Charge: ❏ MasterCard ❏ VISA ❏ American Express ❏ Discover	Tax	
Account Number	Shipping	2.95
☐☐☐☐ ☐☐☐☐ ☐☐☐☐ ☐☐☐☐	Total	

Card Expires
☐☐☐☐   Signaure _____ Date _____

Please add your applicable sales tax: AK, DE, MT, OR, 0.0%—CO, 3.8%—AL, HI, LA, MI, WY, 4.0%—VA. 4.5%—GA, IA, ID, IN, MA, MD, ME, OH, SC, SD, VT, WI, 5.0%—AR, AZ, 5.5%—MO, 5.725%—KS, 5.9%—CT, DC, FL, KY, NC, ND, NE, NJ, PA, WV, 6.0%—IL, MN, UT, 6.25%—MN, 6.5%—MS, NV, NY, RI, 7.0%—CA, TX, 7.25%—OK, 7.5%—WA. 7.8%—TN, 8.25%

Rodgers, Alan

Bone music.

DATE DUE

JUN 1 3 1996			
FEB 08 '96			
JUN 1 1 '96			
SEP 2 8 '96			
DEC 1 0			
GAYLORD			PRINTED IN U.S.A.